QUEEN *of* DIAMONDS

QUEEN *of* DIAMONDS

CATHERINE HUNTER

Queen of Diamonds
copyright © Catherine Hunter 2006

Turnstone Press
Artspace Building
018-100 Arthur Street
Winnipeg, MB
R3B 1H3 Canada
www.TurnstonePress.com

All rights reserved. No part of this book may be reproduced or
transmitted in any form or by any means—graphic, electronic or
mechanical—without the prior written permission of the publisher.
Any request to photocopy any part of this book shall be directed
in writing to Access Copyright (formerly Cancopy, the Canadian
Copyright Licensing Agency), Toronto.

Turnstone Press gratefully acknowledges the assistance of the Canada
Council for the Arts, the Manitoba Arts Council, the Government of
Canada through the Book Publishing Industry Development Program,
and the Government of Manitoba through the Department of Culture,
Heritage and Tourism, Arts Branch, for our publishing activities.

Design: Doowah Design
Printed and bound in Canada by Hignell for Turnstone Press.

Library and Archives Canada Cataloguing in Publication
Hunter, Catherine, 1957
Queen of Diamonds / Catherine Hunter

ISBN-13: 978-0-88801-322-4
ISBN-10: 0-88801-322-1

I. Title.
PS8565.U5783Q43 2006   C813'.54   C2006-905985-3

ACKNOWLEDGEMENTS

Thanks: to Pat Sanders for excellent editorial help and much-needed encouragement in the dead of winter; to Marnie Woodrow (hey, you) and the wordlounge.com for writing advice and support; to Jamis Paulson of the Manitoba Writers' Guild for going above and beyond to make sure I had a place to work; to Melody Morrissette, who listened to hours—nay, years—of talk about this story; to Karen Zoppa for reading the story so observantly; to Nadine Hunter for consulting the oracle with me; to Dean Zoppa of Oz Fine Jewellery for answering questions and letting me hang around his beautiful shop; to Michael Goertzen for research into fraud among the psychics; to Cynara Geissler for research on dozens of topics, typing, shopping, listening, and other assistance; and to the late Don Bailey, may he rest in peace, in whose screenwriting workshop Lorelei was born.

This book is for the Crescentwood Girls

Queen *of* Diamonds

Catherine Hunter

CHAPTER ONE

Through the fine veil of her eyelashes, Lorelei watched the couple seated across from her at the seance table. She had drawn the red curtains in the den she used as a consulting room. But the lingering June sunlight still seeped through, and in the glow of the four candles that burned at the center of the table, she could observe her clients closely. Their eyes were obediently shut, their breathing measured and slow, their age-spotted hands linked together on the tabletop, fingers intertwined. Although they each wore an elaborate gold wedding band, they were not married to each other. Like many of Lorelei's clients, they were both recently widowed and seeking reunion with their spouses. Lorelei knew the man's story already. It was the woman who concerned her. She didn't know the woman well enough.

Outside, a car passed slowly on the residential street, its tires hissing on the pavement. A mother called her children home from play. On the seance table, one of the candles sizzled and sissed in its bed of melted wax. Otherwise, there wasn't a sound. There was a tension in the air, a slight electrical heightening of the senses, but so far the entity they were trying to summon had not shown itself. Lorelei clasped her hands around her own shoulders and raised her head toward the ceiling, seeking inspiration from above. Her body swayed gently, then came to a stop. She opened her eyes. In the mirrored glass of the chandelier, she could see herself and her clients reflected from below.

At twenty-nine, Lorelei had to be vigilant about her appearance. She turned her neck from side to side, inspecting her hair and her complexion. Both were radiant. With artful makeup and a low-cut, but disarmingly simple cotton shift, she had achieved the effect she desired tonight, a seductive blend of mystery and innocence. She gathered her thick dark hair in her hands and swept it back over her shoulders, letting it cascade loosely down her back. With a quick flick of her tongue, she moistened her lips. Then, satisfied with the result, she turned her attention to her newest client.

Penny Johnson was carefully dressed, as if for an evening at the theater. She wore a strand of pearls above the scalloped collar of her dark blue dress and a bracelet of white gold on her left wrist. The linen dress was too heavy for the recent heat, yet somehow the fabric had remained uncreased. Evidently, Penny was the type to stay fresh and cool. Her gray hair, swept up off her face in an old-fashioned permanent wave, gleamed with silver highlights. She wore a light coat of coral lipstick and just enough mascara to darken the lashes. Her face was surprisingly youthful. Though she had to be nearly sixty, her skin was only slightly marred by worry. A few wrinkles at the corners of her mouth and the hint of shadows under her eyes suggested she didn't sleep very well. She tightened her grip on the man's hand and bowed her head fervently, as if in concentration or in prayer. What was it she wanted?

Beside her, Waverley Forbes sat upright, his head held high, his shoulders well back and relaxed. His thick white hair touched the collar of the summer suit jacket he wore over a casual white cotton shirt and blue jeans. As always, he emanated the calm, magnetic warmth that so easily drew others into his orbit. His faith was unshakable, and his strong evangelical streak had brought many converts to Lorelei's door. In return, she had dedicated herself to learning his deepest desires. By studying every tiny facet of his personality, his private habits and his secret dreams, she'd come to know him better than he knew himself.

The larger facts of Waverley's life were public knowledge. As the son of an Anglican minister, he had grown up in the quiet Winnipeg neighborhood of Crescentwood. At age eighteen, while working as a waiter on a cruise ship, he'd met Gloria Brown, the daughter of a Texas oil millionaire. During a six-week voyage through the South Pacific, a mischievous fortune teller, hired as part of the entertainment, had proclaimed the unlikely couple to be soulmates. This sparked a romance that led to their elopement in Hawaii and a scandal in the upper echelons of Fort Worth society. The oil millionaire was unable to force an annulment and finally, after a period of rage, decided to give Waverley Forbes a job. Over the next forty years, Waverley had risen through the company to the rank of CEO, from which position he had amassed his present fortune.

Lorelei had first met him three years ago in San Francisco, where she was offering her services as a psychic healer. Waverley was desperate at the time. His beloved wife and soulmate, Gloria, had been diagnosed with inoperable cancer. It was clear that he was willing to pay any price for the slimmest hope of a cure. But during the examination, Mrs. Forbes had looked right through Lorelei with her pale gray eyes and whispered, "Please. Tell him anything. Whatever it costs. Let him believe, just a little longer." Lorelei had pulled back. For some reason the thought of taking on these clients horrified her. Maybe it was because she and Waverley shared the same home town, and she felt an odd kinship with him. Maybe it was sheer and simple fear of the woman's dying body. Whatever the reason, she'd been seized by a paralyzing doubt. She had returned Waverley's money and told the couple she was sorry. She couldn't help them, she said. It was Gloria's destiny to move into the spirit realm very soon.

Now, three years later, Lorelei was starting to think this was the wisest move she'd ever made. She'd heard of Waverley's suffering, how he'd dragged his poor wife from one quack to another, spending millions of dollars before her inevitable death occurred. Now that he was alone, Waverley had retired to Winnipeg and purchased a mansion, which he shared with his widowed brother, Wayne. Here, he had devoted his time to the study of the afterlife and had formed a local chapter of The Seekers, a society of psychic dabblers that flourished under his leadership and his money. Stung by his failure to find a cure for Gloria's cancer, Waverley was now dedicated to the goal of communing with his late wife in the spirit world. For this, he required the services of a medium. And there was no one he believed in as he believed in Lorelei, the only person who'd been honest with him in his time of need.

Did he believe in her enough to endorse her latest project? He had insisted that Penny come along tonight to witness what he called "the phenomenon," so he was obviously confident it would appear. He had experienced the phenomenon here in this room twice in the past two months, and now that the moon was coming full again, it was time to conjure it once more. If everything went smoothly, Lorelei was prepared to make her pitch tonight. She cast another quick glance at Penny. Everything had better go smoothly. Waverley had invited Penny last night, but he'd only sprung the news on Lorelei this morning. So she was unprepared, and she hated being unprepared. She had invested a lot of time and effort in this latest project; she didn't need any complications.

Last Christmas, when Lorelei was forced to leave California and find a new home for herself and her sister, Nixie, she had thought of Waverley and headed for Winnipeg. It was an inspired move. Since she'd arrived, he had been her most loyal and enthusiastic supporter. In January he had sponsored her trip to Jamaica to investigate a haunting. In March he had made a sizable contribution toward the operating costs of her Psychic Renaissance Foundation and convinced others in his circle to donate as well. But nothing Lorelei had ever asked of him had been as big as her current project. For months now, she'd been preparing the ground, taking him into her confidence, revealing that the foundation was about to embark on an exciting venture to usher in the coming new era of understanding. She'd promised to let him in on the plans once they had the resources to proceed. Waverley's curiosity had been whetted to a keen edge. Everything was moving swiftly toward success and she'd only been waiting for the perfect moment to make her pitch. But over the past few days, he had seemed preoccupied. Something was distracting him, and now Lorelei was beginning to suspect what it was: Ms Penny Johnson.

Until recently, Lorelei hadn't given Penny a second thought. Penny was a member of the Seekers, just another one of Waverley's groupies, impressed by his knowledge of the occult, looking for some kind of meaning in her life. She was an ordinary, aging, middle-class widow. She certainly didn't appear wealthy, so Lorelei had never bothered to invite her for a consultation. Besides, Penny's favorite medium was Yolanda Dawn, a plump, forty-something Hungarian immigrant who ran a business from her high-rise apartment on the bank of the Assiniboine and conveyed to Penny vague but tantalizing messages from her late husband. Penny swore by Yolanda, whom she recommended to all her friends. In fact, Penny had accepted Waverley's invitation to attend this session with Lorelei only on condition that he would attend one with Yolanda. Waverley had agreed. It was a disturbing turn of events, suggesting that Penny might possess something more powerful than money. She might have influence. Lorelei shifted her head, subtly lowering her gaze. Penny's hand was resting comfortably, too comfortably, in Waverley's. His thumb stroked her knuckles, a reassuring, intimate gesture. Yes, it had been a mistake to underestimate this woman.

Lorelei needed to recapture Waverley's attention. It wouldn't be easy tonight, without Nixie's assistance, but Nixie had more important things to do elsewhere, so Lorelei was on her own. In one long, balletic movement, she unfolded her arms and let her fingertips rest briefly under the edge of the table.

Faintly, the mellow jingle of wind chimes sounded from afar. Lorelei moaned softly. She let her arms drift upward and open wide, one hand reaching out to each guest at the table. "Let us close the circle," she murmured. Waverley let go of one of Penny's hands and took hold of Lorelei's. Penny hesitated, but then did the same. Lorelei held their hands firmly, willing their minds to merge with her own. A delicious tingle began to gather along the length of her spine.

The chimes grew gradually more clear, as if they were approaching the house. Penny glanced uneasily at the window, but there was nothing to see. The curtains were closed.

Lorelei let her head loll onto her left shoulder. The chimes rattled against the windowpane.

"What's that noise?" Penny whispered. She drew closer to Waverley. On the wall behind them, their tall shadows loomed and twisted in the flickering candlelight. The chimes grew louder, as if caught in a violent wind storm.

"What *is* that?" asked Penny.

Lorelei felt the release of adrenalin into her bloodstream like sweet wine.

"Shh," said Waverley. "It's coming."

Nixie was strolling through Windsor Park, admiring the green, weedless lawns, the robins flitting from tree branch to birdbath. She had already explored the neighborhood early this morning, noting with quick glances the gates and fences, entryways and windows of the houses she passed. Windsor Park was a monument to cleanliness and tranquility, a carefully planned suburb of duplexes and bungalows, built in the sixties by contractors so obsessed with order that they laid out the crescents and bays alphabetically. Penny Johnson lived in the cs.

Nixie looked like any local teenager as she slouched down Cranberry Bay, headphones at her ears and a pack on her back, eyes locked in adolescent fashion on her own shoelaces. As she'd noted this morning, few of the houses in the bay had security systems. Some didn't even have deadbolts. Penny's bungalow was one of these. Just credit-card entry. Pure and simple. But the infuriating woman had stayed home all day, leaving Nixie no opportunity until now.

As she reached the end of the bay, Nixie casually ducked behind the row of pines that bordered Penny's garden. Within sixty seconds of reaching the back door, she was inside the house, standing on Penny's welcome mat. She pulled on a pair of thin latex gloves, then removed her shoes and placed them in her backpack, in case she had to leave in a hurry. In sock feet, she snuck through the kitchen into the living room. One lamp, turned low, had been left on to discourage burglars. The drapes were closed. She peered out between them, making certain she hadn't attracted any attention before she turned to survey the room.

The couch and matching loveseat were blue, with white doilies protecting their arms, and the blue and white theme was tastefully continued in the flowered wallpaper, the rugs and throw pillows. Every coffee table gleamed as if freshly polished; every surface was neatly dusted. Above the fireplace hung a series of posed, professional photographs, the record of a growing family. In a traditional wedding portrait, the radiant young bride cut the cake with her groom at her side, his hand over hers on the long, white-handled knife. Her honey-colored hair curled up at the ends in the style of the early seventies. The groom was clean-cut, with an honest, open smile and a Cary Grant chin. In the next photo, the young couple held a pair of babies and smiled shyly down at them with adoration. Then came the twins as toddlers, schoolboys, high-school graduates, bridegrooms with smiling brides, and then as new fathers, holding children of their own. The more informal family snaps were displayed on tabletops in stand-up frames. Birthday parties and backyard barbecues. Fishing trips and Halloween costumes. A fat ginger cat under the Christmas tree, wearing a little Santa hat. Nixie sniffed the air and drew a hand across the upholstery. She stepped into the kitchen and checked the floor for a water bowl. There was no sign of a pet in the house.

In the kitchen, fridge magnets held more photographs, a shopping list, and a receipt from the library—*Wuthering Heights, Jane Eyre, The Republic of Love*—with the due date neatly circled in red ink. Penny wasn't much of a cook. The freezer was stocked with low-cal TV dinners, the cupboards with commercial pasta sauces, boxes of cake mix, and tins of deviled ham. She wasn't much of a drinker, either. The lone bottle of scotch was three-quarters full, with a thin film of dust on its cap. In the junk drawer, clipped coupons were sorted into bundles with rubber bands. Loose screws and various metallic odds and ends were stowed in a baby-food jar. Nixie found the utility bills, all paid up, tucked into a letter holder on the table, along with a recent thank-you card from St. Boniface Hospital, honoring Penny for her volunteer work. An excellent find.

As she entered the bathroom, Nixie wrinkled her nose at the smell of bleach. The chrome and tiles were gleaming, freshly scrubbed. In the medicine cabinet, she found four different brands of cream that promised soothing relief of joint pain, a box of nitroglycerin patches, and denture adhesive. On the top shelf, behind a bottle of long-outdated cough syrup, she found a prescription for Valium. But it wasn't Penny's. The name on the label was "Puffball Johnson." The ginger cat? Did cats take Valium? Nixie would have to ask Vivian, the vet at the animal shelter where Nixie had adopted a kitten. Vivian would know.

The jewelry was exactly where Nixie expected it to be. Top right-hand drawer of the bedroom dresser. She ignored the pieces that were well cared for and laid out neatly, ready to choose from. Instead, she reached in to the back of the drawer. Sifting through the tangled chains and broken pins, she found a tarnished silver ring box with a tight clasp. It was not at all easy to open, especially with gloved fingers. It would be too tricky for someone with arthritis, and Nixie guessed that Penny didn't open it often. The lid finally snapped up to reveal a plain, gold ring with a simple raised setting, but no stone. Nixie lifted it out. Folded into the bottom of the box, a tiny card, yellow with age, read simply: "Forever, Raymond." This must be Penny's engagement ring. The stone had come loose and she'd set it aside. Somehow, it had gotten pushed to the back of the drawer with the junk jewelry. Nixie replaced the card, snapped the box shut, and tucked the ring into the pocket of her jeans. She imagined the young man in the living room photographs, down on one knee, reciting a well-rehearsed proposal with a lump in his throat and a pounding heart. She was smiling as she replaced the little silver box and the rest of the jewelry, taking care to recreate the casual jumble she'd found. It wouldn't fetch much money, a thin band like this, but in emotional currency it might be worth a fortune.

Nixie picked up Penny's telephone receiver, punched in the local code to check messages, and got lucky. Penny used the standard local network. And like most innocent people, she had chosen her own phone number as a password. She had two new messages. The first was from a woman, probably in her thirties or forties. She spoke softly, her sentences rising like questions. "Penny? I was wondering if you're home, dear?" Silence for a few seconds, as the caller waited to see if Penny would pick up. Then, "I'm just back from the lake, and I wondered if you'd like to meet for lunch? I'm sorry I missed our reading last week. But we can reschedule, can't we? Yolanda will understand. I simply had to get up to the cottage. There is so much work to be done out there! Could we meet tomorrow? I'll be at the Dharmarama as soon as it opens in the morning. I want to pick up a few little items, and…. Well, give me a ring, dear. All right. Well. Good—goodby, then."

Nixie scrolled through the call display and noted the name of the caller: H. Kellsington. Kellsington was the name of that rich American lady with the fixation on UFOs, the one Penny had recently sponsored into the Seekers. Agnes. The frumpy one. Lorelei had ignored her at first, judging her by her dowdy clothes and her habit of traveling by bus. But when Nixie had looked her up on the Internet, they'd discovered that Agnes and her husband were loaded. Almost in the same league as Waverley. Lorelei had been trying to make up for her mistake ever since, and she'd be glad to learn where Agnes might be found tomorrow morning. But other than that, the message wasn't very helpful.

The second call was more promising. It was from a man with a deep voice, breezy yet businesslike. "Mrs. Johnson? It's Brian from Bader and Bader here. Thanks for your note. We're proceeding toward probate, but I need to tell you that at present we still have not located the additional assets you've listed. I'm calling to ask if you could have young Derek give us a call? In light of the rather, uh, cryptic wording of the bequest, I'd like to have a brief chat with him, but I can't seem to catch him at home. Perhaps he could call me from his workplace during the day? I'd appreciate it. In the meantime, we will continue the search, and I'll let you know if we have any success. Call me if you have any questions. Take care now." He hung up rather clumsily, spoiling the professional effect a little. Nixie grinned. Probate, assets, and financial affairs all sounded par for the course as topics of discussion among Lorelei's clients. But a cryptic bequest? That was a bonus.

Brian Hale knew he shouldn't work such long hours. He knew he should be taking his secretary out for dinner or visiting his nephews or working out at the gym. Even an evening spent slumped in front of the television, munching potato chips, would be healthier than sitting here, obsessing over the maddening Johnson file. Johnson had been a long-term client and Brian had liked him. But since he'd died last year, he'd caused the firm nothing but headaches. As the only surviving son of two successful doctors, the man had inherited a sizable sum from his parents. He had earned well during his lifetime, working as a ski instructor, golf pro, and fishing guide to the rich. And he hadn't been extravagant—aside from paying for his sons' education, he was a penny pincher. The estate should have been large, and as executor, Brian had expected to reap a good profit. But gathering the assets for probate was proving to be more trouble than his two percent was worth. Johnson had taken the idea of diversification to its limit, scattering his stocks and bonds among a dozen different institutions. Then, in the final years of his life, he had become unhinged. He'd behaved like a squirrel stashing acorns for winter—though a squirrel would have kept better records, Brian thought. He sighed as he opened the file once again and read the latest memo. His assistant had discovered a safety deposit box—the last, he hoped, of a total of six—in an obscure caisse populaire in St. Xavier, Manitoba. It contained a paper sack of centennial coins, the title to a rundown bungalow on Ellen Street that would be cheaper to demolish than to repair, a bundle of outdated pawn tickets, and—Brian's personal favorite—a single earring, which, when appraised, turned out to be worth one hundred dollars. The sensible thing to do would be to wind the matter up and bring it to a close, and some of the family were in favor of that approach. But the widow wouldn't hear of it. She insisted there were further assets to be found, and Brian had to admit she was probably right. It seemed unlikely that the estate could be so small. But in the meantime, until all the assets were accounted for, no disbursements could be made.

Brian knew he probably shouldn't follow up on the note his client's widow had sent him. He knew the senior partners would advise against it, and he knew he shouldn't take these particular papers out of the office. Nevertheless, at ten after eight, he stuffed the thick file into his briefcase and carried it down to his car. Tonight he was on his way to an appointment at the home of Yolanda Dawn, a psychic his client's widow was involved with. "If Yolanda holds the papers in her hands, if she touches them where he signed his name," Penny Johnson had written, "she may be able to divine his thoughts as he was signing." Brian hadn't responded to this note, other than to acknowledge receipt of it. He hesitated to agree, officially, to such an unorthodox request. But he had phoned Yolanda Dawn and she'd agreed to see him tonight. Perhaps, as Brian's secretary had warned him, this was a wild goose chase. But Brian didn't see that it could do any harm. It might even do some good. After all, he believed there was more to this world than most people could see from their little nine-to-five perspective.

He drove south over the Osborne bridge and turned right, slowing down to check the address on the note Penny had given him. He found a parking spot on the street in front of the building, a bland but stylish high-rise with a wide stone staircase leading up to double doors. He stepped inside and waited behind two elderly ladies who were using the intercom system. A resident buzzed them in and Brian followed, holding the door politely. In the lobby, he gave his short brown hair an unnecessary pat in front of the gilded mirror, but otherwise he barely glanced at his reflection. He knew he looked respectable in his gray suit and tie. But then, he always looked respectable. The elderly ladies disappeared down a long corridor to the right, and Brian proceeded alone to the elevator. When it arrived, he entered to find that all four of its walls were mirrored and he was surrounded by his respectable self, four lawyers in steel gray suits, crisp white shirts, and spanking new briefcases. He pressed the number sixteen and leaned against the wall, tilting his head toward the ceiling to escape his own image. But he met there only his own green eyes set in his freckled, serious face, with its white-boy good looks. The ceiling, too, was mirrored. Brian closed his eyes as he ascended. There was more to life than this. He just knew it. Beyond this mundane, day-to-day reality, there was a whole universe of possibility visible only to the gifted. Some people truly did have second sight. Brian knew this from experience. If he was lucky, Yolanda Dawn would be one of them.

Lorelei turned her neck, letting her head flop back. Her mouth fell open. The wind chimes jangled frantically against the glass for a moment before they abruptly ceased. The light bulbs in the chandelier glowed with sudden brightness and went out. Then finally, after a full minute of dead silence, the phenomenon manifested itself.

"All things pass away." The voice that came out of Lorelei's mouth was not her own. The gravelly monotone seemed to emanate from somewhere deep within her belly.

Penny drew in her breath sharply. Perhaps she was not as cool and collected as she appeared to be. Her fingers trembled in Lorelei's hand.

"And all return," Waverley answered. He was alert, but

calm. He sat up straight, his head held high. He showed no sign of fear.

"*Yes, all things pass away and all return.*" Lorelei's lips barely moved. Her eyes were open now, but unfocused. She gazed at a point somewhere above Waverley's head. "*Waverley Forbes?*" the voice asked.

"I'm here," said Waverley. "I'm sitting right here."

Penny's neck swiveled as she looked from Waverley to Lorelei and back again. Her eyes opened a little wider every time the voice spoke.

"*Why have you summoned me again?*"

"I want to know," said Waverley, "how to contact Gloria. You said—"

Suddenly, Lorelei's body jerked forward. "*There is interference,*" snarled the voice. Lorelei's spine went rigid and her upper torso veered toward Penny.

Penny leaped from her chair, wrenching her hand violently from Lorelei's grip. She knocked over a candle and red wax spilled onto the white lace tablecloth. Penny instantly snuffed out the flame with her teacup before the fire could spread. She backed away from the table and bumped into one of the tall Victorian lamps that stood on either side of the window. The lamp teetered as she grasped its pole for support.

"Sit down," Waverley told her. "Calm down. It's perfectly all right."

A harsh, guttural noise began low in Lorelei's throat. She stretched her neck, raising her face toward Penny, and her pupils rolled back in their sockets.

"Oh my God!" Penny cried. "Her eyes have gone completely white! Wake her up!"

"It's all right," Waverley assured her. "It's part of the—"

"*There is interference.*" The tone of the voice had dropped even lower, become more menacing. "*I sense the presence of another.*"

Waverley sat up straighter. "Yes," he answered. "I have brought along a friend."

"*Who is this other? What does it want?*"

Waverley reached out a hand toward Penny and looked her in the eye. Keeping his gaze steady and his voice gentle, he said, "Sit down, Penny. Rejoin the circle. Speak to the spirit guide."

Penny sat down. Lorelei's pupils returned to their normal places, but her gaze was still eerily void. The voice was silent.

Penny swallowed hard and cleared her throat. "I'm— I'm Penny Johnson," she said. A tremor passed through her body. But she reached out once again for Lorelei's hand. She kept her eyes fixed on Lorelei's face and spoke up. "I'm here in good faith. I am also seeking guidance through the spirit world."

"Penny can be trusted," Waverley said with authority. "Let us proceed." He was clearly going to brook no resistance from the voice. If he wanted to bring along a friend, he would do so.

Lorelei's body seemed to collapse. A great whoosh of breath escaped from her lungs and blew out another candle. The room was getting darker by the minute. "*Listen carefully,*" the voice commanded.

"I'm listening," Waverley said. "Tell me how to reach Gloria!"

"*You must prepare,*" the voice droned. "*The way is difficult.*" A cool puff of air wafted across the table and Penny shivered. The two remaining candles flickered. One of them went out.

Waverley gripped Lorelei's hand more tightly. "How can I prepare?"

"To prepare the heart, the wise man warms the hearts of others. To open the mind, the wise man opens the minds of his fellow travelers on earth. To learn, you must teach."

"Let me speak to Gloria," commanded Waverley.

"All things come in their time."

The voice seemed to have calmed down, but still Penny kept a wary eye on Lorelei, ready to leap out of reach if need be.

"It's time now," said Waverley. His tone was business-like, firm yet respectful. "It's time for me to speak to her now."

"When the moon is full, you must seek a connection."

"The moon is full tonight," said Waverley firmly.

"Have you forgotten?"

"Forgotten what?"

"You have forgotten," said the voice, sadly. *"The veil descends."*

"No!" Waverley commanded. He let go of Penny completely. He lifted Lorelei's hand from the table and held it tightly in both his own, as if he could wring the spirit of his dead wife from her body. Lorelei's head remained tilted back. Her face was expressionless, blind eyes staring.

"It descends-sss." The voice weakened, dropped to a whisper. *"Remember. After the longest day, the moon comes full again. Gloria asks you to remember the waves, the white birds-ssss...."* The voice hissed into silence.

"Wait!" cried Waverley. He grasped Lorelei's body by the upper arms and shook. She wobbled like a rag doll. Her head flopped forward onto her chest.

"Be careful," said Penny quietly. She laid a hand on Waverley's wrist to stop him.

Lorelei began to stir. "What?" She spoke sleepily, in her own voice. "What happened?" She grasped the edge of the table, struggling to sit up straight. Once again, the wind chimes sounded outside the window, moving away this time, growing fainter.

Waverley went to the window and flung the curtains open. He lifted the sash and leaned out. "Tell her to speak to me," he ordered. "Tell her I remember everything." But there was no response. The chimes faded into the night. The voices of teenage boys drifted in from the playground across the street as they called goodnight to each other. A car passed, rock and roll blaring from its radio. The spell was broken.

Lorelei looked from him to Penny. "I'm so—thirsty. What happened?"

"It's all right," said Penny. She poured water from a pitcher on the sideboard and handed a glass to Lorelei. "It came. It was here. It spoke to Waverley."

"What did it say?" Lorelei asked.

"We had a message from Gloria," Waverley told her. In his excitement, he paced rapidly across the carpet. "We've made a great advance tonight. I believe that Gloria was talking about the night we first met, on the cruise ship. We were out on deck, watching the seabirds in flight. The sun was setting over the water." He shook his head, amazed. "As if I could ever forget!"

"Could we turn the lights on, please?" asked Penny.

"Of course," said Lorelei. She flicked a switch on the wall, and her two clients blinked in the light of the ordinary room. "I'll get us some drinks," she said. "Penny, white wine?"

Penny nodded.

"Brandy," said Waverley. "My God, this is a fantastic breakthrough!"

Nixie completed her tour of Penny's main floor, examining the art on the walls, the plants, the contents of the linen closet. On a shelf in the hallway, she saw a little red vase, with a small plaque that read "Puffball." She realized it wasn't a vase, but an urn for ashes. The ginger cat, like Penny's husband, had passed away.

Nixie noted the titles in the bookshelves, especially the ones beside Penny's bed. Judging by the bookmarks, Penny had several volumes on the go at once. Besides the romances from the library, she was reading *How to Develop Your Intuition* and something called *Abundant Words: Harvesting Your Hidden Creativity*. Most interesting of all was the notebook tucked into a drawer of the bedside table. It wasn't exactly a diary, always a favorite find, but it was some kind of journal. Flipping through the pages, Nixie found fragments of poetry with lines crossed out and rewritten, as well as snippets of conversation, descriptions of people, and observations on all manner of trivial things, such as "An uncracked egg is like a secret" and "Her heart was as wild as an unmade bed." Was Penny an aspiring writer? Nixie looked under the pillow and mattress in case there was a more conventional diary to be found, but had no luck. She checked her watch. She'd better hurry if she wanted a good look in the basement.

The rec room was apparently seldom used. The decor was dated—fake wood paneling, stuffed fish on the walls, and bowling trophies. Nixie ignored these items and went for the closet under the stairs. She tossed aside camping equipment and Christmas decorations. She wanted the things that were buried deepest. Finally, she found a small locked suitcase. Years of practice had perfected her technique, and her agile fingers picked the cheap lock easily without breaking it. She sorted quickly through the papers inside, scanning newspaper clippings, theater programs, children's artwork. She glanced at the boys' old report cards. Their names were Sam and Sal—so who was Derek? In a side pocket, she discovered a bundle of yellowing pages, tied with a blue ribbon. Handwritten letters, no envelopes. She skimmed the words she could make out: *the day we'll finally be together… to look into your beautiful eyes again … Forever, Raymond.* Bingo. Love letters from Raymond. Nixie didn't have time to read them all. But the dust on the suitcase and the boxes piled on top of it told her the letters wouldn't be missed. She placed the whole bundle into her backpack and restacked the boxes under the stairs until the storage closet looked exactly as it had before she disturbed it.

Back upstairs, she slipped out the side door as quietly as possible, resetting Penny's flimsy doorknob lock with a flick of her wrist. She patted her pocket, making sure the ring was secure, and ducked back through the pine trees, emerging onto the front street and strolling nonchalantly to the corner, where she turned and took a circuitous route back to her van. Except for a couple of dog walkers, nobody saw her. She was pleased with herself as she started the engine and began her drive across town. She had acquired some prize assets.

It was still too early to return home, so she drove down Jubilee to the Bridge Drive-In and bought herself a chocolate ice-cream cone. She sat in the van, enjoying the treat, watching the crowd of teenagers gathered on the riverbank. They weren't much younger than Nixie, and most of them were bigger. Some of them munched on french fries from the drive-in. Others puffed on cigarettes. A slim blond in a crop top leaped onto the back of a muscular boy and threw her arms around his neck. Her friends screamed and giggled. The boy pulled the girl over his shoulders, then carried her like a sack of potatoes to the river's edge, where he pretended to toss her in. She shrieked with laughter as the other boys egged him on. Nixie observed their customs as if they were a herd of animals on a nature show. What would it be like to belong to such a gang? To laugh as somebody threatened to drown you, to let somebody hold you like that? These questions made her throat ache. She took a gulp of ice cream and thought of other things.

She bet the engagement ring in her pocket no longer fit Penny Johnson. With all those creams in the bathroom cabinet, Penny's joints were probably swollen. She couldn't wear the ring, even if she wanted to. She had probably had the stone removed and reset. But naturally she'd held on to the original ring, and she'd held on to the little card enclosed with it. "Forever, Raymond." Well, Raymond was dead now, Nixie thought. So much for forever. Still, when Penny realized the ring was missing, she would want it back. And that was Lorelei's specialty, giving people what they wanted. Nixie had seen her do it many times.

Leaving her two clients in the den, Lorelei stepped out into the hallway. For a moment, she leaned her head against the dark paneled wall. These sessions were exhilarating. But afterwards, she often felt used up. Tonight, since she was still recovering from a bout of pneumonia, she felt like a wrung-out washrag. She inspected herself in the full-length mirror. The seance had left her pale and slightly disheveled, so she applied a little blush to her cheeks and combed her hair. Turning, she tried to see herself from every angle. She was proud of her lithe figure, achieved by a rigorous routine of swimming, and her clothing fit her well.

The cotton shift she wore tonight was dark green with a rust-flecked arboreal design. The skirt flared below the waist and swirled about her bare legs, ending at mid-calf. Her jewelry was minimal, just a silver necklace and some silver bangles at one wrist. Her left wrist was bare—she avoided watches, not wanting to seem mired in temporality. Her long, dark hair was neatly trimmed and parted in the middle, a natural look kept sleek with a half-bottle of conditioner every morning to combat the effects of the swimming pool's chlorine. On her scrubbed feet, she wore nothing but clear toenail polish and undyed sandals. The look was intended to be faintly reminiscent of the hippie girls of Waverley's youth. A little subliminal desire never hurt a business deal. But she kept the look sensible and low-key, avoiding the gypsy earrings and turbans worn by some of her colleagues. Clients were charmed by eccentricity, she knew, but no one wanted to invest capital in a kook. Not serious capital.

She smoothed her skirt and then, content that she'd repaired any damage caused by the invading spirit guide, she headed into the kitchen to prepare a tray of refreshments for her guests. But first she paused to peer into the den through a crack between the panels.

In the center of the room, Penny was seated at the table, hands in her lap. Waverley stood beside her, his hand raised above her head. Lorelei saw him stroke her hair, a quick but tender movement that alarmed her. "I told you," he was saying. "Isn't she marvelous?"

"It was as if another—another being—had taken hold of her body," said Penny.

"That's one of Lorelei's gifts. She can move out of her

own soma and allow the spirit guides to use it as a medium for communication."

"It's very…different from Yolanda's methods," Penny said. "I think, all in all, Yolanda makes me feel more…comfortable."

"I truly believe you'll have more success with Lorelei," said Waverley. "How long have you been trying with Yolanda?"

"Nearly a year now."

"Well, I've only been working with Lorelei half that length of time. It hasn't been easy. You heard what the guide said. 'The way is difficult.' But we persevered. And now, well, tonight—you heard. You saw! Gloria managed to get a message to me. And I'm confident that some day very soon she will speak directly to me."

"It *was* amazing," Penny admitted. She reached up and patted Waverley's hand, which he'd rested on her shoulder. "What was all that about the moon?"

"The veil between the dead and the living is thinner and more delicate than most people think," he explained. "But it takes a strenuous effort to move through it. It can be traumatic for the spirits, even dangerous, unless the time is right. One of the things I've learned from Lorelei is that the veil is particularly fragile in moonlight. That's why the light of a full moon is most conducive to contacting the spirits of loved ones."

"I've never heard of that before," Penny admitted. "I've been to several mediums this past year and none of them mentioned the phases of the moon. Yolanda never—"

"Yolanda is old school," he replied. "She's not as scientific as Lorelei. Believe me, I've seen it with my own eyes. The phenomenon occurs most often, and most successfully, on nights when the moon is full."

Lorelei smiled as she continued down the hall. Waverley was an intelligent man and he was learning rapidly. A month or two from now, he would understand even more.

In the kitchen, she poured a shot of brandy into a tumbler and downed it, letting the thick liquid soothe her sore throat. As she prepared a tray, setting out sliced strawberries and Waverley's favorite health-food cookies, she could hear his rich baritone rising in excitement; she could tell he was spinning tales of past encounters with the supernatural and laying plans for future ones. Penny murmured in enthusiastic support. Her dubious tone was gone. As Lorelei knew very well, Waverley's zeal was contagious. She sighed, thinking of the sensuous way he had touched Penny's hair, the gallant way he had defended her presence in front of the spirit guide. He was more attached to this woman than she'd guessed. And Penny was certainly braver than expected. It would be a mistake to try to scare her off. The better way to handle her would be to get her onside, to win her away from Yolanda.

Reaching into the drawer of the china cabinet, Lorelei drew out the bundle of brochures she'd had printed up at great expense last month. The perfect time to distribute them was at hand. In fact, this latest project might be just the thing to win Penny over.

Picking up the top brochure, she examined it critically. Slick, gleaming paper. Bright colors. Very professional. In the cover photo, a beautiful young woman in a long white robe was seated on a bench beside a fountain, surrounded by a blooming garden. She was smiling as she held up her arms to welcome the white light that streamed forth from an unseen point above the letters of the title: "Knowledge Is Faith." The logo of the Psychic Renaissance Foundation was embossed discreetly in one corner. Inside, the text invited readers to imagine a mecca for spiritual research, a beautifully designed and thoroughly modern center for the study of the paranormal that would serve the public during the coming revival of psychic energies foreseen by prominent experts in the field. She caressed the glossy surface, running her fingers once again across the expensive raised ridges of the logo.

"That was an astonishing session," Waverley said, when Lorelei returned with the tray. "Gloria is coming closer and closer. I feel her more strongly every day. But Lorelei, you must try again now, for Penny's sake."

"Not tonight," Penny protested.

"Perhaps another time," said Lorelei serenely. "I believe the spirit guide has retired for the night."

"Do you really think a guide is necessary?" Penny asked.

"Oh yes," said Lorelei. "The guides are advanced entities who have learned to move among the different realms and assist the spirits to speak with the living. Some spirits aren't strong enough to break through the Veil of Ibina by themselves. That's one thing we've learned in this work, isn't it, Waverley?" She smiled at him, and he smiled back.

Penny's eyes narrowed, and Lorelei realized she'd inadvertently aroused the older woman's jealousy. Dangerous. "Gloria's spirit guide seemed taken with you, Penny," she said quickly. "He obviously trusted you and valued your presence, because he kept speaking, even though he didn't address you directly. Or, um, did he?"

Penny and Waverley both shook their heads.

"If we worked together," Lorelei rushed on, "we could make contact with the right spirit guide for you, the one appointed to the person you wish to contact."

"Her husband," said Waverley. "He passed away last year without telling—"

"Waverley, please!" Penny said. "Let me do this my own way."

"But you need to tell Lorelei what you are seeking," he admonished. "That way she can open the right pathways and—"

"I'd rather not say anything just yet," Penny interrupted. "I'd rather…wait and see."

"Of course you must pursue this path in whatever way you wish," Waverley replied.

His sudden deference was alarming. Ordinarily, his was the last word on matters of the occult among the Seekers.

"Sometimes I think it's best to stay quiet and let the psychic take the lead," Penny explained. "Let the truth emerge naturally, without a lot of hints and, well, contamination from the client. That's what Yolanda always says." She gave Lorelei a small smile.

The smile had a sly edge and Lorelei recognized the challenge. So. Penny was a tester. Unlike the skeptics, who simply didn't believe at all, or the doubters, with their tedious crises of faith, the testers truly believed in the spirit world. But they didn't necessarily believe that every person who claimed to be psychic was "the real thing." Penny would want proof that Lorelei was a true medium, with a true gift. She would be a time-consuming client, and Lorelei would need every ounce of wit and charm she possessed to win her over.

After refreshments and an interminable chat about the coming Psychic Fair, Penny said she was tired and wanted to go home. Waverley stood immediately and offered his arm.

This was the moment Lorelei had been waiting for. "I'll

walk out with you," she said as she stood up. "My day's not over yet. I still have another appointment tonight."

"You're going out to see a client at this hour?" asked Waverley. It was nearly nine o'clock.

"My agent," said Lorelei.

"You have an *agent*?" asked Penny.

"A real estate agent." Lorelei led the way down the hall to the front door. "I want to make an offer on a parcel of land in the country."

"You're moving?" asked Penny. She sounded a little too eager for Lorelei's liking. "Surely you're not leaving town?"

"No, no." Lorelei took a light summer shawl from a hook by the door and draped it loosely around her shoulders, tossing her hair free. "This is for a new project." She looked at Waverley, who stood with his hand on the doorknob. "Remember I told you about the Research Center?"

Waverley forgot about opening the door. "You're in the market already? For land?"

"I hope so," she said. "I've found a beautiful location." She picked up her purse and settled it over her shoulder, ready to go. "It's a matter of persuading the owners to sell," she added.

"Why, I had no idea you were moving so quickly with this project. You never said a word! Where is this property?"

"Southwest of here. About three hours. Almost exactly at mid-continent, right inside the vortex of the four energies."

"And you've looked at it?"

"I've been there several times. The Psychic Renaissance Foundation purchased the lot next to it last year, on the advice of our founder, and we've been using it as a sanctuary." She smiled. The legal name of the Foundation was company # 669030330. But Psychic Renaissance, or PsyRen, as Lorelei liked to call it, was more poetic, heralding the dawning new age of discovery into the ethereal realms. It was a shadowy organization, with an international membership and a founder on perpetual retreat in Tibet. "Some of us become world-weary from time to time," she continued. "It's a place to go to reconnect with the ethereal and revitalize the energies. The psychic reception is excellent. Maybe it's the healing powers of nature." She looked off into the distance, as though reliving a fond and private memory. "There's a restorative quality to the air out there." She reached for the door herself, prompting Waverley to recall that he should open it. "Do you have everything?" she asked. "Penny? Your hat? Purse?"

Penny, who'd been concentrating on the conversation, said, "Oh, yes. I mean, no. No hat today." She patted her hips, checking that she had her purse. Penny was a bit stout. Her figure under the blue dress had the sleek, seal-like lines achieved only by an expensive foundation garment.

"Are you telling me you've made this purchase already?" Waverley asked.

The women walked through the door as he held it open. "A small acreage only," Lorelei explained. "With a modest old farmhouse and gardens. Not large enough for the kind of development we envision for the Research Center. The adjacent land is owned by a retired couple living in Mexico. They're willing to rent, but, well…."

"You'd rather buy."

"Yes." Lorelei turned and locked the door behind them. She smiled as she recalled the land she was describing. It was the failed and abandoned flax farm once owned by Lorelei's grandfather. Her Uncle Max had taken her there once or twice when she was a kid. He'd had big plans to fix up the farmhouse and sell the property, but of course that would have required physical labor. The place remained as she remembered it, a broken-down house, an old barn, overgrown gardens, and a muddy pond. It belonged to the government now, since Max hadn't paid the taxes, and as far as Lorelei could tell, the government wasn't making much effort to sell it. She could probably get it for a song. But Waverley didn't need to know all that.

"So," he said, "you're still negotiating, then?"

"Yes. Our aim is to explain our needs more clearly to the owners. To emphasize the benefits to humanity of furthering our knowledge of the ethereal. They're asking a rather large sum, and we want to appeal to their benevolent instincts. Their sense of responsibility to the planet. We even drew up a prospectus to show them our vision." She ushered Penny through the porch and down into the front garden. At this time of year, the sun was still bright at nine o'clock in the evening, and the day's heat still hung heavy in the air. Lorelei regretted donning her shawl.

Waverly followed them. "I'd be most interested to see that prospectus," he said.

Penny walked ahead and stood beside Waverley's Jaguar, waiting for him. He had parked behind Lorelei's new sports car and was blocking her in. But he lingered. He stood at the foot of the steps, beside the budding rose bushes, and turned to face her.

"Thank you for the lovely flower vase, by the way," she said. "I'll soon be able to fill it with roses from the garden."

"Why don't you let me have a gander at the prospectus? Perhaps I could be of some assistance with the planning."

"Oh, thank you," she said. "But you've done more than enough already. Your generous donation to PsyRen will allow us to publicize the project more widely, perhaps hold a fundraiser in the fall." She stepped down the path to the driveway and he followed her.

"But how could I not take an interest? A center for psychic research, right here in Manitoba? I'd be very interested to see the plans. How extensive would the grounds be? Is the location convenient to the public? Why, a place like that could draw thousands of people."

"I really must run," she told him. "My agent's expecting me. She's set up a conference call with the couple's lawyer in Guadalajara." If she'd had a watch, she could have glanced worriedly at it.

"Would you send me some information? The Seekers will be most interested in this."

"Oh, well, if you like, I could let you have one of these." She reached in her purse, pulled out a handful of brochures, and gave him one.

"Marvelous!"

She waved goodby and walked toward her car, fanning herself with the remaining brochures. He called after her. "Do you have any extras? The others might like to take a look."

With a show of some reluctance, Lorelei passed him a bundle of ten. "No problem."

Soon, she told herself, waving as her clients pulled away. Soon, all these months of hard work are going to pay off. She waited five minutes, to be sure they were gone, and then returned to her house.

Yolanda's apartment was number 1601. The long white hallway was decorated with gold-speckled wallpaper and gold sconce lights set at close intervals. The crimson carpet was thick. The halls were silent. Either the soundproofing was excellent or nobody was home. As he rounded a corner, Brian caught the whiff of overcooked meat and heard the faint roar of a television laugh track. He glanced at the numbers. 1610. 1609. He wondered what Yolanda was like and where she'd come from. Her accent on the phone had charmed him. She had a warm voice and a husky laugh. She had been seeing Penny since her husband's death, she said, trying to help her reach him in the "blue beyond," but he was as difficult in death as he'd been in the last few years of his life. Yolanda had chuckled. Perhaps Brian knew what she was talking about? Yes, Brian had said, he certainly did.

The building was larger than Brian had realized, the hallway longer. Yet it seemed empty. As he turned another corner, he saw a second elevator, probably the one he should have taken from the lobby. Its doors were just closing shut and its soft bell rang once discreetly as it began to descend. Other than that, he saw no sign of another person. The scent of meat grew stronger and the obnoxious laugh track louder as Brian continued down the hall. Passing apartments 1605 and 1604, he shifted the briefcase from his right hand to his left, preparing to greet Yolanda with a handshake. She was especially sensitive to touch, Penny had explained. This was why she wanted the original holograph will and as many original signatures as Brian had in the file. So that she could run her fingers across the pages and commune with the mind of the writer. Brian pictured a slender hand, with rings on every sensitive finger, moving across the pages, reading a message invisible to those of ordinary sight.

The door to apartment 1601 was ajar, and Brian realized that the cooking smells and television noises were coming from within. He could hear an actress loudly extolling the merits of a powerful new cleanser. Yolanda must have left the door open so she could hear him over the racket of the TV. Was she a little deaf? He lifted his fist and knocked. The door opened a few inches and the smell wafted into the hall. The overcooked meat was starting to burn.

"Hello?" he called. "Mrs. Dawn? Yolanda?"

Nobody answered. Maybe Yolanda had stepped across the hall for a moment, to borrow a cup of sugar or something. He could see through to the polished hardwood floors and the colorful scatter rugs in her cheerful living room, where a pair of long yellow curtains billowed in off the balcony door. The commercial ended and the dramatic music of the local evening news began. Brian sniffed the air. Something was definitely burning. From somewhere inside the apartment, a smoke alarm began its high-pitched bleep.

Brian entered the apartment, calling Yolanda's name loudly as he hurried down the hall and stepped into the kitchen. He moved swiftly to turn the oven off. As he opened the door, a stream of smoke escaped, but luckily there weren't any flames. He caught a quick glimpse of a charred lump on a pan before he slammed the oven door closed again. Swiping at the smoke with a dishtowel, he glanced into the bedroom, still calling Yolanda. Her room was empty, the bed neatly made, a leather purse sitting upright on the bedspread. The bathroom was also empty. Nothing seemed amiss. He moved down the hall into the living room, intending to turn off the TV so he could hear himself think, but as he passed the open balcony door, he heard a prolonged scream from outside, and a man's voice saying, "Oh God!" Pushing aside the curtains, Brian stepped out onto Yolanda's balcony. It faced north, overlooking the river, with a good view of the legislative building to the east. In the west, the sun was low in the sky, but not yet setting. To Brian's left, a group of guests in party hats crowded together on the patio roof of a neighboring building, holding cocktails in their hands and staring in shocked silence at the ground below. This was where the scream had come from. Brian walked to the edge of the balcony. Gripping the rail with both hands, he peered straight down to the parking lot below. Directly beneath him, on a grassy patch among the shrubbery behind the lot, he could make out a splayed figure. For a moment, he didn't understand what he was seeing. Then he recognized it—a human body in a bright yellow dress, arms and legs outspread. From the ground, the body would be hidden by the tall bushes surrounding it, but it was clearly visible from above. One by one, the other neighbors came out onto their own balconies to investigate, and soon a wall of people had gathered, some silent and some exclaiming in excitement, all of them shaken by the presence of the dead body in the bushes below. As he stood there, hearing the drone of the TV newscaster and the shrill whine of the smoke alarm in the empty apartment behind him, Brian realized he was probably looking at the last remains of Yolanda Dawn.

The sound of sirens and the arrival of an ambulance in the parking lot below jolted him from his state of shock. He backed away from the balcony railing and collided with a plastic lawn chair. He sat down in it heavily, planted his elbows on his knees, and started to rest his head in his hands. But as he raised his palms toward his face, he saw they were covered in blood.

Before he had time to think about what he was doing, Brian had wiped his hands on his pants. Then, horrified to see the red smears staining the fabric, he stood up. He needed to calm down. He took ten deep breaths while he concentrated on getting his bearings. He had entered the apartment without permission, and now he was standing on the balcony of a stranger, a dead stranger, a woman who might have fallen, but…he looked again at the red smears on his pants and the palms of his hands. On the green carpet beneath his feet, he saw small, dark splatter marks. Probably blood as well. Was it likely she'd been bleeding before she fell? Accidentally hit her head and grown dizzy? No. The railing was too high for that possibility. Unless she'd been standing on a ladder. He looked up for any evidence that Yolanda had been changing a light bulb or dusting the ceiling, but nothing caught his eye. Looking down at the carpet again, he noticed for the first time that a heavy pot of geraniums lay on its side, spilling soil onto the carpet. The sign of a struggle? A wineglass, too, lay on the carpet where it had rolled under the railing, perilously close to the edge. If it fell, it would be smashed to dust. But Brian had come to his senses now and he did not touch it.

Down below, a couple of police cars had joined the ambulance, and a group of uniformed paramedics and police officers had surrounded the body. An outer ring of concerned and curious civilians was closing in around them. For a wild second, Brian thought the woman might still be alive, but the lack of any urgent activity told him she must be dead, obviously dead. A couple of the officers leaned back and stared up at the building. At some point, possibly very soon, a neighbor would identify the body and the police would be on their way to apartment 1601.

Although the remaining bloodstains on his hands were dry, Brian used a handkerchief to remove his cell phone from his briefcase. He pressed number one on his speed dial and waited while the phone in his brother's office rang three times and a recorded announcement kicked in. Quickly he disconnected and pressed number two, the restaurant where his brother could often be found in the evening.

"St. Mary's House of Curry," answered Ramya. In the background, the clatter of cutlery and noisy buzz of conversation told him that business was good tonight. "Would you like a reservation?"

"Ramya, it's Brian. Is Tommy there?"

"He's in the kitchen." Ramya laughed. "Sarisha is teaching him to make dal, but mostly he is making a mess. Why don't you come—"

"I need to talk to him right away," said Brian. "Can you get him on the phone?"

"Let's see now, don't tell me," said Ramya wryly. "I suppose it's important. Something that absolutely can't wait until tomorrow?"

"Yes, but...Ramya, this time it really is important."

Ramya, Tommy's long-suffering mother-in-law, put down the phone, and Brian imagined her hips swaying gently as she ambled to the kitchen, in no great hurry to interrupt the cooking lesson. Sometimes, Brian thought impatiently, Sarisha and her family behaved as though Tommy were an employee of the restaurant. But he wasn't. He was a Crown prosecutor, and with a phalanx of police about to start questioning his presence at the scene of a murder, Brian wanted Tommy by his side.

While he waited, Brian began to grow afraid. If someone had pushed Yolanda Dawn from her balcony, where was that someone now? Brian had made only a cursory search of the place when he arrived. He hadn't looked in any closets or under the bed. Someone could still be hiding inside. Planning to hit him over the head, too, and send him plunging to his death. Someone could be creeping up behind him right this second. Was that the sound of footsteps? The hair on the back of Brian's neck began to prickle, and he whirled around to face Yolanda's living room. It was empty.

The hooked scatter rugs and the cozy chairs with their brightly crocheted pillows seemed undisturbed in any way. His imagination was raging out of control. Understandable under the circumstances. Most likely the culprit had run away long before Brian arrived. He wondered when Yolanda had put the roast—or whatever it was—in the oven. Maybe he shouldn't have turned it off. He shouldn't have opened the oven. He shouldn't have touched anything, he realized. He wouldn't touch anything else. He might be destroying valuable clues the murderer had left behind.

This made him remember that he'd left the door to the apartment wide open, so even if the murderer had left, he could come back. Didn't they always return to the scene of the crime? Still holding the cell phone to his ear, connected to the ordinary world by the sounds of laughter and clinking glasses from the restaurant, Brian stepped over the doorsill of the balcony back into the living room. This time, he was facing the far wall of the living room, which he hadn't seen before. He gasped and staggered backward, clutching the glass door with his left hand, forgetting his resolution not to touch anything.

He still gripped the cell phone, though he had let his right hand drop to his side, and he could hear Tommy's voice come on the line, tinny and distant. "Brian? You still there?"

Slowly, Brian raised the phone again to his ear. "Tommy?" he said. "Can you come and get me?"

"Sure, man. But what's up? Where are you?"

"I'm…." Brian struggled to remember the address as he stared at the bright red words that someone had printed in foot-high letters on the wall above Yolanda's comfy, overstuffed sofa: *Burn in hell, witch.*

CHAPTER TWO

Lorelei was exhausted. She carried the dirty dishes into the kitchen but didn't bother to wash up. Instead, she took her cigarettes and a glass of wine into the living room. Collapsing into an easy chair, she slid off her sandals and massaged the sore arches of her feet. When Nixie's black kitten leaped out from under the chair to attack her fingers, Lorelei pushed her away. "Not now, Bitsy." The cat was a pest, but Nixie had gotten it from her latest hero, some vet with an animal rescue shelter, and was hopelessly attached to it.

Lorelei leaned back, lit up a smoke, and immediately began to cough. Damn it. Yesterday, the doctor at the clinic had warned that if she didn't quit smoking, she wouldn't get over the pneumonia. She needed to rest, he'd said. No smoking, no drinking, and swimming was out of the question, at least for another month. The lungs needed time to heal, or a recurrence was inevitable. She stubbed the cigarette out and lay back until her breathing returned to normal. Then she tried again, inhaling more cautiously, until she managed to get some nicotine into her system. That was all she needed. Tomorrow she'd throw the rest of the package in the trash and quit for good.

She felt a powerful urge to sleep, but she didn't want to go upstairs to bed until Nixie was home safe and sound. Nixie had probably gone to a movie or dropped by the animal shelter to help out, her favorite pastime lately. The place was open twenty-four hours and Lorelei never knew when she'd come waltzing in. But she couldn't say anything. She had promised to give Nixie a little more "space" now that she was twenty-one. So she lay down on the couch and covered herself with a light woolen throw. Her eyes closed as she began to dream of all the benefits the research center would bring. But just as she was drifting off to sleep, she was visited by doubt. Did Waverley really believe in her enough to invest in the research center? She tried to quell this thought by remembering the philosophy of her Uncle Max, who had taught her most of what she knew: People *want* to believe in you. They really do.

Uncle Max might not have been the best role model a kid could have, but when Lorelei's parents drowned in a boating accident, he'd been the only one available. Lorelei was only three years old at the time, and Maxwell, her father's younger brother, was a twenty-four-year-old bachelor, serving a sentence for forgery in Headingley Correctional Institute. No doubt Lorelei's parents had been shocked and disappointed when Max was arrested, and no doubt they'd been intending to change the terms of their will and leave the care of Lorelei to someone more suitable. But like most people who intend to change their wills, they had put it off. Like most people, they did not expect to die.

A compassionate judge, who viewed the little girl as Maxwell's possible salvation, had allowed him to leave the prison three months before his time was up, in order to move into his brother's house and care for his orphaned niece. And that was how Maxwell Good came into possession of a fully furnished house in the respectable neighborhood of River Heights, a decent sum of insurance money, a brand new car, and a small, unhappy child to instruct as best he could. As Uncle Max always said, "People *want* to trust you. It gives them hope, and no one can live without hope."

Lorelei wasn't aware of the details behind these events. She knew only that her parents had gone away and she was thrust out of the calm routine of her ordinary life into a sort of endless party. Instead of vegetables and milk, she ate pizza and ice cream; instead of lullabies, she fell asleep to the beat of rock music. And Uncle Max didn't teach her the kinds of things her mother had wanted her to learn, the difference between robins and sparrows, or the rules of hopscotch. Instead, he showed her how to hold a coin between her fingers so that no one could see it, and how to make the queen of diamonds jump up to the top of a deck of cards. Max didn't go out to work, as her father had done. He set up a shop in the basement and went into the jewelry repair business, so that customers came to the house at all hours, sometimes even in the middle of the night. There was also, at first, a series of aunties who came and went. Each one would stay for a while, tidying up the house, fussing with ice-cube trays, giving Uncle Max back rubs. They were all kind to Lorelei, called her a poor, sweet little thing, and sometimes one or another of them would buy her a dress or braid her hair, but in later years when Lorelei tried to recall these women, she couldn't bring any one of them into focus. They blurred together in her memory, a succession of giggles, clicking heels, and beery breath.

As a child, Lorelei had spent most of her time, when she wasn't in school, down in the basement helping Max with his work. Max's shop was an enchanted place where the drawers were full of little glass boxes of precious gemstones—silky, iridescent tiger's eyes, and translucent opals shimmering with subtle colors, and dozens and dozens of cold, brilliant diamonds that twinkled like stars when you held them up to the light. Some of the diamonds were real and some of them were pretend, and Max showed Lorelei how to spot the difference between them. He showed her how to keep everything neat and tidy in the shop and how to lock away the jewels in the safe at night. He also tried to teach her how to do some of the repair work, but Lorelei could never quite get the hang of it. She learned how to run the flexible shaft with the foot pedal and bur out a setting to make a seat for a diamond, and how to push the claws down tightly over the stone to hold it in place. But the work was difficult, the gems were tiny and slippery, and she made a lot of mistakes.

"Try to be more careful, Lori," Uncle Max would say. He never truly lost his temper, but she could tell he was often disappointed in her and her cheeks would burn with embarrassment.

The one thing Lorelei knew she was good at was handling the customers. At this, she was an expert. She learned to greet them at the door and to press the silent buzzer Max had installed at the top of the stairs, to let him know when someone had arrived. She pressed once for a woman, twice for a man, and three times for Max's partner Joey Shaunigan. Then she was supposed to engage the visitors in conversation while Max got ready. She learned how to ask the right questions, to guess their interests and their moods by studying the clothing they wore, the cars they drove, and the expressions on their faces. If Max took too long and a customer grew impatient, she resorted to the sure-fire ploy of asking them to help her with something, like opening a jar or finding a Band-Aid. Most of them, knowing her mother was dead, found these requests impossible to resist. Lorelei discovered she could distract anyone for any length of time until Uncle Max would come up the stairs and say, "oh!" as if surprised to find somebody there. "Don't keep the customers waiting, Lori," he'd say sternly. But she knew he didn't mean it.

Joey Shaunigan worked in a casino downtown part of the time and part of the time he worked with Max. He appeared at the door about once a week, a short, stocky man with curly black hair and bulging eyes, who was easy to distract. When she was a little girl, Lorelei had called him "Uncle Joey." Uncle Joey always brought her candy and he was always willing to empty the soft leather pouch of expensive trinkets he carried in his pocket and let Lorelei play with the contents. Sometimes he'd pin a sparkly brooch to her shirt or drape a necklace over her head and call her "Princess."

"I have a little princess at home, just a little bit bigger than you," he'd say. When Lorelei was a kid, she'd been enthralled by Joey's stories of his princess, imagining her as a crowned, bejeweled creature like the pictures in her storybooks. "Does she wear her hair long?" she would ask him. "Does she have her ears pierced?" But whenever she begged to play with the little princess, Joey would just say, "Maybe someday."

By the time she was ten or eleven, Lorelei had given up

on meeting the little princess, and she had long ago figured out that she was just an ordinary girl named Gail—a miserable kind of girl, according to Max, not even very much fun. Lorelei was also well aware that Joey Shaunigan was not her uncle. None of Max's friends were her real aunts and uncles. But she still called him "Uncle Joey," because he liked the nickname, and she still peppered him with questions about the little princess, because she often had to keep him engaged for a long time before Uncle Max would come upstairs and say, "Lori! Why didn't you tell me Uncle Joey was here?"

Down in the shop, Joey and Max had long discussions about the pieces Joey brought with him, examining them carefully with the loupe, assessing the damage. Each one had a loose stone or a broken clasp, or needed cleaning. While Lorelei watched, fascinated, Max would take out his toolbox and his own bag of stones, which he kept in a safe under his workbench, and set about resizing and polishing and replacing stones. Sometimes he even made a whole new piece that looked, to Lorelei's eyes, exactly the same as the one Uncle Joey had brought, so that Uncle Joey ended up leaving with two of a kind.

Uncle Joey was the only one besides Lorelei allowed into Max's workshop and given access to the safe beneath his bench. But Lorelei was the only, only one who knew about the other safe, the one behind the poster of the Alps in the laundry room, the one with the walls that glittered like the magical hidden diamond mine of the seven dwarves in the story of Snow White. Lorelei was the only one who knew all of Max's secrets and was in on every scheme he invented. Or, at least, that's how it was before Katherine and Nixie came along.

As Brian had feared, it took his brother longer to get across town than it did for the cops to get upstairs. By the time Tommy arrived, Brian was locked in the back of a police car, trying to answer questions he didn't know the answers to. He related his story exactly as it had happened and showed them his ID. But the notion of a lawyer consulting a psychic seemed beyond their understanding. They confiscated his briefcase, ignoring his protests that the contents were confidential. He tried calling Penny Johnson, to get her to verify his story, but there was no answer at her home.

If he hadn't been the brother of Tommy Hale, a prosecutor famous for his fierce support of the police force and his near-perfect conviction rate, Brian was sure he would have been spending the night in jail. Instead, after Tommy swore to bring him back for questioning in the morning, he was released into his brother's custody to spend the night in the spare room across the hall from his nephews.

"I don't understand," Tommy said again as the two brothers sat drinking beer in the kitchen after midnight. Sarisha and the boys had long been sleeping by the time they'd arrived home. "You thought this woman could communicate with the dead guy through his signature?"

"It's complicated," said Brian.

"No kidding." Tommy consulted his notes. "Best thing to do is call Mrs. Johnson first thing in the morning, ask her to come downtown and make a statement. That'll help a lot."

"Think so?"

"Sure. Gives you a reasonable, well...a *legal* reason to have been there, establishes that you didn't know the victim. It'll help. Now, you say you didn't see anybody in the corridor? Nobody at all?"

"Nobody. Just saw the elevator doors close. The east-wing elevator, near Yolanda's apartment. It was going down."

Tommy made a note. "And you didn't touch anything? Besides the stove and the balcony railing?"

"The balcony door. Maybe a chair. I don't know! Oh, Jesus!" Brian hid his face in his hands as his fears came flooding back.

"Calm down," Tommy said. "There is no way you are going to be a suspect in this murder."

"You really think it's a murder?"

"Come on," said Tommy. "*Burn in hell, witch*? Of course it is."

Brian nodded glumly and tilted back his head to drain the last of his beer. "At least I didn't touch that wall. I didn't touch the can of spray paint." He'd been relieved to see that paint can lying on the rug beside the sofa and to realize the ugly message wasn't written in blood.

"Good. But even if you did, you have nothing to worry about, Brian. There will be evidence in the apartment and on the body that will point us in the right direction. They'll probably clear you before you even get to the station tomorrow. Come on, now." He stood up and clapped his brother on the back. "Let's get some sleep."

Brian stood too and gathered the four beer bottles they had emptied. He rinsed them and stacked them in the recycling box, while Tommy wiped the tabletop clean. Even a murder wasn't enough to make them forget that Sarisha was a fanatical housekeeper.

Tommy said goodnight and started up the stairs, but Brian had one more question.

"That message on the wall," Brian said, "isn't that a sort of serial-killer thing?"

"Good question," Tommy said. "It could be, but I doubt it. Serial killers usually address their taunts and insults to the cops or to society at large. But 'Burn in hell, witch' is pretty direct, pretty angry, aimed at the woman. I'm betting it's personal. Intimate. Lover or spouse."

"That poor woman," said Brian.

"I know," said Tommy. "If you can't sleep, pray for her. That's what I do."

Lorelei woke to the smell of coffee as Nixie parted the double pocket doors and tiptoed into the living room with a steaming cup and a whispered warning that it was time to wake up.

"Nix?" Lorelei roused herself from the couch and sat up. "What time is it?"

"Almost eight," said Nixie. "You were sound asleep when I got in last night and I didn't want to wake you. How are you feeling?" She handed Lorelei a cup of coffee.

"Fine. I'm fine, Nix. Better every day." She coughed. "How'd it go last night?"

Nixie sat cross-legged on the carpet and reported to her sister all she knew of the boring life of Penny Johnson. Nixie's memory for detail made her as reliable as a camera, but sometimes, with conventional types like Penny, Lorelei found the long catalog of trivia almost pathetic. As she listened, she eyed Nixie's outfit. Nixie had dressed with her usual carelessness this morning, choosing a hot pink floral T-shirt that clashed with her red hair and a pair of orange capri pants that exposed her wiry, freckled calves. But Lorelei bit her tongue. "Space," she reminded herself. The kid wants "space."

"So," Lorelei summed up, when Nixie had finished, "she's a neat freak, with literary ambitions and a heart condition, a secret romantic, who likes cats." She folded the blanket she'd slept in and picked up her empty coffee cup. "Sounds ordinary as an apple."

"And?" Nixie prompted.

"Arthritis, false teeth, twin sons, and a dead husband."

"And a Derek," Nixie added.

"Right. See what you can find out about Derek. Sounds as if he has ties to the husband's will. I'll take a good look through those letters later today. Right now, I'll head to the Dharmarama and see if I can meet up with Agnes Kellsington. Did you print out that information on her?"

"It's in the file," Nixie said. "As for me, I'm going back to Penny's, sit on the house for a while, see if she goes anywhere this morning. You showed them the brochures last night?"

"It was time," said Lorelei.

"Great. So the seance went well?"

"Gloria got a message through at last," Lorelei told her.

"Great!" Nixie jumped up and danced a little dance, clapping her hands as she headed toward the door.

Lorelei followed her. "I just hope he'll be interested."

"Are you kidding? He'll love it." Nixie grabbed a baseball cap from a hook on the wall. "I'd better get going, in case Penny goes out early." She pulled the lime green ball cap tightly down over her head, and the mass of her unbrushed, flaming curls sprang out wildly from under it. As a finishing touch, she pulled on her crazy, ruby-red high-top sneakers with the silver laces.

"Don't you think you should wear something less… colorful?" Lorelei asked her. "Like, how about the new pair of blue jeans I bought you?"

Nixie looked in the full-length mirror and shrugged. "It's too hot out."

"Just be sure to stay out of Penny's sight, then," Lorelei cautioned. "If she sees you in that outfit, she isn't likely to forget you."

"Don't worry about me," said Nixie. But Lorelei always did.

As she showered and dressed, Lorelei thought about the problem of Nixie. Nixie was good at her job. Hell, she was absolutely gifted. But now that she was older and insisting on her independence, it was getting harder to keep her safe. She didn't listen like she used to. She had her own ideas, and they weren't always sound ones. She wanted to do things her own way, but she had no experience. Lorelei sighed. When she thought about losing control over Nixie, she got a cold feeling in the pit of her stomach.

Over the years she had done her best to protect her little sister. She had fed Nixie green vegetables and yogurt and made her go to school. Even private school, sometimes, when they were flush—Latin and Greek and soccer and piano lessons. Tai chi. And Nixie had been useful. More than useful. Lorelei had to admit, at least to herself, that Nixie's skills had gotten her out of more than one tight corner. The girl had talent. Fingers like the feathers of a baby bird, Max had always said. This used to make Lorelei jealous, but it was true. It was Nixie's fingers that put the magical finishing touches on Lorelei's work. Nixie could slip those little fingers between your first and second ribs and slip out your heart before you even knew it, she was that nimble.

Nixie had come along on the evening of Lorelei's thirteenth birthday, brought by the woman Lorelei came to know as Auntie Katherine. They arrived in the middle of Lorelei's birthday dinner, just as Max was lighting the candles on her cake. The doorbell rang and Max, uncharacteristically, went to answer it himself. Lorelei heard the voice of a woman and then the voice of Uncle Joey, saying something about "a terrible row" and needing a favor for a friend from the casino. In later years, Lorelei figured out that Katherine was running from a bad relationship and that Joey had offered to find her a place to stay. But at the time, she was just upset by the interruption. A whispered conversation was carried out in the hallway while she watched the candles burn down. When the wax began to drip onto the chocolate icing, she wished quickly for Max to hurry up, blew the candles out, and cut herself a thick slice. She had polished off two pieces by the time Max ushered Katherine into the kitchen and introduced her.

"Happy birthday!" said Katherine, when she walked in. At least she was carrying a present, Lorelei thought, something small and heavy and probably breakable, wrapped up in a quilted blanket. "You must be Lorelei! Such a pretty girl." Katherine had long, dark bangs that hung over her eyes, and when she brushed them aside, Lorelei could see a dark purple bruise across her forehead and temple. Wherever Katherine had come from, it wasn't a good place.

"Sit down," Max invited. "Have a piece of cake."

"I have to put Nixie to bed first," Katherine said. "She's out like a light."

"Who's Nixie?" asked Lorelei.

Katherine lifted the quilt and uncovered a pink, sleeping face. "She's four years old," Katherine said. But Nixie seemed too small to be four. She seemed too small to be real. She looked like a porcelain miniature of a child, with fine, sculpted features, a tiny red doll's mouth, and a head of hair like the spun gold of a fairy tale. Lorelei touched the tangle of pale orange curls, and Nixie's delicate, sandy eyelashes fluttered slightly under her closed lids.

"How do you like your birthday present?" Uncle Max joked.

At first, Lorelei loved to help Katherine look after Nixie. She spent her allowance on little dresses and sunsuits and bright green ribbons for Nixie's curly hair. She brushed these curls gently and helped Nixie climb into her new clothes. The tiny limbs, the sprightly little fingers with their wee half-moon fingernails, delighted her. In the mornings, when Max and Katherine slept late, Lorelei would dress Nixie, give her some cereal, and take her out to the playground. Sometimes it seemed to Lorelei as if she really had received Nixie for her birthday. She fed her and bathed her and dressed her up, just as if she were a toy doll. She didn't think it would last. She assumed that Katherine, like all the other aunties, would soon be packing her bags and storming out of the house.

But Katherine stayed on. And Nixie, as it turned out, was not a doll after all. She was a willful little person who demanded not only food and clothing but songs and stories, walks and games and pushes on the swing. Lorelei soon lost patience with all of the dressing and feeding and bathing and entertaining. Nixie became a chore, and then a nuisance, and by the time she had grown out of her pretty little sunsuits, Lorelei was thoroughly sick of her.

Nixie's talents had become apparent quickly. She was mesmerized by Max's shop, and before long she was handling the tools more deftly than Lorelei ever could. She was also fascinated by Max's special cards. They looked ordinary, with kings and queens and spades and hearts like any other deck for playing poker or gin rummy. But they had a complicated pattern on the back, an intricate Celtic design that varied so slightly on every card that Lorelei could never tell them apart.

Yet Nixie could. By the age of seven, Nixie had memorized all fifty-two variations and cleaned out the entire contents of Lorelei's piggybank in one marathon session of crazy eights.

But Nixie's worst fault was the way she captivated Max with her talents. Nixie could cut a deck of cards in two, hold one half in each palm, and then, by slowly releasing the pressure of her thumbs, let the cards fall one at a time into a neatly overlapped stack. When Lorelei tried this, the cards fell in thick, uneven clumps onto the table, and often onto the floor. She practiced hard, taking the cards to bed with her at night and sitting cross-legged in the lamp light while Nixie was sleeping, dividing the deck in two over and over again, willing her thumbs to co-operate. But the cards flipped and flopped in every direction until finally she would give up in despair, disgusted with her own two hands. Meanwhile, Nixie became faster and faster until, at the age of eight, she could shuffle a deck of cards like a professional.

When Max saw this, he began to teach Nixie other tricks, things Lorelei had tried in vain when she was younger. He gave up trying to teach Lorelei anything, and this resignation stung her worse than his former disappointment in her failed attempts. Soon he had Nixie palming pennies, slipping cards and rings and watches up her sleeve with expert skill.

"So nimble!" Max exclaimed. "Look at those little hands. Light as the feathers of a baby bird."

One evening after dinner, Max asked Lorelei to get him a package of cigarettes he'd left on the coffee table. As she walked across the room, Nixie came running in from the kitchen, calling, "Mama!" She ran smack into Lorelei, nearly knocking her over, and Lorelei had to grab the little girl to keep her from falling.

"Nixie, be careful," said Katherine.

But instead of scolding Nixie for running through the house, Max simply laughed. "Say, Lorelei, what time is it?" he asked.

Confused, Lorelei looked at her watch and saw that her wrist was bare.

Nixie, triumphant, was holding the watch above her head. "I did it, Uncle Max!" she cried. "She didn't even notice!"

"Max," said Katherine mildly. "Do you really think you should teach them these things?"

Max shrugged. There were two kinds of people in the world, he said, the cons and the conned, and which kind did Katherine want the girls to be?

Everyone adored Nixie, not just Katherine and Max, but the shop customers and Uncle Joey and all the neighbors. Even strangers on the street would stop to admire her precious face and run their fingers through her coppery curls, which glowed with red highlights in the summer sun.

"Whose little girl are you?" they would ask.

"My mama's."

"And what's your name?"

"I'm Nixie Good," she would say, and everyone would fuss over her and give her candy.

It was the only name Nixie knew for herself. Katherine had taken Max's last name and conferred it on her daughter with no mention of having any other. Whenever Lorelei asked who Nixie's father was, Katherine simply said, "Nobody you'd want to know."

So one day when Lorelei was feeling especially jealous

of her little sister, she told her, "You're not Nixie Good. That's my name—mine and Max's—so don't go calling yourself by our name."

"But Mama said—"

"Never mind what Mama said. You're not a Good."

"Then what *am* I?" asked Nixie. Her lower lip quivered and her round blue eyes filled up with tears, and Lorelei didn't want to look at her.

"You're nobody," Lorelei told her. "You're Nixie Nobody. A little zero, a no one, an absolute nothing."

Lorelei sighed deeply as she remembered this painful scene. Poor Nixie Nobody. The nickname had been unkind, of course, but Lorelei had found it useful when she wanted to get the little girl out of her hair. Oh well, she told herself now, she'd more than made up for it since with all she'd done for the kid.

She gathered up her comb and lipstick and her deck of tarot cards in preparation for her visit to the Dharmarama. As she placed the cards in her purse, she smiled. There was a good reason, after all, why Lorelei did so many things for Nixie. She owed a debt to Nixie's mother. Although at first she was angry with Katherine for bringing Nixie into the house, Lorelei eventually began to forgive her. Because while Max was teaching Nixie how to use a jeweler's graver and pick a person's pocket, Katherine was teaching Lorelei more important things, things that changed her life.

Katherine dug up a patch of earth in the backyard and taught her how to grow tomatoes and tulips. She taught her how to ice skate and bake bread and make soup. She was shocked when she discovered that Max had never taught Lorelei to swim. "After what happened to her parents!" she said. "Max, what's the matter with you?" Soon, she was taking both girls to swimming lessons every week at the Pan

Am Pool. Lorelei became a strong swimmer and an excellent diver. She learned to do a one-and-a-half off the ten-meter platform when the other girls in the class were still afraid to crawl to the edge on their hands and knees. She loved that wild moment just after her feet left the board. It was like flying. And then the terrifying thrill of the fall. The sensation was addictive. Lorelei did it again and again, practicing her high dive to perfection, while Katherine cheered her on from the stands.

In Lorelei's teenage years, Katherine became her closest friend. Lorelei didn't have any real friends her own age. Max had never thought to sign his little niece up for gymnastics or Girl Guides, and he certainly didn't allow her to invite anyone into the house. So Lorelei had never bonded with the other girls in the neighborhood, and by the time they reached high school, she was an outsider. She didn't really mind. There seemed to her to be something insubstantial about those other girls, anyway. Clear-eyed and oblivious to their surroundings, they were somehow transparent. Their thoughts were practically painted on their foreheads, and if Lorelei ever wanted anything from them, she only had to tell them whatever they needed to hear. As for the boys, they were ignorant as lambs and even easier to please. If she wanted to, she could draw them toward her like paper clips toward a magnet, but most of the time she didn't want to. The only boys who interested her at all belonged to a small gang of hoodlums who smoked cigarettes under the school stairway and leered when she passed by. They had a way of looking at her as if they really saw her. But she kept her distance. She had noted their mistakes, the way their minds tended to wander. None of them could get away with anything, because they never paid attention. Lorelei remained outside them all and watched and waited, though she wasn't sure exactly what she was waiting for. And then one day, Katherine showed her what it was.

Lorelei was grateful to Katherine for many reasons. But the main thing, the big thing, the thing that finally made her forgive Katherine completely, was the way that Katherine told stories with her cards. This was something Nixie couldn't share, because Katherine said she was too little to understand. Late in the evening, when the dishes had been washed and Max had gone downstairs to work and Nixie was in bed, Lorelei had Auntie Katherine and her tarot cards all to herself.

The first time Katherine gave Lorelei a reading, the first card she laid down was the Queen of Wands, a noble blond in a golden robe and crown, seated on a tall throne with a black cat at her feet.

"Hmm," said Katherine. She turned over the next card and laid it across the first. It was the King of Cups, a stern ruler, whose throne floated on the surface of the ocean. Behind him, a fish leaped from the blue and yellow waves.

"What?" asked Lorelei.

"Just wait," said Katherine. "Let the reading unfold." She laid out the cards in a pattern, nodding each time she turned one over.

"These first two," she said, pointing to the Queen of Wands and the King who lay across her, "represent your spirit guides. The woman is gentle and wise. See the wand in her hand, how leaves are sprouting from the wood? That's for growth. And the sunflower she holds, that's for light. A light out of the darkness, meaning she knows the way. The man is strong, a protector. The water, that's a sign of life, also. I'd say…." Katherine leaned over the table, looking directly into Lorelei's eyes. "Yes, I'd say these are the spirits of your parents, who want you to listen to their guidance. They're sending you a message through the cards."

Lorelei felt a sudden emptiness in her belly. "My parents?"

"Yes. They care for you very much."

"But they're dead!" Lorelei protested.

"Yes," said Katherine gently. "A terrible tragedy. But see how both of them look to their left?" Katherine's slim fingers caressed the cards. "That is the direction of love. They're watching over you."

"They're dead," Lorelei repeated. "You can't see when you're dead."

"Your parents live on in the realm of the spirits, which is the realm of great wisdom and power. They're much closer than you think." Katherine touched the next card, the Four of Wands. "This picture explains it. You see the two figures waving from a distance? They're calling to you. Don't you hear them?"

"No."

"Are you sure? Sometimes at night, perhaps, just as you're falling asleep. Or in dreams? Why, I can feel them in this room right now. Their warmth envelops you. You haven't ever felt that warmth surrounding you?"

"Never," said Lorelei. But she was no longer so certain. Katherine's voice was soft and low. It made her feel sleepy. And warm. Maybe she *had* heard something, once or twice. A faint rustling in the night. A whisper.

"The veil between the dead and the living is very fragile," Katherine continued. "It's nothing but a cloud of illusion. It can be lifted, if we want to lift it." She laid her cool fingers on Lorelei's arm. "Love can lift it."

Lorelei raised her eyes then and met Katherine's serious

gaze. She could feel the presence of love in the room. "What are they saying to me?" she asked. "Tell me what they're saying."

So Katherine told her. And from that night on, whenever Lorelei begged for a reading, there would be a message from her mother or her father. Telling her to be brave, to be strong, to listen to Uncle Max. They told about the day they met, their love at first sight, their great hopes that Lorelei would remember her chores and learn to be kinder to Nixie.

Lorelei couldn't understand the card pictures herself, but Katherine knew how to translate them. Sometimes she had to work very hard to do it, closing her eyes and wrinkling her forehead, while Lorelei watched in awe and admiration. She repeated to herself the phrases Katherine used, *realm of the spirits*, *cloud of illusion*. When Katherine went out, Lorelei took the cards from their silk wrapper and spread them across the table, memorizing the different pictures and practicing the expressions she'd seen on Katherine's face, the frown of concentration, the wise nod that signaled a suspicion confirmed, the smile of serenity that meant the meaning of a message had at last come clear.

With one red high-top sneaker firmly on the gas pedal, and a twist of red licorice between her teeth, Nixie expertly kept the distance constant between her van and Penny's jaunty blue Dodge as Penny headed north across two bridges, through the downtown area, and north of the city center. When Penny made a right turn onto a short residential block, Nixie passed her and turned at the next corner into an alley. She parked the van in the crumbling back lot of an abandoned grocery store and crept around the corner of the building to scan the front street. Two of the houses were boarded up, and someone had spray-painted the words "Burn me" across one broken front door. On other homes, shingles curled away from the roofs and peeling paint hung from the eaves. Who could Penny Johnson know out here?

Penny's Dodge was parked halfway down the block and Penny was still inside it. Nixie backtracked and ran down the alley. She jumped a chain-link fence into the backyard of a white clapboard house closer to Penny's parking spot. Then she froze. She should have looked before she leaped. Two dog bowls, two mighty chains, and some well-chewed bones were scattered in the dirt beneath her feet. It was pure luck the dogs weren't around. But a tangle of rusted metal blocked her way—an old swing set, hubcaps, radiators, fenders, discarded water pipes and ducts and various unidentifiable engine parts had slid away from a huge scrap heap in the corner and were taking over the whole yard. An ancient washing machine and refrigerator stood in the middle, surrounded by torn remnants of sheet metal, their sharp, rusty edges forming an impenetrable barrier. The yard was not only an eyesore, but a hazard. At least the fridge was locked. A rusty old chain and padlock protected any curious children from climbing inside and suffocating. She spotted a narrow path along the side of a tin shed and picked her way among the bent nails and broken glass into the front yard, trying to keep her balance without resting her bare hand against the burning hot tin of the shed wall.

Penny was still sitting in her car, holding a tiny cell phone to her ear. Nixie bent low and crouched behind a thick caragana bush in the front yard. The car door opened. Penny's knees and the hem of her blue dress swung out of the car, followed by her small feet in matching pumps. Nixie heard the trunk open, the rustle of paper bags, the clink of bottles. Then the trunk slammed shut. Penny came closer, heading for the white clapboard house, directly toward Nixie.

Nixie dropped and rolled right under the bush. A rough branch scratched her just below the eye. She lay still and tried not to breathe as Penny's blue heels came clicking down the walk, inches from her own knee in its bright orange cotton. Lorelei had been right this morning. Nixie should have worn jeans.

Penny spent entirely too long ringing the doorbell of the little white house before she knocked on the front door. When she still got no response, she waded into the scraggly garden under the picture window and banged on the glass.

"Derek?" she called. "Are you home?" She stepped back from the house and tilted her head to look into a higher window on the other side of the front door. "Derek? I have some things for you. Are you there?"

Finally, the front door opened and a shadowy outline appeared behind the screen. Nixie could hear a man's voice, though she couldn't make out his words.

"I just came by to remind you to call the lawyer," Penny was saying. "But I'm afraid I can't stay to visit after all. There's been a terrible accident. A friend of mine's been killed. Yolanda."

Nixie nearly gasped out loud.

"I just heard this morning," Penny continued. "The poor woman. You remember, she—"

The man mumbled something in reply.

"My psychic, of course," said Penny. "Honestly, Derek. You just met her last week. Yolanda Dawn. Anyway, I've just heard the news and, well, I can't stay. I brought you a few things, though. That rum you like."

The door opened and the man stepped out to accept a paper bag. Nixie saw broad shoulders in a tight black t-shirt, a mop of dark hair, dripping wet. She didn't dare move to get a better view.

Penny handed over the rest of her offerings. "I brought a few groceries, too, just in case, and some biscuits for Pirate and Hawk."

Nixie heard the click of toenails on wood from inside the house as two dogs came trotting at the sound of their names. One of them, a Doberman, slipped through the opened door, sniffed the air, and then looked straight at Nixie's hiding place. Its ears flattened against its head and it growled.

"Oh dear," said Penny. She backed out of the way.

Derek dropped the bags and grabbed the dog by the collar. "Hawk! Get back inside! Sorry, Aunt Penny. Hawk!" The Doberman barked and strained to get away. Inside, the other animal, sensing excitement, began to bark, too. Derek was out on the front steps now. He was in his early twenties, tall and barefoot, in oil-stained jeans. Nixie saw his muscles bulge under his T-shirt. She hoped he was strong enough to control his dog.

Finally, he managed to push the Doberman back inside. "Sorry," he said again. He produced a lopsided, uneasy grin. He was kind of cute. "They go nuts with all the rabbits around here. 'Specially when they haven't eaten."

"Well, they're growing boys." Penny laughed nervously.

"I got to feed them," said Derek. "So I guess we, uh, won't be going to that seance Friday night, then? If…."

"Oh dear," said Penny. "No. No, of course not."

"Fine," said Derek. "Friday night's my pub night, anyway." He took his groceries and his bottle of rum into the house, and Penny turned to leave. The Doberman and a German shepherd appeared at the window, their jaws snapping open and shut as they barked and snapped at Nixie. But neither of the humans had noticed her. She watched until the dogs were distracted—probably Derek had opened the biscuits—and then she crawled out from under the bush. Penny's Dodge was just turning the corner, heading back the way she'd come.

As she walked out to her car that morning, Lorelei couldn't resist a wary glance at the windows of her landlady. The duplex they shared was a rambling three-story affair, set back from the street. The yard was large and shady with a small forest of oak trees surrounded by a picket fence, the grass a little too long for this part of town, the branches of the lilacs and honeysuckle overgrowing the front path. It was a perfect location, right in River Heights, just as Lorelei had wanted, but not too expensive. The only drawback was the landlady. Charlotte Trapp had lived in this duplex ever since Lorelei could remember. As a girl, Lorelei had passed it every day on her way to school, and when she was apartment hunting last December, she'd been pleased to see the rental sign in Charlotte's window. Not that the two had ever been friends. Lorelei had only a dim memory of Charlotte as a brooding teenager, rocking her kid on the front porch day in and day out, too wrapped up in her own misery to take much notice of the goings-on in the neighborhood. But Charlotte had turned out to be a little too interested in her new tenants.

Lorelei let her gaze travel up the blue-shingled wall of the house to the upper windows. Nothing. But then a movement below caught her eye. In Charlotte's kitchen window, a pair of white curtains fluttered, and a hand was withdrawn from the sill. Lorelei's presence had been noted.

"Hi, Lorelei!" A voice from behind her.

She turned to see Charlotte's sixteen-year-old daughter, the inquisitive Imogene, on her way to school. As if they didn't know the city was in the middle of a heat wave, the authorities at Sacred Waters Girls' School prescribed a uniform of itchy tights and woolen tunics belted firmly over white, long-sleeved blouses. At nine in the morning, Imogene's blouse was already damp at the armpits, and the tunic had darkened in two wide half-moons under her heavy breasts. She dangled an old-fashioned book bag by its strap, thumping it rhythmically against her plump thighs.

"That's a nice dress," she said shyly.

"Thanks." The deep blue batik sundress was a recent find she was especially proud of.

"Who made it for you?"

"I, uh, bought it," Lorelei said. "From a store," she added lamely. The girl unnerved her. No matter how often Lorelei gave her the brush-off, Imogene persisted in hanging around, asking dozens of questions. Sometimes Lorelei suspected that her mother put her up to it.

"Imogene!" Charlotte had appeared on the porch, a wooden spoon in hand. "You're late!"

Imogene ignored her. "How's your cat?" she asked Lorelei.

"The cat?"

"Yeah, Bitsy. Is she better now? I brought a treat for her." She pulled a greasy paper bag from her satchel. "It's lox. From the deli."

Lorelei took the bag. If Bits was sick, she hadn't noticed.

"Can I come in and visit her?"

"Not right now." Lorelei could see Charlotte marching down the steps, brandishing the spoon.

"I have to go, anyway," Imogene said.

Lorelei nodded. Imogene skirted her mother and slouched away through the oak trees, hands behind her back, the book bag banging against the back of her knees.

"You go straight to school," Charlotte called after her daughter. "You hear me?" Imogene did not acknowledge her.

Charlotte tapped the spoon against her hand as she approached Lorelei. "I'm sorry, but the girl has no time to dawdle. She has work to do."

"Well," said Lorelei. "I have work to do myself."

Charlotte eyed the uncut lawn. "Yard work, I expect."

"Business, actually," said Lorelei.

"Uh huh." Charlotte folded her arms across her chest. "Consulting?"

"That's right." Lorelei had purposefully kept the nature of her business vague when she rented the place. And since every Sunday morning the sanctimonious sermons of televangelists thundered from Charlotte's television set loud enough to be heard in Lorelei's living room, she thought it was best to keep it that way.

Charlotte pointed at the greasy paper bag in Lorelei's hand. "What's that Imogene gave you?"

"Oh, treats for the cat. I guess I'd better go back inside and put them in the fridge before I leave."

Charlotte sniffed. She fingered the gold cross around her neck and frowned, as if cat treats were immoral.

When she finally drove away, Lorelei was tense. In an attempt to shake off her irritation with Charlotte, she took her cigarettes out of her purse and lit up at the first red light, glad she'd forgotten to toss them away. She was going to quit on her thirtieth birthday anyway, which was only six, no seven, weeks away. So there was no point in wasting the rest of this package.

It was true she had planned to quit on her twentieth birthday, and on her twenty-first, and on her twenty-fifth. But those had been times of tension, even danger, and everybody knows you can't quit when you're under stress. Until very recently, she'd been fleeing from one city to another, living on the run with no permanent home. For a long time, she hadn't even had a name to call her own. Depending on the vagaries of chance, she'd been Laura or Laureen or Laurel or once, very briefly, in Sacramento, Lola. But now, she reminded herself firmly, she was Lorelei again, back in her old home town. As she drove past the Crescentwood Community Club, she could see the very playground where she used to push Nixie on the swings until her arms ached. Yes. Life was simple here and streamlined. She had one name, one address, and one single, solitary goal. She was up-front, totally legal, and soon she'd be very, very rich.

Switching on the radio, she was just in time to catch the morning news. To her surprise, the top story was the death of Yolanda Dawn, whose body had been discovered last night in the bushes at the foot of her high-rise. "Ms Dawn, who made her living as a fortune teller, apparently fell sixteen stories to her death."

Lorelei winced. She turned up the volume and learned that police were investigating the death as "suspicious," but that no arrests had been made. Had Yolanda taken on the wrong kind of client? Someone unstable, who didn't like her reading? Maybe some demented killer, a thief or sexual predator posing as a client? It was dangerous to let strangers into your home, and Lorelei herself kept a tiny pistol, a

.38 Special, in a drawer in her consulting room, just in case. Yolanda should have done the same.

Brian drank two cups of coffee as he waited for Penny Johnson to come out of Detective Larraby's office. He had barely slept at all last night on the lumpy single mattress of the bed in his brother's spare room. He'd been plagued by visions of Yolanda Dawn's spread-eagled body in the dirt, the threatening red words on the wall, and her blood on his own hands. And he couldn't stop imagining those last, terrifying moments of her life. Had she been conscious? For some reason, he was convinced she had been. He could imagine it so clearly, the rush of air past her ears like a great wind, the flashing of sunlight on the rows of windows as she fell. He wondered if he had picked up some kind of after-image, the trace, perhaps, of sensations her departing spirit had left behind.

When Penny at last came out, he could see she'd been crying a little. But she smiled bravely at him. "I told them everything," she said. "I'm sure they'll see you had nothing to do with it."

Larraby beckoned Brian into his office. He was an older detective, with twenty years on the job, a heavy frame, and the requisite cynical attitude. He didn't sit in a chair, but simply lifted a thick haunch up onto the edge of his desk—a good sign, Brian thought, that he didn't intend to keep his suspect long. Sure enough, Larraby told him he was free to go, with the usual warning not to leave town.

"Do you have any suspects yet?" Brian asked. "What's your theory on the case?"

"Not at liberty," said Larraby.

"Right," said Brian. Tommy would keep him up to date, anyway.

Afterwards, he agreed to have a cup of coffee with Penny in the cafeteria. It was his third, but he would need it if he was going to get any work done today.

"What's your theory?" he asked her, when they settled at one of the plastic tables with their Styrofoam cups. "Do you know anyone who might have hated Yolanda?"

"Hated her?" said Penny. "You don't think it was…just a burglar?"

"There was nothing disturbed that I could see." he said. "Her purse was lying right there on her bed, unopened. And that message on the wall—calling her a witch, well—"

"A witch?" Penny's dark brown eyes grew round. "A message calling her a witch?"

Brian had a sinking feeling that maybe he shouldn't have said that. Maybe the cops wanted to hold that detail back. But no one had warned him to keep quiet. He described for Penny the gruesome, dripping letters on the wall.

"My goodness!" she said. "How awful!"

"My brother says it was probably someone she knew. Was she married?"

"She had a husband in Chicago," Penny said "But she left him, oh, three or four years ago. Maybe longer. Before she came to Winnipeg. As far as I know, he's never been up to visit her. But that word, *witch*, that reminds me of the graffiti on the wall of the Dharmarama last summer."

"I never heard about that."

"You know Summer Sweet's Dharmarama Boutique on Corydon?"

Brian nodded.

"Well, it started off as a minor nuisance, the word *witch* spray-painted on the brick, but my stars, you'd never guess how hard it is to get spray paint off brick. Summer had to hire a special cleaning service to do it. And then the word kept coming back! It was always *you witch* or *witchcraft* or even once *Satan* in bright red letters on the glass of the display window. Horrible! But then, by the fall, it just stopped. We figured the kids who were doing it must have grown up. And now, on Yolanda's wall…."

"You should mention this to Detective Larraby," Brian said.

"I certainly will. Oh dear." Penny began to sniffle again and paused to blow her nose. "It's just so tragic. She was such a lovely woman. I can't think of any reason anyone could possibly hate her."

She told Brian she'd met Yolanda last year at a retirement party for one of her friends. Yolanda had made a surprise appearance, arranged by the host, and read the cards of the retiree aloud for everyone's amusement. The guests had roared with laughter as Yolanda predicted a new house, trips to Paris, and lavish vacations to exotic islands for the retired part-time librarian with a very modest pension. But a few days later, the woman had won the lottery and all of Yolanda's spectacular predictions came true.

"She became so popular after that," Penny recalled fondly. "I think she was probably the most loved of all the psychics in town."

"*All* the psychics in town?" Despite the somber topic, Brian was a little amused by her turn of phrase. "Are there that many?"

"Oh, there are quite a few, you know. The most famous, I guess, is Maurice Lemoine. At least he's famous now, with his new book and everything. Even his old clients can't get an appointment with him any more. He's been off on a book tour for months now. Then there's Madame Solange at the old DuBois Hotel and Teddy at the Plaza, and of course

Summer Sweet still does the odd reading, though she mostly just runs the boutique these days."

"That's a lot of psychics," said Brian. "Winnipeg can keep them all in business?"

"Oh, yes, and there are more coming up all the time. There's this new one, Lorelei, she calls herself, over on Grosvenor and Lilac. We were there last night, and I must say she was impressive. A bit disturbing, though, her powers are—"

"Lorelei?" said Brian. "I once knew a girl named Lorelei."

CHAPTER THREE

The Dharmarama was a treasure trove of candles, aromatherapy oils, crystals, and publications on everything from vegan barbecuing to tantric sex and near-death experiences—or NDEs, as those in the know called them. Lorelei loved this shop. She attended every open house event and worked hard to maintain a friendship with the shop's owner, Summer Sweet. Summer was generous about letting local card readers use her space. She took a steep cut—forty percent—but her enthusiastic promotion usually made the partnership worthwhile. The Dharmarama was a seemingly endless source of upscale, fashionable women, all flirting with their inner selves and willing to spend good money on the courtship. With Summer's endorsement, and rapid word of mouth, Lorelei had quickly built her client base until she'd achieved her goal of crossing paths with Waverley Forbes. She read cards at the shop only rarely these days, but she kept close ties with Summer, who often dropped helpful hints about her customers' personal lives.

Despite the early hour, the small book section at the

front of the store was crowded. Lorelei recognized several members of the Seekers sitting in a circle on the couches and chairs provided for customers. The news of Yolanda's death must have drawn them together. Summer was seated among them, pouring tea, easy to spot in one of her trademark pink outfits. She had turned forty last year and embarked on a plan of self-improvement. Her graying shoulder-length tresses were now a rich, unnatural magenta-brown. This winter she'd had a bit of a nose job, and recently Lorelei had noticed a startling increase in her bust line. Business must be good.

Summer set down the teapot and handed a cup to Agnes Kellsington beside her. Unlike Summer, Agnes tended to blend into the background. Today she wore a beige, polyester pantsuit, a shapeless thing with a long-sleeved jacket, and a white chiffon scarf tied loosely over her limp, blond hair. Lorelei stepped forward. From what she could overhear, it seemed that everyone was discussing Yolanda's demise.

"I dreamed of her just the night before!"

"I had been meaning to call her that very day."

"I heard she had a restraining order on her ex," one young woman said. "I heard he broke her nose once."

"I thought that was from a car accident," replied a man in a straw hat. "I'm sure she told me it was from an accident."

"Maybe she didn't want to say," the woman suggested.

"Agnes, you've known her a long time," said Summer. "Do you think her ex could have done it?"

"Oh, I don't know," said Agnes. She lowered her eyes to the floor. "I'd hate to think anyone was capable of such a thing."

"You don't think she threw *herself* off?"

"Why, no. I didn't mean that. I only meant, well, perhaps it was an accident?"

Lorelei stepped forward into the book section and smiled at Summer. "Terrible news," she murmured.

Summer smiled back sadly. Lorelei noticed she'd had her teeth fitted with orthodontic braces. Business must be very good indeed.

A few of the other Seekers nodded at Lorelei. Nobody present was a very important client of hers, but she knew most of them by name, except for a bearded man in a checked shirt. She poured herself a cup from the pot of herbal tea Summer always kept hot. She sat and listened, paying particular attention to anything that Agnes said, but Agnes didn't say much.

It had taken some digging on Nixie's part to discover who Agnes really was and how much money she had. Agnes was shy and modest, never comfortable in social situations. She had married late, having spent most of her adult life caring for her sick mother. But Agnes's mother had died last year and now Agnes was a newlywed at the age of fifty-five. According to the society pages of the *New York Times* on-line, Hank Kellsington's recent spring wedding to Agnes Wellford of Chicago, Illinois, had been a gala event, held in the bride's home town and attended by three hundred guests, a string quartet, and a folk ensemble. The ceremony was performed jointly by Dr. Waters of the Living Forever Institute and Guru Vijayan from San Francisco. With her huge fortune, her recently deceased mother, and her interest in spiritual matters, Agnes was definitely a person worth getting to know. But it was unfortunately too late for Lorelei to expect much from her in the way of an investment in the research center. It usually took at least a year to lay the groundwork before a client made a contribution of any significance.

Nevertheless, Agnes was Penny's friend. Lorelei leaned forward and smiled at her. "You knew Yolanda Dawn?"

"Yes, indeed. Yolanda and her husband attended the Living Forever retreat in Chicago several times, back when they were still married, of course."

"And you don't think her husband…?"

"Oh, dear, no," said Agnes. "For one thing, he's a very small man. I hardly think he is strong enough."

"I wonder if you two ladies have met Kent Mason," Summer interrupted. "One of our newest members. Agnes, do you know Kent?"

Agnes smiled shyly. "A little."

The man in the checked shirt held out his hand. "But I haven't met Lorelei," he said. "Though I've heard a lot about you."

"Kent works in television," said Summer proudly, as Lorelei and Kent exchanged pleasantries. "He's doing a piece on the Dharmarama, so you really should talk to him, Lorelei. Kent, you have to interview Lorelei. She has a remarkable gift for personal readings. She can see right through to your inner self. Almost instantly. Her tarot readings are…. Oh, excuse me." The telephone was ringing in her little office at the back of the store and she hurried to answer it.

"Right through to the inner self, eh?" Kent looked impressed. "So, what do you see in Agnes here?"

"Yes," said Agnes. "What do you see in me?" Despite her shyness, she seemed intrigued.

Lorelei reached forward and touched Agnes's shoulder lightly. "Well," she said, "I'd really have to spend more time with you, but I do sense…."

"Yes?"

Lorelei lowered her voice to a confidential tone. "I sense loss."

Agnes looked up, and for the first time Lorelei could really see her face. Her eyes were a clear, bewildered blue.

"You are alone," said Lorelei. "And yet you're not alone."

Agnes's eyes widened.

"That's true!" cried Kent. "Agnes is married, but her husband's away."

"He's in India," Agnes explained. "We went there on a retreat, but I—had to come back."

"You had troubles," said Lorelei. "Yes, I sense—"

"Renovations," said Agnes quickly. "On the house, you know."

"Contractors!" Kent exclaimed in disgust. "Tell me about it!"

"Mmm," said Lorelei. "Yes, I sensed you were apart from your mate, but there's a stronger..." Again, she shook her head and smiled.

"What?" asked Agnes.

"I see someone is waiting for a reading," said Lorelei. She patted Agnes's hand and stepped gracefully past her, making her way toward the back of the store.

There was, in fact, nobody waiting for a reading. The young couple at the back were merely browsing through the gift section, looking for a greeting card.

"How about this?" one asked the other. "It says, 'When a door in the universe closes, a window opens.' Isn't that beautiful? Look at the dove."

"Let me see that."

Lorelei smiled at them briefly before she parted the beaded curtain and entered the booth, where she sat shuffling her tarot cards, waiting to see if Agnes would approach. She loved this booth, with its tent-like frame draped with softly sparkling fabrics from the far East. It was restful and soothing in here and fabulous for eavesdropping.

Through the thin wall behind her, she could hear Summer talking to someone on the phone: "You're flying in on the nineteenth? Have you made appointments in advance? I've got plenty. Just read me the list and I'll tell you. Yes, I've got that one. Yes. Yes. Um, no, I don't think so. Who? Umm, just a sec."

It sounded like a sales call, with Summer checking her inventory for a long-distance customer. The drawer of a file cabinet slid open and Lorelei heard a sound like the flipping of stiff paper. "No, I don't see that one. Who are the others? Yes. Yes. Oh yes, I've got that one, but the price has gone up. That one's gone solid gold." She laughed. "I'll let you know. Depends which way the wind blows in the next little while."

Summer paused, as if listening. Then she said, "It made the news out there? Horrible thing. Poor Yolanda." She listened again. "Of course I knew her. She came in once in a while for— What? No! I don't deal with the locals."

Lorelei mulled over that last bit as she shuffled her cards, hoping to hear more. Summer dealt with local people every day in her store. So what was she talking about?

"I have to go," she said. "I have customers. But let me know which ones you want so I can reserve them for you. It's my busy season."

Lorelei heard her hang up the phone. Then a rustling and the file drawer closing. In a moment, the cash register rang as Summer served customers at the counter.

Lorelei lingered a few minutes longer and soon, sure

enough, Agnes poked her head through the beaded curtain of the card-reading booth. "May I come in?" Carrying an orange net shopping bag bulging with purchases, she stepped inside and said shyly, "Earlier, when you said that I was alone?"

Lorelei nodded. "And yet not alone."

"What did you mean?"

"As I said, I sense you have recently suffered a loss."

Agnes nodded sadly.

Lorelei placed a comforting hand on her wrist. "When a door in the universe closes," she said, "a window opens."

"Oh, that is *so* true," said Agnes. "But what do you mean by 'not alone'?"

"I don't want to upset you," said Lorelei kindly. She folded her hands in front of her and bowed her head. She took a deep breath. "But I sense a presence around you. A female energy. Someone who is…no longer here on Earth."

Agnes stared. She placed her hand over her heart.

"Someone who is…." Lorelei paused, as if uncertain how to broach a delicate topic. "Lingering?"

Agnes seemed to know exactly what that meant. Her head nodded vigorously, as if of its own accord. "Yes. Yes, maybe I should have a reading. Soon." She glanced quickly over her right shoulder, then her left, either to make sure no one was listening, or to catch a glimpse of the lingerer. "You do them, um, in private?" She smiled apologetically. "It's confidential?"

"I'm always happy to arrange private readings," said Lorelei. "For a very small surcharge. In fact, I recommend privacy for a first reading, when it's so important for the vibrations to be pure. The initial consultation is only fifty dollars for twenty minutes." As she spoke, she pulled a card from her purse and pressed it into Agnes's hand. "Shall we say tomorrow afternoon? I'm just over on Grosvenor."

"Yes, but…. Well, I hate to ask, but you see, I'm spending most of the next few days at the lake, getting our cottage ready. It's really not far at all. Two hours' drive, or two and a half. Three at the very most. You could stay overnight, if you like. It's lovely there. Do you know Lake of the Woods? I'm just off the northwest shore."

"I could do that," Lorelei said. It was an odd request. But then readings were always most accurate when she saw her clients in their own homes. "Of course, the travel time…."

"Naturally I'd reimburse you."

"It's a date, then."

"Thank you so much," said Agnes. "I'll call you with directions." She turned to leave, her shoulders stooped, her hands balled into tight little fists at her sides. Something was definitely tormenting her. Lorelei could almost see the gray, wispy apparition that followed her through the door.

What was making Agnes so nervous? And why was she so repressed? Lorelei could discern a slim, curvaceous figure beneath the bulky polyester outfit, a figure amazing for a woman in her fifties. Why did she conceal it beneath such frumpy clothing? Lorelei had met a few eccentrics like this before, guilt-ridden and unwilling to spend anything on themselves. Sometimes they were the ones most eager to give to good causes. If only she'd been more alert, she could have started working with Agnes sooner.

Brian slowed down as he drove through the old neighborhood and past his former high school. He turned left onto Grosvenor, noting the numbers on the houses, watching for Lilac, the cross street Penny had mentioned. As he approached the corner, he glanced to his left and saw two women chatting—or were they arguing?—in a driveway across the street. Who was that? Why, for God's sake, the blond with the garden rake was Charlotte Trapp. That was her parents' old blue duplex. But the dark-haired woman had her face turned away from him, and he could see only the curve of one cheek. Was it her? The car behind him honked, and he had to speed up.

It made Brian sad to remember Charlotte Trapp, a large, boisterous girl, a few years ahead of him in school, who'd been boy-crazy even back in elementary. She would sneak up behind you, wrap her arms around your neck, and demand to be kissed. If you refused, she'd tighten her hands around your neck until you kissed her. Then she'd run off and tell everyone you were her boyfriend. Brian had secretly felt sorry for her, even when—no, especially when—he'd been her victim. But while he'd spat out her germs and made puking noises just like everyone else, his cheeks had burned with shame. And she'd known it. She'd sensed his guilty conscience and it had maddened her somehow, made her seek him out more often. In high school, Charlotte grew tall and voluptuous and the boys had a change of attitude, offering her rides home, inviting her up to their rooms when their parents went out. Behind her back, all the girls had called her Charlotte Tramp. Finally, Charlotte had dropped out of school and later was seen pushing a baby carriage down the sidewalk. Even the meanest girls had shut up about her then.

But the other woman, the one Charlotte had just now been talking to, that brief glimpse of her cheek had spun him into another time and place. One sad afternoon in

June, the day after his father's funeral, when he'd skipped school to lie on the riverbank and mourn in private, he'd seen her high above him, leaning out over the Maryland Bridge, and he'd waved to her. She was the quiet one, the one who rarely came to school at all. The one who finally disappeared entirely.

Brian circled the block and drove past the house again. Charlotte was still standing, arms folded, in the driveway. He saw the dark-haired woman turn on her heels and walk away from her. Brian's eyes met hers for an instant and then she turned to climb the front steps to the porch. Yes, it was her. Lorelei Good. She opened the door and stepped inside without a backward glance.

An old wound that he'd thought long healed opened up in his chest and began to ache.

As Lorelei entered her front hallway, she thought she heard voices coming from within. She put down her groceries and the bag of candles and soap she'd picked up at the Dharmarama. She stepped out of her sandals and walked soundlessly down the hall in her bare feet. When she reached the entry to the dining room, she stopped short. Nixie had company.

Nixie and her visitor were seated at the table, heads close together, books and papers strewn in front of them. Lorelei's brochures had been moved to the sideboard. The visitor was hunched over an open book, twirling a strand of her hair around her ear. It was Imogene from next door. "*Homo sum*," she muttered. She looked at the ceiling. "*Homo sum, Homo sum.*"

"Imogene?" said Lorelei. "What are you doing in here?" She glanced at Nixie, but Nixie avoided her eyes.

"I came to see Bitsy," said Imogene. Bits was curled up in her lap. Imogene stroked the cat's ears and tickled her chin. "And Nixie is helping me with my homework."

Lorelei glared at Nixie. "She's *what*?"

"It's Latin," Imogene said. "It's hard." She sighed and returned to her book. "*Homo sum*," she read, and then looked at the ceiling again, as if the translation might be written there. "*Homo sum*...Some man?"

"*Sum*," said Nixie. "The verb *to be*."

"I am a man?"

"Good," said Nixie. "Or better, *I am human*. And then *humani nil*. You know *nil*, right? Nothing."

Lorelei turned sharply and returned to the entrance for her parcels. She made a lot of noise putting away the groceries. Then she stalked past Nixie and Imogene into the den and grabbed the candelabra. With a pocketknife, she scraped out the stubs of the burned-down candles and replaced them with new ones. She set a patchouli stick in the teak incense holder and then stalked past again on her way to replenish the guest bathroom with aroma-therapeutic soap and towels. What was Nixie thinking, letting this girl into the house? Lorelei regretted the thousands of dollars she'd spent on Nixie's education. And she definitely regretted every kind word she'd ever spoken to Imogene. What was Imogene Trapp to her, anyway? She should have told the kid to get lost long ago. Who knew what trouble this might lead to? She stood in the doorway to the dining room, her arms crossed, looking daggers at the back of Nixie's head.

"*I am human*," said Imogene, reading slowly from her notebook. "*Nothing that's human is alien...to me*? Is that right?"

"That'll do fine," said Nixie. She turned and glanced

nervously at Lorelei. "We're done here," she said. "Imogene's going home right away."

"Good," said Lorelei. "Because I have work to do." She reached over and closed Imogene's notebook and stacked it on top of her Latin text. She stuffed the pen and eraser into her pencil case. "Goodby, Imogene."

But Imogene showed no signs of leaving. She was looking at Lorelei, her wide lower lip drooping open. "I love that skirt," she said. "It's absolutely beautiful."

"We'll see you later, Imogene," Lorelei said. "I'm busy right now."

Imogene looked hurt, but she persisted. "What are you busy with?"

"Nothing that concerns you." Lorelei stepped forward and tucked the books and pencil case into Imogene's bag. "Now scoot."

Imogene remained on her chair.

Lorelei took her tarot cards out of her purse and rewrapped them in the swatch of raw silk she kept for this purpose.

"I know what those are," Imogene said. Her eyes narrowed and she fixed Lorelei with a crafty stare. "My mother says those cards are used to summon demons."

"That's not true," said Lorelei evenly. "Your mother's mistaken about that."

"Then what are you doing with all those candles and—"

"Come on," said Nixie. She tugged at Imogene's sleeve. "Let's go. You can come back tomorrow and I'll help you with that math problem." She ushered the girl into the front hallway.

Lorelei heard Imogene's voice. "I just want to know." The door slammed shut.

Lorelei waited in the kitchen, her foot tapping furiously, as Nixie came back in.

"What the hell were you thinking?" she asked.

Nixie shrugged. "The kid needs help."

"Well, we don't have time to help her. Be realistic." She pointed at the kitchen clock. "I have to get ready. I'm driving out to Agnes's cottage tomorrow."

The sisters sat down at the table and exchanged the news they'd gathered that day. The death of Yolanda Dawn had, of course, made a dramatic change in their plans.

"What happened to her, anyway?" Nixie asked. "I turned on the news, but they didn't have any details."

"From what I heard today, probably a domestic thing. A violent ex."

"Sick," said Nixie. "But it's sort of…."

"Yeah."

Neither of them wanted to say it out loud. But without Yolanda around, Lorelei's plan would work more smoothly. There was now one less rival for Waverley's attention and a better chance of winning Penny over as a client. Knowing the identity of Derek was also promising. Lorelei thought she could move a lot faster now with Penny. But she didn't have time yet to study Raymond Johnson's love letters. She needed to review all the information they had on Agnes Kellsington. Nixie got out the file and they went through it together.

The *Chicago Times* society pages reported with regret that the newlywed Kellsingtons would not be settling down in Chicago. After their lavish wedding in April, the couple planned a four-month holiday to Europe and India, before moving to Winnipeg, Canada, where they were restoring the Kellsington family home, which had stood vacant since Mr. Kellsington's parents had died. Mr. Kellsington, the article added, had been based in New York for the past twenty years. Now that he was married, he planned to lead a quieter lifestyle. It was a first marriage for both of them, even though they were in their fifties.

A little further research revealed that Agnes Kellsington, like Hank, was an only child. Both of them had inherited massive sums. When Agnes's mother died last year, she had left her daughter as sole heir to the Wellford cosmetics industry she'd started in her spare time while her husband had been busy buying up hotels across the United States. Hank and Agnes gave regularly and generously to charity, their favorite cause being the Living Forever Institute, which did important work with those who had experienced alien abductions, teaching that extraterrestrial visitors were a sign of hope for eternal life.

Lorelei went through all the information until she was thoroughly briefed. Her intuition was telling her there was something odd about Agnes's marriage, but she couldn't quite put her finger on it. She would have to get Agnes talking on that topic. It wouldn't be easy to draw such a reserved person into an intimate conversation, but Lorelei would have to try. She needed to divine Agnes's most secret hopes and fears in a hurry, if she was going to impress her on her first visit. Penny Johnson would be looking for a new medium very soon. A recommendation from her good friend Agnes would surely help.

The next morning, Nixie washed the breakfast dishes while Lorelei read the morning news at the kitchen table. She read silently for a while, skimming the tiny article on Yolanda's death, which appeared on page four. No details, yet. The paper had gone to press mere hours after the body was discovered. She turned to the entertainment section and said, "Look at this." She pushed the paper forward so Nixie could see it.

The headline read: "Salem North? Winnipeg Psychics Draw Preacher's Wrath." The photo featured a man calling himself the Reverend Surefire, leading his followers in prayer outside the Hotel Fort Garry.

"Bible thumpers?" said Nixie. "I thought you said they didn't have those up here."

Lorelei read aloud from the article: "The Reverend Surefire has vowed that the city's twentieth annual Psychic Fair will not go unchallenged by the group he calls his 'Soldiers Against Satan.' The group plans a series of protests throughout the city to draw attention to the growing popularity of New Age philosophy and other 'dangerous practices' such as Ouija boards, tarot cards, and of course, the Psychic Fair, which the Reverend Surefire calls 'an open invitation to the devil.'"

"Great. Organized thumpers," said Nixie. "Ready to march, chant, burn your books, and accuse you of satanic rituals."

"I heard this reverend on the radio the other day," Lorelei said. "Some phone-in show for kids. He was warning teens against seances. Says they can attract malicious spirits and demons. Maybe Imogene's mother was listening to that."

Nixie looked closely at the newspaper photograph. "What are they doing?"

"Blessing the hotel to keep evil spirits away."

Nixie groaned. "That kind of stunt could scare customers right off."

"Clients," said Lorelei. "Not customers. And I don't

think it'll scare anyone off. In fact, it's probably good advertising."

Later that afternoon, as Lorelei was taking her overnight bag out to the car, Bitsy came bouncing down the stairs, trailing a length of yellow yarn from her mouth. Nixie leaped up. "Bits! No!" She chased the kitten down the hall and scooped her up. Pulling the yarn out of her mouth, she held it up and said ruefully to Lorelei, "Rapunzel."

"Rapunzel will soon be bald at this rate," said Lorelei as she went out the door. She smoked a cigarette in the driveway, leaning against her car—a 2003 candy-apple red Mercedes-Benz hatchback with a sensuous black leather interior that she didn't want to sully with smoke—and thought about Rapunzel.

Rapunzel had been a Christmas present in a year when the atmosphere was tense between Max and Katherine. They had been arguing a lot and seventeen-year-old Lorelei had been overhearing more than she wanted to. But Christmas morning, there had been a small pile of lovely presents, as usual. For Nixie, there was set of rag dolls fashioned like storybook characters—Cinderella and Rapunzel and a handsome Prince Charming. Uncle Max had given Lorelei a very grown-up piece of jewelry, an onyx brooch in the shape of a prowling black leopard with emerald eyes and spots made of diamond chips. Lorelei loved it. She pinned it to her blouse immediately and kissed Uncle Max on the cheek. But it was the tarot cards that really pleased her. As soon as she tore the paper off, she looked up at Katherine and said, "Oh."

"I know," said Katherine.

For the rest of the day, Lorelei studied the cards and the book that came with them, teaching herself how to interpret the pictures, while Nixie acted out fairytales with her new dolls and a castle made of a cardboard box. Katherine stayed down in the basement with Max for a long time and then she came up to the kitchen and began to cook furiously, banging the pots and pans so hard that Lorelei bundled up Nixie and took her to the skating rink.

That night an argument that had been simmering a long time finally erupted. Lorelei could hear their voices through the air vent as she got ready for bed.

"Max, you're putting us at risk. You're putting the girls at risk. I won't stand for it."

"I've done it before."

"Only with a few pieces," Katherine said. "This is different. If—"

"Katie, Katie, calm down," Max said. "It's only for a short while. It's just until—"

"Until what? Until Joey figures out what you're up to? My God, Max, all he has to do is take a good, close look."

"He won't."

"He might."

"He won't, Katie. He trusts me. Don't you trust me?" Max was using his soft voice, his coaxing voice. "Katie? Love?"

Lorelei heard no answer from Katherine. She heard only the sounds of washing up in the kitchen, the placing of dishes in the cupboards, and then Katherine's footsteps through the house, the opening and closing of doors as she checked the locks. When her own door opened, Lorelei shut her eyes and pretended to be sleeping. Katherine stood there a long time, longer than usual, and Lorelei heard her sigh. Then the door closed, slowly and deliberately, and she was gone.

For a few days, a silence descended on the household. Uncle Max cracked his knuckles more often and smoked more cigarettes. Katherine went out frequently and when she came home, she spent a lot of time on the telephone. About a week after the argument, she called Lorelei into the dining room and set a large manila envelope on the table before her. "I want you to look at these papers," she said. "I want you to study them carefully." She slid the papers out and sorted through them, pulling out three sets of identification, including birth certificates and passports, which she handed to Lorelei. The rest she returned to the envelope. She made Lorelei memorize the birthdays and places of birth, the histories, and the three new names: one for Katherine, one for Lorelei, and one for Nixie. "Just in case," Katherine said.

Lorelei was old enough to understand what "just in case" meant. She had only one question. "What about Uncle Max?"

"Uncle Max can take care of himself," Katherine had answered grimly. "He always does. So it's up to us to take care of us. Up to me to take care of you girls, and up to you and me to take care of Nixie. You understand?"

Lorelei nodded.

"And I would expect...." Katherine hesitated. Then she reached out and grasped Lorelei's hand across the table. "I would expect that—if anything did happen to me—you would take care of Nixie."

Lorelei was surprised. Such an event had never occurred to her, but it was so unlikely that she said, very quickly, "Sure."

"Promise?"

"I promise."

She had kept that promise, she thought now, as she crushed out her cigarette and tossed her bag in the car. Though it hadn't always been easy. As she backed out of the driveway, Nixie waved from the living room and Lorelei waved back. Nixie held Bitsy up to the glass and made her paw wave, too. Lorelei couldn't help smiling, but she also shook her head. No matter how grown-up she thought she was, Nixie was still a kid.

In the car, she turned on the radio only to hear another story about Yolanda Dawn. Rumors were apparently circulating that she had been killed as part of a sacrificial rite. Was everybody going crazy? She switched to an all-music station. She wanted to concentrate on formulating a plan to draw Agnes Kellsington out of her shell. But she found herself thinking instead about Katherine again. She had been thinking about Katherine a lot lately. She guessed it was partly being back in Winnipeg and partly because it was June.

By the June that followed the Christmas argument, Lorelei was beginning to forget about the manila envelope and the promise she'd made to Katherine. At seventeen she had other things on her mind. Since receiving her own tarot cards, and practicing on many of Max's clients, she had given readings for a few of the girls in her class who now regarded her with awe. She'd actually been invited to a party to be thrown by one of the richest, most popular girls in the school, who'd asked her to bring her cards along. So Lorelei was absorbed in observing this girl's circle of friends, learning how to read them. She watched their gestures, charted their blushes, and followed the direction of their most surreptitious glances. She even peeked into their desks at school and listened to their mothers' gossip in the supermarket. She wanted to know them perfectly. Because nothing she'd ever experienced in her life—not even the roller coaster at the Ex or a plunge from the very top of the diving tower at the pool—equaled the thrill she got from the look on their faces when she revealed to them their innermost secret thoughts and feelings. She was also determined to impress a boy named Brian, who was invited to the same party. A few days before, she had made him gasp with wonder, and she longed to see that look of admiration in his eyes again. So on that last day at home, when Uncle Joey came to the door, Lorelei was distracted. She didn't notice, at first, that something was terribly wrong.

"Where's Max?" Joey was yelling before she even opened the door. It was raining and he was struggling in the wind with an umbrella.

Lorelei let him in. She hid her hand behind her back as usual and pressed the silent buzzer three times. "Come on in," she said. "Can I take your coat? Do you want a drink?" Lorelei had discovered that a drink worked best to keep Uncle Joey happy while he waited. His little princess, according to Max, was now working at a strip club and no longer her daddy's favorite topic of conversation.

"Is he down in the shop?"

Joey moved toward the door to the basement stairs, but Lorelei cut him off deftly. "I learned how to make martinis," she offered. She reached forward to remove his wet jacket.

Joey pushed her aside. "Where's Max? I need to see him right now."

"He's gone out." She wasn't sure why she lied. There was something in Joey's eyes she didn't like. She held her thumb to the buzzer and kept it there, a signal to Max that he should stay out of sight.

"Where the hell is he?"

"He's gone downtown," she said.

"Where?"

"Oh, he never tells me much," she said.

"If you know anything…." Uncle Joey shook his index finger in her face.

"He'll be back by dinnertime," she said quickly.

Uncle Joey looked deep into her eyes. Then, seemingly satisfied she was telling the truth, he gave up. "All right," he said. "But I'll be back." He glanced out the window. Through the pouring rain, Lorelei could see a large man waiting for him in the car.

"Any message?"

"You ask him if he knows who he's dealing with," Joey said. "You ask him if he knows exactly who he thinks he's fooling around with."

Lorelei stood at the window while Joey made his way back through the rain to the car. He struggled some more with the umbrella and then, unable to close it, he bashed it again and again on the roof of the car. When he was finished, he threw it against the ground and left it lying, thoroughly mangled, in a puddle. He got into the car and sat there for a few minutes, talking to the driver. Lorelei was afraid they were going to stay there, staking out the house. But eventually they drove off. Just in time. Because a moment later, she heard the back door slam open.

"Max!" It was Katherine, her hair soaking wet and clinging to her face. "Max!" She peeled off her wet clothes, right there in the hallway, even her bra and panties, and Lorelei saw she was soaked to the skin.

"Auntie Katherine, what's wrong?" Lorelei followed Katherine down the hall to the bathroom and watched her towel herself dry.

"Where's your Uncle Max? Where's Nixie?" Katherine didn't wait for an answer. She strode naked to her bedroom and pulled a suitcase from the closet. She flung it open on the bed and began to throw clothing into it—Max's clothing. She didn't bother to fold anything, not even his good white suit.

"Where's Max?" she repeated.

"Downstairs with Nixie. He said—"

"Get him."

Stunned by her tone of voice, Lorelei obeyed.

Nixie was sitting on a stool in the corner, fiddling with a bobby pin and an old lock Max had removed when he bought a new one for the safe. Max was seated at his workbench with one of Nixie's rag dolls laid out before him and a threaded needle between his fingers. The sewing basket was tipped over, its contents spilled across the work table.

"Something's wrong with Katherine," Lorelei blurted.

He didn't look up, but kept his eyes on his work as he asked, "Is Joey gone?"

"He says he'll be back," she told him. "He says to ask you, 'Do you know who you're dealing with?'"

Max looked up sharply.

"Uncle Max is doing an operation," Nixie said. "He's operating on Rapunzel."

"Katherine wants you right away," said Lorelei.

Max resumed his sewing. "One minute," he said, as if Nixie's doll was more important.

"He's taking out her appendix," Nixie informed her.

Nixie was eight. Too old for such a baby game. Lorelei looked at the ragged seam across Rapunzel's cotton skin. She saw the needle dart rapidly across the cloth and something else—a glimpse of something dark inside Rapunzel's belly—before Max stitched the incision closed, knotted the thread, and bit off the end. "There," he told Nixie. "She's all better now. You put her dress back on, okay? And keep her warm." To Lorelei he said, "You stay here."

She snuck up the stairs after him and listened outside their bedroom.

"He knows," Katherine was saying. "He was in the casino looking for you."

"He couldn't *know*," Max said. "How could he know for sure it was me?"

"I don't know, but he does. I could see it in his eyes. He'll be back here soon. He'll tear the place apart."

"He'll find nothing," Max said. "I've cleaned the shop out."

"Then he'll tear you apart. For God's sake, Max, he's got Laugherty with him."

"Jesus Christ," he said. "Mack Laugherty?"

"I've packed your things. There's cash in the side pocket, wrapped in a newspaper. Your wallet's in there, too."

"Jesus Christ," he said again.

"Never mind Jesus Christ," said Katherine. "There's a bus heading east leaves at two o'clock. I've called a cab. Make sure you tell the driver not to go over the Maryland Bridge. You don't want to pass them on their way here."

"Katie—" he said.

"Go! Get yourself safe out of town and then give us a call. We'll meet up with you later."

"Kenora?"

"Farther, I think," said Katherine bitterly.

The door opened and Lorelei hid behind it. Katherine emerged in her bathrobe, dragging Max's suitcase down the hall. Max followed, still protesting. "You don't need to be afraid of Joey," he was saying.

"The cab's here," Katherine said.

"Joey's not going to do anything. I'll talk to him."

"I saw his eyes," Katherine said. "I don't think he'll listen. Besides, do you think Laugherty is going to listen?"

Max put his arms around her then and said she shouldn't worry, that he'd go if that's what she really wanted, that he'd call her as soon as he could. "I'm sorry, Katie," he said.

"I know you are," was all she said. She stood in the open doorway and watched as the driver loaded the suitcase into the trunk and Max got into the back seat. She was still standing there watching, after the cab had driven away. Behind her, Lorelei watched, too.

"It's time," Katherine said, as soon as Max was gone. She lifted a tile from the ceiling of the hall closet and pulled out the manila envelope with the cash and the passports in it.

Nixie came up from the basement, holding her Rapunzel doll in her arms. Katherine knelt down and hugged her. "We're going on a trip, baby," she said.

"Where?"

"You'll see. Now come and get your rubber boots on. Lorelei, you go to your room and pack your suitcase. Be quick, now. Take only what you really need."

Lorelei didn't protest. She understood. Max had made a mistake. A big mistake. Katherine had seen this coming, had taken steps to protect the girls. Lorelei hurried to pack, throwing in first of all her precious tarot cards. Then her favorite clothes. Her makeup case. All the money in her piggy bank, which wasn't much. She snapped the case shut and took it back to the living room. Katherine and Nixie were already dressed in their new raincoats, the matching ones, pale blue with white daisies, as if they were off to an Easter picnic. Katherine was calling a cab. She held Lorelei's jacket out toward her as she spoke to the dispatcher, urging him to hurry.

Lorelei had pushed one arm through a sleeve when the doorbell rang. It couldn't be the cab driver. Not so soon.

Katherine was still holding the receiver in her hand. She replaced it slowly and tiptoed to the door, where she peered out the spy hole.

"Is it Uncle Max?" Lorelei whispered.

Katherine shook her head.

Lorelei's throat went dry.

Katherine ushered the girls into the kitchen. "We're going to be all right. Just get downstairs with Nixie and wait in the laundry room. Don't let Nixie make a sound."

Lorelei obeyed. In the laundry room, she was frightened to see the poster of the Alps torn from the wall and the safe empty with its door hanging open. Uncle Max must have been in a panic, even if he'd pretended he wasn't. From above, Lorelei heard muffled, angry voices, loud bangs, as if someone were overturning the furniture, and then the basement door opened and she could hear two voices clearly.

"He's not here!" Katherine was saying. "I told you, he's gone. He just phoned me from the Green Briar, not ten minutes ago."

"Laugherty's at the Green Briar right now," said Uncle Joey, "and Max ain't there. He ain't at the pool hall, and he ain't at the casino. Now get out of my way and let me down into the shop."

Nixie was sobbing now and Lorelei was fighting to hold her still and cover her mouth. As she wrestled in the darkness with the hysterical girl, she heard a series of thuds and grunts on the stairs above her. Somebody gasped. Katherine said, "No!" And then Lorelei heard the loudest noise she'd ever heard inside the house.

In the silence that followed, even Nixie fell still. She collapsed against Lorelei's chest and lay there breathing harshly, as if she had given up. The front doorbell rang and then Lorelei heard footsteps running through the kitchen, the back door opening and slamming shut.

She crept out of her hiding place and inched toward the stairs, keeping Nixie close behind her. When she turned the corner, she saw the thick trickle of blood descending the staircase, pooling on the landing. Afterwards, she could never remember climbing those stairs, but she must have. Because she was crouched on the kitchen floor with Nixie beside Katherine's still body, trying to rouse her.

"Auntie Katherine!" Lorelei cried. "Come on, we have to go. You said you'd take us away. You promised."

But Auntie Katherine just lay there, all the promises leaking out of her body until they were nothing more than a dark stain across the chest of her new coat, and Lorelei realized she wasn't going to take them anywhere. She was dead.

Lorelei stood up. But before she could think of what to do, she saw Uncle Joey's wide face and intense, bug-eyed stare at the window in the back door. He glowered at her from under his thick black eyebrows and held a finger to his lips in the sign for silence. Lorelei froze in fear. Uncle Joey pointed at Nixie, who was still clinging to her mother's arm, begging her to wake up. He stared straight into Lorelei's eyes as he drew a finger across his neck. Then the front doorbell rang again, and Joey disappeared.

As if it were unconnected to her body, Lorelei's right hand worked to unbutton Katherine's coat, to reach inside and, sticky with blood, remove the manila envelope. Mechanically, she went to the sink and washed and dried her hands. The doorbell rang again and again and then it stopped.

Lorelei tucked the large, bulky envelope under her shirt

and pinned it in place with her black leopard brooch. Then she put on her jacket. Sirens began to sound in the distance. Through the front window, she could see flashing lights reflected on the wet pavement and dark shapes of the neighbors running down the road, arms flailing, as if signaling for help. She walked methodically through the rooms, gathering loose change, matches, Band-Aids, whatever seemed, at the moment, to have some value. She crammed these things into her suitcase and zipped it shut. Then she picked up the suitcase and headed out through the kitchen, toward the back door.

There were two more things that Lorelei took when she left the house. One was the rag Rapunzel with its stitched-up belly and its skein of yellow hair. The other was Nixie Nobody.

CHAPTER FOUR

When she drove across the border into Ontario, Lorelei pulled her Mercedes-Benz into the parking lot of a tourist information center and reviewed the notes she'd scribbled on her cigarette package when Agnes had called this morning with directions to the cottage. She was to stay on the highway until she saw the turnoff to Deception Bay Road. It would be on her right. But she shouldn't turn down the road. Agnes's cottage had boat access only. Lorelei was supposed to pass the turnoff and drive another few minutes until she saw a real estate office on her left. She was to park in their lot and cross the highway on foot to the marina. Agnes would pick her up in a boat. A white Bowrider.

The trip didn't take as long as she'd expected, and when she arrived in the real estate lot, she had time to spare. She parked and got out of the car, lit a cigarette and strolled over toward the real estate building. It was a replica of a log cabin, perched on a hill, with a wide wraparound porch and tall windows facing the lake. Lorelei walked up the hill and climbed the stairs so she could enjoy the view while she smoked. From the porch, she could see across the highway and down the slope on the other side to the marina. Two sailboats and an orange fishing boat were tied at the dock. No white Bowrider. Agnes wasn't here yet. Lorelei had a magnificent view of the sparkling waters of Lake of the Woods, white and blue sails in the bay, the rocky shoreline and the noble scraggly pines that grew upon it, the islands that dotted the lake. She took a deep drag of her cigarette and exhaled luxuriously. This was the life. She wished Nixie could see this spot. Nixie would love it.

According to the sign on the door, the office closed at five o'clock, and it was closed now. Pictures of various properties for sale were posted in the windows. They were all vacation homes, all gorgeous lakeside properties. There were whole islands for sale out here, some of them with buildings already on them, some of them untouched and ripe for development. Predictably, the prices were five and six times the price of the prairie properties she'd been looking at. Millions of dollars. But compared to real estate values in California, these properties were practically giveaways. Not only that, they were pristine, compared to the overcrowded lakeside resorts of the United States. Unpolluted air and water, uncut trees. Fish. The Lake of the Woods was a kind of undiscovered paradise. She remembered rumors of famous Hollywood movie stars purchasing properties around here. It was amazing that rich Americans hadn't grabbed up everything yet. She supposed these places were too remote for most people.

As she studied the photo of an especially lavish estate, a resort with a central lodge and surrounding cabins, something else stirred in her memory. Wasn't there a famous old lodge, not far north of here, that burned to the ground not long ago? She remembered the case partly for the beauty of the historical A-frame lodge, but mostly for the ingenious business machinations involved. Within a single year, the owner had purchased the property, made massive renovations, sold shares, taken deposits, booked conventions, and watched the uninsured building go up in flames. With no insurance company involved, there had been only a cursory government investigation into the fire. The owner's creditors had been forced to share in his bad luck. How had that worked? By a stroke of genius, he had taken out the mortgage with a company he owned himself. Now, if you had the capital, you could—

"Can I help you?"

Lorelei jumped. A man had come around the corner of the porch and was walking toward her. He was smiling, jiggling a batch of keys in his hand.

"I'm afraid we're closed right now, but if there's a particular property you're interested in, I can certainly look into it for you." When he got close enough, he extended his hand for her to shake. "Jack Barnes," he said. He was a short person, bland and blond, with bulging cheeks and a well-fed belly. He was dressed in casual slacks and a T-shirt that advertised a local bass fishing derby. She had the feeling he was sizing her up, assessing her potential as a customer. But she couldn't see his eyes. In his mirrored sunglasses, she could see only a blurred version of herself.

"Lorelei Good," she replied. "I'm just looking today. But I may be interested in the future."

He took a small leather case from his pocket and pulled out a card. "Any time you want to see one of these places, I'd be happy to show it to you." He pointed at the pictures in the window with a jovial salesman's laugh. "Long as you call fast enough."

"Thank you." She tucked the card in her purse. "So, these homes are selling fast?"

"Proverbial hotcakes. The market's gone wild this summer. Where you from?"

"Winnipeg."

"You have a summer place out here?"

"No. Not yet. I'm visiting a friend." She looked out over the bay again. A white, twenty-foot Bowrider had pulled up at the dock, and a woman in a baggy gray sundress was tying it up. "There she is now, I think," Lorelei said. She couldn't see the woman's face, but who else would wear such a dress?

Jack Barnes turned to look. "You mean Mrs. Kellsington? You're a friend of Mrs. K's?" His smile heated up several degrees. "You going out to the cottage?"

"Yes. I'm looking forward to it." Lorelei didn't mention the reason for her visit. Agnes had seemed very concerned about confidentiality.

"I'll walk you down to the dock," he offered. "I should have a word with Mrs. K anyway."

Jack helped Lorelei retrieve her overnight bag from the trunk of her car and assured her she could park in the lot overnight. He insisted on carrying her bag, though he huffed and puffed, even on the downhill slope.

Agnes was sitting on a bench while a marina employee filled her boat's gas tank. She was smiling and relaxed, drinking coffee from a paper cup. "Whatever brings you two together?" she asked.

"I met Lorelei up at the office," said Jack. "She was looking at the properties for sale."

"Speaking of which?" asked Agnes.

"Speaking of which, I might have a couple out to look at your place tomorrow," said Jack. "They're coming up from Detroit in the morning, and I'm taking them out on the lake."

Brian Hale stood outside Charlotte Trapp's duplex on Grosvenor Avenue where he had seen Lorelei Good yesterday. The house was three full stories tall, covered in blue shingles and Virginia creeper. A screened wooden porch, painted white, surrounded each of the two front doors. White shutters on every window. Closed. The house looked cool and asleep. He leaned on the gate and tried to peer into the porch on the side where Lorelei had entered. Affixed to the wall beside the screen door, he could see a hand-painted sign, with a symbol of some kind—it looked like an open eye—and blue letters on a white background: Consultations. Monday to Thursday, 2:00-4:00 p.m. But he could tell no one was home.

He had parked two blocks away, and he walked slowly now, through the old familiar streets, letting the memories come. He wasn't sure when he'd first noticed Lorelei. Grade ten? Eleven? Quiet and dark and a little weird, she had kept mainly to herself. It wasn't until he'd talked to her on the riverbank that day after his father's funeral that he'd really noticed how beautiful she was. But by then it was too late.

She had waved at him from the bridge. Then he'd seen her disappear, and he'd known she was coming to talk to him. He remembered that clearly. Through the haze of his grief, he'd had a bright vision of her walking toward him through the grove of poplars, shielding her eyes against the late slant of the afternoon sun, smiling shyly, saying, "Hey there. What's going on?" Him saying, "My dad's dead." Her touching him. Lightly.

And that was exactly what had happened. The grove of poplars, the sunlight, the smile.

"My dad's dead," he told her.

She had looked at him for a long time and then stated, very calmly, with certainty, "Recently."

"Four days."

"It was sudden."

"Yes."

She had touched him then, the lightest brush of the back of her hand across his forehead, as if she were testing for fever. "He's still with you, though."

"Yes." It was true. Brian felt his father's presence as she spoke.

"He's watching over you," she said. "They always do, the ones who love you."

A breeze had come up then, carrying the sweet scent of roses—a rare event, for the Assiniboine was sluggish and muddy, a breeding ground for mosquitoes, and the banks were littered with the remains of old campfires, broken bottles, and empty aerosol cans. But it seemed as if Lorelei had brought the fresh breeze with her.

He'd heard her stepmother was shot dead a few days later, her father was wanted by the police. How did a person live with that? He remembered with guilt how he had resolved to visit her, to offer some comfort, to say…that was the problem, he hadn't known what to say. He had picked out a card at the card shop down the street, a picture of the sun rising over a beach—sappy. But he couldn't think what to write on it. Finally, he'd dropped it, blank, through the vent in her locker at school. But she had never come back to school. She and her sister had vanished. Foster care, he guessed. A life with strangers. He'd never had the guts to ask. Never had the guts to thank her.

But now she had come back. She had made a life for herself. Was making use of her gifts. And what had he done with his own life? His own workaday, ordinary life. Since his shocking encounter with death the other day, he'd been questioning the meaning of that life even more than usual.

He looked down at the suit he was wearing. It was just like everyone else's suit. Not that clothing mattered, he reminded himself. It was only the outward mark of his profession, nothing to do with his inner self. Yet it seemed ominously symbolic. His tie seemed symbolic. Even his leather shoes and his briefcase seemed symbolic. When he approached his BMW, he groaned out loud.

Nixie drove south and then east across town and parked in the lot behind the St. Boniface Animal Shelter and Clinic. There was only one person, a man with two white Scottie dogs, in the waiting room. The receptionist's desk was empty. Nixie felt a bit silly without any pet beside her. She sat down and opened a magazine, turning to an article on obedience training. One of the Scottie dogs sniffed at her sneaker.

Ten minutes later, a young woman wearing goggles and a white lab coat walked in from the back door. The man with the Scotties got to his feet. "Dr. Logan! I've been waiting half an hour!"

"I'm terribly sorry," the veterinarian told him. "We're having a bit of a problem today. You can bring the dogs in now." She turned to Nixie and smiled. "I'll be a while. Sorry. Do you want to wait in my office?"

"Sure," said Nixie.

She had never been in the office before. It was small and cramped, the desk buried under lab reports and journals. The computer was up and running, tuned to a website about feline leukemia. On the wall, a framed diploma attested to Dr. Vivian Logan's credentials in veterinary medicine. Nixie examined the cluster of photographs crowding a tiny shelf on the wall. She grinned when she recognized Vivian's parents and her brothers from her descriptions of them. She could even distinguish among the five brothers, after the long stories she'd heard about their growing up. The childhood Vivian described was a foreign place to Nixie. Family fishing trips to the nearby creek, diving in the swimming hole, watching the deer come down to the salt lick. Nursing a baby owl with a broken wing. It was all like something out of a movie. A good movie. One you'd watch again and again.

As the vet returned to her office, Nixie turned and grinned. "All done?"

Vivian Logan groaned. "What a day!" She poured herself a cup of coffee from the carafe on the hot plate and removed her lab coat. She wore denim overalls and a white T-shirt, with her blond hair in two long braids, tied at their ends with bright red ribbons. She tasted the coffee and grimaced. "Pure mud!"

"We can get fresh coffee at the restaurant."

"Oh, it will be so good to get out of here. Thanks for coming."

"No problem. How's the mother cat today?"

"Oh Nixie, we couldn't save her." Vivian sat down in the chair and rubbed her temples with her fingertips. "If only they'd brought her in sooner."

"Oh, no." Nixie had been afraid of this. Vivian had told her last night that the cat would likely die. She'd been a beauty, a slinky black and white longhair with a shiny coat, who'd been well cared for until she was injured. Vivian guessed she'd been hit by a car. Someone had abandoned her in the shelter's waiting room in a cardboard box, along with her four kittens. Vivian had operated, but the internal injuries were too severe.

"Any word from the owners?" Nixie asked.

"Nothing. I guess they don't want the bill." Vivian sighed again. "I don't suppose you could take another kitten?"

"No," said Nixie. "I can't. My sister...."

"Your sister."

Nixie hung her head in regret. Then she thought of Penny Johnson and the late, lamented Puffball. "Well, I might be able to find a home for one of them."

"Great! Can you take it today?"

"Maybe next week," Nixie said. "I have to confirm it. Can you keep them for a while?"

"Sure. They're a little malnourished right now, anyway. We'll beef one up for you."

"Great." They beamed at each other. "So," Nixie said. "You hungry?"

"Starving."

At the Good Luck Café down the street, they settled in to a booth and Vivian answered Nixie's questions. Yes, she said, Valium was used for cats sometimes, if they weren't eating. It got them pretty stoned, but it worked to increase their appetite. And yes, she had to agree, dogs were more likely to attack if they were in pairs or packs. Why did Nixie want to know these obscure facts?

"Tell me more about the wildlife refuge," Nixie prompted.

Vivian grinned. "That really captures your imagination, doesn't it?" She had left her white coat back at the clinic, and with her freckled, sunny face and pigtails, she looked more like a high-school student than a doctor.

Nixie shrugged. "It sounds, I don't know, beautiful."

Vivian laughed. "It *is* beautiful. It *will* be beautiful. I'll have to show you the photographs of the land."

"Is it really far north?" Nixie asked.

"Well, not in the Arctic, if that's what you mean. It's on Revelation Lake. North of Riding Mountain."

"Wow."

"There's nothing on it now, of course. It's just scrub brush and swamp. With a wee little falling-down cabin on it and an outhouse. But it's ours! With my brothers splitting the mortgage, we should have it paid up in no time, and then we can start building on it."

"Will you live there?" Nixie asked.

"Oh yes." Vivian laughed again. "Believe me, if I give up my business to take on this crazy project, I won't be able to afford to live anywhere else. The first thing we'll do is we'll renovate the cabin, so I can live there. Then we'll start the fencing. After that, somehow or other we'll figure out how to construct the shelters." She frowned. "Injured animals have to be kept warm. I'll need an operating room. I mean, it'll be horribly expensive. Ah, well, that's all way in the future." She waved the problem away with her hand.

"Maybe you should think about getting some investors," Nixie suggested.

"Investors!" Vivian laughed again. "Where do you get these ideas? Honestly, Nixie, you're a hoot!"

The waiter arrived, bringing coffee and menus, and the women thanked him.

When he left, Nixie said, "Well, I was just trying to think of a way you could set it up sooner. You want to, don't you?"

"Lifelong dream," Vivian confirmed.

"I wouldn't want to wait, if I were you," Nixie said. "I'd want to do what I wanted to do right away. If I was free. I mean, if I had the kind of skills you do. I'd love to be out in the country like that, setting everything up, planning it. Out in the fresh air!" She stopped, embarrassed by her own enthusiasm.

Vivian stirred her coffee, adding a dash of cream. "If you're so interested," she said slowly, "maybe you'd like to come up and see the place?"

"Could I?"

"Sure. We could drive out there some weekend. It's not too far. The cabin's a mess, but it's summertime. We could—"

"I don't know," said Nixie suddenly. "I'm kind of busy this summer."

"We could camp out under the stars."

Nixie looked up. They stared at each other, and a slow grin started to spread across Vivian's face. It was infectious. Nixie felt the corners of her mouth tugging upward. She looked down at her coffee cup, added a teaspoon of sugar she didn't want. "I'm needed at home most weekends," she said.

"I know," said Vivian.

"It's sort of hard to get away. I mean, with the business and all and—"

"I understand. But couldn't you—"

"I might be able to manage a day or two," Nixie said doubtfully. "Maybe later this summer, but right now...."

"I know, I know. Your sister."

"My sister."

"When am I going to meet your sister, anyway?"

Nixie picked up the two menus and handed one to Vivian. "What should we eat?"

"I mean it, Nixie. Aren't you ever going to invite me over to the house when she's at home?"

"Sure," said Nixie. "Soon. You know." She waved a hand in the air, as if gesturing toward the future. "When the time is right."

"I'd like to meet your parents, too."

"Hey, they have milkshakes," Nixie said. "That's what I want. A strawberry milkshake and a plate of fries."

"This place is for sale?" Lorelei asked. She followed Agnes up the tiered, flagstone path that zigzagged up the steep side of the cliff.

"I'm afraid so," said Agnes. "Hank is sorry to part with it. It's been in his family since 1945. But with all the traveling we plan to do, we'll never get out here, so…." She paused, breathing heavily, to wait for her guest. "We're letting it go."

"What a shame," said Lorelei.

At the top of the cliff, the flagstone split into two paths, one leading to a guest house and the other to the screened veranda of the main cottage. Lorelei looked up at it in admiration. The front wall of the two-story A-frame foyer was made entirely of windows overlooking the lake. The cedar trees that had supplied the ceiling beams must have been two hundred years old. The foyer was breathtaking, with a huge stone fireplace, a glass ceiling that filled the room with sunlight, and a cool green marble floor. The decor consisted of white bearskin rugs and white wicker couches and chairs, covered in white and green throw pillows. Six or seven potted trees were strategically placed among the furniture. And this was only the foyer. The Kellsington vacation home wasn't a cottage. It was a luxurious manor.

Agnes introduced Lorelei to her housekeeper, Susanne, a cheerful young woman who showed Lorelei where she would sleep, a second-floor bedroom with enormous windows overlooking the lake and surrounded by a forest of fir and poplar. Susanne gave Lorelei a few minutes to put away her bag and then hustled her downstairs to join Agnes in the living room.

Agnes was waiting by the bay window at the far end of the long living room, perched at the edge of a wing-backed leather chair that was too large for her. Susanne seated Lorelei across from her and departed with the promise of tea and sandwiches. Agnes seemed anxious to begin the reading, but Lorelei encouraged her to talk about herself a bit at first. So Agnes told of her years growing up in Chicago, the schools she attended, and her relationship with her parents.

"My mother was a great beauty," she said. She produced a wry smile. "A gift I'm afraid I didn't inherit."

"Nonsense. You're very beautiful," said Lorelei. "But you're not a materialistic person. You don't need clothing and makeup to feed your ego."

Agnes seemed to like this view of herself. "That's what Hank says," she confided.

"Tell me about Hank," Lorelei suggested.

Agnes seemed to enjoy talking about her husband. She told the story of how she first met him at the First Methodist Church of Chicago and how they'd begun their spiritual journey together. She told of their sojourns among the ashrams and temples of Chicago; their infatuation, and later disillusionment, with the Unitarians; their research into Scientology and the Kabbalah; and finally their involvement with the Living Forever Institute. The couple had bonded during their shared search for the truth and had become engaged. Agnes described the wedding and the honeymoon, which they had organized in great detail to combine romance with spiritual growth.

"We planned to spend four months abroad, an extended honeymoon, you know, while the house was being done. We started in France. Paris first, and then a few weeks in a villa at Bordeaux. Lovely and quiet, but dreary. It would *not* stop raining. So on a whim, we went to Athens. We were simply longing for the Mediterranean sun." She lifted her shoulders. "You know how it is."

Lorelei smiled as if she knew how it was. Agnes was opening up beautifully. Even her manner and tone of voice had changed. She was comfortable being up here alone with Lorelei. The secluded location ensured total privacy. Also, like most excessively wealthy people, she probably tended to relax when the lines of class division were clear. Fortune tellers were in a category somewhere between doctors and hairdressers. One respected and confided in them, relied on them. But one didn't need to worry about making a good impression on them.

"We went north again when the weather warmed up, of course."

"Of course."

"We did Amsterdam, Bruges, Paris again, Geneva…."

"And India?" Lorelei prompted.

"Yes. Hank had made us reservations at the Center for Healing on the ocean outside Mumbai. It's a very modern complex, completely enclosed so you never need to leave the air-conditioned building. Run by the most distinguished gurus in the country. They take care of your every need so that you can concentrate on spiritual healing. Three months with no contact with the outside world. We were supposed to stay until September, but…."

"But you returned alone?"

"Yes, I…." Agnes seemed unable to go on. She turned

toward the window and gazed into the forest, gathering her thoughts.

Lorelei waited, trying not to intrude. She concentrated on Agnes's fingers, which twisted slowly but continuously in her lap, as if she were washing her hands.

"What made you come home?" Lorelei asked softly.

"It was—this *is* confidential, isn't it?"

"Absolutely." Lorelei smiled sympathetically.

Agnes pulled an embroidered handkerchief from her purse and wiped her palms. Then she crumpled it into a ball and held it tightly in her right fist. She raised her head and looked directly at Lorelei. "Because I have to know that you will keep this confidential. Gossip can be very—destructive. Especially to a person in my position."

"I understand," said Lorelei. She looked Agnes straight in the eye. "Over the years I've heard many secrets, and I keep them all here." She touched her heart. "Gossip is a mere diversion for those of little faith. The true path lies in understanding that we're all human, and nothing, um, nothing, that is human can be alien to us."

Agnes seemed to start a little at the word "alien." Wrong word to use on a woman who believed in extraterrestrials.

"What I mean," Lorelei continued quickly, "is that nothing you can say will shock me or make me think less of you. And nothing could persuade me to break the trust that we've established. Without that trust, I wouldn't be able to help you. But if you don't feel comfortable…."

"I do trust you," Agnes said. "Really, I do."

"Then I will listen," Lorelei said, as if she'd just decided to grant Agnes a favor.

"It's Hank," Agnes blurted. "I couldn't stay with Hank any longer. We've had a, a parting, you could say. A parting of ways." She held the handkerchief up to her face, covering her eyes. "And I can't...no one must know!"

Lorelei waited again. She didn't want to push. The conversation was going exactly as she wanted, and she was elated. But she also felt a bit faint. She realized it was hours since she'd eaten anything. The promised sandwiches had never materialized.

Agnes rocked back and forth for a minute, her face buried in the embroidered linen. When she had soothed herself a little, she lowered the handkerchief and spoke again. "This story goes back a while," she said. "I have to explain."

"Go ahead," said Lorelei. Her stomach rumbled. She willed herself not to look at the clock on the wall.

"You know my mother passed away last year?"

Lorelei nodded. "I've sensed your loss. You remember I told you that a female presence—"

"That's just it!" Agnes cried. "It's her presence! Her constant presence! She's always with me, around me, following me!"

"You and your mother had a strong bond," Lorelei said. She was careful not to define that bond. Agnes might be mourning a beloved mother, or she might have hated the old woman's guts. Lorelei didn't know yet.

"We were close," Agnes said. "She taught me everything I know. Everything I believe in."

"So close," said Lorelei. She closed her eyes and concentrated, as if reading a message on the inside of her own eyelids. "So close that sometimes it was impossible to tell the difference between your own thoughts and your mother's."

"Yes! Even now, it's as if she's, well, inside my head somehow."

"Our relationships with each other do not end with death," Lorelei said. "They continue." She wanted to add that love was stronger than death, etc. But she still wasn't sure if this was love. "Especially if someone has a very strong personality."

Agnes was nodding vigorously. "She did. She does!"

Lorelei opened one eye slightly and gazed at Agnes through her lashes. Agnes was leaning forward now, both hands on the table, fully engaged.

"I'm sensing a very forceful personality. This is what is clouding your aura. There is a fusion, an overlap of auras. Your mother's presence mingling with your own." She paused, uncertain which direction she should take. "It's hard for you," she said, finally. That much was obvious.

"Yes! Yes! It's that I always know she's—*watching* me!"

"And I sense she disapproves of what she sees," Lorelei said decisively. She opened her eyes. Agnes was staring at her in wonderment.

Lorelei reached across the table and covered Agnes's hands lightly with her own. "I think I can help you," she said.

"I'd be so grateful," said Agnes.

"First, we must clear your aura. This is what's causing you such stress. If we can untangle your aura from your mother's, you will see much more clearly."

"How can we do that?"

"It won't be easy." Lorelei sighed in anticipation of a long, arduous process. "We must work together. I'll need your full co-operation with all aspects of the ritual, at every stage along the way. And the process may be slow. The presence is very powerful." She concentrated on a spot in the air above Agnes's head. "Your mother was a determined woman. She has a strong hold on you right now. But we must persuade her to let go."

"What do I need to do?"

"First, we must set up a seance, so that we can talk to your mother. This may take some time. The atmosphere has to be just right. We need to gather a number of believers together—perhaps some of the Seekers. And we must wait for the right phase of the moon. Then we can call her forth. We need to ask her what it is she wants—"

"But I *have* asked her!" Agnes cried. "That's the whole problem!"

"You have spoken to your mother? Since she passed over?" Lorelei frowned. "Was it in a proper seance? You see, the presence that surrounds you is only a, well, a sort of electrical current. It's impossible to receive messages clearly when the presence is merely hovering. To communicate with your mother and to interpret her messages correctly, you need an experienced medium. You must contact her in a properly conducted seance."

"But we did that! In Geneva, just before we left for India, we stopped in at the salon of Madame Blassenbaum. You've heard of her?"

Lorelei nodded.

"We went on a retreat. Hank and I and some of Madame Blassenbaum's other clients, we stayed at a chalet on the lake for a whole week. Madame Blassenbaum held seances nearly every night. I assure you they were properly done. She's highly gifted. You can see it, when you meet her. She just glows. A true seer. She's on a different plane than you and me. Well, I mean…." She flushed. "I don't mean *you're* not…."

"I understand. Go on."

"I just mean she's an unusually talented medium, as you must know, with years of experience. Why, she first started channeling spirits when she was a child of twelve! At the chalet, she summoned Hank's dead father and he told

Hank where to find his lost wristwatch, the very watch he'd thought he lost in the airport before we even got to Madame Blassenbaum's salon! She channeled family members and friends of every single person there—even one lady's cocker spaniel. The dead know things about the living. They told what they knew, and everyone agreed it was absolutely accurate."

"And your mother?"

"It took Madame Blassenbaum a while to reach my mother. As I said, my mother is, well, as Madame Blassenbaum said, she's stubborn. But she came, finally, on our last evening there. What a horrible night. I will never forget it." Agnes's shoulders sagged.

"What did your mother say?" Lorelei asked gently.

"It's very personal." Agnes bowed her head. "Intimate."

"Go on."

"It's of a sexual nature," Agnes whispered.

"We are all sexual beings," Lorelei said smoothly. "Sex is nothing to be embarrassed about. It's the earthly manifestation of our love for one another."

"Yes, but you don't understand. It's Hank. The things he wants to do—they're not *normal*."

Lorelei smiled gently. "It's all right."

Agnes suppressed a sob. "In that final seance, Madame Blassenbaum finally channeled my mother. It was my mother's voice, exactly. And what she said! Oh! She knew what we'd been doing. In bed! She described it. In front of everyone. She said the actual *words*. I was never so humiliated in my life!"

Agnes covered her face again with the handkerchief. Lorelei admired the delicate embroidery of the monogram. She stayed silent while Agnes wept. This Madame Blassenbaum was indeed on a different plane—a lower one.

Lorelei wondered what Agnes and Hank had done to piss her off.

When Nixie drove through River Heights, she couldn't help slowing down every time she saw a house for sale. She especially favored the streets closer to the river, like the one she was driving down now. With its stately older homes and leafy boulevards, the whole block radiated soothing vibes. There was a red brick house for sale at the corner and Nixie had a brief fantasy as she waited at the stop sign and admired the leaded windows, the chimney that promised a fireplace, and the fenced-in yard. Once the research center was properly funded and began operations, Lorelei had promised that she and Nixie would get their own, permanent home. They could even get a dog. Nixie could barely wait for that day to come.

She had to admit that things were already looking up. Their lives had been much improved since they'd come back to Canada. Lorelei was making money. There were fewer worries about paying the bills. No scrambling from motel to motel, sneaking out with their belongings in the middle of the night, with Nixie trying to fit in to a new school three or four times a year. They had now been in the same house since Christmas, and in that time Lorelei had bought a brand new van and a fantastic, barely used sports car. Best of all, she'd developed a safe, respectable client base. The residents of River Heights behaved with calm good manners, like people on TV. They believed in fairness and good causes, like saving the rainforests. The women, especially, were unfailingly *nice*. And Waverley Forbes reminded her of a dignified, kindly grandfather, or a handsome actor playing one. She hadn't met him yet. So far, she'd only watched him through the hole in the closet door of the consulting room. But she liked what she saw. He treated Lorelei with respect and embraced her projects with enthusiasm. He was forthright and powerful, not sneaky and mean like the men they'd known in Sacramento. As she pulled away from the corner, taking a last longing glance at the brick house, she saw a father and two sons come running out the door with a football and begin a game of catch on the front lawn. Yes, this was a wholesome place. No arguments erupted in the streets. No tires squealed. Nobody came knocking on the door in a panic, needing cigarettes or money for bail.

Still, she couldn't help remembering that River Heights had not been safe enough for Max and Katherine. She thought of the wild animal refuge that Vivian was going to build. That would be the life. Out in the country. Or way up north. Sometimes Nixie dreamed of making a home in the far north, high above the cities and the desperate scheming, someplace clean and cold, where you could see your breath and know you were alive. Someplace where people didn't steal from you and lie to you and shoot you in the back and leave you to die in a pool of blood on your own kitchen floor.

Pushing this ugly memory out of her mind, Nixie turned onto Wellington Crescent to check out the Kellsington residence. Although it was on the same street as Waverley's house and was built on the same riverbank, Agnes's house was nearly a mile away from his. Her imposing stone mansion, with its twenty windows and three chimneys, was more or less what Nixie was expecting. But the utter chaos of the grounds came as a pleasant surprise. Scaffolding had been built up to the third story along the east wall and draped with heavy tarpaulins. Men in hardhats climbed up and down it, calling to each other. The sound of a buzz saw obliterated their voices. The front lawn had been completely torn apart. It was a mass of upturned sod, mountains of clay-streaked mud, and heaps of gravel. A bulldozer, forklift, and cement truck were parked haphazardly in the midst of the mess. Obviously, the work involved a major restoration.

Nixie drove past the house and parked, returning on foot. A group of workmen stood in front of the cement truck, arguing. Beside them, a woman in overalls and a carpenter's belt sorted through a pile of newly cut lumber. The whole place smelled of wet clay and sawdust. Nixie stood still and stared openly. She figured that turning your home into a construction site was like giving the world permission to stare. In fact, there were two boys across the street doing the same thing. No one would pay any attention to Nixie's presence. She had plenty of time for a security audit. She could see iron grating over the basement windows and motion-detecting lights under the eaves. She walked a few steps closer, scanning the exterior until she spotted the white box of an alarm system attached to the wall inside the glass front door. But the door itself stood open. The system must have been disabled.

She turned her attention to the vehicle parked on the one side of the circular drive that was not heaped with mud and gravel. It was a white panel van, very similar to Nixie's, except that it bore the sign Ten Green Fingers, with a picture of a palm tree. A landscaping firm, or possibly a houseplant service. Rich people didn't have time to water their own ferns. As she watched, the Green Fingers employee got out of the van, carrying a clipboard. He picked his way carefully through the clumps of mud littering the driveway and when he reached the front door, he walked straight through without knocking, as if he owned the place.

Nixie shook her head in wonder as she drove away. The

place was wide open. Whoever Mrs. Kellsington had left in charge was clueless.

Downtown, she parked in an underground lot and rummaged in the back of the van for accessories, finding a blond wig, sunglasses, the high heels she despised, and a makeup kit. Hanging a small mirror from the van's clothing hook, she concealed her freckles with a thick layer of foundation and added lip pencil and lip gloss for a fuller, wider mouth. Then she locked up and walked, unsteadily, through the dark parking garage to the street. The sun beat down on her head, warming the itchy wig and bathing her scalp in sweat. Sam's Undercover Shop was four blocks away, and she hoped she could make it without tripping in these torturous shoes.

Lorelei had mentioned to Waverley and to Summer that she had a little sister, just in case it ever became necessary to explain Nixie's presence. She never mentioned exactly where this sister lived or what she did, and Lorelei and Nixie were careful not to be seen together. If anything ever went wrong, if any clients ever spotted Nixie tailing them around or, worse, caught her inside their homes, they wouldn't connect her with Lorelei. But it was always possible that someone who already knew their connection, the landlady, for instance, might run into Nixie downtown. If so, it wouldn't look good if she was seen shopping at Sam's. It wasn't the kind of place Lorelei's clients should even think about, let alone connect with her.

The man behind the counter—not Sam, for it was a franchise—nodded discreetly as she entered. Nixie gave him a shy smile and began to peruse the merchandise as though she'd never seen such things before. The merchandise included all manner of surveillance and counter-surveillance devices, cameras, tape recorders, binoculars with zoom lenses, even a pair of eyeglasses that allowed you to see what was going on behind your back. These glasses actually worked—unlike the ones Nixie had ordered from the back of a comic book when she was ten years old. A compact voice synthesizer caught her eye. It was smaller than the one they had at home, and would be less obtrusive. She picked it up and examined it. The microphone would fit easily into a person's fist, and the range of effects was quite wide. She moved the switch to "echo" and spoke into the mike. "Hello?"

Her words repeated themselves in a series of overlapping whispers throughout the store. The clerk looked over and raised his eyebrows. "Can I help you?"

Nixie shook her head. She browsed among the cameras and recorders, glancing only momentarily at the signs warning that *the products displayed here are to be used only for legal, legitimate purposes, in compliance with the law. They are not intended for unauthorized interception*, etc. The signs were there to protect the clerks from having to mention this delicate issue out loud. If you were a mad stalker, they didn't want to know about it. She'd been in these places before, in other cities, and she knew the staff never questioned customers about their motives. They pretended to think you were using their merchandise to monitor your store or maybe your household staff. They even called the video hook-ups "Nanny-cams." But of course they assumed you were spying on your spouse. Why else would a person hide a camera in a bedside clock radio? Nixie was intrigued by the latest innovations, tiny cameras concealed in desk lamps, picture frames, smoke alarms, and even, of all things, a camera. But what she really needed was a phone tapping device. The good ones were expensive. At two or three hundred a piece, she used them sparingly, but they were indispensable for long-term surveillance. She read the cards that described the features of each one and decided on a voice-activated digital recorder that could track up to twelve hours of conversation. It was only five inches square, but when attached to the phone jack, it would record not only the conversation, but also the date, time, and phone number of all incoming and outgoing calls. Nixie purchased one and then, on impulse, she threw in the voice synthesizer as well. You never knew when something like that might come in handy.

The Kellsington mansion seemed in such exquisite disarray today that Nixie figured, seeing as she was already in disguise, she might as well drop by right away with a delivery. After leaving Sam's she stopped at a florist and purchased a dozen red roses and a dozen white carnations. She deliberated over the occasion for a few minutes and decided on "Welcome Home," as Agnes had recently returned from Europe. She signed the card with three xs and an illegible scribble and drove straight back to Wellington Crescent.

The front door was now closed, but as Nixie got out of the van and approached with the paper-wrapped bouquet in her arms, a smiling young woman opened it wide.

"Come on in," she said, as Nixie entered. Behind her, a florid-faced young man sat in a highly polished wooden chair in the vestibule, enjoying a beer.

"Hey! Flowers!" he said. "Cool!"

A vase of fresh tiger lilies stood on a table behind him, along with a stack of mail. Through an archway to the right, Nixie could see into a small sitting room where magazines and coffee cups and plates of toast crumbs lay scattered on a coffee table.

"You can put those in the kitchen," said the young

woman. She pointed through the vestibule to a door on the far left. "It's straight through there." She giggled as she teetered slightly and nearly landed in the young man's lap. "You'd better go fire up the barbecue," she said to him.

Nixie walked right on past them without a word.

It must be, as the rich so often said, difficult to get decent household help.

The carpet and furniture in the Kellsington living room were no doubt exquisite, but they were covered with thick, white sheets of canvas to protect them from drywall dust and the dirty boots of construction workers. Nixie stashed the flowers in the kitchen and then snuck up the back stairs to the second floor, looking for a good location. She found a telephone extension in a small sewing room near the back of the house. This room, like several others, was full of cartons from the van line the Kellsingtons had hired to move their things to Winnipeg after the wedding. Agnes hadn't yet finished unpacking. Nixie saw a sewing machine in an open carton. Scissors and measuring tape lay strewn on a tabletop beside a toppled stack of patterns, and bolts of material were propped haphazardly against the walls. There was no chair in the room and no light bulb in the desk lamp. Nixie pushed aside a bolt of orange silk and quickly attached the tapping device to the jack, which was concealed behind the floor-length curtains. Chances were remote that Agnes would be coming in here to sew any time soon. No one would ever see the device, except maybe a cleaning lady, who wouldn't likely pay any attention to it.

When all was done, Nixie simply slipped back downstairs and out through the front door. The young man was lighting a barbecue on a patio at the side of the house, while his girlfriend opened a bottle of wine. Neither of them looked up. Nixie doubted they'd even remember she was there. The flowers were probably doomed.

Back at home, Nixie heated up a can of soup for herself and fed Bitsy some deli scraps she found in the fridge. It wasn't like Lorelei to buy treats for the cat. Most of the time Lorelei ignored the cat. She didn't approve of pets. Nixie had had to beg her to take Bitsy home from the shelter in the first place.

As she'd told Vivian, Lorelei would never agree to a second cat. She hadn't mentioned that Lorelei would never agree to have Vivian over for dinner, either. And it wasn't because she was busy with her consulting business. Lorelei would hit the roof if she found out Vivian had been inside the house. For years, Nixie had trained herself to remove any traces that she'd had friends over. Lorelei didn't want anyone in the house unless she was there to supervise, to make sure no visitors saw anything they shouldn't see—like cords running under the seance table, controlling wind chimes and electric fans or whatever the scheme of the moment might be.

Last week, the landlady's kid had asked a lot of questions when she saw Vivian leaving the house and driving away in the brightly painted Animal Clinic van. Nixie had told her the vet was making a house call for Bitsy, just in case Imogene mentioned the visit to Lorelei.

"But you're not sick, are you, Bits?" Nixie asked, as the kitten rubbed against her leg. She was hoping that Imogene wouldn't mention this particular lie to Lorelei. Only a kid would believe such a thing. House calls for cats.

Nixie sat on the couch and ate a pint of chocolate ice cream for dessert while she watched the news. The Psychic Fair was featured in a clip about local events. Then the newscaster said, "In related news, rumors that popular local psychic Yolanda Dawn was slain by members of a satanic cult were countered today by Ms Dawn's next-door neighbor, who wishes to remain anonymous." Yolanda Dawn's high-rise appeared on the screen, the camera slowly panning up to the height of her fatal fall. "The neighbor told Channel Ten reporters that a gruesome message had been scrawled on Ms Dawn's living room wall, accusing her of witchcraft. The information, if verified, would seem to point to anti-witchcraft forces, rather than Satanists, psychologist Len Frederick confirmed." There was a shot of the psychologist in his office. He said, "Fanaticism comes in many shapes and often disguises itself as concern for the welfare of society's most vulnerable members." The Soldiers Against Satan appeared on the screen, circling the hotel. The camera zoomed in on a protest sign that read "Deliver Our Innocent Children from Evil."

"When reached for comment," the reporter concluded, "the Reverend Surefire had this to say." A grotesque close-up of the Reverend exaggerated his thick lips and wobbly chin as he bellowed, "This is an outrage, led by those who promote wickedness as entertainment, making money off the corruption of our children. And the manipulation of the media—" The Reverend disappeared suddenly.

"Sally Smith," said Sally Smith. "Channel Ten. Winnipeg, Manitoba." The weather report came on. The heat wave was expected to continue.

Nixie snapped off the TV and headed upstairs to bed. It was a relief to have the house to herself and no tasks to perform, for a change. It almost seemed like a normal evening in a normal person's life. Bitsy scampered up ahead of her and darted into the bedroom, as if looking forward to bedtime. Nixie laughed. She washed up in the bathroom and brushed her teeth.

When she entered the bedroom, she could see Bitsy's hind end sticking out from under the bed, her black tail twitching in excitement.

"What have you got there?" Nixie reached over the edge of the bed. "That better not be a mouse," she muttered. She grabbed Bitsy's hind legs, pulling her out.

Bitsy leaped around the room, wild with excitement. A length of yellow yarn dangled from her mouth like a piece of spaghetti.

"Oh, Bits! Not Rapunzel *again*!" Nixie reached under the bed and pulled out the rag doll. Her favorite childhood toy. She had carted it from city to city over the years, and it had become considerably battered. Clumps of its hair were missing and its dress was ragged. Now, during its latest tussle with Bitsy, one of its eyes had come loose and was hanging by a thread.

"Bad cat!" said Nixie. She chased after Bitsy and took away the strand of yarn that she was chewing. "Don't swallow that. That's bad for you!"

She smoothed Rapunzel's dress. She examined the dangling eye and gently tried to pat it back in place. It wouldn't stay. She'd have to mend the doll again tomorrow. Right now it was time to sleep.

Nixie flopped onto the bed and lay down between Bitsy and Rapunzel. She gazed at the rag doll and tried to remember the day her mother had given it to her. Was it a birthday? Christmas? Nothing came to mind.

What kind of a person was she that she could barely visualize her own mother's face any more? Even the smells and the gestures and the texture of her skin were fading, becoming mere words: *soft*, *warm*, *sweet*, a meaningless collection of adjectives. Only a handful of moments remained. Katherine kneeling beside the bed, singing a lullaby. Katherine shouting at Max, racing through the house, frantic, searching for something. Katherine standing in a doorway, backlit and laughing, dancing to music. But Nixie could not remember the music, couldn't recall the sound of her mother's voice. She thought of the photographs she'd seen in Vivian's office. All the family memories displayed in Penny's living room, stuck to her refrigerator door, tucked into her bureau mirror, filling the albums in her bookcase. Nixie had no such albums to refresh her memory. Lorelei had not thought to take one lousy picture out of the house when they left. Not a letter or a handkerchief, not a watch or a spoon, or a single keepsake. Just this old Rapunzel doll, and even then, Lorelei had only taken it because she suspected Max had hidden something inside it.

And he had. That first, terrible night, after Lorelei dragged Nixie through the rainy streets, thunder and lightning crashing all around them, she had checked them into a motel, where they bathed and changed into clean clothes. Then Lorelei took a pair of scissors and slit Rapunzel open and removed the soft leather pouch inside her belly and untied the drawstring, and dozens of shiny, frozen raindrops spilled out onto the bedspread. Diamonds.

CHAPTER FIVE

Lorelei woke to the sweet whisper of poplar trees outside her window and the lapping of waves against the rocky shore below. It was the first time in weeks she had woken peacefully. She lay in bed for a while, under the light, puffy quilt, her head propped up on the feather pillows, enjoying the view and the fresh breeze coming in at the window. She was surprised to see by the clock on the bedside table that it was already nine. She couldn't remember when she had last slept so late.

An old-fashioned photo album lay on the table and Lorelei opened it. Someone had written "Our Summers in Heaven" in white ink across the first of the heavy black pages. Under the words, a black and white photograph depicted a handsome young couple and their little boy, presumably Hank, posing in their bathing suits on the flagstone steps. Looking through the album, she saw how the cottage had changed through the years, both inside and out, undergoing various improvements as the well-dressed Kellsingtons and their guests enjoyed summer after summer of gracious vacation living. As she leafed through pictures of a family fishing expedition, someone tapped lightly on her bedroom door, and she called, "Come in."

It was Susanne, with a cup of tea and clean towels. "Good morning! Mrs. K asked me to tell you she's gone down to the beach for a while. Mr. Barnes is here with some clients and she's helping him show them around."

Lorelei sat up and accepted the teacup. "Thank you, Susanne. These are people interested in buying the cottage?"

Susanne nodded. "Interested in buying the whole island."

"How big is the island?"

Susanne shrugged. "I wouldn't know exactly. A couple of miles long, maybe? I've never been to the other end of it." She folded the towels over a chair. "They'll be another hour or so, looking around. After you shower you can come down for breakfast."

"Are there many people interested in a place like this?" Lorelei asked. She sipped the tea and found it cold.

"Well, you know, it's pretty pricey. Mr. Barnes says there's not too many people around who can afford a whole island. And Mrs. K says she wants to find the right buyers, no matter the size of the offer."

"The right buyers?" asked Lorelei. "What do you mean?"

"Oh, well, she says she'll know when she meets them. Mr. K told her to make sure the vibrations are right or something." She shrugged again. "You know how they are."

"Have you worked with the Kellsingtons long, Susanne?"

"No, ma'am. I mean, yes. That is, I've worked for them nearly six months, but I don't really know them. Mr. K came up from the States and hired me and my sister just around

Christmastime, and Mrs K has only been back for, oh, a few weeks."

This made Lorelei curious. "What have you been doing for six months?"

"Looking after the house in the city, of course. They don't like to leave it empty. And in spring I came out to open the cottage here. I dusted and everything, hired some men to mend the dock and wash all the windows. People around here say Mr. Kellsington hardly uses this place any more. Two or three years in a row now, he's had people out here to air it and clean it and get it ready for summer, and then he never comes. Not even once. They thought he'd come back now that he's married, but it looks as if the same thing's going to happen again this year. He travels too much, I guess. He told Mrs. K to go ahead and sell it. So I've been up here helping her get it ready to show. My sister's looking after the house in the city."

"I see." Lorelei set down her teacup. She reached for her housecoat and got out of bed. "And is Mrs. Kellsington a nice person to work for?"

Susanne beamed. "Super nice! She gives us two days off every week, instead of only one, and she pays us herself, instead of through the agency, so we don't have to give them a cut any more."

"Yes," said Lorelei, as she tied the belt of her robe. "She's a very nice person."

"The bathroom's just down the hall," Susanne said, "on your right."

After her shower, Lorelei descended to the kitchen, where Susanne was attempting to squeeze fresh oranges for juice, without much success. As she waited, Lorelei pulled out her cell phone and tried to call Nixie. But she couldn't get a signal.

"It's tough out here sometimes," Susanne told her.

"Oh, well. It's hardly an emergency," said Lorelei. She was dying to tell Nixie about the possible new location of the PsyRen Research Center, but she would have to wait until she got back to town.

No one could say that Lorelei Good didn't recognize a golden opportunity when she saw one. On the drive home, she went over and over the plan in her head. First of all, the best thing about the place was the optics. Unlike the abandoned flax farm, which would be revealed as an eyesore, if anyone was suspicious enough to go and check it out, the island on Lake of the Woods was absolutely gorgeous, and the cottage had a guesthouse, hot tubs, picture windows, fireplaces—everything a Seeker's heart might desire. Lorelei had taken some photos to show Nixie, and she was already thinking of better angles from which to take photos for a new brochure. For another thing, unlike the flax farm, the place was currently owned by a person who wanted very much to sell it. To the right buyers. A person Lorelei was pretty sure she could control. And even though it was too soon to expect money from Agnes, she might be amenable to giving the PsyRen Foundation a very big discount on the purchase price of the cottage. After all, since their bonding session at the lake, Agnes already seemed to think of the empathetic Lorelei as one of the "right" people. All Lorelei had to do was keep it up. After some mental calculations based on the property values she'd studied at the real-estate office and her knowledge of Waverley's personal wealth, Lorelei figured the deal was entirely feasible.

"So you see," she told Nixie, as the sisters sat down to dinner that evening, "Agnes would invest by dropping the price by a third. The Seekers would invest a third, and

PsyRen would match the Seekers' investment. Three equal partners—with PsyRen as the legal owner, of course—and voila. Instant Research Center."

Nixie was doodling figures on her paper napkin. "But even if Agnes drops the price as low as two million, and even if Waverley can raise one million—"

"He can," said Lorelei. "Remember when his wife was sick?"

"True. But even so, he'll still expect the PsyRen Foundation to match his donation. How are we going to get a million dollars?"

"We'll take out a mortgage," said Lorelei, as she ladled soup into Nixie's bowl.

"A million-dollar mortgage?"

"With a million down? Sure. We have a sound business plan and support from the Seekers. The Kellsingtons might even agree to hold the mortgage for us." She filled her own bowl and carried the pot back to the stove. "There is only one drawback I can see."

"Hank Kellsington," said Nixie. She crumbled a cracker into her soup.

"No. I don't think he's a problem," said Lorelei.

"Isn't it his place?" Nixie sipped soup from her spoon, then used it to crush another cracker into the bowl.

"They're married, so it's Agnes's place now, too." Lorelei frowned. "Well, come to think of it, I suppose she might have to get him to sign something, but if she wants to give us a discount, if she says we're the right people, I doubt he'd object. He's the one who put it up for sale and left her in charge. And don't forget, he's been supporting the Living Forever Institute, and that's *her* favorite cause, not his. So he's obviously willing to subsidize the things she believes in."

"He must believe in it, too," Nixie pointed out. "Donations to the Living Forever Institute are hardly tax-deductible."

"Nor to PsyRen," said Lorelei wryly. "Another case of discrimination. But it's not Hank I'm worried about. It's the cash factor. When we were using the old flax farm as our site, I was hoping for two hundred thousand from Waverley, just to begin with. Maybe another two hundred or so once we parked a few bulldozers out there. And then further instalments as, you know, problems arose. I figured it would keep us in cash for the next two years at least. Steady income. Now if we go with this new plan, we end up with the cottage, but not much cash for construction. Almost everything the Center could possibly need is already there."

"Couldn't we start running programs right away?" asked Nixie. She reached again for the plate of crackers.

Lorelei snatched the plate away. "*Must* you ruin that entirely?"

"Sorry," said Nixie.

"That's a perfectly good vegetable chowder."

"Sorry, sorry. But why couldn't we go legit right away, do some retreats? Seminars and stuff? We could start in the fall. People would come from all over the place, I'm sure. Even in winter. We could take them in by snowmobile. We could invite some of those psychic researchers up from the States."

"Our expenses would be high," said Lorelei. "We'd have mortgage payments, taxes. We wouldn't be rich."

"But look where we'd be living!" Nixie exclaimed. She picked up the photograph Lorelei had taken from the top of the hill, overlooking the lake. "It's paradise."

The smartest course of action would be to flip the cottage as soon as possible, but Lorelei didn't tell Nixie that.

The smartest thing would be to sell it before the taxes ever came due. At first, the cottage would be almost as good as cash. It would need a few renovations, after all, to accommodate all the international guests the Seekers would expect. Naturally, PsyRen would need to purchase its own boat. Then there would be the fees for the decorators, the feng shui consultation, the smudging ceremony. She would be willing to fix it up and operate it for a while, offering seminars and demonstrations, a few group seances. Maybe she'd even invite some people up from the States, as Nixie suggested. But only the very classiest ones. Like those demonologists who had their own TV show. They'd draw a crowd. Then, when the operation became burdensome, she would offer it low on the market—maybe even as low as two million. It would all be perfectly legal. The PsyRen Foundation, otherwise known as Company #669030330, would own it outright. Maybe she could sell it in the dead of winter, when nobody much would be around to notice. Nixie would be disappointed. But she'd get used to the idea. After all, they would be rich. Even if they paid off the mortgage—which was a good idea, come to think of it—they'd make at least a million-dollar profit. With no obligations. For that, Lorelei would gladly change her name again and move to a new town. Nixie would feel the same, she was sure, when the time came.

The first person Agnes phoned when she returned to town was a carpet salesman, who agreed to bring some samples by. The second was her friend Penny Johnson.

"Honestly, Penny, this Lorelei Good is amazing!"

"Do you really think so?"

"Oh yes. Why she's so, so...compassionate. You feel she really understands you, deep down, if you know what

I mean, on a spiritual level. It's as though she can see your aura, without even using one of those special cameras."

"She didn't do any of that grimacing or that…growling I told you about?" asked Penny.

"Not at all," said Agnes. "She was perfectly well mannered. And I must say she has impeccable credentials. The Psychic Renaissance Foundation is a reputable institution."

"You've heard of it before?"

"Didn't you read the brochures, dear? It was established in the nineteenth century. Can you imagine? The founder's great-grandfather actually foresaw the present renaissance of psychic activity and—"

"What do you think of this research center idea?" Penny interrupted. "Waverley is all worked up about it."

"Oh, it's fascinating. Sorely needed in these times. Why, I only hope it doesn't take too long."

"You don't think it's a little too ambitious? The plans are so elaborate."

"Think of the benefits, though. I'm sure it could be built, if enough people pull together. Is Waverley going to get involved?"

"I'm urging him to be cautious," said Penny. "You know what he went through when his wife died. He lost millions seeking a cure, investing in all sorts of alternative therapies that turned out to be, well, bunk. I wouldn't want to see him throwing away—I mean, I wouldn't want to see him hurt like that again."

"No, of course not," said Agnes. "Of course not, dear. You're very wise."

Nixie was impressed. Advances in digital technology over the past few years had resulted in an audio quality unheard of when she'd first started in this business. She played with the volume dials on her computer as she listened to the rest of the calls and discovered she could not only hear every word of Agnes's phone conversations, but also the ambient noise. The ringing of cash registers in the background when Agnes phoned a department store, traffic sounds when anyone called her from their car, and the banging and grinding of the construction vehicles outside her own home. Lorelei was going to love this.

Nixie wished she could tap Waverley's phone as well, but he had a state-of-the-art security system she had never been able to crack. And it was always hard to tap the phones of ordinary people like Penny Johnson, who did their own cleaning. Given the obsessive cleanliness of Penny's bungalow, it was far too risky. It was quite likely Penny kept even the telephone cords in the unused rec room spic and span.

Anyway, Agnes was their main concern at the moment. Lorelei's idea to buy the cottage at Lake of the Woods was so brilliant that Nixie had jumped for joy when she heard it. She'd been dreaming of the place ever since Lorelei described it to her. It was large enough that clients could stay for several nights in a row, leaving their belongings in their rooms when they went out. Once they persuaded Agnes to sell it to them, once they moved in and started a legitimate business, with all the wiring and other work done on-site, Nixie could live there perfectly openly as some sort of research assistant, free to roam the island and explore the lakeshore. And invite her friends to visit. They would have to get a speedboat, of course. Dogs loved speedboats. Especially Labs. Labs were water dogs.

Over the next few days, Lorelei moved slowly toward finalizing her plan. For a while, the Seekers were distracted by a furor in the media. The press had reported the ghastly message painted on the wall of Yolanda Dawn's apartment the night she was killed. The leading newspaper splashed the words "Burn in Hell, Witch" across its front page, a sensational headline that stared at the citizens from the shelves of every newsstand and the glass window of every vending box in the city until it sold out. Kent Mason, who was researching a story on the Dharmarama, saw the link between the killer's threat and the boutique's graffiti problem last summer, and reported it on the evening news. Soon, fear was rippling through the community of Seekers and other likeminded citizens of Winnipeg.

Kent arranged a panel discussion on the nightly news, featuring Summer Sweet as well as the owner of an occult bookstore from the North End and the fortune teller known only as Teddy, who read tea leaves at the Plaza Hotel. When asked whether they feared that someone was targeting local witches, Teddy hotly denied that he was a witch, and the bookstore owner launched into a lengthy dissertation on the history of paganism, Wicca, witchcraft, and the differences among them. "Satanism is in no way related to these ancient, venerable practices," he declared. "But unfortunately, there is confusion among the general public on these matters."

Summer issued a public challenge to those who had defaced her storefront last year, urging them to come forward and confess to the police, in order to lay to rest the rumors of a connection to Yolanda's death. Summer wore a pale pink dress, decorated with a pattern of strawberries, and a matching ribbon in her hair. In this outfit, and with the braces on her teeth, she didn't look much like most people's conception of a witch. She repeated the name of the Dharmarama as often as possible and managed to slip in the address of the store three times.

Another distraction that threatened to interfere with Lorelei's plans was the excited preparation for the most important weekend of the year for the Seekers. Every July, Summer organized a group seance for them, an event they called "Spirit Fest." For the past few years, Summer's sister had been hosting Spirit Fest at her hobby farm outside of Gimli, charging a reasonable fee, and Summer had always hired a celebrity guest psychic from Toronto or Minneapolis to conduct the seance. But recently she'd been hinting at hiring Maurice Lemoine for the occasion. Lorelei had heard plenty about Maurice Lemoine. For years, he had run a small card-reading business out of his mother's basement in the nearby town of Lorette, coming in to Winnipeg only every few months to read tarot at the Dharmarama. He'd been a very minor provincial personality until recently, when he penned a book and managed to get it accepted by a major publisher. Now he was the fastest rising star in the business. So far, he hadn't presented any competition because he'd been away, promoting his book—*Ghost Talk*— across the continent. But he was expected back in time for the Psychic Fair. Summer had mounted a huge display in the window of the Dharmarama. A life-sized cardboard cut-out of Maurice Lemoine's overgrown head sat on a table, the hypnotic eyes a startling, artificial blue, the pointed incisors exposed in an impossibly wide grin, ingratiating and yet supremely confident. He appeared to be gloating over the dozens of glossy hardcover copies of *Ghost Talk* stacked on the table around him. *Ghost Talk* was all the rage among Waverley's acolytes.

Lorelei had been trying to think of ways to neutralize Maurice. Now, with Agnes Kellsington on her side, she believed she could orchestrate a change of venue for Spirit Fest, moving it to Agnes's cottage and getting herself hired as the medium to perform for the occasion. She would put on a spectacular show that would convince all three of her most important clients that the magical atmosphere out at the cottage created conditions under which anything could happen, any wish could be fulfilled. When the Psychic Renaissance Foundation chose Agnes's cottage as the most desirable site for their research center, the Seekers wouldn't be able to resist. Agnes would be sure to offer the discount, and Waverley would be sure to invest.

For the time being, Waverley was away in Boston for a conference on reincarnation and wouldn't be back until the Psychic Fair, a turn of events Lorelei couldn't have organized better herself. She knew it was best that she stay away from him for a while after making her initial pitch. If he feared that plans for the research center were progressing without him, he would be all the more eager to become involved. Lorelei also hoped to have Penny on her side by the time he returned. She didn't want Penny's negative attitude influencing Waverley's decisions.

Meanwhile, she continued to work every day with Agnes, sometimes out at her cottage and sometimes at her residence on Wellington Crescent, where Agnes spent most of her time supervising the renovations. The renovations included repairs to the foundation, the restoration of two chimneys, and the addition of a whole new wing facing the river. It was true that the contractors needed supervision, Agnes said. They were months behind and had botched several parts of the job. But of course it was not true that Agnes had to supervise them herself. She could have hired someone else to do it. Still, the renovations made a handy public reason for her return to Winnipeg, allowing her to keep her marital problems a secret.

Lorelei told Agnes it would be best to wait until the full moon to make direct contact with her mother's spirit. Spirits who take up haunting, she explained, are not well.

She said she didn't like to use the term "ghost" because of its pejorative connotations. Even among the dead, the label "ghost" was considered an insult. But Agnes had to admit, said Lorelei—and Agnes admitted it—Gladys *was* engaging in haunting behavior. The cure for that was similar to the cure for mental illness in the living, though of course drugs were of no use. But talk therapy had proven very effective in certain cases. So Lorelei and Agnes practiced talk therapy on Gladys whenever they got together, and at the next full moon, they planned to perform a ritual that should put Gladys to rest for good. In the meantime, Lorelei gave Agnes a number of affirmations to repeat. These were sentences such as "I am strong" and "My body is beautiful." The affirmations would surround Agnes with a field of positive energy that would keep out any harmful rays emanating from spiteful entities. Lorelei reminded Agnes that discouraging thoughts and negative body messages were actually residual fragments of ionic transmissions that had been distorted through a thickening of the ethereal plane, and that they could be reversed by the output of vigorous thermal forces.

Agnes claimed she was trying as hard as she could, and indeed Lorelei began to notice subtle changes in her manner. With each session, she seemed to gain confidence. Although she was always perfectly polite, she spoke her mind more often. People had to take her into account now. After Lorelei admired some of her snapshots, Agnes decided to take up digital photography as a hobby. She claimed to enjoy it, though she found her new camera hard to understand and the instructions too impossibly tiny to read. She was also receiving a lot of compliments from her small circle of friends, who noticed a new glow to her skin and a straighter spine, which they mistakenly interpreted as weight loss. Lorelei took care not to charge Agnes too much for these sessions, even though Agnes wanted to see Lorelei almost daily and began to consult her on all manner of delicate and uncomfortably personal details involving the problems of her mother and her marriage.

Lorelei graciously listened, providing insights and advice as needed without visibly squirming. But instead of billing Agnes for her time, she told Agnes all about the Psychic Renaissance Foundation, recounting the case histories of people who had been helped by PsyRen. The PsyRen founder, who was currently studying in the mountains of Tibet, had expanded his interests beyond the ethereal realms lately, Lorelei said. He was meditating on the spiritual implications of improving telepathic communication with other beings throughout the universe.

"Beyond our own solar system there are transcendental energies just *radiating* pure spirit," Lorelei said one day when she and Agnes were relaxing in the shade outside the cottage.

"Oh, I'm sure!" said Agnes.

"It is the founder's great hope that our new research center can pursue these questions," Lorelei told her.

"That would be wonderful," Agnes sighed. "How are the plans coming along?"

"Slowly," said Lorelei. "How about your own plans? Have you sold the cottage yet?"

Agnes had not.

"Perhaps you should hold a meeting of the Seekers out here one day," Lorelei suggested. "I can tell from the magnetic pull of the air quality here that it would be an ideal spot for a seance."

"Oh, yes," said Agnes. She invited Penny up for a few days and later reported that Penny had been enchanted with the place. Best of all, Agnes persuaded Penny to book an appointment with Lorelei. Now all Lorelei had to do was impress Penny with her clairvoyant powers, begin a dialogue with the dear, departed Raymond, and try to find out what the hell it was Penny wanted to contact him about.

"I'm so glad you've decided to give Lorelei a try," Agnes told her friend as Nixie listened in on the phone line. "Honestly, Penny, Lorelei Good and the PsyRen philosophy have changed my life."

CHAPTER SIX

In front of the Hotel Fort Garry, a silent band of protesters marched along the sidewalk, spines straight and heads erect. Lorelei enjoyed her first cigarette of the day as she watched them from a parking lot across the street. Although she'd just come from the swimming pool, she was already starting to wilt in the heat. But the protesters were undaunted. They maintained a tight, military order as they proceeded back and forth with their hand-lettered signs, aggravating the doormen, who were trying to push luggage carts and usher guests in and out of taxicabs. Lorelei crushed out the cigarette and headed toward the hotel. As she drew closer, she could make out the lettering on the signs: "Don't play with hellfire!" "Keep Satan out of our City!" An agile teenage boy in a business suit darted forward at intervals, targeting pedestrians with leaflets. He thrust one at Lorelei and she took it.

"Thank you," she murmured. Then she ducked her head as she spotted a familiar figure. It was her landlady, Charlotte Trapp, right in the thick of it all. Charlotte's sign read: "Deliver our Children from Evil." Last night's television feature on the Psychic Fair must have whipped up a furor among right-thinking citizens, like the members of Charlotte's prayer group. Lorelei hid her face behind the leaflet, which explained quite clearly the consequences of black magic, right down to the exact temperature of brimstone: 6000 degrees above zero.

"Wow!" Summer Sweet had arrived, her arms loaded with boxes of supplies from the Dharmarama. "Who knew there'd be so many of them?"

Lorelei spotted a gap in the picket line. "Quick, let's go!" She grabbed Summer's elbow and guided her through, pushing past a slow-moving protester who was hampered by his walker. He pointed a long, bony finger at them and pronounced, "You have been warned!"

"Jesus!" Summer exclaimed.

"Shh," said Lorelei. "Don't *say* that!"

"Why not? Oh, Christ, sorry."

Lorelei led the way past the demonstrators. Summer followed her up the wide limestone steps to the hotel entrance. At the top, Lorelei looked back. It really was a small group, she realized, maybe two dozen at the most. They seemed harmless when viewed from a distance. Charlotte had brought along Imogene, who was listening as her mother conferred with a group of dour men in black suits. Lorelei hoped they weren't planning on storming the place. Imogene was dressed in a pink sailor-suit dress, with matching beribboned hat. Lorelei realized she'd never seen Imogene without her school uniform before. Her outfit today was suitable for a six-year-old. In 1960. The girl resembled a grapefruit. Imogene glanced suddenly in her direction and Lorelei ducked in through the hotel's revolving door.

She and Summer took the elevator to the seventh-floor ballroom, a reception area full of booths where guests could purchase tarot cards or herbal remedies or electronic gadgets for detecting spectral activity. Summer set her boxes down on the counter of her booth beside a stack of shiny copies of *Ghost Talk*. Lorelei picked one up and read the author's bio on the back. Maurice Lemoine, she learned, was a natural conduit to the spirit world, who specialized in the recovery of lost objects. Well, she'd soon have a good chance to study him closely and note his weaknesses. She definitely planned to attend his public performance. And Friday evening, she would even attend a dinner with him, courtesy of Waverley Forbes. Waverley had booked the hotel's most elegant banquet hall to give the Seekers a private audience with the stars of the Psychic Fair. Nixie had managed to get herself hired on to the serving staff for this event, another pair of eyes—and hands—to help Lorelei make the best of it. It was an opportunity not to be missed.

"Have a program for the fair," Summer offered.

Lorelei took one. "Thank you."

"The program is free with purchase." Summer smiled. "You *are* going to buy something, aren't you?"

"Maurice Lemoine's book, maybe. How much is it?"

"It's absolutely fantastic. Kept me up all night." Summer was Maurice's biggest cheerleader. As she rang up the purchase, she chattered gaily about his success. "Isn't it wonderful? Imagine, I said to Penny Johnson just the other day, our very own Maurice. Famous across the nation! Penny tried and tried to get an appointment with him this weekend but he's booked solid. She had to settle for one next week. I remember when I used to let him read tarot cards in the Dharmarama. He used to sit there sometimes hour after hour without a single customer. And now look at him!"

"Yes, it's wonderful," said Lorelei. Penny had an appointment with Maurice! The man was horning in on everything, just as she'd feared. Her only consolation was that she would get a crack at Penny before he did.

She placed the book in her bag and leaned against the counter, leafing through the program. She turned to the page that featured The Amazing Oberon, another star attraction of the fair, who would be at the banquet Friday evening. He had given a performance last night to rave reviews and another one this morning, but Lorelei had skipped them both. According to the program, he would have astounded her. Famous in his native Zubania, Oberon Zolo had revealed his incredible powers at the age of seven, when he'd read the mind of a notorious criminal and helped the Zubanian royal family to recover the kidnapped heir to the throne. She looked for a photograph of the man, but found only more text. Perhaps Oberon wasn't very photogenic. She skimmed the series of testimonials from clients he'd helped. All of them in Europe. He must be new to the circuit, she thought. She'd never heard of him before. In any case, he didn't concern her. As she knew, Waverley viewed mind reading as a mere form of entertainment, interesting but not worth investing in.

Lorelei spent an hour browsing through the display booths and then took the elevator down to the foyer of the Radisson Room, where about twenty Seekers were gathered for a catered reception. They milled about with cocktails and appetizers, discussing the events of the morning. As she made her way through the crowd, she heard Oberon Zolo's name mentioned in tones of awe. Apparently the mind reader had impressed the Seekers greatly with his show.

Waverley was seated at a small table, surrounded on all sides by admirers as he sipped a cup of tea. Penny was nowhere to be seen, but Agnes was seated directly across from him. She wore a pale yellow dress this afternoon, and a matching straw hat that curved low across her face. She had obviously been busy shopping. Her nylon string bag bulged with books and gadgets from the fair's various booths. A magazine peeking out at the top bore the headline, "Could Your Next-Door Neighbor Be An Alien?" Lorelei thought briefly of her landlady, Charlotte. Not impossible.

Waverley was listening as the members of the group discussed the mysterious origins of Oberon Zolo. When he saw Lorelei, he waved and mouthed, "Let's talk," but he was otherwise engaged at the moment.

"Where did you say Zolo was from?" he asked the men beside him. "I've never heard of him."

"Europe," said the man on Waverley's right.

"Zubania," said the man on his left.

"Oh!" said Agnes. Then she frowned. "Uh, where?"

"It's in Yugoslavia," said the first man. "Or is it Estonia?"

"What do you know of him, Lorelei?" Waverley asked.

"I understand he's incredible," Lorelei commented. "Ingenious use of the cross-kinetic undulations of the beta waves."

"Well, Agnes was quite surprised by him!" Waverley laughed. "Weren't you, Agnes?" Agnes simply blushed under the brim of her hat. The Amazing Oberon, Lorelei guessed, had used the old ploy of insinuating that ladies had sexual fantasies.

To change the subject, Lorelei turned her head to speak to Waverley about the research center. But he was already striding away from her, on his way to greet Oberon Zolo, who was just emerging from the elevator with Summer

Sweet. An excited chatter began as they appeared at the entrance to the foyer.

"Excuse me a moment," Lorelei said to Agnes. She rose and followed Waverley.

Oberon the Amazing was a tall, heavy-set man with a full black beard and long mustache. He was a striking figure in a black tuxedo and long, black cloak, lined with crimson satin. As he entered the foyer, the crowd began to gravitate toward him. People jostled each other until they formed a staggered kind of receiving line. Summer Sweet squeezed his arm and he leaned down and whispered something in her ear. She nodded and set off toward the bar. Oberon continued blithely, waving at the crowd, his protruding stomach bumping the elbow of Kent Mason, who was busy scribbling in his notebook, working on the feature he was doing on the fair. Kent dropped his pen and shot an angry glance in Oberon's direction. But Oberon was oblivious. He was addressing his public.

"Good afternoon, ladies and gentlemen!" He spoke in an unidentifiable European accent, with a slight drawl.

Waverley came sweeping through the crowd. "Marvelous exhibition!" he cried.

He clapped Oberon's shoulder. "I hope the exertion hasn't tired you too much?"

"Not at all," said Oberon. "Not at all." He gestured toward the assembled fans, holding his right hand against his heart. "Why, with such an audience, *such* an audience, one is filled up, one is simply *flooded* with positive energy. I feel absolutely refreshed."

"Wonderful! Then you'll join us for lunch?"

"Absolutely!"

"And of course you're joining us for dinner Friday night as well?"

"I wouldn't miss it."

"Just a buffet, you know," said Waverley. "A casual affair." He began to question Oberon about the physiology of the brain.

Lorelei had learned from Nixie that there would be nothing casual about Friday's buffet dinner. As part of the serving team, Nixie had already attended two meetings with the chef and his staff and reported that Waverley's last-minute dinner order had thrown the chef into a tizzy. He viewed it as a crucial opportunity to impress Mr. Forbes, and elaborate preparations for the buffet had been flung into high gear. Lorelei could relate.

"You must meet my guests," Waverley was saying. "Let's see." He turned to survey the room. "Lorelei, there you are. Come here, my dear. You simply must meet Oberon."

Lorelei stepped forward.

"This is Lorelei Good, Oberon. She's a relative newcomer to our scene here, but not at all new to me. I discovered her in San Francisco years ago, and I assure you, she's a natural. Very, *very* gifted."

Lorelei smiled modestly.

"Pleased to meet you," Oberon said. He patted his chest, as if genuinely touched or suffering from heartburn.

"Pleased to meet you, too," she replied. As she offered her hand, she was a little distracted by the thick, utterly black beard that bristled forth from his jowls and billowed down his chest to tickle his belt buckle. It was truly alarming. Could it possibly be real? Then, recovering herself, she glanced up into his eyes. Behind the thick glasses, under the bushy eyebrows, she caught the wild, icy glitter of dilated pupils.

Despite her efforts to appear cool and collected, Lorelei felt her heart begin to hammer. The ice-blue eyes, the bulbous, reddened nose, those grotesque sideburns. This man's name wasn't Oberon Zolo. It was Obadiah Zywyno. And he wasn't from Zubania, wherever that was. He hailed from Tuscaloosa, Alabama, via California and a stint in a Sacramento jail for fraud. Of all the stupid—she stepped backwards, but before she could think of an excuse to slip away, he gripped her hand. Hard.

"The pleasure is mine, I'm sure." Obie wasn't at all perturbed by her presence. Either he was a better actor than she'd thought or, more likely, he'd spotted her earlier and had prepared himself for this moment.

"Lorelei, is it? What a lovely name." His irony was too faint to be detected by anyone else. He released her hand and turned to Summer, who had returned with a frosty martini for him. "Thank you, dear," he said. He raised the glass. "To *Summer*," he said. "Another lovely moniker. Why, it's as light and sunny as your presence." He gulped at his drink.

"So you have met Summer already?" Waverley said. He seemed surprised that any such thing could have happened without his orchestration.

"We met yesterday," Summer said. She turned to Lorelei. "Aren't we lucky, Lorelei, to have such a talented visionary in our midst. So gifted."

Obie was a talented drinker, Lorelei remembered. And a gifted pool shark. She'd once seen him take the entire population of a bar in Sacramento for a total of three grand in one night. And get away with it. She supposed such stunts were behind him now.

As a waiter came forward, bearing a tray of canapés, Kent Mason reached forward to take one. Oberon stepped in front of him. Kent was obviously annoyed. Unlike the Seekers, he did not seem at all amazed by Oberon.

"Are those shrimp?" Oberon asked.

"Prawns," said the waiter. "With a mango-dill sauce, wrapped in—"

"Delightful," said Obie, grabbing a handful. He crammed two into his mouth and sniffed as he chewed. "Lorelei, you must try one of these," he exclaimed with his mouth still full.

"I'm allergic to seafood," she said. She turned away abruptly, nearly colliding with Agnes.

Agnes was looking a little lost in the crowd. "Do you know where the washrooms are?" she whispered.

Lorelei smiled. "No, but I need to freshen up myself. Come on, let's go and find the ladies' room."

As she ushered Agnes ahead of her past the crowd in the foyer, she could see Obie watching her. Head and shoulders above everyone else in the room, he was easily able to keep an eye on her every move. He munched on a prawn, mango-dill sauce dripping from his mustache, as he observed the direction she was taking down the hall.

In the washroom, she took her time washing her face, then rested her elbows on the counter and gazed at herself in the mirror. She didn't like what she saw. Her dark hair was curling in the humidity, and she smoothed it back with her fingers, tucking a few disobedient wisps behind her ears. She wanted to draw together every loose strand, to erase any vestige of the version of herself who had once known Obie Zywyno.

If Lorelei hadn't come so close to a court date in Sacramento, she would never have returned to Winnipeg, city of her unlucky childhood. But life had become very difficult those past few years in California. She had left her psychic healing gig in San Francisco after a few too many disgruntled customers started to make noise. She'd moved to Salinas, where she read past lives and removed curses for a few months. But when Nixie came of age, Lorelei got nervous and wanted to cut back on her little sister's involvement. So she'd moved to Sacramento and turned over a new leaf, choosing a new identity from the manila envelope, and letting Nixie go to college while she read palms and cards at local shops and restaurants.

She'd met Obie at a small bar where she conducted a lot of her business. He was running a number of schemes from the bar, playing pool, making book, and hosting poker games in the rooms upstairs. He was fascinated by Lorelei's tarot readings and introduced her to his friends, who all had various irons in the fire. Lorelei went in on a few jobs with them from time to time. They were rough characters, and there had been some failed jobs, some double-crosses, and then the last terrible straw, an arrest warrant with her name on it. Or rather, Lola's name. In any case, it had been time to take cover. A friend had bailed her out and here she was back in Canada. Her home and native land. Her only refuge, now. The one place she could hide out safely, unknown, disguised as her true self. Or so she'd thought.

The stunt that had nearly cost Lorelei her freedom was a minor crime, really, a dumb mistake. She'd been partners with a couple of Obie's friends, guys who made lottery tickets, and after an especially lucky month of sales, the guys had run off with the profits, leaving her flat. So she'd applied for a credit card under the name she was using at the time, Lola Gold, and it was easy. As long as she kept up the minimum payments, the bank kept raising the credit limit, and soon she took out a card in another name, and then another, until finally some clerk in some office somewhere caught on and called the police. Lorelei had learned a valuable lesson from this experience: don't work with any partners. She vowed that from then on, she and Nixie would rely only on themselves. It was far less risky to use Nixie than to use strangers. The decision to come back to Winnipeg had been made quickly. A few phone calls to determine that Waverley Forbes was still in town, and that "Uncle" Joey Shaunigan was still in jail, and within days Lorelei and Nixie were crossing the border into Canada, leaving the country that had been their home for over a decade.

She thought she had left those days of anxiety far behind her. But the appearance of Obie Zywyno had brought the memories rushing back, and right now, as she returned to the foyer of the hotel, she could feel the tension in her shoulders and the butterflies in her stomach all over again. She wondered what Obie was up to, beyond the obvious. In fact, she realized with surprise, she was dying to know. But she had no intention of asking him. She had something much more significant going on now, something bold and visionary and good for Nixie, and there was no way she was going to let Obie drag her back into his grimy little world of petty crimes. She avoided his eyes as she walked back through the foyer. This wasn't difficult, because he was occupied with Summer, who had separated him from the herd and had him cornered, probably trying to book his act or pitch some angle that would profit the Dharmarama. Lorelei swept past them and took the elevator down to the lobby. She had an appointment with Penny Johnson, a clean and respectable client who was going to become an ally in Lorelei's clean and respectable new venture. She was not about to let Obie contaminate it.

On the front steps of the hotel, she saw that Kent Mason had come outside too. The Soldiers Against Satan had formed themselves into a tight, military wall along the public sidewalk, blocking both entrances to the driveway. This would lead to trouble. The hotel couldn't allow that kind of thing. They'd have to call the police. She scanned the line of protesters and found herself relieved to see that Imogene was not among them. Charlotte was there, but she must have had the sense to send her daughter home. If there was going to be a confrontation, this was no place for a kid.

Lorelei turned toward Kent and was surprised to see he was interviewing the Reverend Surefire himself, in person, not two feet away from her. A camerawoman stood behind Kent, filming the interview. The media loved the Reverend, who was always good for an outrageous quote if the news was slow. Moving out of the range of the camera, not wanting to appear on TV, Lorelei walked backwards down the stairs, keeping her eye on the interview as Kent held the microphone up to the Reverend's red, fleshy lips.

With gusto, and considerable saliva, the Reverend declared to the camera that he was empowered by the Lord to take vengeance against the wicked here on Earth.

"What form might that vengeance take?" Kent Mason asked.

The Reverend glowered at Kent, as if he might demonstrate his methods right there and then. But he restrained himself.

"Channel Ten has recently learned that the police have cleared Yolanda Dawn's ex-husband of any connection to her death," Kent continued. "He was in Chicago at the time. So her murder remains unsolved. Do you care to comment on the fact that a psychic right here in our city, a practitioner of the very arts you have condemned, was apparently thrown to her death from the sixteenth—"

"Toying with the dark side brings its own punishment," the Reverend proclaimed, his face purple with rage. "These witches are doing the Devil's work right here in our city, and I say to the people of Winnipeg, be on your guard! Lock up your sons and daughters! Young people are very susceptible to the wiles of these witches and warlocks, these servants of Satan! They are actively recruiting young people to swell the ranks of their cults."

"How are they doing this?" asked Kent.

"They lurk outside our schools—"

Lorelei didn't have time to listen to any more. She had to hurry home to prepare for her appointment with Penny. She started down the driveway, but she was blocked by the sudden arrival of Oberon the Amazing, who grasped her elbow and propelled her back into the building. He pushed aside a curtain and stepped into a tiny alcove off the lobby, pulling her in with him.

"You're very elusive," he remarked, as soon as they were alone and out of earshot. "I can't seem to get an audience with you at all. Tell me, what are you doing up here at the North Pole? I must say, it's a most inhospitable place, with this preacher fellow whipping up such a fuss. Look at them out there!" He pointed through the window at the protesters gathered around their leader. "And look at the little message the welcome wagon sent me this morning." He reached into the inner pocket of his lapel and pulled out a folded piece of paper, which he handed to her.

The paper was ordinary white bond. The block letters, printed with a red ballpoint pen, spelled "Burn in hell, witch."

Lorelei gasped when she saw it. "Where did you get this?"

"The hotel delivers a complimentary newspaper to its guests every morning. They hang it on the doorknob in a plastic bag. Somebody stuck this inside mine today. It wasn't you, was it? Trying to thin out the competition?"

"Of course not." She handed the note back. "You should take this to the police."

"Hmm. The police? That's a novel idea. Since when—"

"Look, Obie, I'm not kidding. The last person around here who got a message like this is dead."

"Nice try, little one, but I don't scare that easy. I know all about the murder. Everyone does. Including the copycat who wrote this note." He shoved the paper back in his pocket. "One of my esteemed colleagues, no doubt." He placed a gloved hand on his chest and leaned in close. "Speaking of whom, I must say nobody on the circuit seems to know you. They claim you're some sort of local seance queen. Is that so?"

Lorelei backed up into a full-length mirror on the wall. "Look, don't make any trouble for me, all right? Just carry on, do your own thing, and leave me alone."

"But you're not alone, darling. I can see you've weaseled your way into the very inner sanctum. You're positively surrounded by the beautiful people."

"Come on, Obie. Don't cause trouble for me. I've made a lot of friends here."

"Friends?" Obie laughed. He moved in so close she could see the hairs in his nostrils. She stepped sideways. "A certain millionaire and his cronies?" he asked. "A certain Mr. Waverley Forbes and his gang of Peekers?"

"Seekers."

Obie snorted.

"They're good people," she said. "They care about me. If you cause any trouble…."

"They'll rush to your defense, will they? Yes, I'm sure your new friends are captivated by you. Utterly fascinated by your doings—whatever it is you're doing. I'm sure they're dying to become more intimate with, who is it? 'Lorelei Good'?" He grinned and sniffed and removed one glove, which he used to wipe his face. The beard must have been stifling. "Perhaps I could help them to become further acquainted with you."

"What about *you*?" she asked. "What about your ugly little secrets? What's to stop me from busting you?"

Obie shrugged. "In a few short days, Oberon Zolo will cease to exist. As soon as he cashes his checks, poof, he won't care what you say about him. He'll be high in the sky, on his way to—oops!" He chuckled. "Almost let that slip."

So. Obie was pulling a short one. He had nothing to lose. But Lorelei was in for the long haul. She'd invested too much in her current project to let Obie ruin her now, and he could tell. Of all the towns on the circuit, why did he have to end up right here, right now? Would he really expose her past? She watched him closely to see if he was bluffing, but despite the sweat beading his forehead, he seemed perfectly confident.

"How much?" she said.

"Well, let's see." Obie was enjoying himself. He turned toward the mirror, adjusted his bow tie, and brushed a piece of lint from his lapel. "I figure you've got a pretty big fish on the line, here. Forbes is worth millions, and with your particular brand of bait…." He finished the sentence by running his eyes up and down her body, raising his bushy eyebrows in appraisal. "Let's see. Cut me in for fifty grand, and it's mum's the word."

"Fifty!" she said. "You're crazy."

"And you," he said, "are Lola Gold, or is it Lila? Wanted in California for credit-card kiting and fraud and probably a few other peccadilloes I don't know about…yet."

She tried to step past him but he blocked her easily

with a well-placed hammy thigh and pinned her against the wall. She looked straight into his crazed, icy eyes and said, "There's no way you're getting fifty."

"Ah, good." He smiled and relaxed his grip on her. "You're willing to bargain. Because I have a business proposal for you."

"I'm not interested in doing business with you."

"Lola, Lola." Obie shook his head sadly. "I know you think you're better than me. You always did act like some kind of royalty. But in this case you'll see I'm worth your while. I've discovered a veritable gold mine, right here under your nose, and if you don't want to avail yourself—"

She sighed. "What kind of gold mine?"

Obie smirked. "That's my girl," he said. "That's the Lola Gold I know and love." He glanced behind him to be sure the curtain was closed and lowered his voice. "Take a look at this." He opened his outrageous cape and pulled something pink from the inner pocket of his tuxedo jacket. It looked like an index card covered with scribbles in blue ink.

"What's that?" she asked. "Your grocery list?"

Obie wiped his nose on the back of his gloved hand. "A few crib notes," he said. "Courtesy of Miss Summer Sweet. As you may already know, your friend Summer does a brisk trade in the intelligence business. She has a huge cache of information about her customers for sale. Birthdates, hobbies, illicit affairs, objects they've—heh heh—'misplaced' over the years. You name it."

Lorelei eyed him suspiciously. "You don't even know Summer."

"Ah, but I do. This isn't the first time I've been through this town, you know. I first came through about three years ago with an old friend of mine. We were touring the west, me playing pool and him doing a mind-reading gig. He introduced me to Summer and her little sideline—a partnership he found most beneficial. But he's retired now, and being at loose ends these days, I thought I'd give her a call myself. She got me this booking and did the promo. And helped me get to know my clients. For example…." He held out the card and Lorelei took it.

At the top, she recognized the name of Dharmarama customer Bunny Green. But the rest of the card was gibberish, at least at first glance. "Gem. Two sis. Gall blad x. NYC 911 w. hub. Hub x 2004. Car acc 1999—broken ankle." There was more. The card was crammed with writing on both sides, in different colors of ink, as if the notations had been made at different times.

"What is this?" she asked. She read it again. Then she said, "Wow. Mrs. Green and her husband were in New York when the Twin Towers fell?"

"You're very talented, darling." He sniffed. "As I'm sure you can imagine, that experience created distinctive pulsations of her aura for years to come."

"Hmm. Yes. You read her mind today?"

"They don't call me amazing for nothing," said Obie. "Bunny Green will be purchasing my videos and other products by mail order. She's quite astounded—"

"I'll bet she is," said Lorelei. "But Bunny Green is of no interest to me. What else have you got?"

"Name your pleasure," said Obie. He lifted one arm in a gesture of generosity and the crimson lining of his cape extended behind him like a giant wing. "Summer maintains an extensive filing system for the benefit of visiting artists. Facts dating back over ten years." He giggled suddenly. "She puts gold stars—you know, the kind that teachers use—on the ones she calls 'solid gold,' the rich ones. She has boxes absolutely chock full of fascinating gossip, all in alphabetical order. And none of it available to you locals."

"Why not?" asked Lorelei. She was remembering the phone conversation she'd overheard at the Dharmarama, Summer talking about "solid gold" and not dealing with the locals. She must have been talking to Obie.

"Discretion, darling. Less chance of the customers catching on. Summer is scrupulous about maintaining her reputation. Her 'integrity in the community,' as she calls it. It's her livelihood. Now, let's get serious. Summer claims to have valuable intelligence on the Seekers. The crème de la crème, Waverley Forbes and such. So if there's anyone you specially want to get to know…."

"Penny Johnson," said Lorelei, with no hesitation. "Definitely Penny Johnson."

"Now there's a familiar name," said Obie. "That's one of the women who signed up for my workshop."

"Really? Have you got one of these cards on her?"

Obie shook his head. "I couldn't afford it," he said. "Tell me, what's so special about Penny Johnson? She seems like an ordinary customer, worth no more than Bunny Green, but Summer insists she's gone 'solid gold.'"

"She's now dating Waverley Forbes," Lorelei told him. "So anyone who impresses Penny impresses him, too."

"Ah, ha! So you'd pay, say…two grand? Two and a half?"

"I don't have that kind of cash," said Lorelei. "But I can get you a nice piece worth twice that."

"Very well, then," said Obie. "I'll meet you here tomorrow. Same time, same place. Be sure you bring the payment." He turned on his heels, and his cape billowed in Lorelei's face as he walked away.

As she waited a few minutes to avoid being seen with him, Lorelei realized she was still holding the pink index card on Bunny Green. She guessed Obie didn't need it any longer. She placed it in her purse before slipping back out of the alcove and through the lobby.

By speeding, Lorelei managed to make it home in time to tidy up the consulting room. Luckily, given Penny's aversion to theatrics, there were no special effects to set up. Lorelei simply made a pot of rosehip tea and quickly reviewed a couple of Raymond's letters. They were photocopies. Nixie had returned the originals, just in case Penny got nostalgic one day and went looking for them. So far, the letters weren't much help, but they were her only source of information besides the commonplace facts that Nixie had picked up from the house. Raymond had apparently been an ardent, torrid lover, at least on paper. The only other elements of interest were in the letters dealing with the difficult birth of Penny's nephew, Derek. "Poor Ruth, she barely survived the labor," Raymond wrote. "If the boy dies, it will kill her." The baby had been born with a "hole in his heart" and undergone perilous surgery. There were no clues as to where Penny might have been during this time, but Raymond had written to her almost daily, signing his letters, "Missing and pining for you, Ray." Penny didn't seem like the type to inspire pining in a man, but Lorelei had seen stranger things in the course of her career.

Within minutes, Penny arrived at the door and soon she was sitting and chatting comfortably across the same table where, less than two weeks ago, she had jumped away from Lorelei in horror. It was progress. But Lorelei knew she'd better not pull anything too dramatic or Penny might shy away again, and she had to get Penny on board before the next full moon.

Lorelei explained that a tape of the session was available for a small extra fee, and Penny agreed. "With my memory," she said, "it's a blessing to have a record."

Lorelei popped a tape into the recorder. "Many clients find that later, when they listen to the reading after some time has passed, they have a fuller understanding of it."

"That's what Yolanda said."

"Oh, she taped your sessions?"

Penny nodded. "She taped the last one. She said that, even if it didn't make sense to me then…and it didn't, really …I might understand it in the future."

"And…do you?" asked Lorelei. Penny merely smiled. The infuriating woman refused to provide any clues. Yolanda had probably gotten desperate and decided to tape the session so that she could keep a copy of the tape for herself, to study. Well, Lorelei could do that, too. She turned the tape recorder on. "We are not always ready to receive the messages when they come. Sometimes we need to learn more, to grow spiritually, before they come clear to us. Place your hands up here on the table, please." She reached over and gently grasped both of Penny's hands in her own.

"Do you think we'll be able to make contact?" Penny asked. "I noticed, when I looked at the calendar today, that the moon won't be full tonight."

"That's true," said Lorelei. "This is not the most conducive time for summoning—"

"In *Ghost Talk*," Penny interrupted, "Maurice Lemoine says the spirits are not affected by the atmospheric conditions of the natural world."

"A common misconception," Lorelei replied. "But you see, the spirits are part of the natural world, just as we are, and they are bound by the laws of nature. At PsyRen, we are dedicated to the scientific study of those laws so that superstitions, such as those Maurice Lemoine promotes, can be laid to rest."

"But you think you can make contact, even without the right phase?"

Lorelei had no intention of making contact yet. She still had no insight into the nature of Penny's quest. Not one hunch. She said, "We should do a personal reading first, before we seek the right guide, one who can coax the spirits to communicate with us."

"Coax them? But in *Ghost Talk*, Maurice Lemoine says the spirits are eager to speak with us."

"Well, that's sometimes true." Lorelei was heartily sick of Maurice Lemoine. "Let's just sit quietly for a moment, shall we? Let the currents begin to flow between us."

They sat quietly while Lorelei counted to sixty. Penny was alert, her head inclined toward Lorelei, awaiting some revelation.

After a minute had passed, Lorelei let her voice slip into a singsong, feminine chant and recited a series of facts about Penny's astrological sign and her difficult teenage years, always a safe bet. Then she got into a little more detail. "I sense that you have given much of yourself to your family," she said. "Now that your children are grown, you are just beginning to find yourself. You do have children, don't you?"

Penny merely smiled enigmatically.

"You have a son, I believe. But he's…." Lorelei frowned, as if puzzled. "He is a very special person. I'm getting the sense that he is somehow split. It's odd. I'm getting the image of a double heart. Your son is conflicted, wanting two things at once, pulled in two different—"

"Twins," said Penny impatiently. "I have twin sons."

"That explains it. You have given so much to these sons to start them off with every possible advantage. You have depleted your own energies, caring for your family."

Penny made a dismissive gesture with her hands.

"I'm serious," said Lorelei. "We must help ourselves, if we are to help others. I sense you have a deep generosity, an openness of the heart. You give of your time to help those in need. This is very important to you. You are especially drawn to the sick and to the poor in spirit. This is the working out of a mission you began in a previous life. You're on a positive mission, working your way to a higher spiritual plane. I sense you have a love of words, yes, a literary gift. You excelled in English classes and you have a strong appreciation for good stories, with strong characters. I can see an alternate path you might have taken. A literary talent that you might have developed."

Penny smiled at this, a little proudly, and Lorelei was encouraged.

"Your aura has a similar shape and color to those of the great writers, Austen, Brontë, Shields. Virginia Woolf. Yet you never developed this talent fully. You've been too busy helping others. You tend to neglect yourself. You bring comfort and nourishment to others, but you rarely nourish your own inner spirit."

Penny's eyes had widened in surprise at the mention of Virginia Woolf, but her head nodded continuously, agreeing with the rest of it. Like so many aging, middle-class housewives, and Lorelei had met hundreds of them, Penny would be aware, deep down inside, that something was missing from her life. Now that she was approaching sixty, she might be ready to reclaim it. If only someone would give her permission.

"These unselfish acts have manifested themselves in

a weakness of your own heart," Lorelei continued. "I'm sorry but I must advise you to consult a doctor about your heart."

"Oh, I have!" For the first time, Penny seemed impressed by Lorelei's powers.

"Good. There is some danger in this area, but with care will come healing. I also sense a deep ache, an aching in the bones. This comes of too much self-sacrifice. It is the body's way of expressing your spirit's needs. Do you ever feel this? An aching in your bones? In the knuckles, perhaps, or the knees?"

Penny nodded. "Why, yes!"

"You need to immerse yourself in what you truly love," Lorelei counseled. "Open yourself to your creativity. Explore your inner desires! Do something just for yourself."

Lorelei paused, as if on the verge of a revelation. She let go of Penny and lifted her hands, holding up one finger to ask Penny to be silent and wait. She made sure to catch Penny's eye and give her a nice, sane smile, so she wouldn't fear any return of the beastly spirit guide. "Shh," she said.

A quiet but distinct rustling sound came from somewhere behind Lorelei's back. What was that? Lorelei wasn't prepared for that. It sounded like the crumpling of paper or a plastic bag unfolding. Lorelei glanced at Penny but Penny didn't seem to hear. It was Bitsy, she decided. Bitsy was in the hallway batting around a paper bag or chewing up the mail. This thought reminded her of Nixie's plan to provide this client with a new little friend.

"I believe I'm glimpsing.... Yes. I sense a new presence coming into your life. It's very close to you, although you can't see it yet. A kindred spirit. Someone small and quiet. Someone who needs you very much."

"A child?" Penny sounded excited. "Maybe a new

grandchild on the way?"

Lorelei frowned a little. "Somebody lost and hungry. A very quiet soul that cannot speak to you in words. I'm not sure it's human."

"Not human!" Penny was alarmed.

Lorelei quickly shifted direction. "I also sense…." She hesitated, groping for the right words. "I can feel another presence near you, too, a human presence, a loving presence. Very strong. Safe. I think it's male."

Penny leaned forward eagerly.

Lorelei breathed deeply. Her body flooded with energy as she felt Penny moving into her sphere of influence again. "I sense it's someone with a message to convey."

She heard the slight rustling sound again. The curtains? Had she left the window open? "Yes, it's certainly a masculine entity," she said. She stood and began to pace around the table, moving her arms gently at her sides, as though swimming through layers of psychic waves. She swept past the window. It was closed and latched. The curtains hung still.

"It's a protective spirit," she added. "Someone who was bonded to you very closely in life."

"My late husband. Sometimes I believe I can feel him."

The rustling came again. Louder this time. Closer. Lorelei felt a shiver up the back of her neck. What *was* that? Didn't Penny hear it, too?

"But I can't quite reach him," Penny said. "It's as if he wants to tell me something, but he's blocked somehow."

"I see." Lorelei kept walking slowly in a circle around the table, passing behind Penny's back. The rustling seemed to be coming from the closet. If there were mice…. She noticed a crack of light beneath the closet door. Had she forgotten to turn off the light in there? She froze as she heard the tinkle of the wind chimes, then a muffled thud.

This time Penny heard the noise too. "Is that…? Those bells! Do you hear that? Is it him?"

"I don't think so," Lorelei said cautiously. A shadow darted across the closet floor. Too big to be a mouse. Too big to be Bitsy. She remembered something the Reverend Surefire had said about the dangers of seances, how they attracted evil spirits. "Stand up," she said quietly to Penny.

"Whatever for?" asked Penny, but she stood.

"I want you to leave the room," Lorelei told her.

"But if he's here, I want to talk to him!" Penny raised her eyes and turned slowly in a full circle, looking at the four corners of the ceiling.

"It's not your husband, I assure you," said Lorelei. She had to get Penny out of the house without frightening her too much. "It is a misguided spirit. They sometimes tag along by accident when we try to summon someone from the spirit world."

"What do you mean?" Penny was backing slowly toward the door. "Like a, a wrong number?"

"Something like that. Please. Leave the room quickly. Leave the house. You don't want it to attach itself to you. They can be harmful."

"But what about you?"

"I know how to handle these entities," said Lorelei. She was inching toward the desk, where she kept her .38 Special in the top drawer. There was definitely someone in the closet, and it wasn't a misguided spirit. "Wait for me in your car."

Penny made a hasty retreat.

Lorelei opened the drawer and reached for her tiny revolver. She aimed at the closet door. "Who's there?" she called.

There was no answer. Lorelei thought of the gruesome message scrawled by Yolanda's killer. The harsh, forbidding faces of the fanatical protesters. The creepy note left for Obie at the hotel.

"Who's in there?"

Still no answer. Lorelei stepped forward. In her right hand, she kept the gun steady at eye level, aiming it inside the closet while, with her left hand, she flung the closet door wide open.

Out tumbled Imogene Trapp, the landlady's daughter, in her pink sailor dress. Her eyes were round in her wide moon face, and she held her hands up in the air like a captured crook on a television cop show.

"Imogene!"

"Don't shoot me!" Imogene cried, staring up at the .38 Special.

Lorelei lowered the gun. "What are you doing here? Spying?"

"I just wanted to see!"

"I should call the police," said Lorelei. "Don't you know it's against the law to break into someone's house?"

"Is that a licensed gun?" Imogene countered.

Lorelei cursed under her breath as she put the gun down. For Imogene's benefit, she hauled her little-used gun safe out of the drawer and locked up the .38. "There," she said. "Safe and sound. Now you stay here for a minute. I want to talk to you."

"If my mother knew you had a gun in here—"

"Just stay put," said Lorelei. She walked out to the street.

Penny was in her car, talking on her cell phone. "I'll call you back, Agnes," she said, as she saw Lorelei approach. "Are you all right, Lorelei? What happened?"

"I'm fine," said Lorelei. "It's nothing truly malicious. Just a lost soul, a confused entity who needs guidance. I'm afraid I won't be able to finish your reading today. I'm sorry."

"Oh, that's all right. My goodness, if you need to commune with this, this, whatever it is…."

"I should do a cleansing ritual," Lorelei explained. "Just to be on the safe side. May we continue the reading another time?"

"I'm not sure when I could," said Penny. "I'm so busy. But perhaps after my birthday party next week? You could join us for cake. We'll do the reading afterwards."

"I'll be there," said Lorelei. She waved goodby and headed back toward the house, to deal with the confused entity.

Imogene was seated at the seance table, playing with the string of brass wind chimes she'd stumbled over in the closet.

"What are these for?" she asked, as Lorelei came back into the room.

"Oh, for— Give me those." Lorelei took the chimes and returned them to the closet. She locked the closet door.

Behind her, an eerie, distorted voice asked, "And what's this, this, this, this?"

Lorelei snatched the voice synthesizer out of Imogene's hand.

"Wow!" said Imogene. "That's cool!"

"You are in a lot of trouble, young lady, sneaking around like that. When I tell your mother—"

"You can't tell my mother!" cried Imogene. She looked more frightened than she had when the gun was pointing at her.

"Oh yes, I can. We pay rent here, Imogene. This part of the house is off limits to you, and if—"

"You can't tell her! If you do, I'll, I'll tell her you're keeping a gun in here."

"Now Imogene, don't be stupid." Lorelei shook her head sadly. "The gun is perfectly legal," she lied.

But Imogene was wily. "My mother would call the police," she said. "She's already suspicious about you. She thinks you're in a cult. If she found out you were having the cult members over here, having conversations with the devil right under her roof...."

"Then I guess she wouldn't be too happy to know you had witnessed these things," Lorelei retorted. "Now tell me. How did you get in here? Did you steal your mother's keys?"

Imogene turned red. She folded her arms across her chest and stared defiantly at her adversary.

Lorelei folded her own arms across her chest and tried to look stern enough to scare the brat off. They were at a standstill. Finally, Lorelei decided to try reasoning with the girl. "Why did you come down here, anyway?" she asked.

Imogene kicked at the table leg. "I just wanted to see, you know, your stuff. For the readings. I didn't know you were going to be *doing* one. I thought you were still at the hotel."

So much for hiding from Imogene, thought Lorelei. "Did your mom see me there?" she asked.

"Oh no!" said Imogene. "She'd evict you if she knew. I told her I had a headache from the heat and I came home. I was just looking at things, honest. I didn't break anything. When I heard you come in, I hid in the closet. And then I couldn't help overhearing." Imogene looked up at Lorelei. Her bravado seemed to vanish. "Lorelei? How do you *do* it?"

"You want a reading?" Lorelei asked. "I thought you said that was conversing with the devil."

"That's what my mother says."

"But you don't believe that?"

"I don't know." Imogene stopped kicking the table. "Would you give me a reading?"

Lorelei studied the girl. "Would you keep your mouth shut?"

"Oh yes! I would! I promise!"

So Lorelei told Imogene to sit quietly and stop fidgeting while she received her vibrations. "I sense much curiosity," she began. "Curiosity and mischief."

Imogene's eyes flew open. "I want a *real* reading!"

"All right. All right. Settle down, then." Lorelei resigned herself to the task. "Be quiet, so I can sense what's emanating from you. That's better. Yes. I can sense a strong aura—"

Imogene opened her eyes again. "An odor?"

"An *aura*. A vibration, the tangible essence of your spirit."

"Oh."

"Now keep your eyes closed. You need to relax. Make yourself comfortable."

Imogene wiggled her bottom into the upholstery. "How comfortable should I be?"

"That looks good. Now take a deep breath. Let it out slowly. You need to cleanse your chakras."

"My what?"

"Just breathe," said Lorelei. She closed her eyes and began to think about Imogene. Her posture and her gait. The things she said. The way she was always hanging around. "I sense loneliness," she said.

Imogene let out a long, wavering breath.

"Loneliness and…shame." Lorelei watched the girl closely.

Imogene's freckled cheeks were flushed. Her brow was creased; her nose was dotted with blackheads. Despite the humidity, her scalp was flaking and her lips were dry. Lorelei could see the bite marks she'd left when chewing her lower lip. Imogene's fingernails were bitten short, and her hands gripped the edge of the chair so tightly her knuckles were turning yellow. The kid was a wreck.

"Take another deep breath," Lorelei said. Imogene tried, but her back was bent too far forward. Her shoulders were hunched and rounded from trying to conceal her breasts. Lorelei placed her hands on the girl's shoulders and pulled them back. "Sit up straight. Try to relax. Let go. You need to let the oxygen flow through your body."

Imogene breathed more deeply.

"That's it. That's better. You have a lot of nervous energy in your body, did you know that?" She kneaded Imogene's shoulders, digging her fingers gently into the knotted muscles.

Imogene nodded.

"There's an awful lot of tension here." Lorelei paused for a minute. Then she said, "It's fear, actually."

Imogene suddenly sobbed out loud.

"Whoa, whoa," said Lorelei. "There, now. Come on, now." She handed Imogene a tissue. "Calm down."

Imogene squeezed her eyes tightly shut, and one lone tear trickled down her flushed cheek.

"Okay, now I'm getting a better reading," said Lorelei quickly. "I see, uh, a trip in your future."

"Really?"

"Definitely. I see a lot of change coming into your life. Travel, adventure, and many new people. I also sense that you have a gift, Imogene. Your interest in the clairvoyant arts comes to you naturally, because you have a gift yourself."

"Oh!" cried Imogene. "Do I *really*?" She opened her eyes. Her pupils shone and she actually beamed with pleasure.

Against her will, Lorelei felt a soft lurch in her chest. "Sure," she said. "Sure you do. I can tell." She looked at the clock. Half an hour before the bank would close for the day. "Now run along before your mother comes looking for you," she said.

"Obie Zywyno!" Nixie cried, when Lorelei told her. "Not that creep! What's he doing here?" Nixie was standing at the kitchen counter, scooping strawberry ice cream into a bowl. She had worked late at the hotel last night and left the house again early this morning, only coming home now to shower and change and catch up with Lorelei. She'd been hoping for news of a major breakthrough with Penny, but so far the only news Lorelei had to share was the story of Imogene's interruption and the fact that the Amazing Oberon turned out to be one of the old gang of scammers they'd known and loathed in Sacramento. Worse, he was asking for money.

"There's a positive side to this," Lorelei said. "It sounds like he might have some useful information." She told Nixie about Summer's sideline of selling her customers' personal histories and showed her the card on Bunny Green. "I'm tempted to pay him off," she concluded. "After all, he's leaving town in a couple of days. If he can make some money off me, he'll probably be happy to leave in peace. Thank god he hasn't heard about the research center. If he sniffed out that kind of money, we'd never get rid of him."

"But what are you going to pay him with? We're awfully short on cash."

"I know." Lorelei sighed. "In the past few months we've invested more in PsyRen than we've earned. It's going to pay off soon, but in the meantime…for Obie…I'm afraid…." She gave Nixie a regretful smile.

"Not another diamond!" Nixie protested.

"It's unavoidable," Lorelei said. "It's an emergency."

"Yuck," said Nixie. "I hate to waste one on that creep." Nixie hated any expenditure of diamonds. These days, Lorelei kept them in a safety deposit box at the bank. Both sisters regarded them as a shield against possible disaster, their retirement fund, their family heirloom, the only legacy they'd ever get from Max or Katherine. They spent them sparingly. Over the years they had let go of only three, and the thought of one ending up in Obie Zywyno's grubby hands made Nixie angry.

"I know, I know. Just think of the future," said Lorelei. "We have to pay him or he might get pissed and blow my cover. And we can't afford to pass up any information he has. It could be crucial to the project."

"What if he recognizes me at the dinner?" Nixie asked. Obie didn't exactly know Nixie, and he didn't know she was Lorelei's sister, but there was a good chance he might recognize her. He had once teased her about her freckles and red hair when she'd paid a visit to his hotel room in Sacramento. She'd been posing as a maid in order to gather information on some of the card sharps at a poker game he was running. Obie made the mistake of trying to feel her up as she dusted the lampshade. She had bitten his thumb so hard he'd screamed and run to the front desk to complain. It wasn't likely he'd forgotten her wild red hair, or the twelve hundred dollars that had been missing from his room that day when he returned with the mystified hotel manager, who couldn't recall a maid who fit the description Obie gave him.

"I can't show up for work in disguise," said Nixie.

"We can do something with your hair," Lorelei suggested. "I'll help you."

"Good," said Nixie. "I'm not going to blow this chance to watch and listen to the Seekers. Besides, Agnes will be there, and it's a perfect opportunity to borrow the keys to her cottage. You're sure they're in her purse?"

"Yes. They're on the same chain as her house keys. With a little metal heart." It was important to get the keys. The cottage had a deadbolt, and Lorelei didn't want Agnes noticing any signs of a break-in.

"All right, then." Nixie turned over the pink index card in her hand. "And maybe we can do something with this."

"Like what?"

"I don't know exactly, but don't throw it away," said Nixie. "I've got a feeling we can use it." She jumped up from the table. "Look, I gotta go now, or I'll be late for my shift." As she stepped into the hall, Bitsy bounced into the kitchen to investigate her empty dinner bowl. She was closely followed by the little brown and white kitten Nixie had brought home from the animal shelter. The orphaned kitten was destined for Penny's house, but Nixie hadn't yet had a chance to plant him there. "Can you feed them, Lor? I'm late."

"Okay." Lorelei followed Nixie into the hallway. "Hey, is Bitsy sick? Imogene said something about—"

"Nothing serious," said Nixie quickly. "The vet was just doing some tests."

"What kind of tests?" But Nixie was already out the door.

At a quarter to eight, in the lobby outside the hotel's conference room where Maurice Lemoine's performance was about to begin, Lorelei handed over her ticket and entered the hall. She chose a seat near the back so she could watch the members of the audience as they arrived. The stage was low, and the two hundred seats rose above it in tiers. She could feel the buzz of nervous excitement as people filed in, clutching copies of *Ghost Talk*. A smattering of teenagers giggled and hushed each other, but most of the audience were elderly, supported by canes or by each other, as they took their places. The old couple who settled in beside her gripped each other's hands tightly, their faces betraying their anxiety and hope. Lorelei was not happy to see Penny and Waverley settle into the front row. She wondered why Penny was so interested in Maurice. Penny didn't seem the type to fall for his smarmy good looks. Perhaps it was Maurice's specialty, the location of lost objects, that was the attraction. What *did* this woman want?

While she waited, Lorelei opened her own copy of *Ghost Talk* and learned that the spirits of the dead were composed of loose, vaporous molecules, capable of binding to the molecules of the living. Intense emotions, such as jealousy or anger, acted as magnetic forces, compelling the spirits to commune with the living until the emotions could be purged and the souls set free. She managed to read several paragraphs of scientific explanation on this topic before a stunning young red-headed woman sashayed onto the stage like a fashion model. A bouncy theme song began to play as she presented the star of the show to the audience with elaborate arm gestures as though he were a brand new dishwasher to be won as a prize on a game show.

The star himself walked on, looking much like his cardboard cut-out, a little larger, if that were possible, and glowing with healthful energy. He wore an open-necked tennis shirt, chinos, and polished brogues. With his tan and his over-groomed blond head, he looked like an ad for aftershave.

Maurice bowed and held up his hands to silence the crowd. "Good afternoon, ladies and gentlemen," he began. Then he looked toward the ceiling. "Good afternoon, spirits." He smiled at the murmur of surprise he received in response. "Oh yes, the spirits are present. They are with us now." He had a slight French accent and an enthusiastic, booming voice. He seemed barely able to contain his own excitement. "There are several spirits in the room," he continued, "waiting to transmit their messages to the loved ones they've left behind. Parting, as the poet said, is sweet sorrow. But I assure you there is no need to feel sad or sorry for the spirits. This is a joyous occasion for them, an opportunity to communicate, to offer guidance, to those they continue to care so deeply about. For death, though it seems so final to those of us still bound to Earth, is merely a shift in perspective to those in the beyond. In many ways, they have changed very little. Although they no longer inhabit their physical bodies…."

Lorelei scanned the crowd. The place was packed. At thirty-five dollars a ticket, times about two hundred people, minus the room rental, Maurice was making five or six grand today. The fees for the private sessions he was conducting tomorrow would net him another couple of grand. Not bad for a weekend's work. Of course, you had to factor in his agent's cut, the salary of his publicist, the care and feeding of his entourage. But now that *Ghost Talk* was climbing the bestseller list, he was raking it in. Summoning ghosts was a lucrative business, especially if you could summon up a good ghostwriter to go with them.

Maurice cocked his big head. "I'm sensing something over in this corner," he announced. He moved stage left. Lorelei craned her neck so she could see the people he was talking to. She envied his easy patter. Why hadn't she adopted such a cavalier manner from the very beginning of her career? It would have made things much simpler. On second thought, however, she decided such a breezy style wouldn't work for a woman.

"Precisely over…no. Yes. Right over here!" He swept his arm in an arc that encompassed a quarter of the audience. "There's a message coming in, over here from someone with a B name, a name that begins with a B. Or a D. Does that strike a chord with anyone? Madam? The lady in the purple outfit?"

The purple lady shook her head.

"A B or a D? Anyone in this corner?"

Several hands went up. Maurice pointed at a red-faced woman in a sleeveless, sequined T-SHIRT. She was about forty years old and enormously overweight. The flesh of her upper arm wobbled as she waved her hand in the air. "There's someone close to you who has a message for you," Maurice told her. "It's a B or a D?"

"He's a—a D?" the woman said.

"I'm sensing a DA name or a DR. Is it a DA?"

"A DA."

"Is it, I'm sensing it's a male, yes? Is it David? Daniel?"

The woman gasped. The man beside her patted her back. "It's okay, Myrna."

"So it's Daniel."

"Danny."

"Danny is letting me know he has something to tell you. I can tell he was very fond of you. How long is it since he's passed?"

"Thirteen months."

"He wants you to know that he's happy now, he's at peace. I'm getting calm vibrations, there's a serenity about him."

"Serenity? *Danny?*"

"Yes. And he was very close to you. Like, family. A close relation?"

"No," she said.

Maurice continued as though he hadn't heard her. "A close relationship existed between you. He thought of you like family."

The red-faced woman began to cry. Tears trickled down her fat cheeks, and her companion passed her a tissue.

"I feel there was a romance involved, here. Am I right?"

She wiped at her eyes and nodded. "Danny was my boyfriend's foster son. My ex-boyfriend's."

Maurice closed his eyes, communing with the spirit world. The audience was utterly silent, waiting. "In life, Danny was a troubled boy. He had a difficult family life."

The woman looked up in astonishment.

"I sense he died young," Maurice proclaimed.

"Yes!" she cried.

Maurice closed his eyes again. "A tragedy," he said. "It was sudden?" He opened one eye and saw the woman nodding again. Tears were streaming down her face. She blew her nose loudly.

"I see a road," Maurice continued, watching her carefully. "A road of darkness."

"It was broad daylight!"

"But there was darkness in his mind. Confusion. He's telling me now that he didn't mean to hurt anyone. It was an accident. A car accident?"

"Head-on!" she wailed. "Head-on in the middle of the day and no seat belt!"

"Yes. I see it clearly. Painful, very painful. But Danny wants me to tell you that his pain is in the past. He's saying, 'Myrna, I'm grateful for the way you tried to guide me in life. I'm sorry I didn't listen to you. I was young and foolish back then. But I'm at peace now, and I want you to put your suffering behind you, too.'" Maurice paused, as if listening. "Danny also wants you not to blame yourself for the breakup of your romance. He says it was all his fault—the stress his death caused for the two of you. But it was his time to go. And one day you will fully understand the meaning of that."

The woman's mouth was hanging open. She was too surprised to weep any more.

Maurice had her completely hooked. But he didn't stop there. "He's also telling me that there's something about your health. A health issue?"

She nodded again, mouth still agape.

"He's telling me that you need to listen to your doctor. To follow your doctor's advice. There is somebody new in your life." The woman's companion blushed. "A relationship that will blossom. But you've got to take care of yourself. Do what the doctor says, all right?" Maurice smiled and began to back away. His work was done.

"Bless you." the woman said softly. "Oh, *thank* you!"

In the opposite corner of the room, Maurice held out his arm. It quivered like a divining rod. "The airwaves are wide open today! An s, this time. An s name. Or a c?"

Lorelei stood up and slipped quietly from her seat. She'd seen enough. The guy was good. Very good. It wouldn't be easy to best him. If Maurice could work a crowd completely cold like that, what could he do with a targeted client, a client he had a little pink index card on? Armed with facts, along with his superb intuition, he'd be very convincing. He had more experience than Lorelei, a stronger reputation, and a larger staff. But the most dangerous thing about Maurice Lemoine was how easy he made it look, as if chatting to the dead was an everyday event. He needed only to find an open channel to tune in to any particular spirit's voice. The man was a walking cable television. The Seekers would eat him up. Penny, with her practical, no-nonsense approach to the dead, would adore him.

Maurice would have to be discredited. But how?

CHAPTER SEVEN

The following afternoon, Lorelei skipped out in the middle of a demonstration on crystal washing in the seventh-floor ballroom and took the elevator down to the alcove where she'd made her deal with Obie the day before. She loosened the thick tapestry draped across the entrance, to make a more private space, and waited. In the pocket of her dress she had two good diamonds, each in its own velvet-lined ring box. One was to purchase Obie's silence and to place her order. The other, of slightly higher quality, was to pay him off if he came through for her. Together, the diamonds were worth about ten grand, wholesale, and that was her absolute limit. If he thought he was going to get fifty, he was out of his mind.

Nixie had searched the stationery stores for the right shade of pink correction fluid and found an identical match. Delicately, with careful, even brushstrokes, she had removed Bunny Green's name from the top of the index card that Obie had given to Lorelei. Then, taking care to copy Summer Sweet's rounded capitals, she had printed

Penny Johnson's name in its place.

When Obie arrived, Lorelei got straight to the point. "Instead of asking for Penny's card, I want you to ask for several cards," she instructed. "Get Summer to bring out the whole box and then change your mind. Maybe claim you can't remember exactly some of the ones you need. Ask to rifle through, spread them around. Confuse her a bit, you know."

Obie nodded. "Misdirection is my middle name," he said. "But to what purpose?"

"Do you think you could switch this card for Penny's?" She handed him the altered card.

A wicked grin spread slowly across Obie's face as he realized what she was up to. "Smart," he said. But then his face fell as a new thought occurred to him. "Trying to save a few bucks?"

"I'll pay you the same," she promised. She pulled one of the ring boxes out of her pocket and opened it.

Obie gasped. "My God, it's a beauty. Is it real?"

"Real as real can be. Take a look."

Obie took off one glove and picked up the stone between his thumb and forefinger, holding his other hand cupped underneath, in case he dropped it. He held it up to the light and whistled softly. "This is from that bank manager, isn't it?"

"No," said Lorelei. She didn't like to remember that bank manager, to whom Lola Gold had been briefly engaged in Sacramento. He'd given her a lot of gifts, including a diamond ring, before Lola skipped town. Those gifts had since been scattered in various pawn shops across the Midwest. "I inherited it from my dad," she said. "There's another one like it, if you can pull this off."

Obie beamed. He took the box from her hand, replaced

the stone, and snapped it shut. He popped it into his lapel pocket along with the altered index card.

"Very well," said Obie. "Anything else I can do for you?" He bowed low, sweeping the floor with his cape.

Lorelei almost smiled. "See what you can find out about Maurice Lemoine. Is he doing business with Summer, too?"

"Hard to say." Obie leered. "You know, my psychic powers tell me Summer has a bit of a crush on that cad but he's not interested. Anyway, I have heard some tidbits about Maurice. Rumor has it he was involved with that murder victim."

"Yolanda Dawn?"

"Yes. They say she was truly gifted." Obie chuckled. "Even some of the biggest cons believe she was for real. And they say she was in love with Maurice. He's apparently a beneficiary in her will."

"Do the police know about that?"

"You know, lately, the police have failed to keep me informed," said Obie. "All I know is what I hear from my fellow artists backstage. They're all obsessed with the murder. Half of them are terrified of the religious nuts. The other half are convinced Yolanda's husband did her in. Jealous about Maurice. What do you think?"

"I don't know yet," said Lorelei. "Just see what else you can find out."

Nixie circulated among the crowd in the fifth-floor foyer with a tray of appetizers, weaving behind pillars and potted plants. Obie had returned from his meeting with Lorelei and seemed too busy schmoozing with his public to notice Nixie. She was dressed exactly like the rest of the female staff, in a demure uniform of pale apricot and a tasteful little blue apron. With copious globs of gel and a couple of elastics, Lorelei had managed to darken Nixie's hair and pull it back severely so that it lay flat against the scalp. Under the little apricot cap, her hair was almost unnoticeable.

It made her nervous to be so close to Obie, but she was glad to be out of the hot kitchen, away from the hollering, stressed-out chef. Every catering job was the same. No matter how smoothly it began, it always increased in intensity as dinner approached, until everyone's temper was at the boiling point. She preferred housecleaning duties, where she was left alone to do her work unwatched. Getting the keys to Agnes's cottage had been a chore this afternoon. Penny stuck to Agnes like glue, and Penny was always followed by Waverley, who was followed by everyone else. Finally, Agnes had excused herself to go to the washroom and Nixie had managed to bump into her in the corridor and remove the keys from her purse.

Right now, Nixie was trying to maneuver toward a corner where Agnes was talking to Maurice Lemoine. Agnes was wearing a pale peach shawl, pinned closed at the shoulder. She kept her arms crossed beneath it, giving her body a peculiar, lumpy appearance. On a long strap over her shoulder, her purse dangled slightly behind her, conveniently free of her hands. Maurice was holding forth on some theory about the ethereal plane and Agnes seemed enthralled. There was a lot of that going around. While the two of them were occupied, Nixie could probably return Agnes's keys to her purse without attracting any notice. But just as she was easing toward them, she was cut off by Summer, who bounded forward, calling Maurice. Why was he so popular with the ladies?

"Chicken satay?" asked Nixie, turning to Waverley, who was sharing a window seat with Penny. They had already been snacking. Two plates of olive pits and orange rinds sat on the table before them.

"Why, thank you," said Waverley. He took one of the metal skewers from the tray and began to strip it of meat with his knife and fork.

Nixie relieved Penny of her empty glass. "Another melon martini?"

Penny shook her head. "No thanks, dear." She fanned herself with her program. "It's a little warm in here, isn't it? Could you bring me a glass of ice water?"

"Won't be a minute." Nixie turned away and found herself face to face, or rather face to stomach, with Oberon the Amazing.

"Ah, appetizers!" he exclaimed. "Just what the doctor ordered."

Nixie bowed her head and stared at his big shoes while he helped himself to her last three skewers of chicken, loading them onto his plate. She could smell the sweat and cigar smoke clinging to his clothing. His eyes were glazed and bloodshot.

"Thank you, my dear," he said. He patted her greasy head with his greasy hand, but seemed too stoned to see her clearly. He lumbered heavily away as if half asleep.

Nixie turned back toward the alcove, but she was too late. Summer and Maurice were now posing against the backdrop of the hotel's fancy curtains. Maurice raised his head and bared his pointed white teeth and Summer flashed a metallic smile while Agnes, apparently pressed into service for the occasion, was taking their photograph.

Nixie carried her empty tray back to the kitchen, following the twisting corridor behind the staircase. It was a roundabout route, but the chef had forbidden his staff to cut through the banquet hall before preparations were complete. He wanted the table to be perfect before his handiwork was revealed. She checked her watch. Only five o'clock. There were two full hours to go before dinner, an hour for cocktails and then an hour for the guests to freshen up and dress before dinner. She took a deep breath and braced herself as she pushed through the swinging doors.

The kitchen was in chaos. Anxious servers scurried back and forth from kitchen to banquet hall, carting stacks of plates and trivets and butter knives. The chef was screaming at a hapless pantry chef, berating her for lining a serving platter with lettuce while it was still wet. Nixie glided quietly between her harassed fellow workers to the refrigerator and filled a tall glass with ice water. As she closed the fridge, the pantry chef was cursing out a waiter who had set the wrong dessert forks on the buffet table. Nixie was grabbing a lemon slice from the servery when the waiter stopped her.

"Don't carry that in your *hand*!" he barked. He thrust a little silver tray at her and Nixie obediently set the glass on it. The waiter wiped her fingerprints from the glass with a cloth. "It has to stay cold and clean," he said severely. "This is Waverley Forbes's party, you know. If we don't screw this up, we might get to work for him in future."

Nixie nodded wearily.

"Waverley *Forbes*," the waiter repeated. "Do you even know who he is?"

"I certainly do," said Nixie as she hurried back down the corridor.

A few minutes later, as she was clearing dirty dishes from a side table, Nixie spotted Maurice and Summer conferring behind a pillar, hidden from view of the other guests. She piled the dishes on a tray and tried to think of some other task to keep her busy so she could stay close by.

"Did you listen to the tape?" Summer asked Maurice.

Nixie's ears perked up. Tape?

"I listened to it twice," Maurice said.

Nixie knocked over a pitcher. Water spilled across the tabletop and dripped onto the floor. Maurice and Summer looked up for a moment and then continued talking, completely ignoring her as she mopped up. Nixie smiled to herself. The uniform of a menial serving person was like a magic, invisible cloak. She had learned a lot more posing as a maid or a waitress than she'd ever learned in school.

"I don't know why she didn't leave them to me!" Summer sounded resentful. "Surely I'm the obvious choice."

"I told you," Maurice said gently, "she left them to me because we were friends."

"Lovers, you mean," said Summer with bitterness.

"Friends," said Maurice. "We had a pact."

"Whatever," scoffed Summer. "So, anything worthwhile?"

"Promising," said Maurice. "She was one smart cookie. I think I'm starting to see where she was going with this thing."

"You think she knew where he stashed the stuff?"

"I don't think he stashed it anywhere," Maurice replied. "I think the kid took it."

"No!" Summer cried. "One of his own kids?"

"No. The—"

Maurice's next words were drowned out by the crash of breaking glass. Nixie turned toward the sound. One of her fellow servers had dropped a tray of glasses behind the bar. She had no choice but to help out by fetching a broom.

By the time she got back to the alcove where Maurice and Summer were talking, their conversation had progressed beyond the point where she could follow it.

"What's he got against her?"

"I don't know," said Maurice. "Isn't there anything in your files that might explain it?"

"I don't exactly have them memorized," Summer said. She ran a long, pink fingernail slowly down Maurice's chest to his belt buckle.

"Well, let me have a look, then," said Maurice. "For God's sake, surely this case is an exception."

"So this means you've changed your mind? You'll let me hear the tape?"

"I'll bring it over." Maurice sounded as if he'd held out for a long time on this point. "I'll do the exchange this time. But only with this one, mind you. None of the others."

Nixie bowed her head as he walked past her, trying very hard to conceal her interest in their doings. It sounded as if Summer was offering to give Maurice a peek at her files, in exchange for his letting her listen to a tape. This was an exception to her rule against dealing with locals. She wondered what tape Maurice had been listening to and where he had gotten it. Somebody "left" it to him, he'd said. As in a will? Yolanda Dawn? Did Maurice have Yolanda Dawn's tapes? Where was Lorelei?

Lorelei spent most of the cocktail party on the periphery, watching Obie. He was speaking to Penny and Waverley at the moment and she wondered what sort of pitch he was making. Ordinarily, she would have slid right in and charmed Waverley away, but she was too wary of Obie and what he might say or, worse, what he might hear. If he caught wind of the research center project, he'd never leave town.

But she wouldn't have to worry about him for long. Soon, everyone would go their separate ways to freshen up for dinner, and Obie would be over at the Dharmarama, doing her bidding. Then she'd just have to endure the dinner, pay him off, and wish him bon voyage. She ordered a glass of ginger ale at the bar and took it with her into the atrium off the foyer. As she watched the well-dressed Seekers mingle, chatting about ethereal planes and spectral vibrations with complete suspension of disbelief, Lorelei felt a sweet thrill of exhilaration rising through her body. She marveled at how far she had come, working her way up out of the crummy bars of Sacramento to stand here among these lovely believers, at the top of her game. She had nothing to fear from Obie, she reminded herself. This was her territory. She had staked it out carefully and no one could take it away from her.

The long white curtains on the atrium windows had been drawn to block out the glare of the afternoon sun. She pulled one of them aside and looked out the window. The protesters were down there again today, still circling. They were becoming part of the scenery. A stubborn bunch. Fanatics. She remembered Kent's announcement that Yolanda's husband had been cleared. If that was true, her murder was still unsolved. Could one of these extremists really be responsible? It didn't seem likely. Their feet were dragging and their shoulders were slumping. But then suddenly, as if he sensed he was being watched, one of the protesters raised his head and seemed to look straight up at Lorelei. She let the curtain drop and turned toward the crowd in the foyer.

Nixie entered the atrium with a tray of empty glasses. "Anything I can do for you?" she asked. She moved behind a large potted palm and began to wipe spills from a glass-topped table as she told Lorelei of the conversation she had overheard.

Lorelei turned back to the window while she listened,

parting the curtain again, as though admiring the view. "Interesting," she said. "Who could Maurice be targeting?" She glanced back into the foyer. Maurice was exiting down the staircase and Summer followed him. Perhaps Maurice, too, had a pre-dinner appointment to buy information at Summer's boutique this evening. If he was after Penny's card tonight, Obie had better beat him to it. But Obie was seated by the bar, taking his sweet time.

"The crowd is thinning out," she told Nixie. "I'm nervous Obie will spot you. You should get back in the kitchen and stay out of sight until dinner is served."

"But I've still got Agnes's keys in my pocket," Nixie whispered. "I whipped out to the mall on my break and copied them, but I haven't had the chance to return them yet."

"Well, give them to me."

Nixie removed them from her apron and handed them over. "You'll have to slip them back in her purse before she goes home."

There were four keys, attached to the little red heart charm, the same keys she'd seen Agnes use several times at the cottage. She stuck them in her own purse. How hard could it be?

"They go in the inside, zippered pocket," whispered Nixie. "And be sure you hook this ring back onto the key ring in the purse."

"What? Great!"

"Sit next to her at dinner. She'll probably put her purse under the table."

Lorelei nodded. She let Nixie slip out first, then waited a few minutes before she left the atrium.

In the foyer, most of the guests seemed ebullient and unsteady on their feet as they dispersed to dress for dinner. Obie had disappeared. The elevator door was closing on a tightly packed crowd of Seekers who were heading home. Kent Mason was trying to interview Waverley about the founding of the Seekers, but Waverley was having none of it. "Not now," he said. "I have calls to make." He said goodby to Penny, promised to be back within the hour, and took the next elevator down alone. A few partiers lingered, downing the dregs of their cocktails. Penny and Agnes looked sober, but weary. They explained they were going to take a little nap upstairs in the hospitality suite before dinner. In a moment, the foyer was empty and Lorelei was alone.

An hour later, at ten minutes after seven, Lorelei was resting on the hotel stairwell between floors four and five, sneaking a cigarette. She had spent the past hour alone at home, where she'd bathed and changed into a suitable outfit for dinner—a little black number with a single string of pearls. She wasn't sure where the others had spent the hour. She had been looking for Obie since she entered the hotel, wanting to find out if he'd managed to switch the card successfully. But he wasn't in his room, and there had been no sign of him or any of his fans in the lobby or the hotel bar. She hadn't seen Summer, either. Everyone must be in the banquet room by now, she thought. She tried to assure herself that Obie would be there, too, but she couldn't stifle a nagging doubt at the back of her mind. What if the information he had bought was so good, so valuable, that he decided to keep it for himself?

She stubbed out the cigarette on the marble landing and made a half-hearted attempt to scuff it clean with the sole of her sandal, but this only made a larger black smear. For such a classy hotel, this was a lapse. If they didn't want ashes on their floor, they should scatter a few ashtrays around. She popped a mint in her mouth and prepared to breeze into the banquet room with a charming excuse for her lateness. She pushed through the stairwell door and was surprised to find the foyer still full of people. Waverley and his guests had not yet gone in to dinner.

Waverley stepped forward to greet her, with Penny close behind him. They each held a tall glass of water, sensibly trying to dilute the effects of the cocktail hour before they were offered wine with their dinner. Waverley wore a pair of white suspenders over a silk shirt of cobalt blue that made his blue eyes blaze. As concessions to the heat, he had hitched up his sleeves with old-fashioned sleeve garters, and he carried the jacket of his ivory linen suit across one arm.

"Lorelei! I've been looking for you," he cried. "We must talk! Have you spoken to your agent? I was just telling Penny I haven't had a chance to have a real talk with you since I returned from Boston. Have you made any progress with the Mexican couple?"

"We're moving along," she replied. She turned to Penny and smiled. "Did you manage a nap?" She didn't suggest that Waverley might have needed a nap.

"Oh, yes. Agnes and I had a lie-down in the hospitality suite. After those melon martinis, I was out like a light the moment my head touched the pillow."

"You look nice and refreshed," said Lorelei. It was true. Penny was, as usual, bright-eyed and impeccably groomed, her navy-blue party dress crisply pleated.

"Have they accepted your offer?" Waverley asked.

"I'll fill you in later," Lorelei said. "Tell me about Boston. How was your trip?"

"Marvelous, marvelous," he replied. "I made the most astonishing find there. An antique Ouija board, hidden for centuries in the attic of a Boston magistrate. I believe it was fate that led me to it, Lorelei. I arrived in the city the very day it went up for sale. I'm determined we shall try it out at my soiree on Sunday night."

"But the moon won't be full," Penny remarked.

"That's true," said Waverley. "I hadn't thought of that."

"It's a new moon on Sunday," Penny continued. "And you know Lorelei's powers won't work unless there's a full moon."

"It's not that they won't *work*," Lorelei said quickly. She wasn't sure, but she thought she detected a slight edge to Penny's tone. Was the woman challenging her? "It's just that the moonlight thins out the veil between this world and the next, allowing smoother egress."

"We can always give it a try," said Waverley. "No harm in trying."

"No harm unless you accidentally summon the wrong sort of spirit," said Penny gravely. "Lorelei doesn't seem to be able to control what kind of entities her powers are attracting. The other day—"

"That was an anomaly," Lorelei explained. "As it turns out, sunspot activity was extraordinarily turbulent that day."

"Really?" asked Penny. She raised her eyebrows and tilted her glass to her lips, sipping her ice water.

"Interfering with the air waves," Lorelei said. "A rare but disruptive phenom—"

"Oh, yes, I've heard of that!" exclaimed Summer, appearing suddenly at Waverley's side. She was wearing an evening dress of pale rose chiffon, slightly too formal for the occasion, and seemed a little breathless. "What's going on? I rushed to get here, thinking I was late, but you haven't even gone in to dinner, yet!"

Behind her, Maurice Lemoine appeared in a black dinner jacket over a T-shirt and jeans. "Yes, isn't it past time for dinner?"

"Dinner is late for some reason," said Waverley. "I'll go and see what's the matter." He walked off.

Lorelei turned to look at the crowd that was gathering behind her. "Is Oberon Zolo with you?" she asked Summer.

"I haven't seen him," she said.

Kent Mason stepped forward, shaking his head, and greeted them with a sigh.

"What's going on?" Maurice asked him.

"Of all the ridiculous things!" Kent exclaimed. "Dinner's held up. The doors to the dining room are locked, and the manager can't open them! He says the keys are missing."

A sense of impatience was palpable in the room, as twenty hungry guests, most of them a bit tipsy, paced up and down, consulted their watches, and complained. Someone made a timid suggestion that they should mount a detour through the kitchen, and someone else countered that the entrance through the kitchen was locked as well. From time to time, the chef could be heard in there, screeching with rage. The Seekers were not impressed. Such incompetence! The expense Waverley had gone to, only for this! No one was talking about airwaves or the ethereal plane any more. Spiritual matters had been forgotten in light of the rumbling of so many stomachs.

"Here comes the manager now, what a relief!" said Summer. "I hope the food's not cold."

The manager appeared, hurrying toward the doors. He jangled a large, iron ring of keys, reminding Lorelei of the difficult task that still lay before her. She spotted Agnes a few feet up ahead, standing on tiptoe, the better to peer over Maurice Lemoine's shoulder. She had shed the lumpy peach shawl and looked a little more elegant than usual in a rich, chocolate-brown dress with red piping at the collar. Lorelei pushed through the crowd, as if trying to get closer to the dining-room door, and sidled up beside her. Agnes's bag hung over her left shoulder, tantalizingly near. Lorelei studied its gold clasp as she palmed the keys Nixie had given her. Zippered compartment, inner pocket, attach the small leather pouch to the key ring. The challenge was daunting, but everyone was crowded closely together, and Agnes's attention was fixed on the manager as he tried each key in the lock. Lorelei glanced around to be sure no one was watching. She reached out and pinched the clasp between her forefinger and thumb, coughed slightly, and gave it a twist. It opened. Then Agnes suddenly stepped aside to make way for Summer, who was pushing her way through to supervise the opening of the door. Lorelei had to slip the keys back into her own pocket.

"Try the big one," Summer advised the manager. "The brass one. It matches the lock."

"One more moment," the manager said. He turned a key in the lock and pushed open the wide double doors with a flourish. "And voila!"

A gasp went up from the crowd. Across the wide expanse of Persian carpet, the guests could see the buffet dinner laid out like a work of art, gold-rimmed white china and linen-wrapped silverware stacked neatly at one end of the long table. In the center rested the chef's masterpiece, two swans of melting ice, their long necks entwined in the shape of a heart and draped with loops of golden ribbon, their beaks dripping into a cut-glass platter of strawberries and melon balls. Nestled about the swans, a vast array of dishes waited—colorful salads, sculpted mounds of scalloped potatoes and green beans, two enormous, glistening turkeys, and at the far end of the table, among the fruit salads, pies, and fancy dessert plates, lay the very dead body of Oberon the Amazing, face down in the middle of a mocha-almond torte.

CHAPTER EIGHT

Two days after Obie's death, Lorelei still had trouble concentrating. She wandered through the house, from kitchen to dining room to living room, unable to get any work done. She knew she should be sorting her brochures and preparing for Waverley's soiree this evening, but it was difficult to stop recalling images from Friday night's ill-fated banquet. The poor chef had been taken to hospital. According to the local news, he was still there, recovering from a mild heart attack. No word on a cause of death for Obie.

Agnes Kellsington had fainted dead away at the sight of Oberon Zolo's lifeless body. She'd had to be lugged to a couch in the atrium off the foyer. Lorelei had helped out by carrying her purse, taking the opportunity to attach the keys properly inside. It had been easy to do. Confusion had reigned as panic spread quickly through the crowd of Seekers. A number of the women, Summer Sweet included, were hysterical. Apparently talking to the dead was all very well, but having to look at them was too much.

Only Penny Johnson had maintained her calm, trotting

to the washroom to bring cool paper towels to lay on Agnes's forehead, making soothing noises and advising Waverley to get himself a good, stiff drink. Waverley himself had sat still and white-faced on the edge of the potted palm, not moving until Penny guided him to an armchair and made him the prescribed drink at the abandoned bar. She made one for herself, too, and then perched beside Waverley, cool and collected in her crisp navy dress, not a hair out of place, sipping a gin and tonic. You'd never have guessed she'd found a dead body in her dessert that very evening.

Lorelei barely noticed that Bitsy was sharpening her claws on the leg of the sofa. Penny's kitten, or the kitten destined for Penny, swiped at Bitsy's tail and both cats tumbled together across the floor, where Bitsy began to scratch the carpet vigorously. Lorelei didn't even scold them. She returned to the dining room and looked again at her stack of brochures. Would Waverley really invest? Or was she deluding herself? She ran her hand across the glossy paper and suddenly was gripped by doubt. Maybe she was nothing but a big dreamer. A fool. All day she'd been haunted by a stubborn memory of Obie Zywyno, years ago in a Sacramento bar, bragging of his latest scheme to get rich quick. She saw him lifting his beer glass, proclaiming, "All you losers can eat my dust!" A few days later, he went to jail. And now he was dead, he would soon be dust. His family, whatever strange family he might have, would never see him again.

What in the world had happened to him? She recalled his nervous fiddling with his gloves, his sweating forehead and his dripping nose. The way he kept placing his hand against his heart. At the time, she'd thought the gesture was an affectation, but now she wondered. The flu? Drug addiction? He must have come back to the banquet hall, sneaked in to get an early start on dinner—if nothing else, the man was a serious food addict—and been overcome by something. A heart attack? A stroke?

Maybe.

But there was one particular detail from that night that she couldn't shake off.

While the Seekers gathered around Agnes and Waverley, Lorelei had slipped back through the dining room doors to watch the rescue efforts. Obie had apparently been leaning over the table when he'd collapsed. He was bent forward at the hips, his legs dangling, his feet dragging on the floor, and his massive torso planted face down on the table. The hotel manager had hurried to turn Obie's head to one side and clear his mouth and nose of chocolate icing, but everyone could see it was too late. The manager and a waiter then tried together to flip Obie's heavy body over. In the attempt, Obie's jacket flopped open and Lorelei saw that the inner breast pocket was ripped almost completely off the lining of the lapel. She had seen this pocket only an hour before, perfectly intact. Now it was hanging by a thread. And it was obviously empty. The ring box containing Obie's newly acquired diamond—Lorelei's diamond—was gone. In the next moment, an assistant manager shooed all the guests from the dining room, and Lorelei saw no more.

In the excitement, nobody commented on the torn pocket. And nobody ever would, Lorelei guessed. Most likely they'd assume it had torn during the frantic life-saving attempt. And no one would miss the ring box. No one but Lorelei even knew it existed. Well, apparently one other person knew. But who? What had happened? Did someone see Obie collapse with heart failure and then quickly lock the doors and search his pockets? If so, that person had been incredibly lucky. Nixie's theory was that one of the traveling psychics from the Fair had been spying when Lorelei gave the gem to Obie in the alcove and had later followed Obie into the dining room and robbed him. Lorelei, remembering the threatening note he'd shown her, wondered if he'd told anyone else about it before he died. Should she mention it to the police? No, she decided, that would be too risky. How could she explain why a total stranger would show her such a thing? It was better to conceal the connection between herself and Obie. Pretend she never knew him. Most likely the note to Obie had been a hoax, anyway. One of the Soldiers Against Satan had read about the grisly words on Yolanda's wall and sent a copycat note to Obie, as part of the protest strategy. Or maybe a rival psychic, as Obie himself had suggested, had been trying to scare him off. The note probably had nothing to do with his death. It was a heart attack, she said to herself. Heart attack, she repeated. Heart attack, aneurysm, overdose, stroke.

But a logical voice at the back of her mind continued to nag her: what were the chances, realistically, that he would receive a threat alluding to witches burning and then die an accidental death within two weeks of Yolanda's murder?

Zero.

The evening of Waverley's soirée was clear and warm, so his household staff had set up a bar and tables on the patio behind the house. The screened gazebo stood empty as guests milled about in the open air, enjoying a rare mosquito-free evening. City workers had blanketed the area with insecticide the night before. A few people had even ventured into the wooded area below the tennis courts, where the terraced lawns descended to the riverbank and Waverley kept his speedboat tied to the dock, along with a small flotilla of rowboats and canoes. A couple of guests set off for a short canoe ride along the Assiniboine. Their laughter and the splash of their paddles carried clearly across the water. Sunset was still an hour away.

Lorelei had arrived deliberately late. She stood alone at the edge of the crowd, observing and listening, waiting for Waverley to notice her. She could see him seated next to Penny on a wrought-iron bench beside the pool of koi. Penny was doing most of the talking. Waverley seemed to be questioning her and to be taking her answers most seriously. But the chatter of the party guests and the clinking of their cocktail glasses made eavesdropping impossible. Lorelei declined the waiter's offer of a drink. Behind her, one of the servants opened the French windows of the great room as the hired jazz trio, Waverley's latest discovery, began to play "Heatwave." The female singer's sultry voice spilled out across the patio and two or three couples got up to dance.

The music drew Waverley's interest and he looked up. As soon as he saw Lorelei, he began to extricate himself from his conversation. He would be very keen by now to hear about her progress with the couple in Mexico. He had left her two telephone messages yesterday, which she had not returned. She wanted to let him think she was going ahead without his involvement, making decisions, choosing the future site of the research center herself. She would have stayed away tonight as well, except that there was something she wanted to retrieve from his study. The longer she avoided him, she wagered, the more he'd tempted to reassert his authority. Sure enough, as soon as he left Penny's side, he drew himself to his full height and began to stride toward Lorelei. She felt the familiar tingle of excitement run through her body.

"Where have you been?" he demanded.

She smiled. Waverley was a powerful, natural force, like the ocean. A force you had to respect, even as you challenged yourself against it. "What a lovely party," she said. "I'm so glad I could make it."

"Has something come up? Where were you yesterday?"

"Oh, just business." She fanned herself with her hand. "Warm tonight, isn't it?"

"Did you meet with your agent?"

"Yes," she said. "We're making some progress, but I'm not sure the owners really understand our purpose. They're still holding out for a higher price than we can afford. So I've been working on a fuller prospectus. A mission statement. Something to draw more investors." Lorelei scanned the crowd, looking for Agnes Kellsington. "I think I need to sit down, Waverley. Do you think I could have a cold drink? Something with ice. Grapefruit juice?"

Waverley was unable to conceal his disapproval at this show of independence. But there was little he could do at the moment. He walked away to bring her a drink.

Agnes Kellsington strolled by, looking a little lost and alone. Parties were not her forte. She was wearing a button-down dress, the color of overcooked oatmeal, and no jewelry except her wedding band and an ordinary Timex watch. She had made an attempt to be fashionable tonight, accessorizing with a Hermes scarf. But the way she wore it, over her hair and tied beneath her chin, she looked as if she planned to spend the evening dusting or raking leaves. She crossed the grass toward a table and clutch of lawn chairs, where Summer and Kent Mason were enjoying the last rays of the sun. Agnes got out her camera and took several shots of the sun on the river and the boats. Then she wiped a chair with the handkerchief she kept, like an old British nanny, stowed up her sleeve and sat down between Summer and Kent. Lorelei followed and claimed a seat beside her.

The topic of conversation, naturally enough, was the

visiting mind reader who had died at their dinner party a mere two days ago. The close proximity of his demise had created an intimate kind of bond with him in the minds of most Seekers.

"You could tell, when he was doing his readings, that something was unusual," Summer was saying. "I could just feel it. He said he'd never felt the energy flowing through his fingers so effortlessly. It was as if he was closer to the other side already."

"Have you heard anything more about the cause of death?" Agnes asked Kent.

"No more than what we reported on the news. He 'collapsed and was pronounced dead at hospital.'"

"Mysterious," murmured Agnes.

"It's spooky," said Summer, "coming so soon after Yolanda Dawn. It makes you wonder."

Kent shrugged. "It's sad, of course, but I doubt there's anything spooky about it. They didn't know anyone in common. Yolanda was from Hungary, and Oberon was from… Zubania, wasn't it? And let's face it, he was a prime candidate for a heart attack. He was enormous, and I saw him smoking a cigar the very day he died."

That last part was true, Lorelei thought. Obie had a weight problem and a nicotine addiction. Not to mention his dilated pupils, dripping nose, and other signs of drug abuse. He *must* have had a heart attack, she told herself, and some opportunistic robber, maybe one of the kitchen staff, had rifled through his pockets. It was not unheard of.

"There isn't any connection, then?" Agnes asked Kent. "Between Oberon's death and Yolanda's?"

"Not that the police have noticed. Or not that they're telling us. There is the obvious connection that they're both in the same business, but other than that, there's nothing."

"There's the Reverend Surefire and his gang," Summer said. "I just do not trust that man."

"I doubt he's a murderer," Kent said.

"Don't be so certain," said Summer, with sudden vehemence. "Some of those protestors are positively demented. Did you take a good look at them?"

"It's possible, I suppose," Kent admitted, "that one of them might have gone off the deep end. Even someone from outside his group, a disturbed individual watching him on television, for instance, might have taken the Reverend's sermons too literally."

"Sometimes I think that's exactly what he wants," said Summer bitterly.

"Oh, I don't think he means any harm," said Agnes. "He's just ignorant of the true path. Don't you think so, Lorelei?"

But Lorelei didn't answer. She was signaling to Waverley, who was standing on the terrace with her juice in hand, looking about to see where she'd disappeared to.

As soon as she'd caught his eye, he hurried over. He took a seat beside Agnes, and Lorelei had exactly what she wanted. Two of the wealthiest people in the city, ready to hang on her every word.

Brian Hale parked his BMW in the circular drive of Waverley Forbes's residence and walked around to the passenger side to open the door for Rhonda Hill.

Rhonda giggled when he offered his arm. "Oh Brian, that's not necessary." But she took it. "Wow," she said as she took in the impressive façade of Waverley Forbes's home. Of all the mansions on this famous strip of riverfront property, his was the largest and the most imposing, with the most beautiful grounds. Waverley's gardeners shunned the tight, geometrical lines of pruned hedges and brush-cut lawns. The gardens were crowded with luxurious blooms, almost unruly with color, and set about with ponds and statues all the way up the driveway. The grass was green and lush, and the rose beds that surrounded the entire house were a riotous mixture of whites and creams and yellows and every shade of red.

"Mrs. Johnson is *dating* this guy?" she whispered.

Brian laughed. "Not sure how serious it is, yet." He crossed his fingers and held them up for Rhonda to see. "Let's wish her good luck."

"Man," she said. "I had no idea." She looked down at her orange cotton blouse and polkadot skirt. Her bright orange plastic purse. "Do you think I'm dressed okay?"

"You look fine. Come on, let's go in." He was anxious to join the party. He would have come straight here after dinner if Rhonda hadn't wanted to see a movie first. But it would have been rude to slight Rhonda. The dinner and movie were meant as a celebration of her promotion at the law firm. She'd been upgraded from filing clerk to administrative assistant, and Brian had promised to take her out to celebrate long before Penny Johnson invited them to this party. A soiree, she called it. A few days ago, when Penny stopped by to sign some papers, she had invited two of the firm's partners and then, because they were standing there, she had casually extended the invitation to Brian and to Rhonda. Remembering that Penny's circle included Lorelei Good, Brian had accepted immediately.

Rhonda slipped her arm through Brian's arm and they started up the path together. She wasn't his girlfriend, but since the two of them were single, they had fallen into the habit of dinners together after working late, and the occasional movie. Rhonda said Brian was a rare breed, a guy who didn't mind "chick flicks," and Brian had to admit he enjoyed romantic comedies better than the orgies of car chases and explosions that his brother and his nephews were addicted to. Tonight, though, he had barely followed the storyline—some plot about a couple who met through the personal ads—because he'd been thinking about Lorelei. Would she remember him? She had looked right at him the other day without recognizing him. Then again, he reassured himself, she'd barely caught a glimpse of him. He'd been in the car. She'd been busy talking to Charlotte. She would recognize him tonight, for sure. He hadn't changed that much, had he? He tugged at his tie to make sure it was straight. Maybe he shouldn't have worn this tie. Maybe he shouldn't have worn a tie at all, but it was too late now. He escorted Rhonda around the corner of the house, following the sounds of the party in progress.

Agnes and Summer listened intently as Waverley questioned Lorelei on her progress. Penny was on the patio dancing with Kent to "Tupelo Honey." They were too far away to hear. So Lorelei didn't have to contend with Penny's irritating doubts and questions as she made her report.

"I explained to the owners the significance of the site," she said. "Its mid-continental pull is quite strong."

"Mid-continental?" Agnes asked.

"Yes," said Waverley. "Here in the very center of North America, the four energies of the continent merge in a powerful vortex. So we are surrounded by many sacred places."

Summer nodded. She, too, had heard all this before, and was willing to share it with someone new to the area. "The Dharmarama is built on a sacred site," she told Agnes. "Lorelei sensed it the first time she came in the store."

"You mean it used to be a church, or—"

"It was a barber shop," Summer said. "The barber had no idea he was situated at the confluence of so much energy. But when I saw the For Sale sign, well, I must have been guided by intuition, I guess."

"You see, Agnes," said Lorelei, "the vortex at mid-continent exerts a mesmeric pull on the spirits of the dead, allowing them more easily to draw themselves through the Veil of Ibina and enter the consciousness of the living. Sacred spots, where the pull is especially strong, are ideal locations for conducting seances. Because the purpose of the research center is to study the nature of the veil, we hope to build it in the most conducive place we can find."

As Agnes absorbed this information, Lorelei reached into her purse. "If you want to learn more," she said as she handed Agnes an updated prospectus.

"So the owners understand?" Waverley asked. He leaned forward aggressively in his lawn chair, his elbows on the table and his hands clasped under his chin.

Lorelei sighed. "Yes, but unfortunately it only seemed to make them more adamant to raise the price."

"Unfortunate," said Waverley. He sat back again and reached for his gin and tonic. "But perhaps it's just as well. I haven't even seen the property yet. We don't want to rush into anything."

"It would be nice to break soil on the project before the fall," said Lorelei.

"Yes, but there are so many details to take into account. The building has to be designed first, and—"

"Actually," said Lorelei, "that work has begun."

"What?" Waverley stood up. "But you haven't shown me a thing! There's nothing on paper yet, is there?"

Summer swiveled from side to side like a spectator at a tennis match as she listened to this debate. Agnes, absorbed in reading the prospectus, didn't look up.

"I have some small sketches with me," said Lorelei lightly. "It's nothing much. Just a preliminary draft the architects are working up for us." She pulled a few pages from her purse.

"You've consulted the architects already?" Waverley frowned. "What firm are you using?"

"Smith and Waite, uh, Wade," said Lorelei.

"I don't think I've—"

"A Vancouver firm." If she could collect enough money, she'd hire a real firm. "Do you want to see the drawings?" She handed him the pages. Floor plans she'd photocopied from an architecture textbook at the university library.

Waverley spread one of the plans out across the table in front of him. "What's this central area, here?" he asked. "The restaurant?"

Agnes looked up. "Restaurant?"

Lorelei stood and came around the table to look over Waverley's shoulder. "That's the seance room," she said. "We'll commission the building of a large, oval table that can seat thirty people. There will be room for observers along both sides of the room. This way the researchers can set up their instruments without disturbing the vibrations around the table."

"The Dharmarama could supply candles and incense," Summer put in.

"We'll certainly need a reliable supplier," Lorelei said.

"The publicity would be excellent for your business, Summer," said Agnes.

"I could design a little shop for the lobby. Or a little booth," Summer said. "If the rent is reasonable," she added.

Lorelei gave Summer an encouraging smile. But she wanted to keep the conversation on the topic of the plans. "The architects are trained in feng shui," she continued. "They have chosen the northern corner for the seance room because spirit waves travel from north to south. So they'll enter here, at the northern window." She pointed. "And there will be skylights above the table. Here, and here, and here. To let in the moonlight."

"Fantastic," said Waverley. "But where is the restaurant?"

"I hadn't really planned on a restaurant," Lorelei admitted.

"People will have to eat!" he cried.

"You'll need cooks," said Agnes.

"Yes, what about staff?" Waverley asked. "Servers, cleaners…."

"If guests are going to stay overnight, you'll need housekeeping staff," said Summer. "Soaps and towels—"

"Gardeners, of course," Waverley added. "There will have to be gardens."

"It would be lovely to have water nearby," Agnes said. "Soothing to the spirit."

"There is a pond," Lorelei said. "I've been planning a serenity garden to surround the pond. And perhaps an outdoor picnic area."

"Yes," said Waverley. He stood up and faced the river for a few seconds, deep in thought. "I can see it. The Midcontinental Center for Research and Healing. With a large sign in front." He held up his hand and moved it in front of him in a wide arc from left to right, to describe his vision of the sign. "Knowledge Is Faith!" he proclaimed. "Just as it says on our brochure."

Lorelei smiled. The evening was turning out even

better than she'd hoped. But it was time to end this conversation. The sun was sinking lower in the sky. When a waiter stopped by with an offer to replenish everyone's drink, Lorelei excused herself. She had only a narrow window of opportunity, when the grounds would be dark and the house fairly empty of people. Shortly after sunset, she knew, the guests would start flocking indoors. All the chemical poison in the city couldn't prevent mosquitoes from swarming on the Assiniboine riverbank at dusk.

She made a wide berth around the patio, planning to enter the house through a seldom-used side door. Her goal tonight was to liberate one of the handwritten diaries she'd recently discovered in the deep bottom drawer of the massive oak desk in Waverley's study. Gloria's diaries. She hated this kind of work. She wished she could send Nixie in to get the diaries when the house was empty. But Waverley's security was too tight. Most of the time, this didn't matter, because Lorelei practically had a standing invitation into his house. Like tonight, the place was often crowded with guests. When Waverley was busy hosting, it was a simple matter to excuse oneself for brief excursions through the upper floors. Gloria's journals were an excellent source and Lorelei had been reading brief passages during her regular forays into the study. But as the stakes were growing higher now, she'd decided she needed to take them home for a good long study. Early in their marriage, Waverley and Gloria had vacationed at Lake of the Woods. Some concrete details from that time period would be very helpful right now.

But Penny interrupted her plans. She was standing with Summer and a young couple near the piano, listening to the jazz trio. She beckoned, and Lorelei had no choice but to join them.

"Lorelei, I'd like you to meet Brian Hale and his

secretary, Rhonda Hill. Brian says he thinks you went to school together."

Brian offered his hand and Lorelei took it, saying, "Brian?"

"Brian Hale." He didn't let go of her hand. "Don't you remember me?"

"Hale?" She remembered him perfectly. Every detail of his face, his warm lips on her neck and his bare, muscled arms around her. *I feel like I'm floating*, he'd said.

"Yes," he said now. "We—knew each other at school. Kelvin?"

"Good old Kelvin," said Lorelei. "Why, that seems light years in the past." She smiled brightly at Penny. "Brian must have been one of the football stars."

"No, I—"

"The Clippers!" said Lorelei. "They were city champions the year we graduated. I remember the gym was decorated with sailing ships and a sort of, a pirate theme, wasn't it?" She looked at Brian or, rather, through him.

You weren't there, Brian wanted to say, but he said, "Yes. Pirate theme. Bottles of rum and pieces of eight." He won a scholarship to Queen's that year, gave the valedictorian address at the ceremony, took Lucy Whalmer to the dance, and then came home to find his mother drunk and weeping in the bathroom, accusing him of abandoning her. "Good times," he said. He couldn't look at Lorelei. He nodded in the general direction of the other women and excused himself.

He wandered out onto the stone terrace beside the house and inhaled the evening air. He needed to get away from the crowd. The mixture of incense, human sweat, and chemical perfumes was giving him a headache. He swatted a mosquito on the back of his neck and walked down the gravel path through the garden, past the pool of black and golden koi. A white statue of Narcissus knelt at the water's edge, engrossed in his own reflection. It was no mass-produced, garden-center special. It was real marble, an original artwork, with classical lines. A Luke Yeats piece, Brian guessed.

He strolled alone through the gardens for a while, listening to the party from a distance before he drifted back toward the house.

Through the open window, he could hear the inebriated, slightly nasal voice of Penny's friend Summer.

"Hank Kellsington is definitely hot," she was saying.

"Why, Summer, when did you meet him?" Penny asked. "I barely know him myself. He hasn't been up here for years."

"Oh, really?" said Summer. "Well, he was here last Christmas, settling his affairs before his wedding, and he came into the Dharmarama." She giggled. "And we hit it off."

"What's he like?" Penny asked.

"An absolute hunk," said Summer. "Body like a Greek god. It's a mystery why he ever chose that little mouse for a bride."

"Now, Summer," Penny scolded. "Agnes is very nice when you get to know her."

"Comes back early from her honeymoon," Summer scoffed. "To supervise the renovations? Give me a break."

These nasty remarks depressed Brian. He wondered what Summer would say about Rhonda and her plastic purse as soon as Rhonda was out of earshot. Suddenly, the whole glittering crowd seemed less than glamorous. He didn't understand what Penny Johnson saw in these people.

He was bitterly disappointed in Lorelei Good. Did she honestly not remember him? He wondered how she fit into this crowd and whether she knew how the alluring world of the wealthy attracted a sordid, dangerous element. When he heard she had been at the Psychic Fair the night of the mind reader's death, he had been afraid for her. The death of another psychic, so soon after Yolanda's murder, was ominous. Brian had feared that someone was targeting psychics. And since he'd spoken with Tommy, he was even more frightened.

Tommy had told him some dramatic details that hadn't yet been released to the press and Brian had been planning to tell Lorelei a few of them. Apparently the "Amazing" mind reader who had died on the buffet table wasn't who he pretended to be at all, but a convicted con artist and a cocaine addict. One who must have gotten himself in the bad books of some vicious people, Tommy said. Although the hotel staff had not detected it at first, the mind reader had been stabbed in the back and died of a punctured lung. His dark, heavy cape had concealed the wound from view, until the paramedics arrived and discovered it. Blood tests later revealed he'd been heavily drugged. A combination of cocaine and alcohol, along with a dose of barbiturates too large to be accidental, had rendered him unconscious. While he had lain in the torte, someone had lifted his cape and, with a kitchen mallet and a skewer from the hotel's chicken satay hors d'oeuvres, put an end to him.

Whoever had done it must have locked the kitchen doors from inside the banquet room, then twisted the doorknob lock on the foyer door and slipped out into the foyer, mere minutes before the Seekers began to arrive for dinner at seven. In fact, Tommy said, the statements from kitchen staff and guests suggested the Seekers were already in the foyer when the murderer left the banquet room. Yet no one had noticed a stranger. This led Tommy to suspect the murderer must be one of the staff or one of the Seekers, for who else could have slipped through unnoticed by anyone?

Somebody close to these people, maybe even one of the people here tonight at Waverley's soiree, was a killer.

He wanted to warn Lorelei, but his plan to tell her these details had been thwarted. She obviously wanted nothing to do with him. He decided he should rescue Rhonda and head for home.

Lorelei descended from the study to the main floor great room, where the bass player was rosining his bow. The singer sat at the piano bench, picking out a melody, while the piano player sat slumped in one of Waverley's elegant armchairs, taking a belt of scotch. Lorelei stepped past them to the hallway, where she watched the party in progress for a few minutes. As expected, nearly everyone was coming inside to escape the bugs. The house grew noisier as the guests continued to drink. Lorelei stuck to her grapefruit juice. She learned more that way. The doorbell rang and a maid ushered in half a dozen extraordinary tall and vibrant young men and women. Behind her, Lorelei heard the musicians grumbling in low voices.

"Theater people," said the piano player. "They're always late."

"Come on," the singer said wearily. "He wants us to mingle, remember?"

The piano player groaned.

Get used to it, Lorelei thought. If you want to be one of Waverley's finds, you have to let him show you off. She leaned against the wall and let herself relax a bit. She was beginning to feel at home in this house and at ease among these people. She was calculating the approximate cost of an antique vase on the mantelpiece when she was accosted by Summer Sweet, who had consumed a few too many cocktails. Penny was beside her.

"Why, Lorelei!" Summer remarked. "I've been looking for you." Her eyes gleamed with mischief. "He was your date, wasn't he?"

"Who?"

"Brian Hale. He was your date at the high school prom. I could just tell by the way he looked at you." She nudged Penny in the ribs with her elbow.

Penny, disapproving of this unladylike behavior, raised her eyebrows. But she played along. "Do tell," she said.

"Oh no," said Lorelei. "We barely knew each other." Why had she made that stupid remark about the prom? There had been no prom. There had been nothing but one afternoon on a riverbank, the scent of roses. Shade and dappled sunlight under the poplar trees. Brian's breath on her throat, his fingers trailing over her knee….

"He's certainly very handsome," Summer said.

"Is he?" said Lorelei coolly.

"He's still single," Penny said. "Very successful, too."

"Who's successful?" Waverley had appeared at Penny's shoulder and was smiling down on her. He was happy tonight, as the gracious and successful host—one of his favorite roles.

"My lawyer," Penny replied. "Brian Hale. You remember him."

"Oh yes. Nice young man," said Waverley. "Excellent golfer."

"His father was an old friend of the family," said Penny.

"Really?" said Lorelei. "Yes…." Her eyes searched the

room for Brian, but he was nowhere to be seen. "Yes, I always liked him," she said.

Penny's lawyer. Damn.

That night, Lorelei tossed in her bed, tangling her legs in the light cotton sheets. In her dream, she had been walking along the edge of a riverbank with Brian, who was asking her a question, when suddenly the river dropped far below her feet and Brian disappeared, leaving her poised at the brink of a high precipice. And then she was falling, the wind whipping her hair about her face. She tried to scream but no sound came out of her mouth as she tumbled farther and faster, picking up speed, down, down, down, and then *thump*! She woke as her legs, wrapped in the sheets, hit the bed, hard.

She lay still a minute, the air knocked out of her lungs. She opened her eyes and squinted. A sunbeam was shining through the crack in the curtains, right into her eyes. She sat up. She was safe. At home in bed on a sunny, summer morning. But her head was pounding, her chest tight and aching, her throat parched. She put on her robe, made her way to the bathroom, and drank a glass of cool tap water. She hadn't had one of those horrid falling dreams for months. She thought she had beaten the anxiety that used to give her migraine headaches and nightmares. She splashed water on her face and took a few deep breaths, picturing the woman on the front of the Knowledge Is Faith brochure, her beatific smile. Serene and pure. She returned to her bedroom and found her cigarettes, lit one, and sat at the chair by her window, smoking and thinking, trying to plan her day.

She couldn't focus. The image of Brian from the earlier, happier part of her dream kept intruding. But the question he'd been asking in the dream had evaporated. She sighed.

He was probably asking why she pretended not to know him at the party, a move she now bitterly regretted. Penny's lawyer! The person potentially most useful to her at this very moment. Brian from Bader and Bader, who'd left his name on Penny's answering machine for her and Nixie to follow up, if they'd only had the brains to do so! She took a long, angry drag of her cigarette and began to cough. There were so many variables in this current project, with all its tangents and complications. She would have to increase her vigilance.

She tried not to think about the pain in Brian's eyes when she'd ignored him. She honestly hadn't expected that. At the time, she hadn't cared. She'd never imagined Brian would play a role of any importance among the Seekers. So she'd treated him exactly the way she treated anyone from her childhood days, with vague disdain. Force of habit. It was one of the basics of business to keep one's personal life strictly off limits, in order to avoid contradicting oneself. Lying was dangerous and the truth was worse. She made it a rule to drop only hazy hints about her past. The revelation of pedestrian details like high school crushes or ex-con uncles on the lam could put a definite damper on her reputation.

But now that she thought about it, what harm could Brian really do? Like everyone else in the neighborhood at the time, he must have heard about Katherine's murder. But he would be too polite to mention it in public. She didn't think he'd mention their relationship, either. It had lasted less than a day.

She had skipped school that afternoon, too upset over the growing tension at home to concentrate on her studies. She'd stopped on the bridge to take in the view and seen Brian sitting by himself on the bank. She'd heard about the death of his father, a well-known surgeon who'd been on his way to perform an emergency Caesarean section when he was broadsided by a drunk driver two blocks from the hospital. The accident had killed him instantly, and the delay had killed the baby he was rushing to save. The dramatic story was in the newspaper.

Lorelei had been watching Brian from a distance for years, trying to figure him out. He was different from the other boys, kinder and smarter. He didn't take part in the ritual jockeying for position, the snubbing and ostracising that were part of high-school life. He wasn't desperate to forge an identity. He knew who he was. She couldn't remember why she decided to join him on the riverbank that day. She couldn't remember what she had been trying to get from him. Vaguely she recalled that in those days she wasn't always out to get something.

Brian had been devastated by his father's death. She saw it in his pale face, his red-rimmed eyes. He was empty, hollowed out from crying, and she'd wanted to fill him again. Even now, she wasn't sure why she'd felt that need. She'd just been drawn to him.

She remembered the scent of roses drifting from the gardens of the synagogue on the hill up above. She remembered vividly the moment she revealed to him the message from his father. "His spirit is near," she said. "I can feel it all around you."

She ran her hands lightly across his head, his shoulders and arms, and then took both his hands in her own. "He wants you to look after your mother and your—do you have a brother?"

Brian nodded.

"Your brother, Tom. He says you're smarter than Tom. You're stronger, and you need to help him." She reached up and brushed the hair out of Brian's eyes. She cradled his face in her hands, her fingers absorbing his young, male energy. "He says you must forgive the driver. Your anger is weighing you down. It is holding you in place and he wants you, he wants you to soar—"

At that moment, a flock of white pigeons had taken off from their perch under the bridge and wheeled high above the river, circling over their heads.

"He wants you to soar like the birds. To set your spirit free, as he is now free."

Brian's eyes lit up. He let loose a sob. For him, the moment seemed to provide some poignant, mystical comfort. For Lorelei, it was a revelation. The shiver that ran through her blood was deeper, more potent than the one she felt when she told fortunes for the girls at school or for Max's clients. When she saw the light that bloomed in Brian's eyes, the transformation that passed across his face, she knew for certain that the truth was hers for the taking. She could do with it what she willed.

Brian spread his coat on the riverbank and they lay down together, and then he was kissing her, his warm lips on her neck and cheeks, his hands running the length of her bare legs, sending a dangerous thrill through her body. They had lain like that for a long time, necking and talking and falling in love, or what passed for love when you were seventeen.

The media soon reported that Oberon Zolo had been deliberately murdered. The police had discovered among his things the warning note: "Burn in hell, witch." And when news of this discovery hit the press, terror spread among the Seekers. Plans for Spirit Fest stalled as most of the wealthier members decided to take their summer vacations immediately and fled the city as if it were infested by plague. Luckily, Waverley responded to the threat with bravado and Agnes seemed incapable of believing anyone would ever want to harm her. But the general lack of psychic activity in the city put a damper on things. One local New Age magazine, *The Numinous Weekly*, ceased publication for the summer when every member of its editorial staff resigned. Another, *The Mystic*, chose to do a special issue on early Christmas shopping and the joys of returning to tradition, foregoing for the month even its regular horoscopes. Kent Mason interviewed local people on the scene to see how they were coping. Teddy at the Plaza said he had one of the bouncers from the pub keeping an eye on him and his clients during his readings. Madame Solange had left town. Maurice Lemoine cancelled a public appearance at a shopping mall and even a gig on a call-in radio show. Bookstores were stashing their cardboard cut-outs of him in their back rooms. Only Summer bravely kept her display of *Ghost Talk* in her store window. Business at the Dharmarama was dismal, but she refused to close. She was adamant and outspoken about her commitment to her work and said it was a human rights issue. A matter of freedom of speech and freedom of congregation.

Lorelei tried to stay out of it all. She ducked Kent Mason's calls and kept her opinions to herself. If someone was singling out psychics to punish them for their evil ways, she doubted they'd pick on a low-profile person such as herself. But she didn't really believe anyone was targeting psychics for moral or religious reasons. She didn't know what had happened to Yolanda Dawn. But she knew that Obie had plenty of unsavory connections in lots of cities, including this one. Chances were good that his murder was payback for some double-dealing or blackmail on his part and the note was merely an attempt to divert suspicion. She wondered if he had made it to the Dharmarama that last night, if he'd succeeded in switching the cards and, if he had, where the real card on Penny Johnson had ended up. With Penny's birthday rapidly approaching, Lorelei could have made good use of it.

As she left her house early in the evening, Lorelei ran over in her mind the details she needed to remember for her session with Waverley. She was determined to summon Gloria tonight, when the moon was practically invisible, just to prove Penny wrong. Damn that woman and her negative energy! Although Penny had dissuaded Waverley from trying the antique Ouija board at his soiree, Lorelei knew he couldn't wait to test out this latest addition to his collection of spiritualist memorabilia. Tonight's sitting would be an important opportunity. Waverley was always at his most receptive when he was engaging with something new.

Combing through the first volume of Gloria's diary this afternoon, she'd been disappointed to find no mention of Lake of the Woods. The best tidbit she gleaned was an entry about an eagle feather Waverley's father had found on a trip to Sioux Narrows and given to Gloria as a gift. The diary entry had been written five or six years after the event, so Gloria's recollection of the details might have been fuzzy. And Sioux Narrows was many miles south of Deception Bay. But it was on the same lake. It would have to do.

Lorelei was so intent on planning today's session that she failed to notice her landlady coming until Charlotte was standing right in front of her car.

"Didn't you hear me calling?" Charlotte asked.

"What is it?" Lorelei was distracted, searching in her purse for her keys.

"I've been meaning to speak to you," Charlotte repeated. She cleared her throat. "It's about Imogene."

Lorelei looked up. "Yes?"

"I understand she's been visiting you after school."

"Yes, she came a few times," Lorelei said carefully. Did Charlotte know that her daughter had been spying? Was Charlotte *sending* her daughter over to spy? Had Imogene reported that Lorelei had a gun in her consulting room? That Lorelei had sworn the girl to secrecy? She wanted to tell Charlotte to keep the kid out of her house, but she hesitated. She needed to keep Imogene on her side. If Imogene felt rejected, she might betray her.

"I've told her not to be ringing your doorbell any more," Charlotte announced.

"Oh, she's—she's no bother, really. She just likes to visit the cat."

"Cats," corrected Charlotte with a sniff.

"Cats, yes. But the little one is only temporary, mind you. We're just babysitting it." The little kitten had developed an eye infection. Nixie was treating it with ointment, but the vet, whose opinions Nixie worshipped, had warned that the kitten might lose its sight if it weren't watched closely. So Nixie refused to plant the kitten in Penny's yard until the eye was completely healed. Just another one of Lorelei's headaches.

"Well, I've told her to stay away."

"She's welcome," Lorelei said lightly. She studied Charlotte's face. Charlotte's eyes were flat, revealing no flicker of interest in Lorelei or in the contents of her house. Imogene had obviously said nothing to her mother about the gun. Well, give the girl some credit for loyalty, then. Something was wrong, though. Charlotte had apparently forgotten that Lorelei was standing in front of her. Her eyes glazed over and she seemed lost in her own thoughts, completely self-absorbed as if listening to some inner voice. Lorelei wondered suddenly whether Charlotte paid the least attention to Imogene's state of mind. Did the woman not see how unhappy her daughter was?

"Is Imogene in, uh, some kind of trouble?" Lorelei asked. "She seems a bit sad, you know, and…." She trailed off, kicking herself. She didn't want to—she couldn't—get involved. And anyway, what was Imogene Trapp to her?

"Imogene is fine," Charlotte told her. "What I'm trying to say is, I don't want her over to your house after school. She's to come home at four o'clock, to do her homework and help me with the cooking. Four o'clock sharp."

"I'm sorry," said Lorelei. "I didn't know." No wonder Imogene was so miserable and lonely, she thought. Her mother didn't even know her.

It was Wayne Forbes who opened the door when Lorelei rang the bell.

"Ah," he said. "It's the Gypsy Queen. Good evening."

"Good evening," she said. She had learned to ignore his remarks. "Waverley's expecting me."

"We're in the library," he said, and she followed him.

The Forbes library was all polished surfaces and reflections, mirrors with ornate frames mounted on every wall between built-in bookcases of dark, glossy wood, with leaded-glass doors. A crystal vase of white rose buds and a reading lamp stood on each of the gleaming occasional tables scattered throughout the room.

Waverley was standing by the bookcases, looking at a series of black and white photographs newly mounted on the wall. They were grainy, mysterious early-twentieth-century images. Some showed a teenaged girl with white foam streaming from her mouth. The others showed an older woman, her head surrounded by clouds of the swirling stuff, her eyes closed in a deep trance.

"A lot of nonsense," Wayne remarked. "Parlor games for the upper classes."

"It was actually very dangerous," Waverley admonished. "The manifestation of ectoplasm put a great strain on the medium. The practice has since been discontinued. One Winnipeg mystic became severely ill when a foolish observer tried to grab the ectoplasm and feel it with his own hands. She nearly died of the shock to her nervous system."

Lorelei nodded sympathetically. Sometimes she envied those early mediums who performed their works in the golden age before every house was equipped with bright electric lights. Silk or gauze—it looked a little like cheesecloth—could be crushed into tiny packets and concealed in a shirt cuff or corset and then, under cover of utter darkness, be unpacked and made to float above the amazed heads of the sitters. Too risky nowadays, when any skeptic, or even a clumsy believer, could illuminate the entire room with the flick of a switch.

Waverley had laid out the antique Ouija board on a table for Lorelei's inspection. Mary, his housekeeper, brought a tray bearing a silver coffee pot and china cups, milk and sugar and biscuits. As they drank their coffee, Waverley told the tale of his trip to Boston and how, guided by strange premonitions, he'd been led to the very shop and the very shelf on which he'd found the board. It was a steal at five thousand dollars.

"Five grand!" Wayne exclaimed. "Outrageous."

"This piece has great historical value," his brother retorted. "It was preserved in an attic for over three hundred years and only found when the house was demolished.

Someone had hidden it in the rafters. Fear of reprisals, no doubt. As you know, prejudice against witchcraft has long been widespread in Massachusetts. Ignorant superstition held that the Ouija board was a tool of the devil. To be caught in possession of one meant burning at the stake, or worse."

"They thought this was a tool of the devil?" Wayne asked. "It looks like a kindergarten toy. One that's seen better days."

The board was certainly very old. The dye on the hand-stamped alphabet and numerals was faded. The pictures—a sun and a moon and an open eye—were nearly worn away, but the archaic style of the drawings suggested they just might be three hundred years old. The wood had cracked along the bottom edges, and the final Y of the word GOODBY had been split in two.

"It's no toy," Waverley said. "The Ouija board is an instrument for contacting the spirits. It's usually used to gain knowledge of secrets that people have taken with them to their graves. To reveal the location of lost items, for example."

Wayne had stood and was drinking the last of his coffee on his feet.

"You're not leaving?"

"Bridge night," said Wayne. He drained his cup and set it back in its saucer.

"But Wayne, I thought you could be a perfect test case. You never found your gold cufflinks, did you? The ones Queenie gave you. We should try—"

"Don't be absurd," Wayne replied.

"But perhaps, if Queenie could be contacted—"

Wayne dismissed this notion with a wave of his hand. He supposed, he said languidly, that the universe had come to a peculiar pass when those who'd crossed over to the great beyond had nothing better to do than to locate misplaced cufflinks—a feat, he added, that had not been a particular specialty of his own dear wife when she was living.

He strolled happily out of the room, leaving Waverley to shake his head at his brother's stubborn refusal to see the truth.

"Well, Lorelei, I guess it's just you and me," he said.

They rested their fingertips lightly on the planchette, and Lorelei asked aloud to make contact with the spirit world. She was a little uncomfortable with the Ouija board at first. The planchette tended to snag in the grooves and scratches of the old wooden board. She was used to modern, store-bought ones that glided easily across the alphabet to spell out messages.

They asked a few general questions and received only gibberish for answers. The planchette lurched and bumped, stumbled and fell still. But they persisted, and finally it began to travel smoothly and surely across the board in answer to their questions, as if it were possessed by a conscious entity. Was there a spirit in the room? YES. What did it want? The spirit didn't answer that one. The planchette squatted silently on the board.

"What is your name?" Lorelei asked. There was no response.

"Are you from Boston?" Waverley asked. Again, no reply.

They looked at each other. "Shall we ask it—" Waverley began.

The planchette darted suddenly to s. Then it spelled out SHE IS HERE.

Waverley looked at Lorelei. "What does that mean?"

The planchette began to move furiously, over and over. SHE IS HERE. SHE IS HERE. SHE IS HERE. Then suddenly it flew out of their hands and across the room, landing upside down on the Persian rug at the foot of the stairs.

Waverley tore his eyes from the planchette to look at Lorelei. She was beginning to slump in her chair. Her eyelids began to flutter. "Lorelei?"

Her head fell back, a low rumbling began in her throat, and her body shook with tremors. After a minute, she spoke. But not in her own voice. "*Waverley?*"

He gasped.

"*Waverley. Are you there?*" The voice that was now inhabiting Lorelei's body was entirely different from the voice of the spirit guide he had heard before. It was a soft, feminine whisper, barely audible.

"Gloria?" Waverley asked.

"*Yes, it's me. I've been trying….*"

"Oh my God, Gloria! Is it really you? Tell me, what is our special song? What is your middle name?"

"*I have only one name, Gloria.*"

Waverley gasped. "And where were you born?"

"*In the house. My father's ranch outside Fort Worth.*"

"My God, it's you at last," he said, grasping Lorelei's hand. "Are you all right?"

She emitted a long, soft sigh. "*Tired,*" she breathed. "*Difficult. Journey.*"

"Yes, yes of course." He stroked Lorelei's hand, caressed her cheek. "I've been trying to reach you for so long. Gloria, I want to tell you, darling. I was wrong, I—"

"*Can't stay,*" she whispered. "*The veil…it's too heavy. Meet me where the white birds fly, in the moonlight. After the longest day. Look for my sign. In your father's book.*"

227

"Gloria!"

But Gloria was gone. Only Lorelei remained, groaning a little as she came to. Waverley chafed her wrists and then rang for Mary to bring her some water. He was so excited he was barely able to tell her all that Gloria had said. But he got it right, word for word. Then, while Lorelei was recovering, Waverley sprinted upstairs and returned triumphant, a long white eagle feather in his hand.

"Where did you find that?"

"My father's Bible," he said. "It always lies open on a bookstand on the landing outside my study. Wayne put it there, under our father's portrait. But as I've told you, I never touch the book. Our father forced us to read it every night and every morning when we were children. We both grew sick of it. Since I became a man, I haven't so much as opened it. But Gloria must have kept this feather between the pages. My father gave it to her years ago. He found it on Lake of the Woods. That's what she was trying to tell me. She wants me to be out on the lake." He paused and walked to the table, sat down and buried his face in his hands as the full meaning of his dead wife's message dawned on him. "Gloria loved the Lake of the Woods," he said.

"She did?"

"Yes. My God, when she first sent those messages about the waves and the moonlight, I was thinking only of the night we met. On the cruise ship, off the coast of New Guinea, and the seabirds. But I see now she meant the waves on the lake. I always promised I'd take her back there."

"To Lake of the Woods?"

"Yes. The first year we were married we came up to Canada for a camping trip. In a way it was a disaster. A rainstorm came up. The tent leaked. We were soaked. But Gloria loved it. In the morning, we walked through the forest. We spread our things out on the beach to dry. We watched two eagles fishing in the bay." He looked up. "I had forgotten."

Lorelei smiled. Her favorite client never ceased to surprise her. His interpretive powers were amazing.

"I promised her we would return," he said. "But we never did. I was always too busy, always too damn busy, and somehow—" He slammed his fist on the table. "I have broken so many promises, and I have never told her how sorry I am."

"It's all right," Lorelei said. "It's okay. We will contact her again. You'll be able to tell her yourself."

"But when? How? She isn't very strong. It's so hard for her to get through."

"We'll try again on the next full moon," said Lorelei, "when the veil is thinner."

Waverley covered his face in his hands, and Lorelei felt a pang of sympathy. But she had no intention of explaining. Waverley was a highly intelligent man, and she much preferred to let him figure things out for himself.

"The spirit guide keeps telling us to try again at the full moon," he said. "But it doesn't seem to work, Lorelei. We've tried twice, now, at the last two full moons, and yet today was the only time we've been able to contact her directly—and the moon is still new. It's barely begun to wax. Perhaps Penny is right. The phase of the moon doesn't—"

"But the next full moon is the most powerful of all. It is the Moon of Takara."

"Takara?" Waverley was always intrigued by new vocabulary.

"Yes. The first full moon after the summer solstice. A time when the veil becomes especially transparent. It is said that the Moon of Takara was an ancient Druidic holiday, a night for sacred rites of passage into knowledge.

Meteorologists have actually reported a slight thinning of the Earth's atmosphere during the twenty-four hours following moonrise on that night."

"Really?" Waverley's enthusiasm returned in full force. "Why, we should definitely hold a seance at that time." He stood and strode over to the cherrywood desk where he kept his calendar. "It would be an ideal night to schedule Spirit Fest. We should try to book a place out on the lake." He flipped through the pages. "The solstice is the twenty-first, so the next full moon is…." He turned a page. "It's…July… eleventh. My God. July eleventh."

"What is it?" Lorelei asked.

Waverley sat down at his desk. "It's my wedding anniversary," he told her.

When he had recovered from this astonishing coincidence, he sat at his cherrywood desk and made a production of writing a check to PsyRen for two hundred thousand dollars.

"Toward the research center," he said. "I feel very strongly there is nothing more important a man could be doing for his fellow travelers on Earth than to further the investigation into the properties of the veil."

As she drove home from Waverley's house that evening, Lorelei knew she should have been elated. The two hundred grand was a good headstart on funds for the research center. And she knew from experience that the more money the client invested, the more committed the client became. But something nagged at her. Waverley had been happy to make contact with Gloria at last. But compared to his behavior in past sessions, he had been strangely subdued. Waverley believed absolutely in Lorelei's powers. But his chief enjoyment with these sessions was showing off her performances to others, especially to Penny. Ordinarily, there would have been at least a couple of other Seekers present, but attendance at psychic events, even in the privacy of people's homes, was dropping off. Without an audience, Waverley was robbed of half his joy. Telling people about it afterwards just didn't provide the same rush as showing it to them. Amazing them.

She sighed. The murders had put a general pall over everything. With so many Seekers dropping out of the plans for Spirit Fest, like rats deserting a sinking ship, it was hard to keep up the group dynamic that helped to build momentum. She hoped an arrest would be made soon so life could get back to normal. In the meantime, she had to convince Penny that her powers were reliable and accurate, that Penny needed her. Without Penny's support, Lorelei didn't think she could bring this project home.

Tense and depressed, she passed her usual turnoff and took a slight detour. She continued west for a few blocks and then turned south on Oxford Street, slowing down as she approached her childhood home. It was a simple, white-stucco, two-story house with a red door, and someone had recently put a new roof on it. She drove past it once in a while, she wasn't sure why, just to look at the place that had once belonged to her parents. Tonight she was keyed up, wanting a cigarette. She parked across from the house, climbed out of the driver's seat and lit up.

Leaning back against the car, she massaged the kink in her neck. Across the street, lights snapped off in the upstairs bedrooms of her former home. Mom and Dad were putting their children to bed. A few minutes later, the eerie blue glow of a television filled the living room window. She imagined the young couple snuggled together on the couch, watching a movie. She had seen the family once or twice when she'd been driving by. Husband and wife and daughter and baby son. The kind of family her real parents might have had, if there were any mercy in the universe.

The curtains in the dining room windows were closed, but Lorelei knew what was behind them. A wide archway that led to the kitchen and beyond that a staircase that led to the basement where two girls had once hidden, clinging to each other. She straightened up and flung her cigarette to the ground. Why did she linger here? What did she think? That Joey Shaunigan would come bursting through that door again, only this time Lorelei would be able to stop him? That she could bring Katherine back?

She got into her car again and closed the door, but she didn't start the engine. She just sat there for a while, trying not to remember, and remembering. Uncle Joey had surely wanted to shoot her and Nixie dead right there in the kitchen. She didn't think he had hesitated out of pity. He was just scared off by the doorbell. By a weird stroke of luck, some stranger had heard the shot that killed Katherine and tried to come to the rescue. Someone, maybe the cab driver they'd been expecting or maybe a neighbor, had rung the doorbell and called the police, saving the girls' lives.

She knew little about what had happened to Joey, except for the sketchy details she'd read in the newspapers. A few months after Katherine's death, he was arrested and eventually convicted of smuggling and trafficking cocaine. He was sentenced to twenty-five years. But the police never made the connection between him and Katherine, and Lorelei had no intention of coming forward to make it for them.

To this day, the main suspect in Katherine's murder was her common-law husband, Maxwell Good, who had disappeared along with his two daughters the night of her death and hadn't been seen for a dozen years. Lorelei had no idea where Max was or even if he was still alive. There were no dedicated cold case detectives on his tail, as far as she could tell. In the movies, there was always a contingent of outraged, grieving relatives, egging the detectives on. But no one was seeking justice for Katherine. Not even Lorelei. If the police ever hunted down Max and charged him with murder, Lorelei supposed she'd be forced to come forward and tell the truth about that horrible night. Then Joey Shaunigan would come after her and Nixie for sure. She imagined him picking up Nixie's little body in one of his ham-like fists and slitting her neck as he'd promised in his final gesture. He wouldn't hesitate. Maybe, she thought, that was why Max had decided to stay away. To protect his family, at long last, with his absence, something he hadn't managed to do when he was around.

Lorelei watched from the kitchen window at Cranberry Bay as Penny circulated happily among the guests in her backyard, celebrating her fifty-eighth birthday with a cake she'd baked herself. About twenty guests sat on lawn chairs in the shade of the lilac and honeysuckle bushes or in the shade of the pick-up truck Penny's nephew Derek had parked in the back driveway. Derek himself sat in the front seat of the truck, his plate of cake balanced on his tool box, drinking a beer and listening to a ball game on the radio. Lorelei had tried to engage him in conversation earlier, but learned nothing. Except for a knowing smile, as he drank in every contour of her body from breasts to ankles, he wasn't interested in communicating. Penny stopped here and there among her friends to receive their congratulations and to introduce them to her new beau, Waverley Forbes, who was enjoying himself immensely, charming all the ladies. Penny seemed carefree enough at the moment, but what was she hiding?

In the course of her profession, Lorelei had met hundreds of widows and widowers. Listening to their confidences and confessions, she'd learned a strange truth: the happier the marriage had been, the more easily the survivors bore the loss. They suffered, of course, but the miracle was that the pain eased, ever so slowly, over time. The grieving softened, gave way to the consolation of memory. It was the ones who'd been miserable in their marriages who couldn't recover. They were the ones who were still consulting the psychics two, three, six years after the funeral. It was the same with the ones who had feared their parents, mistreated their children, sinned against their brothers and sisters. The ones with unfinished business. Waverley, for instance, who had promised Gloria he'd find a cure, that he wouldn't let her die. That foolish, arrogant promise kept him bound to her, a slave to her spirit. It was the guilty clients who paid the most, and the most often, for the chance to apologize, to be forgiven, to be rid of regret.

But Penny? According to all the evidence in her house, her marriage had been blessed, unblemished by guilt or resentment. So why was she so desperate to contact her late husband's spirit? What message was she expecting?

Summer Sweet came swooping across the lawn, waving her camera, insisting that Penny pose with her friends. Penny gathered three other women around her, then gestured to Agnes, calling her to be part of the photo. Agnes demurred, shaking her head and lowering her eyes to the ground, but Penny insisted, pulling Agnes to her side and wrapping an arm firmly about her waist. Penny squared her shoulders in a show of bravado and lifted her head to face the camera. Agnes bent her knees and lowered her head as if, like a hedgehog, she could make herself smaller. Although she'd been gaining confidence, she still wore the baggy clothes. It would take a few thousand more affirmations to overcome those fifty-odd years of virginity and that killer combination of a sexually repressed mother and a sexually adventurous husband.

Penny glanced up and saw Lorelei watching from the kitchen window. She waved gaily. Lorelei was in her good books again. Waverley had impressed her with his account of the visitation from Gloria and the proof of the eagle feather. Even more important, Penny had been greatly amazed by the arrival of the quiet, needy, non-human kitten who had landed in her mailbox. He must have been climbing the honeysuckle bush beside her mailbox, Penny explained when she phoned to tell Lorelei the news, and he had tumbled right in. Luckily it was just before her regular mail delivery so he wasn't stuck there for long. She had named him "Honey" and was spoiling him rotten. Lorelei's incredible prediction of Honey's arrival was fast becoming a legend among the Seekers.

While Penny said goodby to the last of her party guests, Lorelei waited in the living room to resume the interrupted reading. As she waited, she flipped through a travel brochure on the coffee table, a thirty-page full-color ad for luxury cruises to Alaska. The bold photos showed snow-capped mountains and pristine waters. On board, well-dressed travelers drank champagne in opulent staterooms, played tennis, and placed bets at a roulette table. It was a vacation far beyond Penny's means, but apparently this woman liked to dream big. When she came back and settled on the couch, Lorelei apologized for the other day's disruption.

"I'm sure it couldn't be helped," Penny said, as she lit

the candles. "I must say your powers seem a bit muddled at times." She sighed. "I suppose these things happen, though, what with spirits crossing over into your soma and so on. But you *do* have a gift, however strange." She produced a warm smile. Not only did she adore her new kitten, she had also quit her volunteer job at the hospital and signed up for a creative writing class instead. She was feeling bold and liberated. Entitled.

During today's session, Lorelei reinforced some of her earlier messages about Penny's talents and made some references to past troubles, working in an amazingly accurate account of a time in Penny's life when she'd been traumatized by the illness of a tiny new soul very close to her.

The usually tight-mouthed Penny exclaimed, "My nephew, Derek! Yes! He was born with a defect in his heart and nearly didn't survive. That was a terrible time."

Lorelei then tried to turn to the topic of a loss in Penny's past and a quest she was on. But Penny prompted her to return to the protective male spirit she had sensed at the previous reading. She insisted that Lorelei try to tune in to her husband's spirit again.

"You miss him very much," Lorelei said. "I sense that you still grieve—"

"Do you think we can contact him?"

"It's always possible," Lorelei said. "Let me concentrate." She thought fast. It was too early to start dwelling on Raymond. There was obviously something left unfinished between Penny and her late husband, but what? These things took time to ferret out. Patience was the key, and if you waited long enough, the truth would always come to light. But in this particular case, she didn't *have* time. The complication of Waverley's attraction to Penny, and Penny's influence over him, had blindsided her at the last minute. Her preparations had been cut short, and with two murders, a blackmail attempt, and a case of pneumonia to contend with, it hadn't been easy to concentrate. Not to mention nosy little Imogene. All these disruptions left her with the nebulous fear that she was missing something important. She shook the feeling off. She had to be at her best. The important thing at the moment was to put Penny at ease, make her feel comfortable enough to start talking. If the woman would only start talking, Lorelei felt sure she could draw her out, gain some clue about what it was she was seeking.

After two minutes of silence, Penny asked, "Is he—saying anything?"

At that moment a strong breeze came in at the window, ruffling a stack of paper party napkins on the coffee table. Both women jumped at the movement.

Penny's eyes grew large. "I knew it," she whispered. "He's here!"

Lorelei nodded. "Just as I thought," she said.

"Does he—have a message for me?"

Lorelei grasped Penny's hands again. "Let us listen," she said. "Let us open our hearts." Long silences on the tape were not good, she knew that. But she couldn't relay any messages from Raymond. Not yet.

Penny was entirely caught up in the moment, her eyes shining with that particular longing Lorelei knew so well.

The breeze came again, and this time lifted a few of the paper napkins from the top of the stack. Two or three of them drifted across the room and then fluttered to the floor. But one of the napkins sailed straight into the flame of the candle and caught fire. The women stared as the burning napkin flew up toward the ceiling. Then, as the breeze died, it crash-landed on the carpet. Lorelei jumped up and stepped on the flame with the heel of her sandal. It was a small fire and easy to smother. In seconds, nothing was left but a singed and tattered scrap of paper, black ashes, and a scorch mark on the carpet.

"Oh my," said Penny. She swiveled in her chair, looked behind her, then up at the ceiling. Her eyes flitted around the four corners of the room. "He's here right now!"

Lorelei's heart beat rapidly. The incident had unnerved her. She blew out the candles and closed the window.

"What do you think he's trying to say?" Penny asked. She peered at the small mess on the carpet, as if it were some kind of code. "Do you think he's angry?"

Lorelei sat back down and folded her hands demurely in her lap to conceal their shaking. "I feel only a sensation of warmth," she murmured. "No anger. A great sensation of warmth, love. No specific message, just a kind of—I'm sorry." She sat up straight. "Whatever it was, it's gone. The connection's broken."

"Broken? But you must try again!"

"I'm sorry," said Lorelei. "There's something blocking the vibrations. Perhaps some other time."

"But he was—so close! Can't we try again?"

"Not today. But perhaps, if you're willing to try at the full moon…."

"Oh, I will. I just know he's trying to communicate with me. I can feel it."

"It will happen," Lorelei assured her. "If we concentrate, on the night of the full moon, Raymond will come again."

"Raymond?" said Penny.

"Yes, I sense he has something to tell you."

"Ray—*Raymond*?" Penny stood up so fast she knocked her chair over. She backed away from Lorelei, her hands clasped over her mouth, and her eyes wide with horror.

CHAPTER NINE

Most of the calls to and from Agnes's house concerned boring inquiries about paint chips and draperies or calls from telemarketers, who were dispatched unceremoniously by the housekeeper, Susanne. But other calls made Nixie sit up and listen carefully.

One of these had come in at 10:46 a.m. today. It was Summer Sweet, in her capacity as secretary to the Seekers, phoning to inform Agnes of a meeting about Spirit Fest to be held at the Dharmarama. Would Hank and Agnes be able to come, she wanted to know. Agnes explained that Hank was still in India, but said she would come if she could. Many important decisions had to be made, Summer reminded her, such as which place to rent and who to hire. Summer was unable to resist putting in a plug for her favorite. "I'm sure the Seekers will agree that Maurice is the only medium we want for the occasion. After all, he's decided to settle here in Winnipeg. He's bought the cutest Cape Cod bungalow in the south end and he'll be reading regularly at the Dharmarama. Spirit Fest would be the ideal way to welcome him."

"Oh, I don't know," said Agnes. "Some of the girls really prefer Lorelei Good."

"Lorelei's great. Don't get me wrong," said Summer. "But an association with Maurice Lemoine would really raise the profile of the Seekers."

And the Dharmarama, Nixie thought, as she listened. She could just picture Summer using her little pink index cards like flash cards to prep Maurice for an exam. If he passed, Maurice would become the darling of the Seekers. Then Summer and her sister would have a cut of his business for years to come.

"Thank you for the invitation," Agnes told Summer. "I'll attend if I can find the time, but you know I am terribly busy with the house."

"Don't put yourself out," Summer said.

Pretty catty, thought Nixie. She would have expected Summer to suck up to a rich lady like Agnes Kellsington. But Summer was obviously ticked with Agnes. Maybe she resented Agnes's refusal to support her pet psychic.

The next call, fifteen minutes later, was an outgoing one, Agnes to Waverley. After some preliminary courtesies, Agnes steered the conversation toward the plans for Spirit Fest. "I'm certain you feel as I do," she said, "about the obvious choice for a medium to conduct the seance. Surely Lorelei Good is the one we want."

"I have every confidence in Lorelei," said Waverley. "She's the best I've ever seen. I endorse her without hesitation."

"I agree," said Agnes. "And I want you to know I'm quite willing to host the event. The house isn't in any shape for guests, of course. But I was thinking that the cottage would make the ideal—"

"Perfect!" cried Waverley. "Right on the lake! Then it's

all settled. This will be the most spectacular event in the history of the Seekers. I'm so glad you've—"

"Won't we have to consult the other Seekers?" Agnes asked. "Summer was just telling me that some members want to hold the event with Maurice Lemoine, out at her sister's farm."

Waverley cleared his throat. "Naturally, we have to discuss it with the others," he said quickly. But his tone clearly indicated that the others would not pose a problem. He continued, "Agnes, there's something else I especially wanted to consult with you about. Privately."

"Certainly. What is it?"

"It's this center Lorelei is planning to build. Have you thought about it?"

"I have to admit," said Agnes, "it intrigues me. I wonder about the location, though. As Penny says, it would be wise to view the site for ourselves before we make any decisions, don't you think?"

"But you're interested?" he asked.

Nixie thought that "interested" must mean *planning to invest*.

"I'm interested in the concept, yes. And I'm sure Hank will be, too. His only reservation about moving back north was the lack of facilities up here for doing really serious work."

"I knew I could count on you," Waverley concluded. "The other Seekers will of course participate. But you and I need to move on this together."

That meant: *you're the only one besides me who's rich enough to invest*. The conversation gave Nixie hope. It sounded as if Agnes and Waverley were both on-side. And now that Penny seemed to be coming around, everything was falling into place.

But a moment later, Nixie's hopes sank when Lorelei came bursting into the room. "Her husband's name is Roland!" she shouted. "Roland Harold Johnson! Not Raymond!"

"Oh brother," said Nixie. She was lying in bed in her pajamas, eating a bowl of frozen blueberry yogurt and drinking ginger ale, while she listened to Agnes's phone calls on her laptop.

Lorelei was too upset to care about Nixie's bad habits at the moment. She flopped onto a chair, letting her purse fall to the floor. "Roland, for God's sake. And there I was in her living room, babbling on about messages from Raymond! After that stupid interference with Imogene the other day, she must think I'm a total flake."

"So who *is* Raymond?" Nixie asked.

"I don't know." She told Nixie the story of the flaming napkin. "When I said the name 'Raymond,' Penny turned pale and hustled me out the door."

"Some old boyfriend, I guess," said Nixie.

"I guess," said Lorelei. She was starting to calm down. "And he must have been an important one, or she wouldn't have kept his letters all those years."

"Maybe she still has feelings for him."

"Yes," said Lorelei. She sat up a little straighter. "And maybe *he* still has feelings for *her*."

"What are you talking about?"

"I'm going to take another look through those letters." Her sense of purpose renewed, she picked up her purse and moved toward the door. "I have an idea Raymond might help us out."

"But we don't even know where he is," said Nixie.

"No, not yet," said Lorelei. She shot her sister a grin.

"But I'm going to find out. And wherever he turns out to be, let's just hope he's dead."

The following evening, over dinner, Lorelei suggested taking a closer look at Penny's nephew Derek. "Raymond mentions Derek so often in the letters," she said. "I wonder if Raymond was a family friend. Maybe even a relative. If so, Derek might still be in contact with him." She ladled the last piece of broccoli onto Nixie's plate. "But I don't know if Derek could be persuaded to talk."

"He might talk to a stranger," said Nixie. "A little friendly conversation. A few too many beers. The talk turns to, oh, say…." She waved her fork in the air. "Broken engagements? Aunts who spend too much money on psychics?"

"But Derek has already met me," said Lorelei.

"He hasn't met *me*."

Lorelei stood up. "No way."

"Yes way. You're too old for him, anyhow."

"I wouldn't say that." Lorelei smiled to herself as she began to clear the table. "But he *has* met me. Penny introduced me as Waverley's psychic. So he's not going to reveal any family secrets to me, not without telling Penny about it."

"He might talk to me."

"You stick to surveillance," Lorelei said. She carried the dishes to the sink. "Leave the talking to me."

"Come on, let me do this, Lorelei. Please?" Nixie followed her into the kitchen. "I really want this plan to work. I want that cottage. You don't know how bad I want it." Suddenly she stopped. "Hey! I just remembered. Derek said Friday night's his pub night." She took off down the hall, sliding in her sock feet.

Lorelei sighed. Would Nixie be safe with Derek? Could

she get him to talk? She filled the sink with hot, soapy water and put the dishes in to soak. She wiped the dining room table and put the leftovers in the fridge. Then she followed Nixie upstairs. The bed was already covered in a jumble of wrinkled clothes in clashing bright colors. Nixie stood in the closet, pulling more from the rack. "Help me pick something to wear."

Lorelei's head began to ache. Finding something suitable for Nixie to wear wouldn't be easy. Her wardrobe was hopelessly childish, and she was too small to borrow Lorelei's clothes. Yet Derek wouldn't look twice at her unless she had some sex appeal. The thought made Lorelei recoil. She never imagined she'd be sending her little sister out to bars to get information from strange men. But there wasn't time to think about that now. It was six o'clock, Friday evening. If Nixie wanted a chance to catch Derek on his pub night, she'd have to leave soon.

Nixie waited until she saw Derek emerge from his little white house. He wore the same oil-stained jeans she'd seen the other day and a tight black T-shirt. Heavy steel-toed boots. A bright green pack of smokes bulged from the T-shirt pocket. He approached the shiny black pickup truck in his driveway. Nixie turned her own key in the ignition, ready to follow him. But Derek wasn't driving anywhere. He reached into the front seat and lifted out a tool box. Then he locked up his truck and disappeared behind his house. What was he doing? Fixing something? She heard the dogs begin to bark in the back, the banging of metal and the clanking of chains. Finally the dogs fell silent. She assumed he was feeding them before he went out for the evening. When he emerged from the back yard, he walked past his truck, pausing to comb his dark curls in the side-view mirror before he strode off down the street. She'd have to follow him on foot.

Derek was at least six foot two, athletic, with long legs and an agile gait. Effortless and aggressive. Nixie had no problem staying well behind him, and she didn't have to do it for long. He turned in at a bar on the next corner. The Palace. Nixie peered through the one spot of the windowpane that wasn't covered by posters. Not much resemblance to a palace. Dim lighting, pool tables, a jukebox. A long bar, where Derek was seating himself on a tall stool, lifting a finger to order a drink. Two young women in tight clothing passed behind her and paused at the entrance, fluffing their hair and tugging on their blouses. One of them held the door open and turned to Nixie. "You coming in, honey?"

Nixie entered The Palace. The air was cool and dank and smelled of fried onions. Willie Nelson was on the jukebox. At one end of the bar, hot dogs turned on an electric spit beside a greasy plastic vat of popcorn. Two young couples played doubles at the pool table. Others sat around laughing, sharing pitchers of beer. Only Derek was alone. The stool beside him was unoccupied but Nixie didn't want to seem too eager to sit beside him. She strolled casually over to the jukebox and began to read the selections. This was her chance to approach him, get him talking. But talking wasn't her strong point and she hadn't been in a lot of bars like this. She wasn't sure how to act. She tried to remember how women did it in the movies. Usually they had a problem of some kind. They'd been stood up or stranded in some way. They sort of glided into the bar and looked helpless. She could handle that.

She had to grip the edge of the bar in order to hoist

herself onto the stool. So much for gliding in. But he didn't seem to notice. He was watching the Twins beat the Mariners on the television behind the bar.

"Do you know what time it is?"

Very slowly, Derek swung around on the stool and glanced at her. Silently, he pointed at the wall behind the bar. Nixie looked up. She was sitting right in front of a giant clock.

"Gee, eight, already," she muttered. She felt like an idiot.

Derek turned around again. "What's that?"

"Eight o'clock," she said.

"Meeting someone?"

"Yeah. He's—you haven't seen him, have you? Tall guy, blond. Probably wearing a cowboy hat."

"Sorry. I just got here." He turned away again, his eyes on the baseball game.

Nixie started rummaging in her pockets. "I don't suppose you—"

Derek raised his open palms, as if to ward her off. "Not if you got a boyfriend coming."

"My cousin," she said quickly. "I'm meeting my cousin. He's always late, but he'll show up. He'll pay you back."

"Yeah?" A slow, crooked smile. "I guess I could spot you one. What are you drinking?"

"I'll have a beer, please. Canadian."

He ordered one for her and another for himself. She had his attention now. He turned away from the game and propped an elbow on the bar, leaning in her direction.

"So," she said. "Do you work around here?"

"Yeah. You?"

"I go to the U of M."

He lifted his eyebrows. She was a long way from the U of M.

"My cousin works near here," she said quickly. "He's a mechanic."

"Oh yeah?"

"Yeah. But he's always late."

Nixie took a sip. It was good beer, cold and sweet. She missed beer. There was never any beer at home. Lorelei said liquor interfered with the concentration. She wouldn't drink when she was in a situation she was trying to control, and there was never a situation she wasn't trying to control.

Nixie downed the beer quickly as she told Derek about her cousin and the many times he had let her down. The more she drank, the more easily the stories unfolded. She ended up with an anecdote about the huge phone bill he'd racked up by calling the psychic hotlines.

"Family!" she complained.

"Don't I know it," said Derek. "You want another beer?"

Back home in her living room, Lorelei paced the floor, hoping she hadn't made a mistake. Could Nixie pull this off? Would Derek see through her? It didn't seem likely that Derek could possibly jump to the conclusion that Nixie was the little sister of his aunt's boyfriend's psychic, sent to spy on him. But she worried nevertheless. When the telephone rang, she rushed to answer it. But it wasn't Nixie. It was Agnes Kellsington.

"Why hello, Agnes. How are you? Is everything all right?"

"Yes," said Agnes. "Or rather, not exactly. I was wondering if we could talk?"

"Certainly." Lorelei sat down on the couch and reached for her cigarettes. Counseling Agnes was becoming a regular pastime. By the time payday came for this job, Lorelei thought, she'd have earned every dime. "What can I do for you?"

"It's something we shouldn't discuss on the phone," said Agnes. "I was wondering if you'd be free to drop by the house."

"Tonight?"

"If at all possible."

"If you're experiencing uncomfortable activity, you should practice your affirmations," Lorelei advised. "Ten or twelve repetitions should clear your aura in no time."

"It's not that. It's about the research center plans." Agnes sounded dangerously grim. "It's about this property you're calling an investment opportunity. Penny and I have been discussing it—"

"Penny!"

"Yes, and we've decided there are some inconsistencies."

"I see."

"Certain things that don't add up," Agnes continued. "It just so happens that I'm reconsidering my investment options at the moment, and before I make a decision, I'll need you to account for certain factors that are, let's say, discomforting. Certain red flags."

"I'll be happy to answer any questions at all," Lorelei said. Her mouth went dry. "I can be there—" She began to cough. "Excuse me. I can be there by eight."

"Thank you," said Agnes. "I'll be waiting."

Lorelei hung up. She walked across the room and stood looking out the window. Imogene was sitting on a swing beside the lilac bushes, dragging her feet in the mud. Lately, she'd been agitating for a lesson in how to read the tarot, and Lorelei had been putting her off. If Charlotte caught her teaching the tarot, there would be hell to pay. Lorelei was sure she'd be evicted. But if Imogene got mad and decided to tattle, things could get infinitely worse. Lorelei's left temple throbbed with pain. Everything was going wrong. It had all started with that blasted Penny Johnson and her negative attitude about the moon. Now she was pointing out "red flags" in the research center plans. What next?

Lorelei tried to hold in her mind the pattern of the plan she had tried so hard to put into place. It had been like a delicately balanced castle of sand, but she had compromised a little, cut a few corners, gotten careless, and now there was movement on the periphery, things were shifting, sliding out of her control.

Halfway into his fourth beer, Derek told Nixie that his father had walked out on his mother shortly after Derek was born. "Left her for another woman," he said. "There was my poor mom with no car, no money. A sick baby. And he walks out!"

"You were sick?"

"Heart problem," Derek said. He thumped his chest and grinned. "All better, now. But I had five operations before I was two years old." He talked for a long time about how his mother worried about him all his life, how she had struggled to raise him alone, working two jobs, how she'd worn herself out.

"She's in a nursing home now," he said bitterly. "Massive stroke at the age of fifty. Half the time she doesn't even recognize me." He drained the rest of his beer and plunked the empty bottle heavily onto the bar. "Costs me six hundred bucks a month just to keep her on a decent ward. So now...."

He grinned softly to himself. "Now I'm the one who's working two jobs."

"And your dad?" Nixie asked.

"Dead," Derek told her. "Drank a quart of whisky and drove his car into a train when I was four years old. His slut broke it off with him. My mom wouldn't take him back, and he couldn't stand the guilt, I guess. Oh, well. No loss."

He turned away and began to watch TV. The baseball game was over and the bartender had turned the sound off. The local news was on, its pictures rolling silently over the screen. Nixie saw the mayor attending a powwow, a scientist holding up a test tube, two mangled cars on the highway. How could she keep Derek talking? She remembered that Penny had brought groceries for Derek and biscuits for his dogs. Maybe if she brought up the topic of kindly aunties, Derek would provide some information about his own aunt. "Family is so important, though," she said. "My mom was sick when I was a kid, and I was lucky to have an auntie who looked after me. I guess you must have had relatives who pitched in to help out when you were little, eh?"

Derek made a noise that was somewhere between a grunt and a snort.

"How did the rest of the family feel about what your father did?" Nixie asked.

He looked at her curiously, then turned back to the TV.

The face of the Reverend Surefire filled the screen. It seemed that he was a part of every local newscast these days. Nixie saw the Soldiers Against Satan marching outside a store. Was that the Dharmarama? In a flash it was gone, and there was only the talking head of the Reverend.

"The rest of my family?" said Derek. He didn't turn around. He seemed to be talking to the Reverend Surefire. "There was no rest of my family. There was just us."

"You didn't have a grandma to help out, or an uncle, or an auntie or anything?'"

"The worst of it was that, well, the other woman? She was married to my dad's brother. He was screwing his own brother's wife. Can you imagine?"

"Disgusting," said Nixie, as the bartender placed another two beers in front of her. They were cold, and the bottles were covered with condensation. She slid one over to Derek. He caught it in his hand.

"Yep," he said. "Good old Auntie Penny. What a bitch."

Despite the increasing chaos of the construction work and the less than stellar talents of her housekeeper, Agnes was keeping the entrance to her home as neat as possible. The gleaming hardwood floor of the vestibule had been freshly polished and a tall vase of orchids graced the table beside the antique umbrella rack. Susanne was up on a ladder, cleaning the crystal beads of the chandelier when Lorelei rang the bell.

Susanne climbed down and ushered Lorelei into the sitting room off the vestibule, the only room in the house not affected by brick dust and overrun by construction workers. As Lorelei sat down to wait, it occurred to her that Friday evening was an odd time to be polishing a chandelier. Dust must be a constant problem with the renovations.

"Susanne," Agnes was saying as she entered, "bring us tea, will you?"

"Yes, ma'am." Lorelei heard Susanne collide with the ladder as she hurried out to the kitchen.

"As I said, I've been reading over the materials you gave me." Agnes closed the door, shutting off the light from the vestibule, and switched on two small lamps ensconced in the wall above the tea table. She pulled out a chair opposite from Lorelei, but remained standing, her hands resting on the chair's back. "I've been discussing your plans with Waverley and with Penny," she said. "In fact, all the Seekers have been talking about the research center. There's a great deal of excitement in the air, and I just wanted to speak with you further about, well, the actual practical details of the plan, before I…make any decisions."

Lorelei smiled. "That's always wise."

"Waverley is committed to the project," Agnes said, "and of course I trust his judgment, but I'm just not sure whether Hank would understand. He's trusting me to handle our finances while he's away. He's put me completely in charge." She stepped away from the table and walked toward the wide windowsill, where she picked up a framed photo of Hank and clutched it to her chest. She began to pace as she spoke. "It's quite a responsibility." She laughed nervously. "I don't know what I'd do without his lawyers and accountants to advise me!"

"You seem to be struggling with a decision," said Lorelei.

Agnes ignored this remark. "Waverley has donated two hundred thousand toward the center," she said.

"Toward purchasing the property, yes," said Lorelei.

"And he's suggested I match that."

"Why, that's wonderful!"

"But the property you're proposing…I just don't know," Agnes said. "We drove out to take a look at it."

Lorelei forced her voice to remain calm. "You did? Really?"

"Just this morning. Penny thought Waverley should look at the site before he invested any more money, and they invited me to go along. When we saw it, we all thought, well …. Tell me, honestly, how long do you think it will take to develop that place into a center like the one you're planning? Isn't it rather desolate out there?"

"It's a place of immense serenity."

"Yes, but you see, we were hoping for a project that wouldn't take quite so long to complete." Agnes twisted her hands together and leaned forward. "None of us is getting any younger. And forgive me, but I also think—to build the center out there would be—well, as Penny pointed out, there's nothing *growing* there. There isn't even any water."

"We plan to sink a well," Lorelei said. "We've consulted a diviner, already. A highly gifted—"

"And the farmhouse," Agnes rushed on. "I hate to say it, but it's practically crumbling. The roof looks ready to collapse."

"The contractor has assured me the structure is sound. The farmhouse will be renovated and expanded." Lorelei pulled out one of her architect's drawings and spread it on the table. "You see, there will be an addition here, larger than the original structure." She pointed out the various features, skylights and balconies, the courtyard with its central fountain.

"Yes, it's lovely," Agnes admitted. "We were all so taken with the plans, but contractors sometimes promise things they can't accomplish. And how long would it take? The Seekers are hoping for a center we could use right away."

"All things in their own time," said Lorelei.

Agnes held the photo of Hank against her heart, hugging it. Then suddenly she seemed to make a decision. She sat down across from Lorelei and leaned forward conspiratorially. "We came up with an idea. It was Waverley's idea, really."

"Yes?"

"Well, would you consider our cottage?"

"Your cottage on Lake of the Woods?" Lorelei asked. "Why, I'd have to think about that."

"So Raymond and Roland were brothers," Nixie explained to Lorelei. "Raymond was married to Derek's mom, and Roland was married to Penny. Penny had an affair with Raymond—her husband's brother! All those love letters and that engagement ring, those weren't from her husband, but from her lover—who killed himself when she broke up with him! Derek secretly hates her."

"Secretly?"

"Around Penny, he pretends not to know about the affair," Nixie said. "He was only a baby at the time. When he grew up, his mother told him all about it, the suicide, everything. But Penny doesn't know he knows. He acts like a dutiful nephew, talks about missing his dad and such, and takes advantage of her guilt feelings to get her to bring him steaks and beer and bottles of rum. She's making the payments on his truck, too. And there is something about Roland's will he was chortling over, as well. It must be that 'cryptic bequest' mentioned in the phone message from Penny's lawyer. But I couldn't get any details out of Derek on that. Whatever it is, Derek loves it because he says it's driving Penny crazy with guilt."

"Wow," said Lorelei. "No wonder she was so shocked when Raymond showed up on her birthday. Imagine how she must have felt! Her deep, dark secret suddenly brought to light by the wandering, napkin-burning spirit of her dead, illicit lover!"

"Well, at least he's dead," said Nixie. "So your reputation as a psychic is unstained. It's not your fault if Raymond's haunting her!"

They both laughed. They were giddy with excitement

since Agnes had made the offer of her cottage. Projects were always so much more successful when the clients came up with the idea by themselves—or when they thought they had. Lorelei had promised to get back to Agnes once she consulted the founder of the Psychic Renaissance Foundation. He, naturally, would respond that the cottage was a teensy bit too costly. But by that time, Waverley and Agnes would have their hearts set on the place.

Nixie looked at her watch. "Is the news on yet?" She turned on the television. "I thought I saw an item about the Soldiers Against Satan and the Dharmarama. Are they picketing Summer's store now?"

"Oh yes," said Lorelei. "They marched around the store all afternoon and this evening Summer went on the offensive with a press conference. She's convinced it was the Soldiers Against Satan who defaced her store last year, and she's saying some pretty inflammatory—there she is. Turn it up."

Summer was using the front counter of her store as a podium. "These protesters have no right to harass and intimidate my clientele, who are respectable, law-abiding citizens taking part in wholesome, environmentally safe practices." She pounded the counter with her fist. "The Reverend's tactics are nothing but irresponsible hate mongering. The police have cleared all previous suspects in the death of Yolanda Dawn. They have no suspects in the death of Oberon Zolo at the Psychic Fair. But it's clear that these two murders were hate crimes. Whether it is the Reverend himself, or his followers, or some misguided member of the public who listened to their cant, the Reverend Surefire has blood on his hands. And the media is not blameless!" The station cut to a commercial.

Lorelei needed all the information she could get about Penny Johnson. Roland's will was obviously involved in some mysterious way with her reason for trying to contact him in the afterlife. And if Lorelei was going to interpret Roland's messages correctly, she'd have to know what the will said and what was in the estate. What strange legacy had Roland left for his nephew? Lorelei knew she would have to face Brian Hale. As Penny's lawyer, and an old family friend, Brian could help. And yet she hesitated.

Lorelei had been hovering over the phone for half an hour, sometimes starting to dial Brian's office number before she hung up. She didn't understand her own reluctance. All she knew was that she felt relieved when her own phone rang and it was Waverley, inviting her over for lunch. Obviously lunch with Waverley took priority, so she showered and dressed, took extra care with her makeup, and brushed her long dark hair until it shone. She suspected that Agnes had told him about her offering the cottage for sale to PsyRen. She was right.

After a lunch of grilled salmon and asparagus, Mary served fruit and coffee in the library while Waverley told Lorelei his ideas for the center. He became more and more animated as he unfolded his vision to her. The island location would necessitate a certain rustic flair to the ambience, he pronounced. But they could make that work. He had a particular interior designer in mind. Had Lorelei ever heard of— Their discussion was interrupted by the distant sound of the doorbell and, a moment later, Mary ushered in Penny, who had apparently decided to "drop by" for a visit, once she'd heard Lorelei was there.

Penny greeted Waverley warmly with a hug. She gave Lorelei a tight smile.

Waverley urged Penny to take a comfortable seat where

the sunlight wouldn't shine in her eyes. He adjusted a pillow behind her back and asked Mary to put on the kettle for tea, as he knew Penny didn't care for coffee.

"We were just discussing the research center," he said. He seemed too keyed up to sit down again. "Plans are moving much faster than I anticipated. Lorelei tells me the founder is ready to secure a property. So it's time for the Seekers to come forward to the Psychic Renaissance Foundation with a substantial contribution. If we don't get in on the ground floor of this thing, we'll regret it."

"But Waverley, you saw the site yourself. It's just not suitable."

"There's been a positive development there," said Waverley. In his excitement, he spoke rapidly, pacing across the floor. Now, with Penny here to listen, he was even more energetic than before. Forty years seemed to have dropped from his frame. "Agnes proposed her cottage as an alternative site, and Lorelei is simply waiting for the founder to approve the idea. The more I think about it, the more convinced I am we should purchase the Kellsington cottage. I've already given two hundred thousand toward the center—"

"You have?" said Penny. She shot a disapproving glance in Lorelei's direction, too fleeting for Waverley to notice. "Are you sure that's wise?"

He appeared not to hear this interruption. "And if we can get the cottage," he continued, "I'd happily pledge five more. Six if necessary. Think how many people the place would attract. And we'd have the whole island for expansion. It's perfect."

"But that whole island? On Lake of the Woods? It must be worth a million dollars!" said Penny.

"Place like that," Waverley corrected, "more like three million. But imagine the crowds we'll bring in! People from all over the world. Luminaries in the field. With the center's mid-continental location and the natural beauty of the lake, we'd find ourselves hosts to the very top stars in psychic research."

"But it's way beyond our means. The amount we've saved so far is…wait a minute." Penny searched through her purse and pulled out a checkbook. She paged through it. "Since we started taking up a collection toward the research center, we've raised our savings account, but it's still nowhere near enough for such an extravagant— Here it is. We have a total of twelve thousand and fifty-five dollars. And that's before we take expenses out for Spirit Fest."

"Well, surely we can—what? *Really*?" He was silent for a minute. "Only twelve?"

"That's it. And it's taken us two years to accumulate."

For a few seconds, all three of them sat in silence. Lorelei held her breath. Should she propose a solution? Or stay out of this? She sipped her coffee thoughtfully and tried to look serene. Before she could decide what to do, Waverley seemed to rally.

"Where there's a will, there's a way," he pronounced. "I didn't get where I am through negative thinking. Why, I'll simply have a talk with Agnes. I'm sure we can come to an agreement." He looked at Lorelei. "Perhaps the Kellsingtons could be persuaded to drop the price for the sake of a good cause."

Lorelei expressed surprise at this novel idea and suggested such a move would be very good for Agnes's karma.

"Oh, I don't know, Waverley," said Penny. "Agnes *does* seem interested in the research center. I know she's planning to invest. But to practically donate the family cottage? It's been in Hank's family for years."

"He's selling it anyway. This way he can continue to use it. And we could tell her, *suggest* to her, that she could have a hand in naming the center." Waverley paused for a minute, thinking. "She could name it after her mother."

Lorelei nearly choked on her tea.

Later, when Lorelei rose to leave, she refused Waverley's offer to walk her to the door, insisting she could see herself out. Penny said goodby sweetly—too sweetly, Lorelei thought. Penny seemed eager to be rid of her.

Lorelei walked down the corridor more noisily than usual. When she reached the foyer she opened and closed the front door without leaving. Then she stepped out of her sandals and carried them in her hand to the kitchen doorway. If Mary saw her, she'd claim to have a blister. But Mary didn't see her. Mary was busy rolling out pastry. In her bare feet, Lorelei padded back down the corridor to the library and flattened herself beside the archway, listening.

"She's just not reliable," Penny was saying. Just as Lorelei had suspected, Penny was bad-mouthing her the minute she left.

"You'll see, Penny," Waverley said decisively. "At Spirit Fest, when all the conditions are just right, you'll see exactly the amazing things that Lorelei can do. Why, with the confluence of the lake waters and—"

"But let's say that we don't get results at Spirit Fest," said Penny. "What if I get another garbled reading? With her summoning the wrong spirit? That was so disappointing! It happened twice! Or what if nothing happens? And I don't count growling and vague messages. I want real results. Proof. What if you invest in this idea and then Spirit Fest is a failure? Then what are you going to do?"

"I'm sure that won't happen," said Waverley. "But naturally, if we can't contact the spirits, even when all conditions are ideal, then I suppose it's probably…not the best location after all, even though it *is* so beautiful."

"So you wouldn't invest any more funds in that case?" asked Penny.

"I suppose not," said Waverley reluctantly. "No, of course I wouldn't."

"Then you should wait, Waverley. You've already pledged enough. Don't sink any more assets into the PsyRen scheme until you get some proof that the site is viable."

"You're right as usual, my dear," he said. "I'll hold off on any further investment until after Spirit Fest."

That hypocritical bitch, thought Lorelei. *She doesn't want him spending his money!* She found it difficult to contain her fury but she forced herself to tiptoe back to the front door and exit quietly. Once in her car, she slammed the door and revved the engine, shooting off down the quiet crescent. The true nature of Penny Johnson had been revealed. Despite her volunteer work, her creativity, and her love of cats, she was nothing but a money-hungry gold digger.

The Kellsingtons' lawyer had drawn up the papers, as Agnes requested. But he obviously disapproved of the sale of the cottage at such a reduced price. When Susanne ushered him into Agnes's sitting room, he greeted Lorelei coldly. He quickly took control of the meeting, treating Agnes with a proprietary, condescending manner and Lorelei with frank suspicion, requiring her to show her identification before he would even take the papers out of his briefcase. He had been representing Hank for twenty years, he explained, and was almost part of the family. Hank's interests were his top priority. He then proceeded to ask numerous probing questions about the reasons for the price reduction. He finally relaxed a bit when Agnes explained that this was her way of making a donation to the good cause of the PsyRen Institute. He was apparently used to the Kellsingtons' good causes and tolerated them with a paternal kind of resignation.

"Very well, then," he said, as he took out the papers. "Let's go over a few details." He looked over the offer to purchase and frowned. "I understand the financing isn't in place yet," he said.

"Not quite," said Lorelei. "The PsyRen treasury is experiencing—"

"We'll need a substantial deposit then," said the lawyer. He wasn't interested in the PsyRen's cash-flow problems. "Certified check preferred."

"Um, it's ten percent of the purchase price, right?"

"Normally," he said. "But Jack Barnes insists, and I agree with him, that until the financing's firmly in place, we'll need a meaningful deposit." He smiled at her. "Show of good faith."

"How meaningful?"

"Five hundred thousand," he said. "It's only fair. If Jack is going to hold the property, and turn away legitimate purchasers—"

"Lorelei is perfectly legitimate, Harry!" Agnes interrupted.

"I'm sure she is," he said calmly. "I only meant the word in a general sense, in terms of a guarantee of purchase. If the offer is conditional on financing, Agnes, you are expected to require a substantial deposit to ensure the purchaser is serious and to compensate you for potential losses. It's only fair business practice."

"Oh," said Agnes. "All right, then. That's all right, isn't it, Lorelei?"

"Certainly," said Lorelei. She was rapidly revising her

calculations. The deposit was three hundred thousand more than she'd anticipated.

"There's the Family Property Act to consider, as well," said Harry.

"What's that?"

"Manitoba law. Both spouses have to agree to the sale."

"Hank will agree, I'm sure," said Agnes. "He wants to sell."

"That's fine. But we still need his signature."

"But Harry, he's in India! On a spiritual retreat. I told you, he's not to be disturbed."

"He'll have to be, if you want to sell the property."

"But he's only to be contacted in case of an emergency."

"Hank might consider a million dollars an emergency," the lawyer said dryly.

"What do you mean?"

The lawyer sighed. He looked at Lorelei. "Ms Good, I'm going to be frank." Then he turned back to Agnes. "Agnes, you're selling this cottage at a greatly reduced price. It's worth at least three million. Last week I did the paperwork on a similar property that went for four point five. It had road access and a swimming pool, but still—this deal you're making, with your friend here, it's an incredible steal. Even if it weren't, we'd have to consult Hank. The law requires his signature on the papers."

Agnes looked at Lorelei. "I don't quite know what to do," she said. "I thought it would be so simple."

"You really can't phone him?" Lorelei asked. "E-mail?"

"In an emergency, I'm supposed to reach him by telephone, through the ashram's main office. But I hate to interrupt his meditations with business matters. I promised—"

"I'll accept a faxed signature," the lawyer said. "I know

Hank's signature. If we can fax him the papers, we can do it. Otherwise, I can't help you."

"I suppose I could," said Agnes. "I hope he won't mind."

"Fine," said the lawyer. "Contact him. Give him the details. Then give us the fax number of the ashram, and we'll take care of the paperwork."

He smiled at Lorelei. "And now, Ms Good, if you'll sign here and here and give us a check for the deposit, we're done."

Back at home, Lorelei stood at the window, gazing into the oak grove beside the house. She had no way to get a certified check for five hundred thousand dollars and no ideas about how to get around that bulldog of a lawyer. She sighed and tapped her fingers idly on the glass. She could see Charlotte Trapp walking resolutely along the path, returning from the store with two bags of groceries, as if their weight were a punishment she was enduring for a higher purpose.

"Imogene!" Charlotte called. "Come and help your mother!"

Lorelei heard the door slam on the Trapp side of the duplex and saw Imogene clump down the path in her school uniform to help her mother. The backs of her knees looked dirty. Lorelei studied the girl's gait and noticed she was limping. She looked again at her legs. There was a purplish tinge to them, visible even from across the yard. That wasn't dirt, it was bruising. What had happened to the kid's legs?

Lorelei turned away. She had bigger problems. How could she raise a deposit so that Agnes would hold on to the cottage for her until she could put the financing in place? She had assured Agnes that PsyRen had a mere minor cash-flow problem that she could clear up in a day or two. Agnes's lawyer was not at all happy with the delay, which he seemed to interpret as a sign of PsyRen's financial instability. Seeing as they had to wait for Hank's signature anyway, he had not made an issue of it. But if this dragged on too long, Lorelei was afraid he'd advise Agnes to withdraw from the deal.

The Seekers had only twelve thousand to contribute up front. And Lorelei knew that Penny wouldn't release even that paltry amount in advance—not since she'd turned Spirit Fest into a Spirit Test. Lorelei still had Waverley's two hundred thousand dollars in her PsyRen account. In the old days, she would have skipped town the minute that check had cleared, but she was smarter now. She was going to do this all legally. But where could she get the other three hundred? She had nothing else in the bank, except money for household expenses. And the diamonds. If she sold the entire bag, she could raise three hundred thousand. But Lorelei couldn't sell *all* the diamonds. The thought made her queasy. There had to be a better way. She considered going to see Waverley. He had said that he'd up his donation to five or six hundred thousand *if* they could get the cottage, but would he be willing to put that much forward as a deposit? She didn't think so. He was a faithful believer, but he wasn't stupid. If PsyRen couldn't even come up with the deposit, he might pull out altogether. But she had to try. She went to see him.

Waverley was busy. He was poring over a set of brightly colored pamphlets from his travel agent, trying to decide where to stay during his upcoming business trip to Greece. "I've had to change my reservations," he told her, "since I postponed the original seminar until after Spirit Fest."

Lorelei was impressed. Twenty-five of the world's top oil executives had been forced to change their plans so that Waverley could keep his date with a ghost on the Moon of Takara. Now *that*, she thought, is what it means to be wealthy.

He pulled out a brochure for a luxury resort on a Mediterranean beach and sighed. "These places are really meant for couples," he said wistfully.

"I met with Agnes's lawyer yesterday," Lorelei said. "It looks as if PsyRen's offer on the cottage has been accepted."

"Wonderful! We'll have to get together the minute I return from Greece, Lorelei. You know, I was out at the cottage a couple of times, and I've come up with some splendid ideas for improvements to be made." The telephone rang, and he answered it without even pausing for breath. "Yes, Debbie? Debbie, dear, could you book me in to the Ithaca? A seaside room. Yes. Thank you, dear. And you'll take care of the tickets? Wonderful! You're a doll." He hung up. "Now, where were we? Oh, yes. Agnes called to ask about borrowing some of my staff for Spirit Fest, so I'll ask Mary to take care of that. I thought the cook and some of the servants could pack up and come along on the new boat. Make a holiday of it!"

"You bought a new boat?" Lorelei didn't like the sound of that. New toys had a tendency to distract Waverley from his pursuit of spiritual matters.

"Mmm hmm." He shuffled papers. "A Sundancer. She's a beauty. Twenty-six-foot sportscruiser with hot water and cooking facilities. I thought the staff could bunk on the boat, and—"

"You bought a yacht!" exclaimed Lorelei.

"It's only an entry-level yacht," he said. He looked up. "You sound like Penny." He laughed. "She says I should be more 'prudent.' Prudent! What an ugly-sounding word."

"Yes, well, about the purchase of the cottage…there's a bit of a snag."

"I'm in no mood to brook any snags," Waverley said. "You know me, I want to be surrounded by positive thinking!" The telephone rang again and he picked it up immediately. "Yes? Ah, good, Debbie. Now, listen, can you do one other little thing...."

Lorelei stopped listening. This was obviously no time to be making a pitch for any more money. If everything went smoothly at Spirit Fest, she felt sure that Waverley would pour plenty of money into the project in the future. But would everything go smoothly?

CHAPTER TEN

The offices of Bader and Bader grew somber late in the afternoons, as the hustle of morning meetings and phone calls subsided and lawyers bent their heads to paperwork. Brian found it a depressing time of day. Or was he just depressed? He sighed, sharpened his pencil, and stared out the window of his twenty-sixth-floor office at the green canopy of trees that hid from view the residential streets across the river. If he ever bought a house, that's where he would live, among those hundred-year-old trees in the "flats" near the river, where bicycle paths snaked along the riverbank and baseball diamonds dotted the fields.

"Hi Bri!" Rhonda smiled as she entered his office, handing him a sheaf of yellow messages. She leaned over his desk and began to play with the snow globe he used as a paperweight. "You want to catch some dinner with me?" she asked.

"Wish I could, but I have to wrap up these memos." He turned back to the file he was working on. "You go home, now, you hear? It's late."

"Okay," she said wistfully. "Good night."

Brian sorted through the messages. Finally that kid Derek Johnson had returned his calls, just ten minutes ago. He reached for the phone and, at last, caught Derek at home.

"We wanted to ask you," Brian explained, "if you could remember any other bank accounts your uncle might have had, any other financial institutions or storage companies he had dealings with."

"Sorry, man," said Derek. "Aunt Penny already asked me that. I can't think of anything that's not on that list she gave you."

"You don't know of any friends he might have trusted with his valuables, or possibly anyone he might have lent money to?"

"No."

"He didn't…lend you money?"

"No. Like I told Aunt Penny, I think she should give up, quit looking for more stuff and get this will on probation."

"Probated."

"Whatever."

"Well, thank you for calling," said Brian. Privately, he agreed with Derek. Penny Johnson was holding out too long. She should get it over with. Move on with her life.

He spent the next three hours writing memos and then locked up his desk and walked down the hall of the law office, calling good night to two lawyers and an articling student who were still working in the library. He drove to St. Mary's Curry House and parked in the lot, too tired to get up and go in. Through the window, he could see his sister-in-law, Sarisha, waiting tables. Tommy was coming out of the kitchen, balancing two trays piled dangerously high with steaming plates of curry. This was Tommy's idea of a night off.

When he entered the restaurant, Sarisha's mother greeted him warmly. "Tommy says you'll eat with us tonight," she said.

"I can't," said Brian. "I have to take it out. I'm sorry."

She gave him a mock frown and shook her finger at him. "Work, I suppose?"

"I'm afraid so."

"You're going to ruin your health," she scolded. "It's too much stress, these long hours. You need to learn to relax."

Brian laughed. "Is that what you're doing? Relaxing?" He raised his arm to indicate the crowded, noisy restaurant, Tommy and Sarisha dancing around each other, trying to avoid a collision as they served tables, the din of clattering silverware and chattering customers rising around them.

"At least we're together," she said.

A party of six entered the restaurant. When she hurried to greet them, Brian put out a hand to slow her down. "Honestly, Ramya, don't save a seat for me. I have to go. I'll come next Friday night, all right?"

"All right," she said. "But bring your girlfriend this time!"

"She's not my—"

Ramya hurried away without listening and Brian sighed. He asked one of the waiters for a takeout order of vegetable korma and managed to sneak out the door without being spotted by Tommy.

At home, he turned on the television and had just settled down with his takeout dinner and a cold glass of beer when his telephone rang. Who would be phoning him this late at night? It could only be work, he thought. Some crisis at the office. He was shocked when he heard the voice of Lorelei Good on the line.

"I hope I'm not disturbing you."

"No," he said. He walked into the kitchen as he spoke and placed the plate of curry on the kitchen table. "No, not at all."

"I've been meaning to call you ever since I saw you the other night," she said.

"I'm glad you did."

"I wanted to explain—"

"Wait a minute," he said. "How did you know my number?"

"You're in the phone book."

"Oh. Yes. Well, it's good to hear from you. I thought you didn't recognize me the other night when we met at the party."

"How could I not recognize you?"

"That's exactly what I was asking myself," he said. "Are you angry at me for some reason?"

"Of course not. I was just taken by surprise. After all these years. And you were with your girlfriend, so I just—"

"She's not my girlfriend," he said quickly.

"I see!" She was laughing at him. But in a sweet way. She sounded a lot more sophisticated than the seventeen-year-old girl he'd kissed on the riverbank twelve years ago. Other than that, her voice was exactly the same, light and teasing and mysterious.

"Where have you been?" he asked. Then the questions came rushing out of him before he could stop them. "Where did you go? What have you been doing all this time? Have long have you been back in town?"

"That's a lot of questions," she said. "This might take some time."

"I've got time," he said. He took a salad bowl out of the cupboard and turned it upside down over his dinner to keep it warm. "Tell me how you've been."

An hour later, Brian was humming as he took his vegetable korma out of the microwave. His depression had lifted and dispersed, like the steam that rose from his plate. He had a date, a dinner date, next Friday night, with Lorelei Good.

A week before Spirit Fest, Agnes called Penny to discuss details and last-minute arrangements. The two women began to discuss their choice of a medium for the seance.

"I really believe Lorelei was the right choice," Agnes said. "Now, I know you favor Maurice, but—"

"Don't talk to me about that awful Maurice!" cried Penny.

Nixie and Lorelei, who were listening to the call together, exchanged a look of glee. The mighty Maurice had fallen from grace? They listened eagerly.

"Why?" asked Agnes. "Did something go wrong with your reading yesterday?"

"Everything went wrong! The man is nothing but a sham. His reading was completely off the mark. The only thing he had right were a few insights about my nephew, Derek. Otherwise—"

"What did he say about Derek?" asked Agnes.

"Well, he was right that Derek is troubled," conceded Penny. "And I'm sorry to say he was right that Derek once spent some time in juvenile detention. But Derek has outgrown the problems he had as a youth, and that's what I told Maurice. Yet he insisted I should look more closely at Derek, that Derek is concealing something from me, and it's very upsetting because, well…."

"Yes, dear?"

"Because Yolanda said the exact same thing before she died. Derek came to one of my readings with her, you know, and she told me afterwards she could sense he was holding something back. Hiding something. There was…what did she say? Something cold about him. Or he was out in the cold?"

"Cold?" asked Agnes. "Did she mean emotionally?"

"She said he wanted to hide things in a place that was no longer cold. Something like that." Penny sighed. "She was sometimes a bit mysterious, I must admit. Still, she was a paragon of clarity compared to that Lorelei girl. And Maurice!"

"What else did Maurice say?"

"Oh, the rest was utter bunk," said Penny. "I don't know what he thought he was doing but he certainly didn't contact Roland. He couldn't even get my sign right, saying I was a Gemini! Everyone knows I just had my birthday. I'm a Cancer. What else? Oh, that I had two sisters and a gall bladder operation. Really! My gall bladder is perfectly intact, thank you very much, I said to him. But the silliest part was his message that Roland and I witnessed the terrorist attacks on the World Trade Center."

"Very odd," said Agnes. "Where in the world did he get that idea from?"

Lorelei and Nixie knew exactly where he'd gotten it from. Bunny Green's card: "Gem. Two sis. Gall blad x. NYC 911 w. hub."

Whatever else Obie had done on his final night on Earth, he had switched the cards, just as Lorelei had asked him to. He must have switched them at the Dharmarama and then, after his death, Summer had unwittingly sold the altered card to Maurice. In that case, the real card on Penny Johnson was still unaccounted for. It would have been in Obie's pocket when he was killed, and the killer would now have it, along with Lorelei's diamond. Was the pink index card the real motive for Obie's murder? Any psychic might want that card, to impress the girlfriend of an oil millionaire with his powers of divination. But would any psychic kill for it? Or did the card contain some deadly information, a secret somebody wanted to know, or wanted to conceal?

On the evening of the murder, Summer claimed she hadn't seen Obie between the reception and the dinner. She had probably been lying, to cover up her shady dealings with him at her store. But what if she'd been telling the truth? What if Obie had been murdered for the card before he even got to the Dharmarama? In that case, the real card on Penny Johnson would still be sitting in the files at the Dharmarama. And the murderer could only be the person in possession of the fake card—Maurice Lemoine.

For days, the D in the pink neon sign in the display window of the Dharmarama had been burned out, so that the sign read "HARMARAMA," and now finally the rest of the letters had fizzled out. At two o'clock in the morning, the display window was dark and no one could see into the store. In the lane behind the building, a van had been parked so that it blocked the rear entrance from view. A dark curtain covered the rear window. Nixie thought that conditions couldn't possibly be better for a break in—until she tried the door and found it unlocked.

The lane was only partially lit by a streetlamp half a block away. The windows of the houses across the lane were dark. Nixie turned the handle and eased the door open a crack. A light flashed briefly behind her and she spun around, but she saw nothing. A passing car's headlights, she thought, flashing between the buildings. Otherwise, there was no one around. She waited in the doorway, listening, in case Summer or one of her salesclerks was working late. But she knew that was unlikely. In the candles and incense business, there wasn't much call for overtime. She peered inside. The store was utterly silent and pitch black. Pulling her flashlight from her pack, Nixie stepped in and let the door close behind her. A streetlamp cast a dull glow through the display window at the front of the store. As her eyes adjusted a little to the dark, Nixie could make out the dim shape of the card-reading booth in front of her.

Nixie made her way carefully around the booth toward the door to Summer's office. Her goal was the filing cabinet where Summer kept her index cards. If the real card on Penny Johnson was still in the cabinet, then Maurice was the murderer, and this made Nixie uneasy. If Maurice was killing off rival psychics, Lorelei could be in serious danger. But it would be better to know the truth. And if the real card was there, then Nixie planned to read and memorize it before she wiped it of prints. She was also going to look for a tape, and if she found it she'd replace it with the blank tape she carried in her backpack. The longer it took Summer to figure out anything was missing, the better.

If she and Lorelei were guessing right, then all the clues they'd overheard and pieced together added up to a theory that Yolanda had taped her last reading with Penny. It had something about Derek on it. Maurice had inherited the tape. And he had possibly lent it to Summer in exchange for one of her cards. Nixie kept thinking about the conversation between Maurice and Summer at the Psychic Fair, about a tape Maurice had listened to twice. Something about an item not being hidden but taken. By a kid. But not one of the sons. If that was the tape of Yolanda's last reading with Penny, what would that mean? By all accounts, Yolanda was highly intuitive. She might even have had a real gift, though Lorelei was skeptical about that. Nixie slid her feet along the floor, keeping one hand raised in front of her face like a blind person, to prevent herself from banging into anything. Summer's office was windowless, so once Nixie got inside it and closed the door, she'd be able to turn on the light and relax a bit, take her time looking around.

The door to the office was ajar and Nixie slipped inside. She closed the door behind her, knelt down, and pulled out a towel she had brought along to block the light from escaping under the door. She stuffed it into the crack between door jamb and floor. Then she stood up and felt along the wall for the light switch. Where was it? She swept her arm in a wide arc twice, then a third time, before her fingers found the switch. She flicked it on.

Then off again.

The room filled suddenly with the sound of her own ragged, frightened breathing. The pounding of her own blood against her eardrums. It was pitch black but every detail of the image she'd just seen was seared into her mind. Three feet in front of her, the desktop was scattered with blue and pink index cards. A cup of tea had been broken and tea spilled across it. The telephone had been pulled from the wall. Behind the desk, a wide-eyed Summer Sweet sat upright in her swivel chair, her pink straw hat on her head, her pink dress soaked in blood, and a knife in her chest.

A loud crash came from the rear of the store. The tinkle of shattering glass.

And then it happened. The loud boom and whoosh of an explosion, a force that blew the office door open and sent Nixie flying. She sailed across the desk and smashed head-first into the cold, dead body of Summer Sweet. Her cheek struck the handle of the weapon protruding from Summer's chest. Nixie screamed and pushed herself away. Staggered backwards, struggling to keep her balance. She clasped her hands together and felt the slime of congealed blood that coated them. *Murder*, she thought. But she couldn't think anything else. She was afraid to move. As she stood shuddering uncontrollably in the dark room, she caught the smell of smoke. The Dharmarama was on fire.

The gift section at the back burned first. Nixie stepped to the threshold of the office to see an entire shelving unit, holding nothing but wicker baskets full of dried flowers, go up in smoke. The flowers were vaporized instantly in white puffs, and the baskets were incinerated almost as quickly. In seconds, the fire jumped from the gift shelves to the gauzy fabric that covered the card-reading booth. The booth was transformed into a flaming tower, shooting sparks and flames at Nixie. She leaped through a shower of sparks and ran toward the front door. The store was small, she should have made it. But as she ran, the gauzy curtains that stretched the length of the wall caught fire. Nixie saw the flames race past her. As the rugs and tapestry decorating the front entrance caught fire, she realized she was trapped. Smoke rapidly filled the building.

Nixie sprinted for the one last escape route. The front window. She threw aside the iron bookstand in the display area, scattering copies of *Ghost Talk* across the floor, and kicked the window pane. She coughed. She had never imagined smoke could get so thick so fast. She kicked harder. But she was never going to break this glass with a hundred and ten pounds of force and a pair of rubber-soled high-top sneakers. Jumping out of the display window, she ripped the cash register cord from the wall, heaved the register over her head and hurled it at the window. It didn't smash through, as she had hoped. But it cracked the glass, leaving a hole in the middle about six inches wide. That was a start. She smelled the cool night air for a second before the smoke closed in around her again. Blindly, she bashed at the crack with the wrought iron bookstand and finally made a hole big enough for herself. Ten minutes after she'd entered through the rear door, she smashed out through the front window.

Bleeding and coughing, she ran down the street to a parked pickup truck. It was a landscaper's truck, full of rolls of sod. She lay down in the back and covered herself with a tarp. By the time the fire engines came screaming down the street, she was invisible.

Later, when she dared to peek out from under her cover, the Dharmarama was already a lost cause. It was engulfed in flames. Firefighters could do nothing but keep it from spreading to neighboring buildings. When they entered in the morning and began to sift through the rubble, they would be in for a horrible shock. Would any incriminating evidence remain to tell them who had killed Summer Sweet? The firebomb had been thrown with that one purpose in mind, Nixie realized: to burn up every shred of evidence. She hoped that any evidence of her own presence would burn with it.

For the next two days she stayed in bed, recovering from the shock to her system. Her arms and legs were covered in cuts, her ribs were sore, and her cheek, where she'd smashed into the hilt of the knife, was badly bruised. Lorelei applied bandages and ice and read up on the Internet about smoke inhalation. Nixie seemed to have gotten out in time to avoid any serious damage from the smoke. Lorelei would have liked a doctor to look at her ribs. But that was out of the question at the moment. Nixie had to lie low.

The media went wild with the news of Summer's murder and the firebombing of the Dharmarama. The incendiary device, as they called it, had been a kind of Molotov cocktail, and the newspaper printed a sidebar about the availability of recipes for explosives, how any teenager could access such instructions on the Internet.

Kent Mason produced a tasteful half-hour tribute to Summer Sweet, her contributions to the community and her battle against bigotry and fanaticism. Part of his script was read at her funeral service, where there was a heavy and obvious police presence. Family and friends were bewildered by the large crowds. Hundreds of customers and even complete strangers had been drawn to honor Summer at the service. She had become a symbol of rebellion against repression, a martyr to the cause of free speech and freedom of religion. Her interviews were replayed on television and the whole issue of the Soldiers Against Satan was again at the top of the news. The Reverend Surefire, contacted by Channel Ten, had no comment.

"Why won't he even say he condemns the attack?" Brian asked Tommy one night over dinner. "I don't understand why he will not distance himself from it."

"I think he believes it was an act of God," said Tommy. "He can't condemn an act of God."

"Brian's right, though," said Sarisha. "He should speak out against these attacks. Three innocent people dead!"

"I'm not so sure how innocent they are, really," said Tommy. "Most people in that line of work have a shady side."

"And televangelists don't?" Sarisha challenged.

"Are the police at least investigating him?" Brian asked.

Tommy nodded. "Of course. But he has a solid alibi for the time of all three murders. Besides, he's too obvious. Murderers don't usually make speeches on television condemning their victims."

"He scares me," said Brian. "I have a friend who does psychic readings and seances with the Seekers, and I worry. How much danger do you think these people are in? I tried to warn my friend but she won't listen. She—"

"She?" asked Sarisha. "You mean Rhonda?"

"No, not—for God's sake, Sarisha, I know more than one woman!"

Tommy and Sarisha raised their eyebrows and looked at each other in mock surprise. "And where did you meet a woman?" Tommy asked him. "Hiding in your filing cabinet?"

"Go to hell," Brian said. But he couldn't help smiling. "No, I—" He didn't want to say she was a high-school friend. That sounded too lame. They'd tease him. "I met her at a party. With the Seekers." They were looking at him skeptically. "A client invited me to a party and I went, okay? It was fun."

"A party with the Seekers?" Tommy asked. "Oh, come on, Brian, you don't still believe in that stuff, do you?"

Brian shrugged.

"You're so naïve," said Tommy. "You are so incredibly naïve."

Brian ignored him. Prosecutors, like police officers, grew cynical over time. It was inevitable.

That night he called Lorelei. "I worry about you with these fanatics on the loose," he said. "You're keeping your doors locked?"

"Of course I am. Are you?" she teased him.

"I hardly think I'm a target," he said. "But that crowd you are involved in, they're in some danger, obviously. Even the police believe now that there's a killer targeting psychics. Three people, all involved in occult practices, have been killed in less than a month. It's frightening."

"Yes," said Lorelei. But she didn't think anyone was targeting psychics. She didn't know much about Yolanda Dawn, but she was sure that Obie had plenty of enemies, and Summer was making a living selling people's secrets, a dangerous business, bound to run some serious risks. Summer had been playing with fire—was that part of the murderer's message? And she had not played well. She might have given away the wrong person's secrets. Or she might have given the wrong secrets away—was it Summer who gave that altered card to Maurice? Would he have sought revenge for his humiliation? But no matter who it was or what was going on out there, Lorelei was determined that Nixie should stay close to home from now until Spirit Fest. Winnipeg, a city she'd chosen mainly for its peace and quiet, was no longer safe.

After she finished speaking to Brian she went upstairs and checked on her sister. Nixie was asleep, her face flushed, her red curls tumbling over the pillow. The bruise across her cheek would fade in time and the cuts would heal. But what damage might have been done to Nixie's spirit? When she thought of the danger Nixie had been in, she became enraged. She could have killed Summer if she weren't already dead.

CHAPTER ELEVEN

Lorelei watched from the window as Brian chatted with Charlotte Trapp in front of the duplex. Charlotte was weeding the flowerbed when Brian came to pick Lorelei up for their dinner date. He was late. The driveway was blocked by Nixie's van and Lorelei's car, and every parking spot on the street was taken. He had been forced to park a block away and so arrived on foot. Charlotte stood as he came walking up the front path. He held out a hand for her to shake. Lorelei saw Charlotte's mouth open in a round oh of surprise as she recognized him. She decided to get out there before the evening turned into a high school reunion.

"Oh Brian, I thought you'd never come!" Charlotte was saying as Lorelei approached from behind. "I mean, I never thought you'd come here. Oh my goodness." Her hands were muddy from her work in the garden, and she wiped them on her apron.

"I came to see Lorelei," he said. "I understand she's your tenant now."

"You're here to see *her*?" Charlotte leaned in close and her voice took on a conspiratorial tone. "You know that

Lorelei has changed, don't you, Brian? She's not the same at all. She belongs to a cult!"

"Oh, I wouldn't call it a cult," Brian said. "It's just a little experimental—"

"It's a *cult*," Charlotte hissed. "I can hear her in the night, casting spells. I told my daughter—" She left off suddenly, when Lorelei coughed loudly, and resumed her weeding.

Lorelei insisted on driving, so Brian got into the passenger seat of her Mercedes. He waved to Charlotte, but she merely stared. "Have you noticed anything strange about her?" he asked Lorelei.

"Strange?" said Lorelei. "Yes. It's too bad. Charlotte was always such a *nice* girl." She turned on the radio and fiddled with the tuning until she found a classical music station. "Now, where did you say we were going for dinner?"

"St. Mary's Curry House. On St. Mary's. It belongs to my brother's in-laws, so we're sure to get first-class treatment."

"Lovely!" said Lorelei. She detested Indian food, but India was such a spiritual country that she could never admit it.

Nixie was disappointed in herself. She'd been so proud of the information she had coaxed out of Derek last Friday that she'd gotten up her courage to return to The Palace tonight to try for more. She had dressed in her best outfit—a black satin tank top and her orange capris—and made an attempt to conceal the bruise on her cheek with some of Lorelei's makeup. She even borrowed Lorelei's lipstick—after she'd left on her date with Brian, of course. Since Nixie's close call at the Dharmarama, Lorelei wouldn't let her go anywhere further than the grocery store. But Nixie thought she could find out more about Penny and Roland from Derek. Unfortunately, the evening had not worked out as she'd planned.

"Hey, kid," was all that Derek had said when he saw her. He walked right past her and sat at a table in the far corner. Nixie ordered a beer and planned to follow him. But then everything had gone wrong. First of all, there was a different bartender at The Palace tonight, and he had humiliated her by asking loudly and rudely for her ID. Then, as she was fumbling with her wallet, a tall, lanky redhead in a tight black dress and killer heels came gliding past, swaying her hips, and sat next to Derek before Nixie could get anywhere near him. He had greeted the red head with a soft "Hi, babe," a kiss and a squeeze. Nixie had felt crushed.

Unfortunately, she had already ordered a beer, so she had no choice but to sit at the bar and take a few swallows before giving up and slinking out the door when Derek wasn't looking.

Defeated, she was trudging back to her van less than an hour after she'd parked it. She had blown her chance and she might as well go home. Maybe she would make herself a huge plate of spaghetti and meatballs. Or pick up a pizza on the way home. With Lorelei out for the evening, she could eat whatever, and wherever, she wanted. Maybe she'd rent a movie and rest. She was still achy and easily tired after her ordeal in the Dharmarama. There was nothing else she could find out from Derek tonight, anyway. She certainly had no intention of entering his house when he was out. She would love to snoop through his personal belongings, but she'd seen his dogs. Pirate and Hawk would be formidable security guards.

She had parked the van in a weedy, gravel driveway behind the abandoned grocery store down the street from Derek's house, and as she cut through the lot, she realized the back alley was terribly dark. Why? She looked up. The bulb was burned out in the streetlight. Or had it been smashed? Curious, Nixie took a few steps forward, to see if any broken glass was littering the ground. But then she heard a tiny noise, like the scrape of a shoe on cement, and she stopped.

In the open doorway of a garage directly across from Derek's backyard, she saw a figure leaning out into the alley. The man had his back to her. Instinct made her dart behind a garbage bin before she even had time to think. She pressed herself tightly against it, despite the rust and the stink of rotting vegetables and fish. Her heart began to beat faster. Who was this person? Was he watching for Derek? Lying in wait? She crouched and peeked cautiously out from behind the bin, keeping close to the ground. He was dressed in dark clothing and seemed to carry something in a sack that dangled from one hand. But it was hard to tell in the darkness. The fat, waxing moon was obscured by fast-moving clouds, and its light was intermittent. The man leaned out further around the side of the garage. He didn't turn around or notice Nixie. His body was taut, on high alert. He was intent on watching something down the lane. Nixie didn't dare to move.

After a few minutes, the man stepped out into the alley and approached Derek's back fence. The dogs barked. As the man came closer, they barked louder, more viciously, and began to leap into the air, throwing themselves against the chain link fence. The man turned around to make sure he was alone and Nixie got a look at his face. It was

Maurice Lemoine, esteemed author and famous psychic, creeping around in the alley like a criminal. Nixie shuddered. Maurice reached into the bag and tossed something over the fence to the dogs. Both of them immediately began snuffling the ground and then gobbled whatever it was he'd given them. Maurice came closer and dumped the whole contents of the bag over the fence.

As the dogs wolfed down their food, Nixie expected Maurice to make a run for the back door of Derek's house. She assumed he intended to break in, or that he had somehow lifted a key. But instead, he retreated to his post in the doorway of the garage across the alley. Why wasn't he entering the house? After going to the trouble of distracting the dogs with meat, why wasn't he trying to take advantage of the opportunity? Maybe he wanted the dogs to trust him in the future. But such a plan seemed like a lot of work. What made Derek worth all this trouble? Nixie thought back over all the clues she had picked up over the past few weeks.

Maurice could very well be the killer. He had profited from Yolanda's death, ending up with her tapes. He was one of the last people to see Obie alive. And if Summer had sold him that card full of false information on Penny, he would have been furious with her. He could have killed all three of them. Nixie wondered whether he'd seen her in the Dharmarama. She thought back to that night. The open door, that flash of light just before she entered. Someone had been out there waiting to throw the firebomb into the store to destroy evidence of Summer's murderer.

After they finished eating, the dogs sniffed the ground, looking for more, then Hawk, the Doberman, began walking in slow circles until he curled up on the ground to sleep. Pirate, the German shepherd, began to do the same. Nixie could see the dog was wobbly on his feet. He lurched sideways and seemed to fall to the ground. Maurice stepped out of the garage again. He approached Derek's chain-link fence, curled the fingers of both hands through the links, and shook. The resulting rattle should have woken the dogs. Instead, they remained motionless on the ground while Maurice unlatched the gate and crept into the yard. He had drugged the poor animals. Or worse.

Strangely, Maurice did not approach the house. Nixie watched, mystified, as he headed toward the heap of scrap metal that desecrated Derek's backyard. She heard a clatter and a clang, as his movements disturbed the balance of the junk pile. But the dogs didn't stir. Maurice slowed down and proceeded more cautiously through the hazardous jumble of debris. But before he had gone very far, he suddenly stumbled and fell. He thrust out his arms and caught hold of the handle of the old fridge that stood in the midst of the debris. He might have narrowly escaped a nasty gash and a tetanus shot, but he'd dislodged a cascade of car parts, pipes, and assorted junk that came tumbling down with a hideous racket. Maurice froze. He crouched low beside the fridge, hiding himself from view. But it wasn't necessary to hide. No one came to investigate the noise. Apparently the neighbors didn't care.

It pleased Brian that Tommy was impressed with Lorelei. Tommy had jumped to his feet right away to greet her, bowing ever so slightly when he shook her hand. Then, when the women weren't looking, Tommy had given Brian the thumbs-up.

Sarisha was a little cooler. She annoyed Brian by asking about Rhonda before they had even ordered their food.

Somehow she managed to mention Rhonda again twice during dinner, implying that Brian brought her to the restaurant often. Well, he did bring her to the restaurant often, but it was hardly polite to mention that in front of Lorelei. Luckily, Lorelei didn't seem to notice. She was happy. Every time he caught her eye, she smiled at him. But she didn't eat much, and she never finished her one glass of wine. She was quiet tonight, very demure and a little shy.

During a lull in the conversation, Brian tried to draw her out. "What's this new project you're involved in?" he asked. He pulled from his pocket the pamphlet Penny Johnson had given him. "Penny told me you're building a school of some kind?"

"It's just a little center for meditation," she said.

"What kind of meditation?" asked Sarisha. "Yogic? Transcendental?" She smiled as she picked up the pamphlet, and Brian was pleased with her change in attitude. She seemed genuinely interested.

"Oh, it's just a retreat, really," said Lorelei. "A place for relaxation and spiritual contemplation."

Brian frowned. "I thought it was for teaching or research or something. Penny said Waverley was investing in it as an educational thing."

Tommy looked up from his plate. "Waverley Forbes? The oil millionaire?"

"Yeah," said Brian. "Hey, did I tell you Penny Johnson's been dating him?"

"You're kidding!" said Tommy. "Well, good for her." He lifted his wineglass in a salute. "More power to her."

"So, you both know Penny Johnson, then?" asked Lorelei.

"Family friends," Brian explained. "Penny's husband

was a guide up at a lodge where our dad used to fish, and they got to be close. You remember him, Tom. He came up to the lake for Dad's last birthday, remember?"

"Of course. Pickerel feast," Tommy said. He sighed. "Those were the days."

Sarisha reached out and rubbed Tommy's upper arm. The couple looked at each other with kind, sad smiles.

Brian felt a stab of loneliness, watching them. "Anyway," he said, "this meditation center sounds like an exciting project." He poured himself another glass of wine. It was an excellent Pinot Noir Sarisha's father had sent to the table. Delicious. And Brian wasn't driving tonight, so he felt free to indulge himself. "I'd love to go there once it's built."

"Yes. Interesting," Tommy said. He too was imbibing a good share of the bottle. "And Waverley Forbes is investing?" He looked at Sarisha. "You know, honey, if Forbes is investing, maybe we should look into it, too."

"Our advisor did tell us to diversify," she answered. She opened the pamphlet. "Beautiful pictures. Where is this place?"

"That's an artist's conception," Lorelei explained. "The actual property hasn't been purchased yet. We're hoping to acquire a resort on Lake of the Woods."

"Penny would love that," said Tommy.

"Actually," said Brian. "It's the Kellsington place." He turned to Lorelei. "Roland was a guide for Hank Kellsington, too," he told her.

"Really?" she said. "Oh, yes. Penny mentioned that."

"How do you know Penny?" Tommy asked her. "And Waverley Forbes?"

"Like I told you, Lorelei does psychic readings," Brian said. "Waverley and Penny are clients of hers."

"Ah," said Sarisha. "My mother is into that. Do you do tarot readings?"

Lorelei nodded. "I work out of my home, on Grosvenor. I don't have my book with me, but I could give you my number, if you want to make an appointment."

Sarisha smiled, then returned her attention to the pamphlet. "Tommy, look at this." She passed it to her husband.

As he reached for the pamphlet, Tommy knocked over his wineglass, spilling a bit on the tablecloth before Sarisha righted it. "Oops," he said. He wiped the pamphlet clean with his napkin, though there wasn't a drop on it, and handed it back to Lorelei. "Can you give us your number? Maybe we'll give Sarisha's mom a reading for her birthday."

"She'd love that," said Sarisha.

Lorelei wrote her phone number at the top of the pamphlet. "It may not be…exactly the kind of reading she's used to," she said.

"Oh, she's open-minded," said Sarisha.

After dinner, when Tommy and his wife both stepped away from the table for a minute, Lorelei suggested a nightcap at the lounge of a nearby hotel. "Just the two of us?" she asked. She wanted to get away from Sarisha, who made her nervous. Sarisha's interest in Lorelei's business seemed forced, and Lorelei was afraid that she could see right through her with some kind of mystical Indian wisdom. Worse, she might trap Lorelei with tricky spiritual questions. Brian happily agreed to go. He was a little drunk, and Lorelei ushered him out the door before Sarisha's mother, no doubt even wiser, could waylay them.

They chose a booth in a quiet corner, and Lorelei sat beside him instead of across the table. After they settled in with their drinks, she began to talk about her work and how glad she was to be back in her home town, meeting so many interesting people and making friends. She returned to the topic of Penny, her favorite client, and how much she wanted to help her. "We have had a few readings so far," she said. "But it's difficult for Penny to relax. You know how anxious she is to find Roland's things."

Brian closed his eyes and groaned. "I'd like to forget about Roland Johnson's things for a while, if you don't mind."

"Penny showed me photographs of everything, of course."

"She has photographs of his stuff?" Brian frowned.

"For insurance purposes. Lots of people do it. And the photographs are a helpful guide during the readings. But I must say—" Lorelei sighed. "I must say that I doubt the things are as valuable as she believes they are. But I guess they have sentimental—"

Brian laughed. "You don't know much about jewelry, do you? Those are black pearls on that necklace. It's worth more than your sports car. It belonged to Roland's beloved mother, but after she passed away, he wouldn't even let Penny wear it out of the house. And that sapphire dinner ring—" He stopped himself. "I shouldn't talk like this," he said. "Penny is a client."

"She's a client of mine, too," said Lorelei smoothly. "I'm trying to help put her in tune with her husband's wavelength, but it isn't easy."

"Tell me something." Brian leaned forward. He was a little drunk by this point, and his speech was starting to slur. "How exactly do you do it? Can you hear Roland's voice?"

She laughed. "Not exactly." She laid a hand lightly on his arm. "It's more a matter of picking up the vibrations, or the traces of vibrations, that he left behind. For example, I could tell immediately that Roland was a strong-willed person."

Brian laughed. "That's one way to put it."

"And he had very specific desires regarding his estate. But he was also, well, you know…."

"Crazy," said Brian.

The scrap heap served as a primitive kind of burglar alarm, Nixie thought, but what was it protecting? It was at least twenty feet away from Derek's house. She was intensely curious about what Maurice was up to. She stole a little closer. She didn't want to risk being seen. Who knew what this dog-drugging scum might do to her if he caught her spying? But she wanted to check on the animals. Maurice had his back to the dogs, so she was able to creep close enough to hear the Doberman snoring. She thought she could see the shepherd breathing, but it was too dark to be sure. What if he'd given them an overdose?

Quietly, she backed away from Maurice and made her way into the lot where she'd parked her van. Maurice couldn't see or hear her from here. She took out her phone and gave him a call on his cell. He didn't answer at first. Naturally, he would have his ringer turned off. Burglary 101. But she hoped he was keeping it in his pocket, set to vibrate. When his answering service kicked in, Nixie hung up and dialed again. And again. On her sixth try, he answered in a harsh, frustrated whisper.

"What is it?"

"Mr. Lemoine?" said Nixie.

"Who is this?"

"I'm Sally Smith," she said, "from Channel Ten News. I'm standing outside your house right now, and—"

"My house?"

"I wondered if you'd care to comment on the possible involvement of the Soldiers Against Satan in the arson—"

"Arson? What's going on?"

"Well, the blaze seems to be under control now, but it's still too dangerous for the firefighters to enter your home."

"What the hell!" Maurice hung up. A few seconds later Nixie heard him come running down the lane. She ducked her head as he raced past and stayed hidden until she heard him gun his motor and peel away. Immediately, she dialed another number.

"St. Boniface Animal Clinic."

"Is Dr. Logan there?"

When Vivian came on the line, Nixie described the situation. She lied a little, telling Vivian she'd been looking after the dogs for a friend who'd gone away for the weekend. "I think they've been drugged. Or maybe even poisoned. Can you come?"

Vivian took down the address and said she'd be there as soon as she could.

Nixie grabbed her tool box from the back of the van and hurried to Derek's backyard, scrambling through the junk to the fridge. A quick glance showed her that Maurice had been trying to remove the padlock that held the chain on the fridge door. He had managed to saw it almost in half already. Nixie didn't have the proper tools to continue with that operation, but she thought she might be able to pick the lock. She wondered how much time she'd have before Vivian showed up.

"I wouldn't say that Roland was crazy, exactly," said Lorelei. "But it is sometimes difficult to determine exactly what he wanted."

"That," said Brian, "is an understatement. Poor Penny, she has no idea where he's stashed the rest of his stuff or what he wants her to do with his estate once she gets it all together."

"Yes, and that odd passage in the will certainly doesn't help."

"She showed you the will?"

"Of course. It's important I get to know Roland in order to communicate with him."

"And did reading the will give you any insights?"

Lorelei tried to gauge his tone of voice. There was an edge to it, a bit of cynicism that wasn't like him. "A bit," she said.

"A bit! That thing is a document in madness! She should sue the lawyer who drew it up."

Lorelei remembered the voice message Nixie had heard about the cryptic bequest. "Well, yes, the part about Derek is, oh!" She dropped her coaster and bent to retrieve it.

"You have to wonder," said Brian, "if it's animosity at work, or if it's all just part of the illness."

"I don't believe he was actually ill," she said with confidence. " I think he had his reasons."

"What possible reason could he have had?" Brian asked. "Except to create trouble between his nephew and his wife."

"Yes, how did he word it? 'I bequeath….' How did he put it? It was really quite…cryptic."

"'After the estate is consolidated,'" Brian recited. "'I bequeath to my nephew Derek Johnson the portion or percentage deemed by my wife to be his desert.'"

"His desert. Yes. What he deserved. Very strange indeed."

And very nasty, Lorelei thought, though of course she didn't say so. Roland must have known full well about his wife's affair with his brother, and he'd chosen to leave Penny a big guilt trip as legacy. She wondered what portion Penny *would* deem to be Derek's desert. She also wondered whether Derek knew the contents of the will.

"Have you talked to Derek?" she asked Brian.

"He thinks we should take the estate to probate without the missing items," Brian said. "He's willing to forego his share of their value, just to give Penny some closure."

So, Derek did know the contents of the will. "Yes, Derek is very helpful," she said. "He has been very cooperative."

"Well, he helped her search her house. He even helped her search *his* house, in case Roland had left the things there, and he went up to the cabin before she sold it and helped her search there as well. I think he's a bit tired of all this, and frankly so am I. Let's hope you'll have a breakthrough so we can put an end to it."

"To think that Roland hid away such a lovely necklace and ring." Lorelei looked pensive. "I suppose those are the most important pieces to find."

"The coin collection's worth more than you'd think, too," Brian said. "Roland's grandmother started the collection at the turn of the century. The appraiser who looked at the inventory was blown away."

Lorelei hid her smile in her wineglass. "Yes, that's exactly what Penny told me."

Lorelei's car was parked in the driveway, so Nixie knew she was back from her date with Brian. Lorelei always drove her own car wherever she went. But the house was dark.

Knowing Lorelei, she was probably asleep on the living room couch. She always tried to wait up for Nixie, but rarely managed to stay awake. Nixie glanced at her watch. Two in the morning. She turned her key in the lock with care. "We'll have to be quiet," she whispered, "so we don't wake up my sister."

"I feel like a teenager," Vivian whispered. "Sneaking in late after curfew." She tried to kick off her runners in the dark hallway and lost her balance, colliding with Nixie. The two women giggled.

"Shhh," said Nixie. "Wait here a second. I'll turn on some lights." She lugged the backpack up the stairs to her bedroom and put it in her closet. She'd told Vivian the pack was full of books, but it was clunkier than books. After she'd managed to pick the lock and open the fridge, all she'd found inside was Derek's tool box. Locked. Nixie had not had the time to open it there, so she had stashed it in her van just before Vivian arrived. She was grateful to Vivian. Vivian had examined the dogs and stayed with them until she could pronounce them in no danger. Someone had given them a mild sedative, she said, but they were breathing well, and their hearts sounded fine. The Doberman was even beginning to stir before they left.

So Maurice, Nixie thought, was probably not a killer. If he'd taken such care to give the dogs only a low dose, he was unlikely to throw people off balconies, stab them, and set them on fire.

Now, as she'd predicted, Lorelei was asleep. Nixie and Vivian had the night free and the place to themselves. They were going to make popcorn and watch the old movie channel on the TV in the basement. She tiptoed back downstairs, intending to close the pocket doors to the living room, so as not to wake Lorelei up. It was dark in the hall, and a spurt of irrational fear flared in Nixie's chest. She suppressed it. There was nothing to fear in her own home.

Then she paused. Voices. The television was on. She recognized the voice of a famous talk-show host. But there were live voices, too, and muffled laughter. It sounded like Lorelei's laugh, a happy laugh—a sound Nixie hadn't heard for years. She stepped into the living room. In the blue glow from the television, she saw two bodies lying entangled on the couch, one on top of the other. What the— Nixie snapped on the light.

The two bodies flew apart. It was Lorelei and a man. Lorelei shrieked. Her blouse was off, she was wearing only a lacy bra and a very disheveled skirt. "What are you doing up?" she yelled at Nixie. "You're supposed to be—"

"What's the matter?" Vivian had come running down the hall at the sound of the shriek. She had grabbed a purple umbrella from the front hall and now brandished it as a weapon.

The man sat up and handed Lorelei her blouse. He grinned at Nixie. He must be Brian Hale, she thought. What the hell is Lorelei doing?

"Are you all right?" asked Vivian. She searched Nixie's face for any sign of injury or pain.

"Yeah. Yeah. Everything's fine." Nixie put her hand on the umbrella and lowered it gently toward the ground. "This is my sister Lorelei."

Lorelei was sitting up now, too, buttoning her blouse as fast as she could. Vivian and Nixie stood motionless in the hallway, the umbrella limp in Vivian's hand. On TV, the studio audience erupted in cheers as a movie star bounded onto the stage.

"Nixie's sister? Pleased to meet you at last," said Vivian.

She stepped forward, as if to shake Lorelei's hand, then thought better of it.

Brian looked confused. "Your *sister*? This is your little sister?"

"Who are you?" Nixie asked.

Lorelei held up her hands. "Stop. Hold on, everybody." She ran her fingers through her hair, trying to smooth it back into place. She found the remote and switched off the TV. "Nixie, this is my friend Brian Hale. Brian, this is my sister, Nixie, and her—"

"My, uh, vet," said Nixie. "Bitsy's vet, Vivian."

"Vivian," said Lorelei flatly.

"Pleased to meet you," said Brian. If he thought it was odd that Bitsy's vet was visiting at two in the morning, he didn't say so.

After Vivian and Brian went home, the two sisters glared at each other.

"And *you* won't let *me* have anybody over!" Nixie began.

"Don't you know how risky it is to let people into the house? First you bring in Imogene! And now this, this, animal doctor that you're so in love with! Just because she—"

"She is a good person," Nixie shouted. "She is a fine person. She's, she's clean!"

"Clean! What are you trying to imply?"

"You think your lawyer isn't a risk?"

"Brian is Penny's lawyer, I'll have you know. So I was working."

"You were working, all right," Nixie said. "Working him up nice and good."

"Don't you *ever* talk to me like that!" Lorelei shouted.

"At least I was trying to work on this case. At least I was trying to get us ahead. While you're running around with Dr. Dolittle. Bringing her into the house! When are you going to understand that we can't afford to take risks like that?"

"For your information," said Nixie. "I *was* working. I was at Derek's house and I found something very important."

"What? Why didn't you say so? What did you find?"

Nixie sighed. "I don't know, yet," she said. "Come up to my room and take a look." They both forgot their argument as she led the way upstairs.

As Nixie tried to open Derek's tool box, the sisters recounted their evenings to each other. Then Lorelei waited, taking in the pictures on Nixie's bulletin board. She'd never really bothered to look at them before. They were almost all pictures of animals, a few landscapes. There was the vet, Nixie's idol, a photo Lorelei had seen before, but now she looked at it more closely. There was something about the smile that was…compelling. Strong. Lorelei felt something give in the pit of her stomach. If she ever had to go up against this woman, she wasn't sure she could win.

She left Nixie working on the lock and went down to the kitchen to make drinks. She found a bottle of vodka that had been sitting in the freezer since Christmas and decided to mix a couple of Bloody Marys. Her date with Brian had tired her out. The psychological strength it took to keep a step ahead of him had drained her. At first, he'd been alert to the danger of talking about his client, but as the evening wore on, he'd relaxed. Once he believed that she already knew everything, he had folded with pleasure. He was glad to let down his guard, and the wine and cocktails had eased the transition. But Lorelei was unable to relax. She had to stay at a distance from him and she found that strangely difficult, especially when she was in his arms. He still possessed whatever it was that had drawn her to him twelve years ago. The green eyes, maybe. The smile that made it so hard to resist sinking into him. The way his hands moved over her skin, as if she was the first and only woman he wanted, as if he needed her.

She gulped at her Bloody Mary and realized she'd finished it off still standing at the counter. She made herself another and sipped it more slowly, massaging the back of her neck with her fingers, trying to rid her body of tension. The effort of reading Brian's reactions, noting every shift in his mood, had left her with knots in her muscles.

As a matter of fact, all the readings she'd been doing lately were stressing her out, giving her headaches. She was working so hard for her clients, she barely had a moment to herself. Nixie didn't understand how difficult it was to read these people. You had to know them as no one had ever known them before. You had to learn to speak their language, and when they lacked a language, you had to invent one for them. The mental focus and emotional energy required were immense. Especially with Penny, who would give away absolutely nothing. Interpreting Penny was like struggling to read a book in the darkness. Straining every nerve.

Nixie would never understand the effort that Lorelei exerted for her sake. Nixie's part of the job was simple. She worked with her hands. Sure, she was clever, but the tasks she performed were rote. They involved none of the anxieties and exhaustion that plagued Lorelei. It was Lorelei who did all the planning, carrying this operation on her own shoulders.

A risk? Vivian was a risk? Nixie looked at the picture of Vivian she kept pinned to her bulletin board. Vivian's hair was loose in the wind and her smile was broad and open. Behind her, cumulus clouds tumbled in the clear blue sky. What was risky about that? She wiped away a tear and cursed her sister as she struggled with the lock on Derek's tool box. What did Lorelei know about risks? It was Nixie who took the real risks, picking pockets, picking locks. It was Nixie who did all the work. It was Nixie who crept into buildings and cut up her arms and legs by jumping through windows, while all Lorelei had to do was talk. And talk came easily to Lorelei. She could talk anyone into anything. Always could. It was a gift she'd been given. It occurred to Nixie that Lorelei had talked her into a lot of things, too. It was Lorelei who sent her in and out of those buildings. Then she had the nerve to talk about risks. If Nixie ever got caught, she'd be charged as a common thief, and she wasn't even sure whether her identification papers would hold up under the scrutiny of an arrest. She didn't even know her own real name. Most of the time, Nixie dealt with this eventuality by refusing to think about it, but once in a while, especially when Lorelei was in one of her moods, Nixie had paranoid fantasies about being arrested. Being deported. But to where?

She was getting nowhere with the pick she was using. She tossed it back in the box and tried with a darning needle. Her fingers were starting to cramp and her wrist still ached from the contortions she'd gone through to get the padlock off Derek's blasted refrigerator. She put down the needle and flexed her hands and fingers. She couldn't afford to injure her hands. She needed them for her work. Lorelei would never understand the discipline required to maintain the dexterity of the fingers, the hours of tai chi and piano practice, the mental effort of getting the energy flowing through the veins and muscles of the body. Nixie was tired of it. Most of all she was tired of not being appreciated for it. It took years of dedication to fine-tune the skills necessary to pick a lock. While to unlock a secret took only a few simple lies.

Without Nixie, Lorelei was nothing but a storyteller.

"Take a break and have a drink," Lorelei said as she stood in the doorway, holding two frosty glasses. "Is it a tough lock?"

"It's a cheap enough little lock," Nixie said, "but it's getting the best of me. Stupid Canadian Tire Special!" She pounded the top of the safe with her palm and suddenly it sprang open.

The two sisters stared at the contents. They stared at each other. Nixie laughed out loud, then covered her mouth with her hand.

"That dirty little thief," said Lorelei. She crossed over to the bed as Nixie began to lift items out of the safe.

Their argument was forgotten and their anger at each other vanished as they sat down together to examine more closely the coin collection of Roland Johnson and the long-lost pearls and sapphire ring of his beloved mother.

CHAPTER TWELVE

In retrospect, Maurice's actions made perfect sense. Although he had blown the minor details of Penny's life, thanks to Nixie's pink correction fluid, he had known the larger, more pertinent facts. Putting those facts together now, Lorelei and Nixie figured it out. Derek hated Penny for ruining his parents' lives and resented her for living a comfortable lifestyle while he worked two jobs to support his sick mother. When Roland died, Derek had stolen his choicest treasures and hidden them away. He probably considered them his due. He might have planned to sell them someplace far away after Penny had given up trying to find them. In the meantime, Penny had the estate to deal with. She knew the coins and jewels existed, but she didn't know where they were. She had searched everywhere—even in Derek's house. That was probably when Derek had transferred his spoils to his tool box. He had taken that box with him everywhere, Lorelei remembered. He'd even had it with him at Penny's birthday party, right under her nose. When he couldn't take it with him, he locked it in the fridge, which was hidden in plain sight and surrounded by rusted metal and two watch dogs.

Yolanda had known somehow. She had divined that Derek was hiding something. Maurice had wanted to pass along these words of wisdom, to be the one to lead Penny to the fridge. But when he botched Penny's reading, she would no longer listen to him. So he'd planned to get it himself and reveal it in some other way. Then he'd been interrupted by Nixie's phone call.

"Maurice must have freaked when he got back to Derek's and found the fridge empty," said Nixie.

"He probably thinks Derek has moved his stash somewhere else," Lorelei speculated.

But Maurice had given up looking for this particular stash. After the horror of the fire at the Dharmarama and the phone call that clearly threatened his own home with firebombing, Maurice announced he was leaving town. Reporter Kent Mason and his television crew caught up with him outside his Winnipeg home, where movers were loading a van with Maurice's newly purchased rugs, lamps, and furniture. The For Sale sign was back on the front lawn. Maurice was returning to his mother's house in Lorette, he told Kent, and his things were going into storage while he reassessed his life. He would not be staying in Lorette, he said pointedly into the camera. He and his fiancée were taking a tropical vacation and then moving to a larger center, someplace free from "provincial attitudes and religious terrorism." His fiancée came to stand by his side and he snuggled her under his arm. Lorelei recognized her as the assistant who had introduced him at his performance.

"That's the girl from the Palace!" Nixie cried when she saw the assistant's face. "The one who was flirting with Derek."

"That figures," said Lorelei. "It was her job to distract him while Maurice broke into the fridge—Yolanda's 'place that was no longer cold.'"

Because of the fallout from the murders, several Seekers had backed out of Spirit Fest. But others had signed on, saying they felt safer being out of town than in the midst of the "psychic wars," as Kent Mason had dubbed them, in Winnipeg. Kent was coming as well, and to make up the shortfall, Lorelei had recruited Brian. Waverley's people were taking care of the meals and wine. Only Penny, though thoroughly disillusioned with Maurice Lemoine, was still not sold on Lorelei Good. Penny spoke at length about the unreliability of Lorelei's methods, her dependency on the full moon.

"But if we hold Spirit Fest on the Moon of Takara," Waverley declared, "that won't be an issue." He held forth on the topic of the sacred, festive evening, its history and spiritual significance. Several of the Seekers, to Lorelei's great surprise, claimed to know all about it.

"Oh yes," said one newcomer. "It's in the writings."

"What writings?" asked Penny.

"The ancient writings, of course," was the reply.

Nixie and Lorelei had gone over their own plans again and again, purchasing equipment, gathering information, anticipating problems, and inventing backup plans. Surely nothing would go wrong. Their future depended on the results of this seance. If Lorelei could produce proof that the spirits were present, the deal would go through, and they would become the proud owners of a luxury lakeside resort worth over three million dollars. Surely a sapphire ring, a string of black pearls, and a nineteenth-century coin collection constituted that proof.

Spirit Fest was only three days away when Agnes phoned to ask Lorelei if she had gotten the deposit together yet. "Hank signed the papers, so everything's in order," she said. "But something else has come up." She told Lorelei that Jack Barnes had received an offer on the cottage for three point two million, and neither he nor Agnes's lawyer were inclined to turn it down in order to hold it for someone who was only offering two million—someone who couldn't even make the deposit. "I'm sure if you could only give us the deposit, we can keep holding the cottage for you. But I'm afraid, with the season getting later, and no other offers on the horizon, we can't hold it forever. Hank does want to sell it. He'll be ever so angry if we're stuck with it for another winter."

Lorelei and Nixie discussed their options. At this point, they were confident that Lorelei could pass the Spirit Test, but they still had no way to raise the necessary deposit, except to sell the diamonds. But it wasn't possible to sell them all at once. Any legitimate dealer would demand proof of ownership before turning over that much cash, and the arrangements would take time. They would have to find the right buyer. After all, Max's diamonds were undoubtedly stolen property, and they had most likely been stolen in Winnipeg. The police might very well have a detailed description of them. If the stones were identified and their source traced, things could get very ugly.

Finally, Lorelei went to the bank and got a certified check made out to Agnes for two hundred thousand. Then she took the diamonds out of the safety deposit box and carried them over to Agnes's house herself. She made sure that the door to the sitting room was locked, to prevent Susanne from barging in, and opened the velvet bag, tipping the jewels gently out onto a chamois cloth.

"Our founder brought them over from South Africa last year," she said. "A gift from a grateful client."

"Harry will find it a bit unorthodox," said Agnes. She picked up one of the diamonds between her thumb and forefinger. "Very well cut!" she remarked.

"We always prefer to deal with the natural elements of the Earth, such as minerals," said Lorelei, "rather than having to deal with money."

"Oh, of course," said Agnes. "Guru Vijayan was the same way."

"They do have monetary value, of course. They're worth at least three hundred thousand, wholesale. So along with the check, we are giving you a deposit equivalent to the five hundred thousand your lawyer requested."

"Oh, yes, of course. Harry is sure to see reason," said Agnes. "I'll make sure of it. Let me just write you out a receipt." She pulled papers and a pen from her desk.

"Tell him it's only temporary," said Lorelei. "Just to secure the cottage. You'll hold the diamonds only until our cash-flow problem is resolved and then I'll gladly replace them with a more conventional down payment."

"I'll stand up to him, if I have to," said Agnes. "After all, it's our money, not his. Honestly, I feel as though sometimes Harry bullies me. But I'll not be bullied. Not any more. Since you and I have been working together, I feel so much stronger." She placed the diamonds in the Kellsington family safe, built into the wall of the dining room.

It was true. Agnes actually looked stronger. She stood taller, with her shoulders straighter. She had even bought herself a cheerful red headscarf, the first hint of color Lorelei had seen her wear. The power of her mother was diminishing, thanks to Lorelei's talent and hard work, and Agnes was grateful. She admitted to Lorelei, in confidence of course, that she was no longer ashamed of expressing her love for Hank in a physical way. She accepted his desires as her own. She was starting to look forward to Hank's return, instead of dreading it.

The following day she sent over official acceptance of Lorelei's offer to purchase, all signed and witnessed. "Harry was livid at first," she confessed over the phone. "He insisted on having the diamonds appraised."

"That's only natural," said Lorelei. "I don't blame him. He's looking out for your best interests."

Nixie rented a twelve-foot fishing boat in Kenora and towed it by trailer to the marina at Clearwater Bay. The lake and surrounding landscape were breathtakingly beautiful, but she didn't have much time to enjoy the view. She took her boat around the opposite side of the island from Agnes's cottage, beached it, and camouflaged it with branches. Then she hiked up to the cottage, unpacked her tools, and got to work.

With a screwdriver, she removed the grate on the air vent and placed a small tape recorder inside it. She inserted a tape, replaced the grate, and stepped across to the other end of the room to test the remote. When she pressed play, nothing happened. She adjusted her aim, and the first few bars of piano music filled the room. Too loud. She turned down the volume and rewound the tape. This time, the opening strains were almost inaudible. They rose in volume gently and then faded out completely. She waited sixty seconds until the vocals began, rising and falling before the tape subsided into silence. It took a long time to affix the remote to the underside of the table in exactly the right location. Finally, it was perfect. But that was only the first of the little tasks she had to complete in order to set the stage for the most important performance of Lorelei's career.

The following day, when the Seekers arrived, there was no sign Nixie was on the island. They all wandered through the foyer, admiring the skylights and the high, spacious loft enclosed by its cedar railing, behind which they could see a pair of massive stereo speakers and the glint of bottles from a well-stocked bar. Agnes led the way through to the rear of the house, where the back staircase split in two. East wing to the right, west wing to the left. As promised, Agnes gave Lorelei the room she'd slept in on her earlier visits. Penny was right across from her, while Kent Mason and Brian Hale bunked together in a room down the hall. The others were in the west wing. For Waverley, who hadn't yet arrived, Agnes had reserved the master bedroom. For herself, she preferred the ground-floor guest room. "The sound of the waves lapping at the shore is heavenly. It always lulls me to sleep."

From her bedroom window, where she sat planning her evening's performance, Lorelei could hear the Seekers gathered on the flagstone patio for a casual lunch. Their various conversations overlapped as the breeze carried their voices through the trees.

"Summer Sweet was always so welcoming," she heard one woman say. "I barely knew her but she always took *such* an interest in me, asking about the kids and—"

"Oh, yes, she was a lovely woman. It's just tragic to think that her life was snuffed out by those awful fanatics."

"Once I've wrapped up this business with the estate," Penny was telling someone, "I'm selling the house and moving to Victoria, where it's sunny and warm nearly twelve months of the year."

"Have you ever been up the Sunshine Coast?"

"I'd absolutely love to!" said Penny. "My hairdresser went up to Gibson's Landing last summer, and he said it was charming. And of course I've always longed to go farther north. I saw a beautiful film about Haida Gwaii on the television. Have you ever seen pictures of it?"

Lorelei smiled to herself in the privacy of her room. Down below, the white bow of Waverley's entry-level yacht was pulling up at the dock. Everything was perfect.

CHAPTER THIRTEEN

"*I'm here*," said a voice from somewhere deep in Lorelei's throat. Her lips were barely moving. She felt Brian's grip tighten on her hand, squeezing her fingers together.

Waverley's hand tightened, too, and she sensed his excitement.

"Gloria?" he asked.

"*I'm here.*" The voice was hollow and strangely disembodied, though it clearly emanated from Lorelei.

"Oh my God," whispered Kent Mason.

"Be quiet, Kent," said Waverley. "Gloria? Is that really you?"

"*My love….*" Lorelei slumped forward on the table, letting her body go limp. Her hands slipped out of the hands of Waverley and Brian, and fell beneath the table.

"Are you all right?" asked Brian. He placed a hand on her shoulder.

"Will you speak to me, Gloria?" Waverley asked the air. "Oh, darling, I've been trying to reach you, to tell you how sorry I am, how wrong I was. I shouldn't have promised I could find a cure for you. Lorelei was right. It was your time to move on into the spirit world, but I didn't give you time to prepare. I was in denial."

"*It's all right, Waverley,*" said Gloria's voice. She sounded calmer, gentler. "*I am at peace now. You should be at peace, also.*"

"Are you really…all right?" Waverley sounded astonished. He had spent so much time convincing himself that Gloria was suffering from her untimely death that he couldn't believe what he was hearing.

"*Yes, Waverley, I must tell you the truth. I was fully prepared to die.*"

"Prepared? But I told you to have hope," Waverley cried. "I kept you believing in those faith healers and vitamin salesmen. Those charlatans. Even on that very last day, in the last hour of your life, I was deceiving you."

"*You were only deceiving yourself,*" whispered Gloria.

"Myself?"

"*Yes, darling. We deceived each other. In those last months, I knew I was dying. I said nothing to you because I wanted you to have hope. But in my heart, I was preparing myself. Dying is natural, Waverley. It is a path we all take.*"

"I only wish we had said goodby honestly to each other," said Waverley.

"*We can say goodby now, my love, for now the truth has been told. It is time for you to let me go and to open your heart to another.*"

"I could never…." said Waverley, but even as he said it, his eyes darted across the table toward Penny.

Penny was rapt, hanging on Gloria's every word. Perhaps she had only hated Lorelei for being the conduit to Gloria, the last remaining link to the woman Waverley loved above all others. If Gloria was going to release him from his wedding vows, Penny didn't want to miss a single syllable.

"I don't want to say goodby," Waverley confessed.

"*I will still watch over you, Waverley. I will still speak to you from time to time, when you call me. But I can no longer be your wife. I have moved beyond that. You have no idea…how beautiful…it is here.*" Her voice was beginning to fade out.

"Oh, this is so wonderful," said Waverley. "But—is it really you? How can I know? Send me a sign—let me know …." As he spoke, the high notes of a piano sounded in the background, barely audible above his voice.

"Is that music?" Kent asked. "Do you hear that?"

"Shhh," said Penny. The piano fell silent.

Brian was the only person moving. He was rubbing Lorelei's back, his fingers circling gently between her shoulder blades. She felt his fingers move down to her wrist and feel for her pulse.

For a full minute, the Seekers sat still around the table, straining their ears.

Then quietly, gradually, the unmistakable voice of Sam Cook, singing "You Send Me," filtered into the room.

"Our song," whispered Waverley.

The voice echoed with unearthly beauty through the air ducts. Even Lorelei felt the hairs on the back of her neck begin to rise.

In the silence that followed, they heard nothing but the wind caressing the poplar trees outside the cottage.

From her pup tent in the forest, Nixie could see the cheerful lights of the cottage and hear the tinkle of silverware, laughter, and conversation, all evening long. She ate a cold sandwich and drank a warm beer. She couldn't even light a fire to keep the bugs away, so she was imprisoned in the tent.

Through the screen door, she could see a small corner of the sky, with its wild conglomeration of stars. The Seekers were right about one thing. It was great to be out of the city, away from all that light pollution.

Nixie thought of the things Vivian had taught her about the world. When the sky is scudded with clouds like mackerel scales, it's going to rain. When the leaves on the trees grow pale, a storm is coming, and if you count the seconds between lightning and thunder, you can tell how far away it is. If the sky turns green and hail begins to fall, take cover. A tornado's on its way. Lorelei didn't know any of those things, and the colleges Nixie had gone to didn't teach them. You had to be outside in the summertime to know them. There were things to learn about winter, too, and Nixie looked forward to that.

Soon, she would go camping with Vivian up at Revelation Lake. Once Spirit Fest was over, Lorelei could spare her for a few days. Nixie hadn't had a vacation since, well, come to think of it, she had never had a vacation. She imagined camping out under the stars and telling Vivian all the stories she had learned from books about the constellations. Cassiopeia and Orion were her favorites. She wondered if Vivian had ever noticed how many animals were up in the sky. There were spiders and bears and rams and bulls and fish…. She wondered what sign Vivian was. Vivian was twenty-five years old, but Nixie didn't know when her birthday was. She tried to guess, but then she decided it didn't matter. There would be lots of time to find out. Once Nixie was living out here on this island, not in a tent but in the cottage with its magnificent view of the lake, she would have Vivian over to visit whenever she wanted. She wouldn't have to pretend that Bitsy was sick.

Lorelei took some time to recover, but soon she was "on" again. After a round of drinks to refresh the Seekers, they gathered again at the dining-room table and took turns asking questions of their loved ones in the beyond. Most of the spirits chose to communicate by giving Lorelei their messages telepathically, and she passed them along in her normal voice. Spirit guides, as she had explained earlier, were usually unnecessary during the Moon of Takara. Some Seekers, such as new member Mary Jane, received mild messages of encouragement from distant relations. Others, like Kent Mason, were disappointed. Kent's late grandfather was not answering his summons this evening, Moon of Takara notwithstanding. Agnes's mother, of course, was never summoned in public. Agnes's nerves wouldn't be able to stand it, for you just never knew what Gladys might say. About an hour into this second session, when everyone was weary and ready to quit for the night, Lorelei suddenly demanded complete silence.

"I'm getting a signal," she said. "An entity who has been trying to get through all evening. Someone with a message for…Penny."

"Oh!" said Penny, as if she'd been stuck by a pin.

Waverley squeezed her hand. "Listen carefully," he said.

Penny squirmed in her chair. "Who, who is it?"

Lorelei made her wait. She raised her head and stared up into the shaft of moonlight that came pouring through the open window. After a while she nodded. "Yes," she said. "I see. All right." She turned to face Penny. "Penny, there is someone here to speak to you."

Penny seemed paralyzed. "Who—who is it?" she managed to ask.

"It is the spirit of your husband, Roland," said Lorelei.

Penny's shoulders sagged in relief.

Waverley put his arm around her. "I told you," he said. "You see? It's happening."

"He says he has been listening every time that you asked him questions, but he did not come before because he was angry. He says there has been another spirit interfering. A spiteful entity who can't let go because you have held on to certain things of his. Certain feelings and…objects. Certain tangible objects. Do you know what they are?"

"I don't know!" said Penny. She seemed panic-stricken. She stood up and began to back away from the table. She seemed terrified her affair was about to become public knowledge.

Lorelei decided to make her suffer a little. Payback. "He says you do know," she said. "I am getting an image of a staircase or a suitcase. Papers and…blue ribbon?"

Penny raised both hands to her mouth. She stepped backward, banging her head against a stuffed fish on the wall.

"They belong to a spirit who resents your attempts to contact your husband. With this type of intense possessiveness, it's usually a romantic attachment."

Penny blushed and Lorelei decided she'd better back off. Penny was just vain enough to believe that her rival suitors continued to vie for her affections in the afterlife. But if she suspected that Lorelei really knew her secrets, she would hate and fear her more than ever.

"But Roland says if you promise to burn these objects, he will help you to find what you have been seeking all this time. It is closer than you think."

"Oh, my."

"Do you understand?"

"Y-yes. Yes, I do know what he means, and I'll burn

them, all of them, I promise! Oh, my! I had no idea what I was doing."

"He has forgiven you now."

"Oh, thank goodness," cried Penny.

"He says he has summoned you here for a reason. He has guided us all to this place because—"

"Roland!" Penny cried. She raised her hands into the beam of moonlight. "Tell me, please. Where is the rest of your mother's jewelry? Where is your coin collection, and what did you do with the savings bonds?"

Lorelei remained silent for a long time. In all her years of conducting seances, she'd never seen anyone interrupt a spirit before. She thought it might be wise to discourage the practice.

"What's happening?" Penny demanded.

Lorelei decided to relent. "He's saying that what you are looking for is right below you."

Penny jumped to her feet. She picked up the chair cushion and checked underneath.

"He is saying something about fish," said Lorelei. She turned to Penny. "Is he a Pisces?"

"Taurus," said Penny. She bent down and looked under the chair.

"He's saying something about a fishing boat," said Lorelei. "Water and a boat or a house by the water. A houseboat?" She turned to Agnes. "Is there a houseboat?"

"Not that I know of," said Agnes.

"Oh, it doesn't make any sense," said Penny in despair.

"Oh, dear, he's fading," said Lorelei. "I can barely hear him. He's…fading out."

"Wait, Roland!" cried Penny. She held up a hand as if hailing a taxicab. "Come back!" She crossed the room to the window and stood in the moonlight, wringing her hands.

"He's…oh, he's gone," said Lorelei.

Penny whirled around and glared at her. "Get him back!"

"Now, Penny," said Waverley. He left his chair to go to her side. He put an arm around her shoulder. "Take heart, Penny. I'm sure he'll come back. You must be patient."

"Wait," said Lorelei. "At the end, there, when his voice was fading, I was receiving images, instead of words, a series of pictures flashing past." She rubbed her eyes.

Brian handed her a glass of water. "You need to rest," he said. "She needs to rest, everybody."

"Wait. What did you see?" Waverley asked. He drew Penny back to the seance table.

"Something bright and shiny," Lorelei said. "I was getting the image of, well, fish hooks, and lures. Bright, shiny lures—and a blue stone of some kind."

"A blue stone!" Penny cried. She pulled away from Waverley and looked about the room. "Where is it?"

"Perhaps we should look down by the lake. In the boat shed!" Agnes suggested. "Roland used to come fishing up here with Hank!"

After much animated discussion, Waverley lit a kerosene lantern and led the way down the steep flagstone steps to the Kellsington boathouse. Brian took up another lantern and offered Lorelei his arm. Penny and Agnes came next, followed by the rest of the Seekers, carrying as many flashlights and candles as they could find.

There was only room in the boathouse for two. Agnes entered first and Penny followed. The others waited outside, listening, as the two women poked around. They heard them overturning crates and rummaging through heavy objects. A pair of oars fell to the ground.

Lorelei finally peered inside to offer assistance. "Fish

hooks and lures," she reminded them. "Are there fish hooks anywhere in here?"

"Hank's tackle box," said Agnes. "It should be somewhere…." She shone her flashlight along the shelves near the ceiling and finally illuminated a battered red tackle box, on the highest shelf. "I don't think I can reach it."

"Let me," said Waverley. The women moved out of the shed to let him enter. He reached up and took the box down from its shelf. "It's heavy," he said. He brought it out and set it down on the dock. The Seekers all crowded around, training their lights on the tackle box as Waverley unlatched it and lifted the lid. Inside, among the tangle of fishing line and lures, an array of scattered coins and necklaces lay glittering like pirate's treasure. In the center lay an enormous, brilliant, blue sapphire, set into a thick gold ring.

"Incredible," breathed Penny. She kneeled to get a closer look, stroked a string of black pearls with one finger. "Why, Lorelei…." She turned to look at Lorelei, her eyes shining with gratitude and wonder. "It's here! It's been out here all along!" She turned back to the box, lifting out the sapphire ring and placing it on her finger. "Why would he leave it here? In a tackle box? I can't believe it!"

"I can," said Brian.

"Derek is going to be *so* surprised!" said Penny.

Nobody else said anything. They all gaped at the long-lost coins and jewelry. Lorelei could hear their ragged, irregular breathing, imagined the wild beating of their hearts. Exhaustion washed over her. She closed her eyes, savoring the lake breeze on her face. Soon, she would sleep. But for now, she waited, listening to the steady, vigorous lapping of the waves on the shore, the far call of a loon. Then a sudden thud as Penny, overcome with wonder, sat down heavily on the boathouse steps. Lorelei's victory was complete.

At two o'clock in the morning, the muted beeping of Lorelei's travel alarm woke her, and she shut it off with a flick of her finger. She sat up and pulled her black silk dressing gown around her shoulders. Then, in her bare feet, she crept down the hall. She wanted to remove a few items from the dining room, just in case someone got curious and decided to nose around. She didn't entirely trust Kent Mason not to attempt some kind of exposé. He had been pretty ruthless in his reporting lately. As she passed Penny's room, she noticed the bed was empty, still made. Unless she was very much mistaken, Penny was tucked up tight beside Waverley in the master bedroom. Last night, Lorelei had listened in as Waverley cornered Penny alone and invited her to his room for a nightcap. Penny had put up a few practical arguments, but the attempt was feeble, and Waverley had easily persuaded her. In her state of elation, Penny had been in no mood to resist him. Yet another reason for Waverley to be thankful for Lorelei's powers.

Downstairs in the dining room, Lorelei used a penlight and a tiny screwdriver to remove the tape recorder and replace the vent cover. She peeled the remote from under the table and placed all the evidence in the deep pockets of her bathrobe. Then she padded back upstairs. No one was stirring. She was the only one awake. Or so she thought. Just as she was two feet from the door to her own room, she heard a low voice.

"Lorelei?" It was Brian. "What are you doing?"

"I couldn't sleep," she whispered.

"Neither could I. I've just been lying in bed thinking about everything that's happened tonight. It was so amazing." He was moving toward her.

She backed away, but he followed her right into her room. "You're so amazing," he said. He was reaching for her. He was going to put his arms around her. He would feel the tools and the tape and the remote in the pockets of her dressing gown.

In one quick movement, she unbelted the gown and let it fall gently to the plush carpet. It made barely a sound. She stood naked before him.

"Oh wow," he said. "Baby."

Lorelei backed up all the way to the bed. And he followed her, kicking the door gently shut behind him.

Lorelei and Brian slept late. By the time they awoke, the other Seekers were already up and out, enjoying the woods and the lake. Although the seance was over, Spirit Fest would continue for another few days of meetings, relaxation, and spiritual cleansing, traditionally accomplished in a hot tub with an iced drink or two for nourishment. Waverley was going home early, as his flight to Greece departed tomorrow at the crack of dawn, but he was leaving his yacht anchored in the bay with his cook and other staff on board to make sure the Seekers had everything they could possibly want.

Lorelei stood at the window, luxuriating in the sensation of the sun's warm rays, the smell of pine trees, and the happy sounds of Seekers splashing in the lake. She could feel a tightness in her chest, and the familiar coppery taste in her mouth that hinted of a fever. But she tried to ignore it. She was too happy to let these minor symptoms ruin her day. "Let's go for a swim," she suggested. But Brian had fallen back to sleep. Quietly, she put on her bathing suit, slipped a sundress on over it, and stepped into beach thongs.

As she passed Agnes's room, she saw her hostess rummaging in her closet. Her suitcase lay open on the bed and the bedspread was covered with her belongings.

"Oh, Lorelei!" Agnes called. "You'll never guess what's

happening. It's Hank! He's come back. I'm going home right away. I'll catch a ride into town with Waverley and Penny."

Susanne had called from Winnipeg, she explained, to say that Mr. Kellsington was returned from India and waiting at home for his wife. He'd been home since yesterday morning, she said, but Susanne hadn't been able to reach Agnes by phone—the connections were so poor out here. As Agnes stuffed a handful of blouses into the suitcase without even folding them, Lorelei noticed her hands were shaking.

"You're not afraid, are you?" she asked quietly, prepared to prescribe some soothing affirmations.

"Oh, no," Agnes confided. "I'm just so excited, I'm trembling. I've been sending Hank messages, through the ethereal plane, sending him vibrations of love and, well, you know…and he must have received them. From halfway around the planet. It's a miracle."

"That's wonderful."

"Agnes!" called Waverley from down the hall. "If you're ready, I'll send someone down with your bags." He was waiting in the living room, having coffee with Penny. His servants began to cart the bags down the steep shore to the Bowrider. "One more thing before we go," he said. "There's the matter of the purchase." He handed Lorelei a check made out to the Psychic Renaissance Foundation. Eight hundred thousand dollars. "That brings my contribution to one million," he said. "With Agnes's generous donation of a million, in the form of a discount, and PsyRen's million, this makes us all three equal partners."

"Yes," said Lorelei, though it wasn't exactly true. The title to the cottage would be in her company's name. An electric buzz emanated from the check she held in both hands and vibrated up her arms into her chest.

Waverley raised his coffee cup to Agnes and Lorelei.

"This is a great day," he said. "We are making a giant step toward furthering human knowledge of the ethereal and bringing the truth to the world. Remember, Lorelei, what the spirit guide told us? 'To open the mind, the wise man opens the minds of his fellow travelers on earth.'"

"To learn, you must teach," she replied.

Beside him, Penny was beaming happily, all her reservations gone. A good thing, too, because Lorelei had the feeling Penny was going to be with Waverley for a long time to come. She was holding her purse in both arms, clutching it tightly to her chest, and Lorelei guessed the pearls and the sapphire ring were stowed away in there. Lorelei would have to warn her somehow about Derek. It would only be right. And she'd also look into this matter of the savings bonds that Penny had mentioned. Then there was Raymond's ring, and some secrets of Gloria's still to come. Agnes, too, would need further help. Her psyche was deep and complex, a rich mine of repression and guilt. Yes, there was lots of work for the future. And then there would be all the new clients the center would bring in.

Lorelei said her goodbys to Penny and Waverley. To Agnes, she said, "I'll drop by the bank as soon as I get into town tomorrow. Then I'll come by the house and we'll finish the paperwork, all right?"

"No rush," Agnes said. "Stay a little longer at the cottage, if you like." She gave Lorelei a sly, suggestive smile. Her eyes flicked toward the stairs to the upper room where Brian lay sleeping. "Enjoy yourselves. We can finalize things any time next week."

Lorelei had no intention of leaving it until next week. She wouldn't be able to raise the remaining million dollars tomorrow, of course—she'd have to stall Agnes a bit longer on that. But now that she had Waverley's contribution, she could put down enough cash to get her diamonds back. Hank Kellsington's return made her nervous. Would he convert to PsyRen as easily as his wife had done? She hoped he'd be grateful for the change in Agnes's attitude toward physical expressions of love. But she also feared he'd be suspicious of the unconventional arrangements surrounding the purchase of the cottage. After all, he was a sophisticated businessman. If he changed his mind about the real estate deal before Lorelei could raise another million through a mortgage, he could bring the whole project to a halt. She had worked so hard to set up the flax farm and then the cottage as the ideal location for the research center. It would be impossible, she thought, to start all over again, making the same claims for a third piece of property—at least not with this same group of people.

As he stepped into the bathroom off Lorelei's room, Brian noticed her bathrobe had slipped from its hook. He picked it up and saw Agnes's nylon string bag lying underneath. Agnes had been in such a hurry, she'd forgotten it. He smiled as he remembered how excited she'd been to hear her husband had returned. She'd come rushing through the bedroom an hour ago, waking him up, searching for some last minute necessity. Back in his own room, he placed Agnes's bag into his own suitcase to take it back to town for her. As he finished dressing, he gazed out the window, admiring the view all the way to the lakeshore. Lorelei was there, in a white bathing suit, diving off the end of the dock. Deciding to join her, he changed into his trunks and made his way down.

Others had had the same idea. Kent Mason and some of the younger new members were dog-paddling around in the bay. One of them floated in a huge inner tube. But Brian couldn't see Lorelei. He splashed water on his face and chest and jumped into the deep water at the end of the dock. He hadn't gone swimming for a while, and the shock of the cold water took his breath away for a moment. Then he began to swim. He kept himself parallel to the island, following a curve in the shore, and when he rounded the turn, he saw her. She was standing on a rocky outcropping high above and overhanging the beach. She bent her knees and bounced lightly on her feet. She raised her arms above her head. Then she kicked off, her body arcing through the air. With her spine straight as an arrow, she shot into the water. Brian was impressed. He began to swim toward the cliff, to join her. She emerged from the water before he got there, pulled herself out onto the rocks and lay back in the sunshine, resting. She looked beautiful there on the rocks, and memories of their explorations together last night in her bed rushed through his mind. He swam slowly, trying not to splash. He wanted to surprise her, to pull himself up on the rock beside her and take her in his arms.

But she heard him coming. He saw her raise herself on her elbows and lift her hand to her forehead to keep the sun out of her eyes as she looked for the source of the splashing. Then she saw him, and she smiled. She sat up on the rock, the sunlight gleaming in her wet hair, and beckoned him toward her.

CHAPTER FOURTEEN

A fleet of shiny, expensive summer cars lined the length of the circular drive in front of the Kellsington house, and Lorelei had to park in the street. She hurried past a Sunbeam, a Jaguar, and a Triumph, ran up the stone steps, and peered through the glass pane of the front door. The white curtains were swept aside and she could see into the vestibule. A large trunk lay open on the Persian rug, with a man's overcoat folded on top. On the table, beside the usual vase of exotic flowers and the neatly folded daily paper, sat a man's briefcase and hat. There was no sign of their owner. Lorelei rang the bell and waited.

She knew she wasn't expected. But she'd decided she couldn't wait until tomorrow morning. After her swim in the lake, she and Brian had spent a pleasurable hour in bed, but afterwards, lying there, Lorelei had become restless. The more she thought about Hank Kellsington, the more she worried. She began to wonder why he had returned so early. She doubted he was responding to Agnes's love vibes. She was afraid his lawyer Harry might have contacted him. Was Harry becoming suspicious that PsyRen was bilking Agnes?

Perhaps Hank was flying home to investigate this new coterie his wife had become so deeply involved with. So, a mere two hours after Agnes had left the cottage, Lorelei followed. She and Brian caught a boat ride with a couple of other Seekers and were on their way in no time, much to Brian's disappointment—he'd looked forlorn as they'd parted in the Deception Bay parking lot to drive home in their separate cars. Back in Winnipeg, she'd stopped at the bank, deposited Waverley's check, and now she was here to redeem her diamonds. It was only four o'clock in the afternoon.

A needle of pain shot through her chest and she shivered as she waited on the front steps, though the heat of the sun was intense. The stress of the past few weeks was taking its toll. She would have to rest, she told herself, to ward off a recurrence of pneumonia. As soon as she got the diamonds back, she would go home and sleep for eight hours straight. A few minutes passed and she had to ring the bell again before a middle-aged woman in a white uniform came hurrying to the door. A new employee? Lorelei didn't recognize her. The woman paused to wipe her hands on the tea towel she carried, then held it behind her back with one hand as she opened the door. She stood on the threshold and smiled primly, her eyebrows raised.

"Yes?" she asked in a thick, English accent. "May I help you?"

"Is Mrs. Kellsington at home?"

"May I ask who's calling?"

"Lorelei Good. I need to speak with her."

"Lorelei Good," the woman repeated. She paused, as if trying, and failing, to recollect the name. "Well, I'm afraid Mrs. Kellsington is very busy at the moment."

"Just tell her I'm here, please." Lorelei stepped past the woman into the house. From behind the closed living room doors, she could hear classical music playing softly on the stereo. Then the murmur of voices, glasses clinking. Agnes was evidently entertaining. Lorelei started to move toward the entrance to the living room, but the woman quickly blocked the way with her stout little torso.

"If you'll just wait here, ma'am." She placed a firm hand on Lorelei's arm. "I'll tell her you've come."

Lorelei tried to push past her, but the woman held fast.

"You must be new here," Lorelei said coldly. "Where's Susanne?"

Before the woman could answer, the doors to the living room parted and a handsome face peeked out. "Who is it, Molly?"

"A Ms Lorelei Good, sir. She says she's here to see Mrs. Kellsington."

The man pushed the doors wide open and strode forward, smiling. He was tall and tanned, with broad shoulders. "Well, Molly, if she's a friend of Mrs. Kellsington's, don't leave her stranded at the door, for heaven's sake."

"I'm sorry, sir, but she's not on the guest list, sir, and you said—"

"Never mind that. Go on up now and tell Agnes she's here."

As Molly scurried away, the tall man held out his hand to Lorelei. "Sorry about that. I don't believe we've met. Hank Kellsington. Agnes's husband."

Lorelei shook his hand. "Lorelei Good," she said. "I'm sorry to interrupt. I didn't know you had company."

"A little welcome-home party, arranged on the spur of the moment," he explained. "Just a few of my old friends, really," he added politely. "But you must come and join us." He placed an arm around her shoulders and steered her toward the living room. "Agnes will be down soon. Or at least I have high hopes that she will. The woman takes hours to dress."

Hank Kellsington was muscular. His body was strong and warm against hers, and Lorelei tried not to think of the intimate details Agnes had divulged about him. She followed for two steps, then hesitated. Someone at the party had turned up the music, and a great wave of laughter swelled through the door. This was not the time or the place to be conducting business with Agnes. She needed to see her alone.

"Perhaps I'll just wait here," she said. "I really don't want to intrude."

"Nonsense!" He propelled her forward, but she resisted.

"No, really, I'd rather just wait here. I only need a quick word with Agnes and then I'll be on my way."

"Well, now." He looked down at her, studying her face. "That sounds serious." He waited for her to respond, and when she didn't, he said, "Very well, then. But do come into the den, at least, and sit down. I'll tell Molly to bring you a drink." He settled her on a sofa in the den and went to rejoin his guests.

Lorelei sat down to wait. Hank hadn't seemed to recognize her name. But the papers had probably listed Psychic Renaissance as the purchaser. The sounds of the party waxed and waned as people opened and closed the doors to the living room. Several times she saw a guest or two pass through the vestibule. They would peek through the door and give her a curious glance before they went on their way. Every one of them was tall and tanned and groomed to the nines, glowing with diamonds and gold and that sleek, well-fed skin of the very rich. She had never seen any of them before, and she guessed that Hank and Agnes led very separate social lives. None of his friends were her friends. At least, not yet. They were certainly opposites. Confident, beaming Hank and skittish, mousy Agnes.

Molly appeared with a glass of red wine and set it down on the coffee table. "Here you are, ma'am," she said stiffly.

"Thank you," said Lorelei. "And Molly? I'm sorry about—you know, before."

Molly simply pursed her lips.

"It's just that I was expecting Susanne to be here," Lorelei continued, trying to soothe the older woman's wounded feelings. "Is Susanne not well?"

"If you're meaning Susanne Chambers, the housekeeper, she's been let go."

"I see," said Lorelei. Well, that was no surprise. But it was inconvenient, as Susanne had been a good source of information. "That's too bad. But she *was* a little sloppy, I suppose."

"Sloppy?" Molly snorted. "She were a thief!"

"Susanne? A thief?"

Molly nodded. "We came home to find she'd been skimming the wages of the workers on the estate. The books were a terrible mess. And the entire contents of Mr. Kellsington's liquor cabinet vanished!"

"Oh dear," said Lorelei. "She didn't steal any…valuables, did she? Any cash or…or…jewelry?"

Molly wiped her hands on her apron and smiled smugly. "Luckily, we placed the valuables at the bank before we went overseas."

"Oh, you were overseas, too, Molly? In India, too? How interesting for you." Lorelei hardly knew what she was saying. But she knew her own diamonds had not been among the valuables placed for safekeeping at the bank. Her head whirled. "Whatever is taking Agnes so long?" she cried.

"I'll fetch her, ma'am," said Molly.

Lorelei grasped the wine and downed half the glass. It was a fine Merlot, but she scarcely tasted it. She repeated to herself all the reasons she had nothing to worry about. Susanne could not be accomplished enough to crack Agnes's safe. Even if she had, Agnes would have insurance. Lorelei had a receipt. She reminded herself to breathe slowly. Everything would be fine. Her thoughts were interrupted by a low, musical voice at the door.

"Hello? Hello there!" It was one of the tall, tanned creatures from the party. She was barefoot and dressed in a red and gold silk sari, the theme of the welcome-home party. Her streaked blond hair had been swept up off her forehead with a red silk hairband and allowed to cascade in a casual jumble of variegated curls below her shoulders. It was a style too youthful for her age, which Lorelei guessed to be nearly sixty. She gave the woman a noncommittal smile, hoping she would go away.

But the woman stepped into the room, eyeing her critically. "You're one of Hank's friends, I suppose?"

"I've just met him," Lorelei said. "I'm waiting—"

"I see that you're waiting," said the blond. "The question is, what are you waiting for? There's a party going on here, in case you hadn't noticed."

"I noticed," she said. She forced a smile. Must be polite to the friends of Hank Kellsington. "And I don't mean to intrude. But I'm here on business, and I must—"

Hank Kellsington strode into the room and said, "Ah! Here you are!" He handed the woman a glass of white wine.

"This lady is here on business," the blond said to Hank. She raised the glass to her lips, spilling a drop on one sari-clad breast. "Oh dear." Hank handed her a serviette, and she dabbed at the drop, frowning. "You don't think it will stain, do you?"

"What kind of business?" Hank asked pleasantly.

"It's about the cottage," said Lorelei wearily. She, too, took another sip of wine. Why did this have to be happening in the middle of a party? "Just some minor details. It won't take a minute." She wondered again how much Agnes had told him.

"You're interested in the cottage?" the blond woman asked. "This really isn't very good timing. I'm sure Hank could arrange for a real-estate agent to call you at some later date. Why don't you leave your number with Molly?" She smiled. "Hank will see you out."

Hank stepped forward, as if to do just that.

"You don't understand," said Lorelei. "I've bought the cottage already, I just need—"

"What?" said Hank. "*Our* cottage? On Lake of the Woods? What do you mean?"

"Let's start all over again," said the blond. "From the beginning. Now, who did you say you represent?"

"I don't represent anyone," Lorelei said. Her neck ached with tension and her forehead was beginning to throb. "I'm Lorelei Good, a friend, and—"

"A friend?" asked the blond. "Of whom?"

Lorelei rubbed her temples and tried to remain calm. She took a deep breath and appealed to Hank. "Look, would you please just tell her that Lorelei Good is here, and I need to speak with her immediately."

"Speak with *whom*?" the blond stretched both her arms wide, holding up her hands in wonderment. "Whatever are you talking about?"

"Agnes Kellsington," said Lorelei firmly. "I need to speak with Mrs. Agnes Kellsington."

"But my dear," the blond cried. She was clearly exasperated. "*I'm* Mrs. Agnes Kellsington!"

"A terrible misunderstanding," Lorelei muttered. "The wrong address. Forgive me." She tried to rise, but was overcome with dizziness and sank back down into her seat.

The noises of the party whirled around her. The party guests were calling out for their hosts. "Hank! Agnes! Where are you hiding? The honeymoon is over, you know!"

Two women came laughing into the sitting room. "There you are!" one cried, pulling at Mrs. Kellsington's hand. "I thought you said you came back because you were so terribly *bored* with solitude and meditation. Well, come and join the party!"

Mrs. Kellsington turned to Lorelei, bewildered and amused. She shrugged and smiled and said, "These mix-ups happen, I guess. Molly will see you out." Then she went off with her guests, towing Hank Kellsington along behind her.

Lorelei leaned forward in her chair and watched them through the open door. Agnes and Hank laughed as their friends dragged them back into the living room. The doors were pulled closed, and the sound of the piano was once again muted. She could see the open trunk in the vestibule. Yes, on a second, closer look, she saw there were women's things in there, as well. A woman's sun-hat, a flowered scarf. Agnes and Hank Kellsington had just returned from three months abroad together. So who had Lorelei been talking to these past few weeks? Who was the mousy blond in the beige pantsuits and the hideous, shapeless dresses? The one who looked so miraculously young for her age? Lorelei's head throbbed with pain. She stood up and staggered toward the front door.

"Are you all right, ma'am?" Molly had come bustling back, carrying a tray of hors d'oeuvres. She set the tray down on the table. "You look pale. Sit down, sit down."

"Thank you, Molly. I'm fine."

"Can I get you anything?"

"No. Well, Molly, can you tell me what Susanne Chambers looks like? Is she a blond?"

"I thought you knew her," said Molly. "You said you did."

"Yes, but I'm not sure now," said Lorelei, "whether it was really Susanne I saw. Perhaps it was only one of the maids. I wouldn't want to misjudge one of the honest girls, you know."

"Well, you can see for yourself," said Molly. "She's right here in this picture, unpacking the kitchen things. Just a few days after he hired her." She handed it to Lorelei. "We had a better likeness, but we gave it to the police."

The photo was blurry and out of focus, and Lorelei's head was still spinning slightly. But she could make it out. There was Hank Kellsington, looking comically confused, standing amidst a sea of cartons in the kitchen, knee-deep in packing paper. Beside him, a servant in a staid blue and white uniform was kneeling on the floor, pulling a kettle from one of the boxes. "That's Susanne?"

"That's the little thief. Susanne Chambers. She was bonded, too! She was sent to us from The Cleaning Bee on Main Street, and they're usually ever so reliable. You can't trust anyone these days, ma'am. It's a terrible thing to be saying, but it's true."

Lorelei studied the photograph. The servant's head was bowed and it was hard to see her face. But she could see enough to tell it wasn't the Susanne Chambers she had known, the one who'd opened the door so many times to let her in. It was Agnes, or the one pretending to be Agnes. The one she'd just given half a million dollars to.

CHAPTER FIFTEEN

Speeding toward The Cleaning Bee on Main Street, with the photo of the imposter in her pocket and the .38 Special in her glove compartment, Lorelei still couldn't believe that she had given away Max's diamonds, the diamonds she'd protected for twelve years, to a con artist. Just handed them over. Practically begged her to take them. Nixie would freak. At the moment it was Lorelei's intention to get the diamonds back before Nixie found out.

The Cleaning Bee was located in a dingy cement building that also housed an exterminator's business and a vacuum repair shop, both closed for the evening. The hallway stunk of chemical lemon cleaner and microwaved leftovers. At the far end, a man in orange coveralls mopped the floor in a desultory fashion, an unlit cigarette hanging from his lips. Lorelei stalked past him and entered the offices of The Cleaning Bee, which advertised "industrial, commercial and residential services." The sign on the door boasted of "Bonded Professionals."

"Never seen her before," said the receptionist when she looked at the photo. Lorelei got the same answer from the four cleaning women who were waiting around in the office to be picked up for the night shift. She had claimed to be the woman's parole officer, checking up on her, but the ruse yielded no results. The Cleaning Bee staff had never seen the woman in the photo or heard the name Susanne Chambers, either. The manager had everyone's records on his computer, they said, but he was out for dinner. They weren't sure which restaurant he was at or when he'd be back. The wary glances they exchanged with each other suggested the manager usually had a long liquid dinner at a nearby bar and that he might not want a parole officer knowing about it.

Lorelei fumed. Time was crucial. By her calculations, the woman posing as Agnes had been taken off guard when the real Kellsingtons returned unexpectedly early from India. Otherwise she never would have let herself be caught with an empty liquor cabinet and shortages in the household books—amateur mistakes unworthy of an artist of her caliber. Judging by the time she left the cottage today, fake Agnes, whoever she was, would so far have had little time to figure out a change of plans. She'd be scrambling, and the faster she had to scramble the more mistakes she'd make. Lorelei had to pick up her trail right away. She wished she had Nixie to help her, but the minute she'd decided to take the gun along, she'd had to leave Nixie out of this. It was too risky.

She left The Cleaning Bee and stood on the street, smoking, trying to formulate a plan. Should she wait for the manager, or start searching through the nearby bars? She groaned, remembering how many bars littered this particular part of town. Then, in her peripheral vision, she sensed a person standing in the glass doorway of the building she'd just exited. Someone was watching her. Without letting on she was aware of his gaze, she turned her back to him and used the reflection in the window of a parked car to check him out. It was the janitor of the building, the man she'd seen mopping the floor when she'd entered. She recognized his short, dumpy figure. He was leaning on the stringy floor mop, watching her, taking an unusual interest in her presence. She decided to show him the photograph, see how he reacted.

Quickly, before he could slip away, she turned around and opened the door to the building again. He stepped back, out of her way, and ducked his head.

"Excuse me?" she asked. "Could I ask you a couple of questions?"

He looked up, and when her eyes met his, he started to run in the opposite direction. Lorelei chased him. He'd been wearing mirrored sunglasses when she saw him last, but she recognized his plump little cheeks and his thinning blond hair. The man with the mop was Jack Barnes, the real-estate agent from Deception Bay. Barnes ran to the end of the hall and Lorelei struggled to keep up, slipping on the wet, sudsy floor. He turned into the last office in the hall, a door marked "copy room," and Lorelei followed. She found him in a tiny office, empty except for a photocopy machine, a rickety table, and some shelves of office supplies. He was crouched behind the table. Cornered, he lifted his dripping mop, as if prepared to do battle with it.

"What do you want?" he asked.

Lorelei kicked the door closed behind her. She couldn't pull the parole officer ruse with him. He knew who she was. The game was over. She pulled the .38 Special from her pocket and aimed it at his head. "Put that down."

Jack Barnes opened his hands and the mop clattered to the floor. He backed up against the wall. "What do you *want*?" he asked again.

"I just came from the Kellsingtons' house," she said. "And it turns out there's been a thief living there. I want to know who she is and how she pulled it off and I want to know where she is now. Right now!"

"Her real name's Abby," Jack said in a rush. "Abby Baker. She came in here—I think it was M-March or so. She wanted me to set her up with papers so she could work as a housekeeper." He stopped and gulped air. His carotid artery throbbed with fear. "I used my access to the files, here—the forms and everything—to make her up fake credentials. We gave my cell number as the contact person for the, uh, The Cleaning Bee. Do you have to point that right at my face?"

Lorelei lowered the gun to his chest. She saw he was sweating profusely. The armpits of his janitor's uniform were soaking wet. "Keep going. Faster," she said.

"We gave, uh, a couple of friends as references. And we got her hired. It was easy. Then she set herself up there as the lady of the house. The real lady was off in India."

"Nobody noticed?"

"Nobody knew her here, this lady. She was from Chicago. Her husband came up here a couple of times to hire staff for the house and do a little business, but nobody much knew him, either. Abby kept a low profile. Nobody asked any questions. If the neighbors saw her goin' in and out of the house, they just figured she was the housekeeper." He let out a nervous rush of air. "Which she was."

Lorelei shook her head. That explained the dowdy clothes, then, and the reason that "Agnes" took the bus everywhere. The construction workers would have known her as the housekeeper, of course. There were probably quite a few tradespeople and some of the neighbors, who had met her as the housekeeper. It wouldn't do for them to see the housekeeper dressing in Mrs. Kellsington's fine clothes or driving her Ferrari. She remembered how long it had taken her to catch on that "Agnes" was rich. The woman had laid a nearly perfect trap. The places she passed herself off as Agnes Kellsington weren't generally frequented by people likely to know the real woman. The only danger might have come from people who knew Hank Kellsington, people like Penny. But Hank had not yet introduced his bride to Winnipeg society. He had taken her straight from Chicago to Europe and then to India. Just as the newspapers said he did. Penny had simply accepted Abby's word that she was Hank's new wife.

Lorelei's blood pressure soared as she remembered the hours she'd spent listening to a litany of embarrassing marital problems that didn't exist. This Abby Baker had quite the imagination.

"Does she do this often? Did you set her up in other houses, so she could rob them as well?"

"Nah. She only wanted that house, that particular place. She worked on it for weeks. There was a couple other places empty on the same street, but she wanted that one."

"Why?"

"She was looking for someone rich who was into all this New Age stuff, this psychic mumbo-jumbo. There was a particular woman she was after, who ran in those type circles. That's who Abby was looking to get, really. I'm surprised, honest, you telling me she took stuff from the house. Something must have gone wrong. She didn't go there to steal from the house."

"This woman she was after," said Lorelei. "Tell me about her."

"Somebody Abby knew a long time ago."

"Yolanda Dawn?"

Jack recognized the name immediately and panicked. "I

don't know nothing about that Yolanda woman!" he blurted. "Or none of those psychic murders. No way!" He looked wildly about the little room, but there was no escape. Lorelei and her pistol stood between him and the door. "All's I know is Abby asked me to say I worked at that real-estate place there, up at the lake. She gave me some business cards and told me to wait for you there. That's it! That's the sum total of what I did. I don't know no more about it. You got to let me go. I got a kid, and a wife, and—"

"Shut up," said Lorelei. She was thinking about Yolanda Dawn. Of course Abby didn't know Yolanda. It was Agnes who knew Yolanda. The real Agnes, from Chicago, who had attended Living Institute retreats with her. So when Penny Johnson had invited the fake Agnes to a reading with her old friend Yolanda, "Agnes" had made a series of excuses, cancellations, and then finally...Yolanda fell sixteen stories to her death.

"So if it wasn't Yolanda," she said slowly, "then who was it Abby knew a long time ago?"

"All I know is she set this whole thing up so she could get back at someone for something done to her father."

Lorelei stood very still. "Who's her father?" She tried to calculate the number of men who might want revenge on her. Too many to count.

Jack only held up his hands. "That's all I know. I swear. If you want to find Abby, try her ex-husband. Mike Baker. He's the one pretending to be her lawyer. He lives over on Marion Street. The Marion Apartments."

"So Baker is her married name. What's her maiden name?"

"I don't know, but Mike is at number 99. First suite on the right."

"He'd better be," said Lorelei. "Seeing as I'm sure you'll

be easy to trace from your little job here, you'd better be telling the truth."

Brian sat in his BMW in the driveway of the Kellsington mansion, trying to process the nature of reality. He held in his lap the nylon mesh bag he had just tried to return to Agnes Kellsington—only to discover that he didn't know Agnes Kellsington at all.

"There was a young lady here, oh, hour and a half ago, making the same mistake," said the lady of the house to Brian. "I think she had us mixed up with the Kingsleys next door." She had stood in the doorway, wearing a sari and leaning languorously against the doorframe, while her husband, holding a wineglass in each hand, leaned against her. They were both drunk. "Why don't you ask over at the Kingsleys'?" She pointed across the wide lawn to another mansion barely visible beyond the trees.

"Maybe we should look into this, Agnesh," said her husband. "It's awfully shtrange."

"Tomorrow," said the real Agnes Kellsington. "We can look into it tomorrow. Today we're celebrating." She hiccupped loudly and closed the door in Brian's face.

Whatever the hell was going on, Brian knew damn well it had nothing to do with the Kingsleys next door. Who was the real Agnes Kellsington? Maybe there was some kind of clue in this bag, if the woman who owned it, whoever she was, had truly left it behind by accident. Still sitting in the Kellsingtons' driveway, he reached into the nylon bag and pulled out a zippered makeup kit. He rummaged through it, tossing aside lip balm, eye shadow, and a bottle of perfume. There was also a padded envelope in the nylon bag, with the word "Insurance" written on it in felt marker. He reached in and pulled out a couple of photographs. One was a picture of a young woman in a red peasant blouse and flowing skirt, walking past a man seated at a piano. Her long dark hair covered her face but Brian knew who she was. The next photo showed her gliding up a spiral staircase. He recognized it as the staircase that led up from the great room in Waverley's mansion. He recognized Lorelei's clothing and he recognized the piano player. These pictures were taken the night of Waverley's soiree. Agnes had been circulating with a camera that night. But why would she photograph Lorelei from the back, when she wasn't even looking? Was she some kind of spy? But why? Who would spy on a group like the Seekers?

Brian tipped the envelope again and let all the photographs fall out onto the passenger seat. The first one he picked up showed an enormous bewhiskered man in a black cape, towering over a waitress who was serving him something from a tray. Brian recognized the mind reader, Oberon the Amazing, whose distinctive image had been in the paper at the time of the murder. The next photo showed Summer Sweet's Dharmarama. In flames. Brian realized his hands were shaking. How did Agnes get this picture and why would she be carrying it around? He looked closely at the photo of Oberon and swallowed hard when he realized what the man was holding. In his left hand, he brandished two long objects that might have been shish-kabob. In his right, he held a half-eaten one to his teeth and Brian could see the bare metal skewer—the very weapon Oberon had been murdered with.

Could this Agnes imposter be an undercover police officer? Brian found that hard to believe. But why else would she have two photos, each taken at the scene of a crime? She couldn't possibly be involved in the murders. Agnes, or the person he had met as Agnes, was such a nice lady. He stopped himself. God, it was true. He was just as naïve as Tommy said he was.

The Agnes imposter was possibly an undercover member of the Soldiers Against Satan. Was she an assasin, sent by the Reverend Surefire? Where was she now? Where was Lorelei?

He stepped on the accelerator.

The Marion Apartments were little more than boxes of wood and stucco, sixteen boxes, as much like one another as the buildings in a game of Monopoly. They hardly looked like they might be harboring hundreds of thousands of dollars worth of diamonds. But Lorelei had to try. Mike Baker lived in a ground-floor suite. Stupid. If he wouldn't open the door, she could easily kick the window in. Her fury was in no way diminished by her encounter with Jack Barnes. She burned as she remembered "Harry" the lawyer and his conservative manner, how protective he'd been of Agnes's interests, all the while upping the ante bit by bit. When she thought of how grateful she'd been to him for accepting her diamonds instead of cash, she was tempted to kick the window in right now, before she even knocked on the door. But she knew she should avoid a disturbance. She should calm down. Let the anger fuel her purpose, not control her. She walked around to the back of the building, trying to see into the apartment. The lights were on, but every window was covered with blinds or curtains. Was Abby in there? Lorelei fervently hoped so.

As she waited, a man walked up the back steps of the building and pressed the intercom beside the entrance. She sidled up behind him and took the opportunity to get inside when someone buzzed him in.

Mike Baker answered the door on her first knock. With

a day or two of stubble on his jaw, and a pair of ratty slippers on his feet, he seemed an entirely different person from the clean-cut "Harry" she'd met at the Kellsington mansion. Instead of a suit, he wore blue jeans and a black hoodie with the name of a soft drink on it. But he was the same man. The look of shock on his face was gratifying. He had obviously been expecting someone, but it wasn't Lorelei. He must have thought she was still out at the cottage, unaware of Abby's scam.

As she'd done with Jack, Lorelei pulled the .38 Special right away and immobilized him. Like Jack, he was terrified. He answered all her questions.

Abby had gone to the airport, he said. She was on her way to Toronto and she had the diamonds with her. He looked at the clock. "Her flight leaves in an hour," he said. "If you hurry, you can probably catch her before she boards the plane."

Lorelei watched his face carefully and asked, "Where are my diamonds?"

"They're not here. I told you. Abby has them."

Something about the way his eyes slid sideways told her he was lying. Her heart beat faster. The diamonds were here. In the apartment. She just knew it.

"Where are they?" She moved to the odd, long closet on the kitchen wall and opened it. It contained only an ironing board and iron. She slammed it shut.

"Look," he said. "You don't understand. If I give them to you she'll kill me."

"And if you *don't* give them to me, *I'll* kill you." She moved to the cupboards, keeping the gun trained on his forehead. She threw open door after door, until all six of the kitchen cupboards stood open, exposing a collection of mismatched plates and coffee cups. Then she walked along the counter, banging them shut one by one, each bang making Mike Baker cringe as if it were a gunshot.

"Make up your mind," she said. "Which is it going to be? Me or her?"

"Oh, Jesus," he moaned. "Why me?"

"Where are they?" She held the gun to his head and clicked off the safety.

He reached into the pocket of his hoodie and pulled out a dark blue velvet bag, Lorelei's bag, and tossed it on the table.

"She'll kill me," he said.

Lorelei's mood was soaring crazily high now. With one hand she kept the gun aimed at Mike while with the other she picked out one of the gemstones and held it up to the light. She hefted the bag, judging its weight in her palm. "Are they all here?"

"All but one."

"Where is the one?"

"Jack Barnes."

"Damn it!" But she didn't really care at the moment. She'd been lucky. For the main part, she had regained her rightful treasure. She tucked the velvet bag in her purse and felt some measure of control returning to her. She'd been running entirely on rage for the past hour and a half, and now that it was dissipating slightly, she could barely believe what she'd done in such a short time. A wave of nausea passed through her as she remembered the sweat pouring through Jack Barnes' uniform. And right now, here in front of her, Mike Baker was breaking down in tears. His legs were shaking so hard he had to sit down at the table. He didn't know she'd been bluffing. Lorelei wasn't sure herself whether she'd been bluffing. She thought she was going to be sick.

"Get into the closet," she ordered him. "If you stay in there, you'll live."

He nodded. He tried to stand up, but his knees failed him. "Jesus," he said. "I—I can't. Oh, God, Abby is going to murder me in cold blood."

Tears were rolling down his cheeks. He didn't seem like a hardened diamond thief. But she didn't want to let her guard down, in case he tried to jump her, so she kept the gun on him. "How did you get mixed up with her, anyway?" she asked him.

"My wife," he said. "I knew the minute I saw her she was bad news."

"Who is she?"

"Abby Shaunigan." He wiped snot from his nose. "Christ, I wish I'd never set eyes on her."

"Shaunigan?"

"Yeah. When I first met her, that's what she was calling herself. S-H-A-U-...."

She let him spell it out, though there was no need. It wasn't a name she'd ever forget. Abigail Shaunigan would be Gail Shaunigan. Uncle Joey's daughter. The little princess. As she stood there gripping the gun, threatening the life of a pathetic, babbling little man for the second time today, she remembered all those stories Joey used to tell her about the "little princess" he had at home and all those unkept promises to invite Lorelei over to play with her. Well, Lorelei had played with the little princess at last. Max had been right. She wasn't much fun.

There was no answer at Lorelei's house. Brian wanted to wait for her, but he didn't want to park in the driveway or on the street, in case he got cornered by Charlotte Trapp. He didn't want to get drawn into a conversation with Charlotte tonight. He drove around the block and found a spot on the next street over, where he could watch Lorelei's driveway through the oak trees. He'd spot her red car from here when she got home. He wondered where she'd gone and whether she knew yet that Agnes wasn't Agnes.

While he waited, he called Tommy at home and Sarisha said wearily that he was working late again. But there was no answer at Tommy's office, so Brian left a voice mail message, explaining that someone had been impersonating Agnes Kellsington. Or at least it looked that way—Brian was still uncertain about the drunken woman in the sari. He suggested an officer be sent to the address to ask a few questions. "Call me back when you get this message," he added. "I'm on my cell."

He hung up and continued his search of fake Agnes's nylon bag. There was nothing else of interest so he gathered up the photographs and studied them closely. There were several more pictures of Oberon the Amazing, all taken at the same fancy reception as the server moved through the crowd with her tray of hors d'oeuvres. He identified Waverley and Penny easily, and several Seekers. Were these scenes from the Psychic Fair? He peered more closely, examining every detail. In every photo, he noted, the server was the same. In fact, she seemed to be the main focus. And she looked familiar. She looked like…yes, it was. Lorelei's little sister, Nixie. Huh, he thought, she was working at the reception? I wonder why Lorelei never mentioned that.

The next photo made him sit up straight and gasp. It was Nixie again, in a dark alley at night. The lighting was dim, but in her dark clothing she was visible against the pale panel van parked behind her. He recognized her small shape. The date, July 4, and the time, 2:06 a.m., appeared in the corner of the photo. What was she doing? From her stance, she didn't appear aware that her picture was being taken. The next few photos showed her approaching the rear of a brick building. She was peering in at the darkened window. Then she was opening the door. In one photo, a flash had captured her perfectly, her face turned toward the camera, her mouth a round "oh" of surprise. Brian had never been in the rear of this building, but he recognized the distinctive white brick and the word "Dharmarama" visible on the pink door.

As he flipped through the next few pictures, he realized they formed a series. Most likely, they'd been taken originally in video mode and these were stills someone had printed. He thumbed through them again and again, unwilling to believe what he was seeing. But the camera's sophisticated zoom lens left no doubt. And although Lorelei did not appear in any of the pictures, it was plain to see she had been deeply involved.

On her way back home, Lorelei called Nixie. The phone rang again and again, but Nixie wasn't answering.

Mike Baker had sworn Abby was out of town for the night, not at the airport but up at Stony Mountain where she could visit her dad at the penitentiary, presumably to give him the good news in person. Of course she couldn't get in there with a bag full of stolen diamonds, so she'd left them with Mike for safekeeping. First thing in the morning he was supposed to bring them to the train station and the two of them would take off together for Vancouver. Trains were the safest mode of travel, if you were carrying contraband. No security check.

As far as Abby knew, Lorelei was still up at the cottage, oblivious to her scam. Mike had sworn he wasn't going to warn her or tell her what had happened. He said he was going to use the time he had to get as far away as possible. But Lorelei didn't trust him. He might have meant it when he said it, but once Lorelei and her gun were gone, he'd get to thinking about those diamonds and how much they were worth and whether he wanted to be the one to cross Abby Shaunigan and her father.

She called Nixie again. Again no answer. She tore through a red light and sailed over the Norwood Bridge, narrowly missing a collision with the guard rail. Where was that girl?

Five minutes later, she parked her Mercedes recklessly, almost sideways, in the driveway of her home and raced up the front stairs. She was furious when she saw Nixie sitting on the couch on the screened-in porch, with Imogene Trapp. She stormed in.

"Hi Lorelei," said Imogene. She looked up and Lorelei saw that her eyes were red from crying. One side of her face was mottled with red and purple welts.

"What happened?" Lorelei asked. "Nixie, are you all right?"

"I'm fine." Nixie looked up, too. Besides the bruise from her night at the Dharmarama, she seemed unharmed.

"Was she here?" Lorelei asked. Her eyes scanned the front yard and her hand hovered above the pocket of her dress where the .38 Special was concealed. How could Abby possibly have made it here so fast?

"Who? My mom?" said Imogene. "She's out at a prayer meeting." She blew her nose and Nixie patted her arm.

Nixie looked at Lorelei and shook her head ruefully. "Poor Imogene," she said. "Her mother was really angry with her this afternoon."

Lorelei was beginning to understand. "Imogene, go on home now, all right? I have to talk to Nixie."

Nixie, seeing the look in Lorelei's eyes, said, "Yeah, Imogene. I'll see you later, all right? You can come over and play with Bitsy later."

"Probably not tonight," Lorelei added. She tugged at Imogene's arm.

Imogene stood reluctantly. "Nixie said you'd help me."

"We will, we will," said Lorelei. "But later. We'll help you later."

"Okay." With excruciating slowness, Imogene thumped down the stairs and back around to her own side of the house.

Lorelei realized she was still shaking with anger. She had the diamonds back and here was Nixie right in front of her, safe and sound, and she was still on fire with rage. It wasn't only the theft or the threat to Nixie that were fueling her anger, she realized. It wasn't only the interruption of her plan, either, though that was maddening. It was the whole set-up, the way that Abby Shaunigan had taken control of the plan and molded it to her own aims. Abby had caused a sudden, irreversible shift in reality.

Dizzy, she sat down on the couch and hung her head in her hands. As she endured the sickening sensation of adrenalin draining from her bloodstream, she cringed with shame to think how deluded she'd been, believing she was manipulating Agnes.

"What's wrong?" asked Nixie. "You got them back, didn't you? Please tell me you got them back."

"I did. I've got them. Where's Rapunzel?"

"Up in my room."

Lorelei handed the velvet bag of diamonds to her sister. "You've got some sewing to do," she said.

"Shouldn't they go back in the bank?"

"Not now. Come on. Let's go inside."

But Nixie didn't move from her seat on the porch. "What's going on?"

"Well, the thing is, Nix, you see, we're going to have to go away for a little while. We have to pack a few bags."

"What? No! I don't *want* to go away for a little while, Lorelei! I've got things to do. I promised Imogene I'd help her. Do you know that her mother has been beating her for years with a wooden spoon? And today she attacked her face! You saw her. I promised I'd stand by her if she gets up her nerve to stand up to her mom, and I'm going to do it. Besides, we can't leave now! I'm going up to Vivian's land tonight, and then we'll be moving into the cottage and—"

"I'll explain inside. Let's go."

"No," said Nixie. She remained in her seat. "Explain now."

Lorelei stood above her, taking stock of the situation. Nixie's little bow mouth was set in a stubborn frown, her baby blue eyes staring defiantly at her sister. She wasn't just sulking. She was in a state of brazen rebellion. There was only one way to reach her.

"Agnes isn't Agnes," said Lorelei.

"What are you talking about?" Nixie stood up.

"Agnes isn't the real Agnes. That woman we thought was Agnes Kellsington? She's a fake. A con artist. She doesn't own the cottage at all. It was all a huge set-up."

"But you got them back!" Nixie shook the velvet bag in front of Lorelei's face.

"I did. But this woman, she'll be coming after us. She'll—"

"Who is she?"

Lorelei weighed the pros and cons of telling the truth. She didn't want Nixie to panic, but this defiance was worse than panic. Much more dangerous. She needed Nixie to understand the risk. "It's Abby Shaunigan," she said. "Uncle Joey's daughter."

Nixie turned white. She put her hands over her mouth and said, "No."

"Nix, I'm sorry," said Lorelei.

A shadow suddenly moved across the screen door. Lorelei whirled around, her hand reaching for the gun in her pocket. Nixie screamed.

Brian Hale was standing on the front steps, looking at them through the screen door of the porch. "Who's Abby Shaunigan?" he asked.

Lorelei drew in her breath sharply when Brian showed her the first photograph. They were sitting together alone in the living room. He had wanted Nixie to take part in the "talk" he wanted to have, but Lorelei had begged to speak to him in private. The look on his face was chilling. She didn't know what he knew, but she knew it wasn't good. So she'd sent Nixie upstairs with a directive to "work on your sewing project." She'd locked all the doors and closed the curtains and sat down to listen to what he had to say. But he hadn't said a word, merely handed her the photo.

She was still staring at it. Nixie breaking into the Dharmarama. She had to think fast. They could say that Nixie had been working for Summer. That would explain why she was going in through the back door. No one could contradict the story.

"Where did you get this?" she asked.

But before Brian could answer, his cell phone rang. "Hello? Tommy! Yeah. Yeah. No. Yeah, she's all right." He glanced at Lorelei. "Did you send someone over there? Good. The Kellsingtons wouldn't listen to me. I found out something else, too. Got a pen?"

Lorelei reached for Brian's sleeve, but he turned away from her.

"Wait," she whispered. "Don't—"

"Her name's Abby Shaunigan. That's right. Uh…." He looked at Lorelei again.

She clasped her hands together in a gesture of pleading.

"Uh, found the name in some of the papers she left behind. Right. No, we're okay. I'm here with her now at her house. Okay. Keep me posted."

He hung up. "Geez," he said. "I'm lying to my own brother."

"It's okay, Brian," she told him. "Everything's going to be okay. Where did you get these pictures? Let me see them."

"In a bag Agnes left behind, or Abby, or whoever she is." He waved the stack of photos at her. "I think you should call Nixie in here, and we'll look at them together. Then maybe you'll tell me who Abby Shaunigan really is and why Nixie reacted so strongly when you said her name."

"Brian, I've never heard of her before."

"No more lies," he said. "Get Nixie in here and let's take a look at what Abby Shaunigan was carrying around in her little mesh bag. Unless you want me to take these down to the police station right this minute."

"I can't get Nixie involved in this, Brian. I just can't." She reached for his arm.

He shook her hand away. "She's already involved."

As she walked upstairs to Nixie's room, Lorelei briefly considered taking her sister and running. But that was not a practical plan. She needed time to think, to figure out how to handle Brian. She needed to figure out what it was he wanted.

Nixie was sitting on the bed, with Bitsy in her lap. "I heard," she said, indicating the heat register near the floor. "How bad is it?"

Lorelei stood in the doorway. "Not sure yet. Are you done?"

"All done." Nixie held up the naked Rapunzel, who now had a new scar running sideways across her chest. Bitsy leaped up in an attempt to attack the doll, but Nixie held her out of reach.

"Remember what Max said that day?" asked Lorelei wryly.

"Keep her warm," said Nixie. She put Rapunzel's dress on and wrapped her in a flowered kerchief as a blanket.

"And keep her close," Lorelei added.

"Right," said Nixie. She placed Rapunzel in a canvas bag she used sometimes as a purse and slung it over her shoulder.

Bitsy bounded after them down the stairs.

"You do the talking, all right?" said Nixie.

"Of course."

The last photos were the worst of all, showing Nixie inside the boathouse. Through the open door, you could see her virtually pouring coins from a glass jar into Hank Kellsington's old tackle box. Among the jumbled treasure, the brilliant blue sapphire ring was clearly visible. Judging by the angle, the photo had been taken with an expensive zoom lens by Abby or, more likely, Jack Barnes, from the deck of any one of the innocent-looking boats that were always sailing in the bay. Lorelei was beginning to understand the extent of the set-up, the pains Abby had taken. Abby and her partners must have been watching the island closely in the days before Spirit Fest, just waiting to catch Nixie and Lorelei setting up.

"I can explain all this," said Lorelei to Brian.

"You don't need to explain it," Brian told her. "I can see for myself exactly what you've been doing. And I know why. I was at the seance, remember? I know all about the research center plans. In fact, didn't I help you out myself, by telling you exactly what Penny was looking for?"

Lorelei lowered her eyes and tried to blush.

"Where did you find Roland's things, by the way?" he asked. "Despite myself, I'm impressed. We searched for that stuff for months. I even hired a private investigator."

"Derek had it."

"Derek? Penny's nephew?"

"He hates her," Lorelei told him. "She broke up his parents' marriage, and he blames her for his father's death. He figured he deserved the jewels and coins because they belonged to his grandmother. He knows about the weird clause in the will and there is no way he trusts his Aunt Penny to give him his just deserts."

"So he stole them. And you found all this out by sneaking around." He waved the photos in the air and slapped them against his palm. "Okay. I get it. Now, who is this Abby Shaunigan? She's in this same business with you? Duping people? If you know how to find her, you'll have to tell the police."

Nixie and Lorelei exchanged glances. "I know I lost a lot of money," Lorelei began.

"Waverley Forbes's money!" Brian corrected.

"Yes. Waverley and I were partners in this investment and I'm sorry about that. But don't you see, it's just not worth the trouble of tracking Abby down."

"Not worth the—what are you talking about? This woman just ripped off Waverley Forbes and the Seekers for a million dollars. Worse, she might be a killer!"

"Yes, but—"

"Don't you understand? As soon as I take these photos to the police—"

"Brian," said Lorelei. She moved closer to him, placed her hand on his knee. "You *can't* take those pictures to the police. I can't let Nixie get involved. They'll change us with fraud."

"Fraud?" Brian was incredulous. "They will charge you with *murder*!" He stood up, out of her reach, and rifled through the photos in his hand. "Here's a good one," he said, tossing it into her lap. "Here's your sister serving food to Oberon Zolo the night he was drugged. Here she is handing him one of the skewers used to kill him!" He tossed another photo on top of it. "Here she is breaking into the Dharmarama, the very night Summer was killed in that very store."

"But Brian, I told you—"

"And here she is with the stolen property of Penny Johnson, client of Yolanda Dawn, who was murdered after she taped a session with Penny!" He threw this last photo wildly, and it hit the edge of the couch and drifted to the floor. His green eyes blazed with righteous anger. "This woman has labeled these photos 'Insurance,' another word for blackmail, and left them there on purpose for you to find. She'll have copies. This is not the kind of thing you can hide!"

She could see there would be no stopping him. He would call the police, they would launch an investigation, Lorelei's schemes would come to light. Unless…. Maybe there was one way to stop him. "Brian," she said. "Can I talk to you in private?"

Nixie jumped off her chair and left the room, carrying her canvas bag on her shoulder. Bitsy followed her.

Lorelei needed Brian's help, and it looked as if he wanted the full story before he'd consider giving it to her, so she told him a little about how she had started on the path she was on. She mentioned her aunt with the tarot cards, her uncle with his questionable morals. Katherine's terrible death and Max's disappearance. She had never seen Max again, she said, and she probably never would. This was the truth and brought a genuine tear to her eye. She had been afraid to go to the authorities, she said. She played up the poverty, the responsibility of caring for Nixie. Her only gift was the telling of fortunes, she said, and if sometimes her gift wasn't working, well, she'd fallen into the occasional stretching of the truth, just to please her clients. It was her only means of support for herself and her sister.

"I was scared and I was alone," she said at the end of her story. "I know I've made some bad choices, but I was young. Do you think you can ever understand that?"

"I'm disappointed," Brian said truthfully. "I never wanted to fall in love with a—a—someone who would do things like that. But I am falling in love with you, Lorelei. I think I've been in love with you for twelve years."

He sat for a while with his elbows on his knees and his head in his hands.

"I'm sorry," she said.

"I believed in you. We all believed in you."

"I'm sorry," she said again. Maybe if she repeated it, it would come true.

"How did you ever get into these crazy schemes?" he asked suddenly. "You really do have a gift. I know you do."

"Yes. But it doesn't work the way people think it does. I mean, I can't really talk to ghosts and ask them where they've hidden their sapphire rings." She reached for his hand, stroked it.

"No, of course not," he said. "It sounds ... absurd, when you put it that way."

"If you can help me out of this mess," Lorelei said, "I'll be glad to give up this awful business. It all started as a kind of lark and now I've just gotten myself in too deep."

"I think I can help you," Brian said. "But you've got to promise me you'll come clean with the people you tricked, and then you'll give up this crazy business."

"I want to give it up. I really do. But expenses are so high."

"If you don't have enough set aside, if you can't support yourself, you can live with me. Both of you, of course. I'll take care of you while you look for a job." He put his arm around her. "Tommy is tracking down Abby Shaunigan right now. If we find out where she lives, maybe we can get Waverley's money back for him."

"That would be wonderful," Lorelei said. She wasn't concerned about getting Waverley's money. But Abby would want her diamonds back. The diamonds Max had stolen from Joey so many years ago. Diamonds Lorelei couldn't mention to the police. It was for those diamonds that Abby had gone to so much trouble to set Lorelei up, to make her take them out of the bank. And that was why she would return, looking for Lorelei, as soon as she discovered she'd been had. Lorelei did some quick calculations. If Abby had gone up to Stony Mountain, she couldn't possibly be back yet, even if Mike had called to warn her right away.

"But first, I insist you tell Waverley the truth," Brian was saying.

"Oh, I couldn't face him!"

"I'm sorry, but you'll have to face him. Otherwise I can't help you."

"What about Penny? When she finds out, she'll have my head on a platter."

"In the case of Penny Johnson, you've done nothing wrong. In fact, you helped her. I'm sure she will consider the small sums she paid you fair compensation for the stolen valuables that you recovered for her. But you have to tell Waverley the truth. Tell him we'll do everything we can to get his money back, and if we can't get it back, then, when you get a job, you can make restitution. Regular payments."

"Brian, please!"

But he had gone far enough. He wouldn't budge on this one last point. If Lorelei wanted him to keep these photos from the police, she was going to have to come clean with Waverley Forbes.

When the doorbell rang in the middle of their negotiations, Lorelei leaped up from the couch. Plunging her right hand into the pocket of her dress, she took three huge strides to the bay window and then slowly began to lift a corner of the curtain.

"Lorelei?" Nixie appeared in the doorway. She cradled her kitten in one arm. In the other, she held Rapunzel. "There's a man at the door."

"Are you sure it's a man?" Lorelei was trying to peer sideways through the bay window into the front porch.

Brian simply walked out into the hall and looked directly through the window. "It's okay," he said. "He's a cop. Detective Larraby. I met him when Yolanda was killed."

"Don't let him in."

"Of course I'm going to let him in," Brian said. "Tommy must have sent him."

"Don't tell him anything!" she cried.

Brian folded his arms across his chest. "Will you come clean with Waverley?"

"Yes. I promise. Just don't say anything about the photos. Please?"

"Promise? We'll go to Waverley's house tonight and you'll tell him everything?"

"Everything."

Brian opened the door.

Lorelei steered Larraby away from the living room, where the photographs were still scattered across the couch and coffee table. "Come on into the den," she said. "Where it's cozier."

The den was crowded. Nixie settled herself cross-legged on the rug in front of the window, between the twin lamps. Brian and Lorelei sat down side by side at the seance table.

Lyle Larraby plunked his huge bulk down in the third chair and then seemed to regret it. He shifted uncomfortably, barely able to fit his girth into the narrow wooden seat. He set his briefcase down and opened it, took out a couple of files. Then he leaned toward Brian and Lorelei, his elbows on the seance table as if it were his desk at the office. "So Tommy tells me you've run into Abby Shaunigan," he said. "Bad break for you. Good break for me."

"You know her?" Brian asked.

"Here's the facts," said Larraby. He opened the file and read from the covering memo. "Thirteen years ago, Josh Stonefield of Canadian Diamond Imports was leaving his home with a package for delivery. It was, let's see, a package of sixty 'one-carat diamonds of vvs2 clarity and a body color of E to F,' whatever that means. Expensive. He was robbed. Shot dead right outside his own house. Right in front of his wife and two kids."

Lorelei felt as though she'd been doused with ice water. She glanced at Nixie and their eyes met in terrible recognition. Nixie, already pale, turned white. Lorelei felt sick. She didn't want to hear this story. But Larraby kept talking.

"Died right there in his driveway," he said. "Bled out before the ambulance arrived." He shook his head. "Should have hired an armored car."

"What's that got to do with Abby Shaunigan?" asked Brian.

Larraby held up a hand to silence him. "Hold on. See, Tommy didn't recognize the name Shaunigan. But some of the older guys did. I sure did. This little tiger is Abigail June Shaunigan. Her father is Joseph Anthony Shaunigan, doing twenty-five years for cocaine trafficking. Now, Joseph Shaunigan is the one who shot that diamond dealer. We know it was him. We knew it then. We know it now. Trouble is, we never had enough proof. He stashed them diamonds somewhere. That's the reason thieves love jewels. They're easy to stash and hard to find. See, this haul is worth about three hundred thousand bucks, maybe three fifty, yet it'd fit in your jacket pocket. Each one's about, oh…." He drew a little circle on the back of his hand with a pen, about half an inch in diameter, and shoved it in Brian's face. "You seen anything like that lately?"

"No!" said Brian. What had he gotten himself into? He looked at Lorelei. Her face was white, and she was shaking. Brian put his arm around her and squeezed her waist gently. "It's okay," he said.

"How about you?" Larraby asked her. "You seen any sign of them? She wearing anything like that?"

"No," said Lorelei.

Larraby looked at Nixie, but the girl just shook her head. She said nothing, just sat there, open-mouthed, with her kitten and her rag doll in her lap, looking a little slow. Bitsy started chewing on the doll's head, and Nixie said, "Bitsy! No!"

"Well, we're real interested in this Abby Shaunigan, let me tell you. We've been watching her for a long time now. We have arrested her on a number of occasions over the years—drug charges, shoplifting, impersonating a police officer—five separate occasions. And every time we have searched her home and vehicle and her person and come up with nothing."

"Maybe they sold the diamonds?" Brian asked.

"Nope. My guess is they're holding them for Daddy, who is due for another crack at parole less than a year from now."

"And you want to find the stash from the robbery before he gets out," said Brian.

"And charge him with murder," said Larraby. "Oh yes, I surely do. Now, if I might be so bold as to ask you, what do you know about Abby Shaunigan? Tell me everything."

An hour later, Lorelei was sitting in the passenger seat of Brian's car. She hated sitting in the passenger seat. But Brian would not allow her to drive. He had allowed her to shower and change, though. She had chosen a simple outfit, hoping for a penitent look, a plain white blouse and a blue denim skirt embroidered with white flowers. One thin gold bracelet. She turned it over and over on her wrist as Brian drove down Wellington Crescent, telling her how much better she'd feel when this was over.

Detective Lyle Larraby had taken his sweet time in

her house, she thought. First he wanted to hear the whole story of the cottage. Then he had a number of mug shots he wanted to run by them. Lorelei picked out the two women who had called themselves Agnes Kellsington and Susanne Chambers. These were Abby Shaunigan and her cousin Tina, Larraby said. Lorelei recognized Jack Barnes and Mike Baker, too, but she didn't admit it. She didn't recognize any of the others. Abby's other boyfriends and past accomplices weren't familiar to her. But Larraby made her keep turning the pages.

When they reached Waverley's mansion, Brian parked on the street. Lorelei said nothing as she got out of the car. Her legs felt heavy as she trudged up the long driveway, the slanted rays of the sun in her eyes. In the garden, she lingered awhile, knelt and trailed a hand through the fish pond. The black koi nudged her fingers, searching for food. Beyond the statuary and the labyrinth of rose gardens, she could see the sun dancing on the river's surface, sparkling like diamonds. She would miss this place. She felt keenly that she'd barely arrived in this world before she was to be exiled from it. But there could be no more delay.

An unfamiliar maid opened the door and eyed her suspiciously, asking, "Who may I say is calling?" For a moment, Lorelei had a terrible, sinking sense of déjà vu, imagining that Waverley, too, had been an impostor. But no, there was good old Mary behind her, smiling in welcome, and there was Waverley. She could see him in the sunroom off the hall, sipping a martini with Wayne. The second he saw her, he got to his feet.

"Lorelei! Come in, come in. Why, I was just about to call you. Penny and I have had an idea, and we want you to—Oh, Brian! Good of you to come. Mary, another martini, would you?"

Lorelei turned around, surprised to see that Brian had entered behind her.

"I thought you were going to wait in the car," she said.

His only reply was a sad smile and a shrug.

"We want you to consider a proposition, Lorelei," Waverley continued. "On second thought, Mary, be a doll and bring the pitcher. We have a lot of business to discuss." He placed his hands on Lorelei's shoulders. "But let me look at you, my dear. Are you all right? You're a bit pale. Is anything wrong?"

Lorelei smiled and shifted away.

"Lorelei has something she wants to tell you," Brian said.

Waverley and Wayne exchanged a look.

"Bad news, is it?" asked Waverley.

"I'm afraid so," said Lorelei. "It's a rather long story." She hung her head. "Could I speak to Waverley in private?"

"Certainly," said Wayne. "Of course." He nodded at each person in turn and exited into the billiards room.

Mary arrived with a pitcher of martinis on a tray and a poured a generous portion into a chilled glass for Lorelei. She took it gratefully.

"You'll excuse us, Brian?" asked Waverley.

"Yes, but first there is something I think you should see." Brian waited until Mary had left and then reached into his jacket pocket and pulled out the photo that showed Nixie planting Roland's treasure in the boathouse. He handed it to Waverley.

"What is this?"

"Lorelei will explain," Brian told him. He began to back away toward the door. "Lorelei? Look at me."

She looked at him.

"Sorry," he said. "I just wanted to—remove any temptation you might have."

She said nothing.

"I'll be parked right out front," Brian said. "I'll be waiting right there, no matter how long it takes. I won't leave you."

"I know," she said finally. "I know you won't."

"Right." Brian lifted a hand in farewell and left.

Waverley took another look at Lorelei's face and lifted the pitcher from the tray. "Perhaps we'll take this with us, shall we?" He led her into the library. "I think we're going to need it."

Waverley listened to Lorelei's confession with bewilderment. If it was hard for her to tell him the truth, it seemed even harder for him to accept it. When she told him that Agnes was a fraud, too, he sputtered like an old man for a minute before he recovered his dignity. At times, during her recitation, he fell silent and seemed to brood. At times he became argumentative, disputing the facts. When she told him that she had orchestrated the whole discovery of Roland's treasure in the tackle box, he could take no more.

"But Roland's spirit reached out, letting you know where it was." He threw up his arms and spread his hands wide in an elaborate, challenging shrug. "I saw it with my own eyes. Penny saw it. There were witnesses. Those are truly Roland's jewels and coins. An appraiser has verified them."

"You don't understand." Lorelei didn't want to persist, but she had to. "The jewels? Roland's coins? We brought all that stuff up to the lake ahead of time, hid it in the boathouse."

"You…what? Why?"

Lorelei sighed. "So that I could reveal it," she said. "At the seance."

"When the time was right," said Waverley.

"Yes."

"I see." Waverley placed his fingers to his temples, as if he had a headache.

"I'm sorry," said Lorelei.

Waverley remained frozen, his face unreadable. He turned away from her and began to pace. He walked to the far end of the library, then continued along the south wall until he came to the row of psychic photographs mounted above the display cabinet. He reached up and touched one, straightened its frame. Then he placed his hands behind his back and resumed pacing until he had circumnavigated the room and returned to face her.

She was surprised, and a little frightened, to see that he was smiling. He placed a hand on her shoulder, with his fingers a little too close to her throat. "You wanted to time it right," he said. "For dramatic effect?"

"Yes."

"To tell the truth, I don't see the harm in that."

"You don't understand—"

He held up a hand to stop her. "Yes, I do understand. I understand perfectly. You're an artist. Like all artists, you have a flair for the theatrical. It's not only natural, it's charming. In fact, it's only right that you should take such care in presenting your work. I know that Penny would agree with me. Why, that was the most wonderful night of our lives. Absolutely astounding. If I live to be a hundred, I'll never see anything like it again." He smiled to himself and then added in a whisper, "Nor will I need to."

"But, Waverley, if you'd listen—"

Again, he stopped her. "No. You're the one who needs

to listen." He walked to the south window and peered down both sides of the driveway. "Where's your car?"

"I got a ride."

"I see. Young Hale drove you here. He put you up to this?"

"He said you might forgive me. If I paid you back."

Waverley sighed. "Young Brian Hale. That boy has no imagination." He drained his martini glass. "He's a bad influence on you."

Lorelei could only stare at her former client. Brian Hale, a bad influence?

Waverley turned his back to her again as he poured himself another drink.

She looked out the north window toward the river bank. It was starting to get dark now, and the Japanese lanterns were lit. She wanted to get home to Nixie.

He turned again to face her, filled her glass from the pitcher and said, "Look. Roland didn't tell anyone where the jewelry was, did he?"

"No."

"He died before he told anyone, didn't he?"

"Yes."

"And you found it."

"We didn't exactly—"

"You found it, right?"

"True."

"Where did you find it?"

"In the city." She didn't want to get into the story of Derek, that whole mess.

"Well, then," he said, "you *did* find it."

"Yes."

"Can you explain how you found it?"

"Not exactly."

"Can you think of any rational explanation for it at all?"

Lorelei thought about the whole convoluted story. Penny's long-ago affair and Derek's twisted revenge. Maurice Lemoine lurking about, drugging dogs. The refrigerator. Was any of that rational? "No," she said, truthfully.

"You see? The spirits led you to it. Don't ever forget that, my dear. You might have employed some of your craft—a little sleight of hand—when you presented the truth to us. But ultimately the spirits led you to it. Roland wanted Penny to have her treasured memories. Gloria wanted to reveal her truth to me. And with your help, your gift, they overcame the very border of death to make us see. Don't you *ever* doubt that." He pointed a finger at her heart. "Don't you *ever* lose your faith."

Bitsy hated her cat carrier. In her short life, she'd rarely been inside it, but she knew it meant nothing but confinement and car sickness. She complained loudly as Nixie carried her to the van. The back of the van was still stuffed with Nixie's camping equipment from her stay on the island. She pushed it aside to make room for the carrier. Imogene had looked after Bitsy while Nixie and Lorelei were on the island, but now Nixie wanted a more permanent home for the kitten. Who knew what crazy Charlotte Trapp might do to the witch's black cat? Who knew what she might do to Imogene? Imogene would have to move out on her own somewhere. But she was only sixteen. Nixie groaned as a sharp stab of guilt cut through her stomach. She had promised Imogene she'd help her and instead she was going to abandon her. She would try to talk to her this evening, explain about foster homes and shelters, but she wouldn't be around to see her through the ordeal.

She looked up at the girl's bedroom as she drove away. Imogene was staring morosely out the window. Nixie waved and Imogene waved back without much enthusiasm. The girl had too many problems right now to look after a kitten. Bits would be much better off at the shelter with Vivian. Once Vivian realized that Nixie wasn't coming back, she'd find her a good home.

"It's just for a few days," she'd told Vivian on the phone. "While Lorelei's redecorating. She's worried about Bitsy getting into the paint or the turpentine. I don't want her around the fumes, anyway."

Nixie wasn't going to think about Bitsy any more. She had made a mistake, that was all. She had let herself believe that she and Lorelei were going to settle down, and she had let Bitsy come pouncing into her life. Lorelei had warned her not to. Lorelei had warned her against Bitsy and against Imogene and against Vivian, and in every single instance Lorelei had been right. Nixie leaned on the horn and blasted the car in front of her for waiting too long at the light. Who did he think he was?

When she pulled in behind the Animal Clinic, Vivian came out into the lot.

"You brought your camping stuff! Great!" she said, as she reached in to retrieve little Bitsy. She handed the cat carrier to Nixie and pulled out Nixie's purple-spotted sleeping bag and her cooler. "I'll put these in my van."

Nixie had promised to go up with Vivian to see the site for the wildlife shelter. They were supposed to leave tonight, right after Vivian's shift. She followed Vivian into her office and sat down, wondering what her friend would think if she knew who Nixie really was, the things she'd done.

Vivian took a small stack of photos down from the shelf. "Look at this. My brother made me copies of a bunch of the pictures he took when we were up there this spring." She shuffled through them and handed one to Nixie. "This one shows Revelation Lake. That's the shoreline, about fifty feet from the front door. Well, what's going to be the front door."

Nixie looked at the photograph. There was Vivian leading a horse down to the lakeshore to drink. The sun was setting across the water and the clouds in the sky were fiery pink. In the foreground, Nixie could see little dots of blue and yellow and red among the tall grass. Wildflowers. "It's beautiful," she breathed.

"You can keep that one, if you like," said Vivian.

"Thanks."

"The pictures don't do the place justice, though. The light up there, it's indescribable. I can't wait to show it to you."

For half a minute, Nixie allowed herself to picture the place, the cold, rushing river, sun shining on the flanks of horses, Vivian coming toward her through a field of wildflowers, calling her name. Then she gathered herself together and stood up.

"I'd better get going," she said.

Vivian remained seated. "And look at this one. This is a bobcat we found last summer, just a kitten. Its paws were—"

"I have to go," Nixie said firmly. "I'm late."

Vivian stood up and looked at her, her brown eyes serious. "I thought you were free tonight," she said. "I was going to ask if you wanted to get some dinner. My break's in ten minutes."

"I can't, really. I have to go."

"All right then." Vivian bent down and spoke to Bitsy

through the bars of the cat carrier. "She'll be back tonight, Bitsy, so don't you worry."

Nixie turned and left without saying goodby. Without even thanking Vivian for taking Bitsy. For being the first friend Nixie had ever grown to love.

"Don't be late!" Vivian called. "I want to leave the minute my shift is over."

Nixie turned and waved. She didn't trust herself to say anything.

"And now," said Waverley, "practical matters." He sat at the cherrywood desk and opened the top drawer, pulled out his checkbook. "I'll have to stop payment on the last check, of course," he said, "if PsyRen can't purchase the cottage." He meant the eight hundred thousand.

"Of course," said Lorelei. She'd expected that.

"But earlier you gave two hundred to this imposter?"

"Yes," said Lorelei. "Last week. Certified check. I'm sorry."

Waverley shook his head once. "Well, you'll need to be reimbursed, then."

"What?"

"You'll need to be compensated for that loss," Waverley insisted. "You'll need a sum available if you find another property."

Lorelei nearly dropped her drink.

"The research center absolutely must become a reality," he said. "I am one hundred percent committed to it. But may I make a suggestion?"

"Naturally."

"It's a matter of climate," he said. "I don't mind the cold myself, but for Penny, well, the thought of facing another winter here is hard on her. We're planning to relocate. After the wedding."

"To Victoria?" asked Lorelei. She smiled. "I've always thought Penny belonged near the ocean."

"Well, you see it's her—"

"Arthritis? Makes it difficult getting around the icy streets."

"Yes. And we thought we'd spend our honeymoon—"

"On the Sunshine Coast," said Lorelei. "Maybe sail up to the islands of Haida Gwaii?"

"My dear, you are amazing." Waverley opened the checkbook. "I'll give you another two hundred toward the establishment of a center. But I only ask that you do me the very great favor of reconsidering the location." His pen hovered above the paper.

"I see," said Lorelei slowly. "To the west coast?"

"Yes. Don't you think an ocean-front resort would be more conducive to the kind of work you're doing?" The pen did a tantalizing dance.

"The spiritual force field at the ocean shore," said Lorelei decisively, "is in fact preferable to the mid-continental force field." She bit her lip to keep her smile from spreading across her face. "Ions," she added.

"I thought so," said Waverley. He uncapped the pen. "And there's one more thing."

"Yes?"

"Once we're settled, Penny wants to invite some of the Seekers from the west coast chapter along on a cruise up the coast. To Alaska. As a gesture of friendship. A way to introduce ourselves and make sure we get…."

Control over them, thought Lorelei. "Acquainted," she said.

"Exactly. We'll make an event of it, hire a band, get the best chef in Vancouver. Would you be available?"

"To go on the cruise?" Lorelei recalled the rich people in the travel brochure at Penny's house, their evening gowns dripping with jewels.

"Yes, as resident psychic for us both—and for our guests. It would give me a chance to introduce you to some new people."

"I believe I could clear my schedule," she said. "If the founder agrees."

"I knew you would," he said. He wrote out a check for two hundred grand and handed it to her with a smile.

"You're the most unpredictable person I've ever met," said Lorelei.

"I know, my dear, but you love a challenge, don't you?" He smiled, and for a moment, Lorelei thought he winked.

"Waverley," she whispered, as she hugged him in the foyer of his gracious home, "you may have saved my life."

"Well, that," he said, "would be only fair, wouldn't it?" He turned around as Penny came down the staircase in a yellow terry bathrobe, yawning. "Seeing as you saved mine." He kissed Lorelei's nose and ushered her toward the front door.

"Maybe I'll just slip out into the back garden for a bit," she said.

"Be my guest." He gave her a last affectionate pat on the head before Penny claimed his attention entirely.

Lorelei stepped out the side exit onto the patio and walked a few feet until she could see around the curve of the driveway. Brian had gotten out of his car and was leaning against the hood, hands in his pockets, gazing up into the dark, overhanging branches of a giant American elm.

Probably thinking that his apartment was too small, that he would have to buy a house, get Nixie a dog at last, send her to university. Maybe law school. Lorelei smiled. Waverley was wrong about Brian, she thought. Brian had a great imagination. And he had taught her so much. She would never forget that look on his face all those years ago the day she had given him a message from his dead father. A person could not have greater faith than Brian Hale, not even if he saw the veil between life and death lifted into the air and torn in two before his very eyes.

Behind her, she could hear someone in the house playing "Heart and Soul" on the piano. The moon was very round and bright. She stepped back behind the house and looked at the string of Japanese lanterns that illuminated the path down past the tennis courts and the white statues casting long shadows in the moonlight across the tiered lawns that stretched all the way to the riverbank. She walked past Narcissus and Orpheus and Pan. The piano music faded as she approached the dock, drowned out by the lapping of the river. When she did not think she could be seen from the house any longer, she bent and untied the canoe.

CHAPTER SIXTEEN

Brian arrived at the police station anxious and tired and wondering why Tommy had insisted he come in to talk to Detective Larraby again. Tommy had called while Brian was still waiting outside Waverley Forbes's mansion. Brian had wanted to take Lorelei with him, but when he went to the door to collect her, Forbes said he wasn't quite finished with her yet. He had looked grim. Lorelei had obviously confessed, as she'd promised to do. Brian could only hope Forbes could be persuaded to wait. With luck, he'd get his money back and maybe he'd choose not to pursue the matter further. After all, Brian reasoned, if this case became public, it would be very embarrassing for everyone involved. Including himself. He sighed heavily. Well, this was what life with Lorelei was going to be like. At least at the beginning. But he loved her and he was willing to endure it. Now he braced himself as he entered Detective Larraby's office, wondering what other shocks he was in for before this night was through.

"Tommy asked me to fill you in on a few things that

have come up in the investigation," said Larraby. He came out from around his desk and offered Brian his large hand to shake.

Brian shook it. "It's appreciated."

"You're welcome." Larraby hiked himself up and sat on the edge of his desk. "But first things first. I'm afraid I have to tell you that the person you know as Lorelei Good is a fake."

"Oh?" said Brian. He tried to look noncommittal.

"Her real name is Lola Gold," Larraby continued.

"*What*?!"

"Sorry, man," said Larraby. "You've been had. I hope she didn't take you for too much money."

"No, she—I didn't give her any money," Brian said. "I was—I was dating her."

"Oh, man," said Larraby. "I am truly sorry. But at least you caught on before she fleeced you. She took a bank manager in Sacramento for a five-thousand-dollar engagement ring. Plus, let's see here…." He flipped through the pages of the memo. "Identity theft and mail fraud. She was also operating a credit-card kite."

"A kite?"

"Like a check kite," the detective explained. "She had seven different credit cards going in her own name, plus twelve more in aliases. It's like a circle, taking cash advances on the new cards to pay off the minimum balance on the older cards. Eventually, of course, the kite crashes, and the banks lose out."

"That sounds…complicated."

Larraby shrugged. "It would take some doing to keep track of it all, I suppose. But it beats getting a real job. That's the trouble with these people, they don't want to work. They figure they're better than you and me. Too good to sweep floors and sling coffee."

"How do you know she's Lola ... Lola who?"

"Lola Gold. We know it's her from the fingerprint on that pamphlet you gave us."

"What pamphlet?"

Larraby opened a file folder and showed him a plastic bag stapled to it with one of Lorelei's Knowledge Is Faith brochures inside it. Lorelei's phone number appeared across the top in ink, just where she'd written it for Sarisha that night in the St. Mary's Curry House.

"Nice, shiny surface," said Larraby. "Good for lifting prints."

"She gave that pamphlet to Tommy!" Brian protested. "You had no right—"

"Hey, look! Tommy asked me to check her out, so I checked her out. Her prints are on file in the US database of outstanding warrants. She was arrested in California last December. Jumped bail and ended up here, posing as Lorelei Good." He paused and turned awkwardly to shuffle papers on the desk behind him. "There *was* a real Lorelei Good, by the way." He tapped a second file that was sitting on his desk. "The real Lorelei Good has been missing for twelve years. She's most likely dead."

Brian opened his mouth. Then he closed it.

"That's what these identity thieves do, you see. They pick someone who died young, send away for their birth certificate, and then start up a whole file—social insurance, driver's licence, passport, even. Next thing you know, they're taking out bank loans, credit cards, mortgages. What's the matter?"

"Just—surprised, is all," said Brian. Over the years, he'd

lost touch with his intuition, but lately he'd been getting it back. Right now it was telling him to shut up.

"Tommy and his wife, see, they suspected her for a scam artist soon as they saw that brochure," Larraby said. "They bagged it right away, in the restaurant, and set it aside, just in case she had a record."

"Jeez!" said Brian. "He didn't even tell me."

"Today, when it turned out she was mixed up in this Abby Shaunigan case, Tommy gave it to me and asked me to look into it. I'm making up a report for him."

Brian sat and listened to the long catalog of details about Lola Gold's crimes and Larraby's theories about her connection with Abigail Shaunigan. Larraby thought they were partners in crime who had turned against each other. "Blood might be spilled," he said, as Brian at last stood up to leave. "You know she'd actually be safer if she turned herself in. Are you one hundred percent sure you don't know where she is?"

"One hundred percent," said Brian. It was hard to walk out of the station without telling the police the truth. But he was still hoping Waverley Forbes would listen to reason, that he would calm down and make some private arrangement that didn't involve turning Lorelei over to the police. As for the Lola Gold theory, Brian knew damn well Lorelei wasn't Lola Gold. He had known her since high school. He couldn't understand how her fingerprints could match the prints of an identity thief from California, but he was sure there was some rational explanation. Maybe this Lola Gold was in town and somehow she had touched the brochure. Tommy couldn't claim he had followed the strict chain-of-evidence rules in this case.

As he walked down the steps outside the station, Brian released his pent-up breath and tried to relax his tense shoulders. He had never lied to the police before. He'd barely lied to anyone his whole life. Never needed to. But right now he had a feeling it was best to let Larraby believe that the real Lorelei Good was dead. At least until he knew what was what.

He intended to find out what was what as soon as possible. He hurried out to the parking lot. He was going straight back to Forbes's place to wait for her.

Lorelei paddled her way down to the Maryland Bridge and tied the canoe to a tree on the riverbank behind the Unitarian church. The bank wasn't steep, but she had some trouble climbing it. Her chest was tight, her lungs congested. She definitely had a fever now. She felt light-headed, unreal. She started toward home on foot, it was only a few blocks, thinking over what she was going to do. She was free, at least until Abby was arrested and ratted her out. But for now she was free. In her purse was the booty she'd just scored from Waverley, which she could easily convert into negotiable bonds and cash. In the Rapunzel doll at home was another three hundred thousand in diamonds. Almost any way you wanted to look at it, she had won this game.

And yet....

She didn't think she'd ever be able to forget about the diamond dealer who'd walked out of his house on a sunny September morning to go to work. She wondered how old his children had been when they saw him gunned down, and where those children were today. She couldn't forget the image of Jack Barnes sweating or Mike Baker crying. The violent way his arms and legs had quaked. And Nixie's face was haunting her, too. That little rebellious mouth and the way Nixie had walked upstairs with those diamonds and sewn them into that doll and stayed there, not even trying to escape, just waiting for Lorelei to tell her what to do next. That bruise on her cheek, like the bruise on Katherine's cheek when she'd first come to stay so many years ago. Lorelei slowed her pace and tried to breathe easy. All these things were connected, and connected, too, was that photograph on Nixie's bulletin board of Vivian the vet, smiling, nothing behind her but the blue and white prairie sky.

The truth, obvious now, was that Lorelei couldn't keep Nixie safe. Not any longer. She never could keep her safe, any more than Max could. Because Lorelei was just like Max. She couldn't give up the game. As she'd walked across Waverley's lawn this evening with his check in her purse, she'd known she would never give it up. And it wasn't the two hundred grand. Two hundred grand can come and go, as she knew very well. No, it was the look on Waverley's face that told her she had played well and he admired her for it. She and Waverley were two of a kind, she thought. She got a charge out of pitting herself against someone so powerful. He got a charge out of showing her off. Together, they controlled everyone around them.

That was something she'd been craving ever since the day Joey Shaunigan had shot her mother. Yes, Katherine had been a mother to her, though she'd never called her by that name before. Ever since the day Joey Shaunigan had shot and killed her mother and then stared at her through the window with his grotesque bug eyes and threatened her sister, drawing his pudgy finger across his neck, Lorelei had been paralyzed, drowning, desperate for some measure of power. She had exercised that power over Nixie, over her clients; she had used her charm, her wits, her gift, and her gun, and still it was never enough.

But now, at long last, Joey Shaunigan was going to come under her control.

Lorelei was careful to avoid the front driveway in case anyone was watching the house. She walked down the alley and entered the yard through the back gate. She slipped through the rear door into the kitchen, calling Nixie's name. Nixie didn't answer. Her bags were packed and piled by the front door, but there was no other sign of her. Lorelei went upstairs. It was time for her to pack, too. She filled her large leather purse with valuables. On impulse, she pinned the leopard brooch onto her white blouse. It didn't suit her outfit at all, but Lorelei for once was not concerned with her fashion statement. Nixie wasn't in her room. Where was she? Lorelei went back downstairs.

The pocket doors to the living room had been drawn shut. Maybe Nixie had lain down in there for a nap.

Lorelei pushed the doors open a crack, slowly in case Nixie was sleeping.

She saw the w first, a bright red w on the living room wall above the couch, and she thought she was going to be sick.

"Nixie?" Her heart turned over as she shoved the pocket doors apart and the whole message was revealed: *Burn in hell, witches.* The room was empty.

"Nixie!" Lorelei went pounding up the stairs to Nixie's room, then searched the whole second floor before she came pounding back down again. At the bottom of the staircase, she stood paralyzed for a moment. Which way to turn? The consulting room.

As she opened the door, an electric shock of fear raced through her body.

Nixie was bound to the pole of the heavy Victorian lamp with clothesline, as if tied to the stake, gagged by a white cloth around her mouth. Her blue eyes pleaded with Lorelei to save her. She was trying to communicate, but produced only desperate, muffled sounds. Her arms were tied behind her back and her ankles were bound together. At her feet lay a stack of kindling—newspapers, ripped cardboard, and some broken sticks she recognized as the smashed pieces of the consulting room chairs.

Sitting at the seance table, toying with a glass of red wine, was Abby Shaunigan, aka Agnes Kellsington. She had shed her disguise. She wore tight black denim jeans and a bright blue T-SHIRT. She wore no makeup, no hat or shawl, no effort to conceal her face or the curves of her figure. Her blond hair was pulled back loosely in a practical ponytail. She was about thirty-five years old. She sipped her wine and gave Lorelei a sweet Agnes Kellsington smile. Casually, she pulled a cigarette lighter from the pocket of her jeans.

"The Soldiers Against Satan are getting more authentic," she said. The shy hesitation had completely vanished from her voice. "They're recreating the original witch hunts of Salem now." She pointed at the matching lamp across the den. "The other stake's for you."

"Let her go," said Lorelei. She lunged at Abby, but Abby drew a handgun on her. It was no dainty .38 Special, but a heavy, well-oiled .45 with a big barrel.

"When I saw the name 'Lorelei' in the window of that hocus-pocus shop last winter, advertising your fortune-telling gig, I just knew it had to be you," Abby said. "I remember my dad used to get his cards read by that crazy Katherine. The last time he saw her, she said he was in for a run of good luck. Hah! The next day he finds out his diamonds are fakes. Max has replaced them with cubics. Some luck!" She took a swig of the wine and sat back. "Where is Max, anyway?"

"I don't know," Lorelei said.

"Hmm." Abby looked at her shrewdly. "Maybe you don't. Anyway, to hell with Max. You're the one with the diamonds now. At first, I was afraid you might have sold them, but I decided to follow you around anyway. Join your circle. See if you still had them stashed somewhere. I figured all you needed was something worth buying."

"So you made up a plan to draw them out," said Lorelei. "Clever." She saw Rapunzel lying on the floor beneath the seance table, as if she'd been flung there during a struggle. Abby obviously had no idea what was inside her.

"It took you long enough to take them out of the bank!" Abby said. "You were driving me insane with your paranoia. Why the hell didn't you just give them to me for a deposit? I was beginning to think you didn't have them." She shook her head. "I almost gave up. I probably would have, if Obie hadn't shown up. That creep. When I saw him take you aside, I knew he was blackmailing you. So I followed you around until I figured you paid him off and then I offered him a special little cocktail before dinner. And Jesus, do you know how long that bastard took to die? I gave him enough reds to kill a horse but he was so huge it didn't faze him." She suddenly burst into giggles. "Kept on going like a wind-up toy. Left the hotel with Summer Sweet and was still standing an hour later. I couldn't believe it when he came back to the hotel for dinner. Of course he was walking like a zombie, but he was still upright—and still hungry!" Again, Abby sputtered with laughter and fought to recover herself.

Lorelei was hoping she'd lose control completely, but Abby kept the gun steady. This was a woman who had held it together for the past four weeks, pretending to be Agnes Kellsington, with barely a crack in the façade.

"Anyway," Abby continued, "I suggested to Obie we steal into the banquet hall for a little taste before the other guests showed up, and he went for it. Finally, he keeled over on the table. And when he checked out, I found the proof in his pocket. One lousy stone. But it meant you had the rest of them stashed somewhere. Probably in the bank. Where are they now?"

"You murdered him," said Lorelei. "For no reason. You drove a skewer into him when he was passed out and killed him."

"Yeah. Got blood all over my shawl, too. I had to ball it up and stuff it in the garbage can in the ladies' room. Hell of a hassle retrieving it later."

"You killed him just to find out if he had a diamond on him?"

"I killed him," said Abby, "because he was blackmailing me." She swallowed the rest of her wine and poured herself another, filling the glass to the brim.

Lorelei watched her closely, trying to figure out what she wanted, besides the diamonds—and burning her and Nixie to a crisp. Abby seemed to be enjoying herself. She was proud of what she'd accomplished and she wanted to talk about it. Lorelei hoped to keep her talking while she figured out what to do. She glanced at Nixie. The girl was still fearful, but no longer panicking.

"Obie knew you, too?" Lorelei asked Abby.

"He recognized me," she said. "I played a little pool with him and sold him some coke a couple years ago when he was in town. Christ, who'd have thought he'd show up in those posh circles you were running in. He nearly exposed me right in front of Waverley and everyone at the Psychic Fair. I had to offer him a connection to shut him up."

Lorelei remembered that Agnes had seemed uncomfortable around Obie. She'd chalked it up to embarrassment. "Poor little Agnes and her sexual hang-ups," Lorelei said. "Her low self-esteem and her fainting spells. What a crock of—"

"My diamonds," said Abby. "Now."

"They're not your diamonds."

"Those diamonds belong to my father," she said.

"He stole them, Abby."

"And your father? I suppose he climbed down a mine shaft in Africa and dug them out of the wall with a pickax?"

"He didn't kill anybody to get them," Lorelei said. She glanced over at her sister again. Nixie was sagging. She had gone beyond panic and desperation and was sinking into despair. Lorelei looked deep into Nixie's eyes, tried to send her a message to calm down, that everything would be all right. If only she could keep Abby talking.

"What about Yolanda Dawn?" Lorelei asked. "What happened to her?"

"Yolanda knew Agnes," said Abby dismissively, as if Lorelei should have figured this one out. Her casual manner was chilling. "Agnes Kellsington was one of Yolanda's favorite clients in Chicago, as I heard over and over again from that insufferable Penny Johnson. Penny kept trying to arrange for us to get together."

"And you kept putting it off."

"Until finally I just couldn't put it off any more. Yolanda was phoning the house. Asking for Agnes. She was going to blow my cover."

"And Summer?" asked Lorelei. "What about Summer Sweet? She didn't deserve to die like that."

"She was driving me crazy, too!" said Abby. "With her little pet Maurice. For one thing, I should have killed her just for causing so much delay. What's the matter with you, you can't compete with amateurs like them? You should have got rid of them both. They dragged the whole thing out for days."

"You killed her because she was causing delay?" Lorelei thought of all the people who had died for these diamonds, starting with the diamond dealer, Josh Stonefield. Then Katherine, Yolanda, Obie, Summer, and now maybe Nixie and herself.

"I killed Summer because she asked too many questions," Abby said. "Summer had a goddamn thing for Hank Kellsington. And she hated me because I was his wife. She caused me trouble from the day I showed up in her stupid Dharmarama. Then as things were moving along, she sent Hank a fax to his ashram in India, to 'alert' him to certain 'developments' concerning his wife's 'activities.' I know because the Kellsingtons had arranged to have every fax and letter forwarded back to the house to be screened. They paid me extra to screen their mail! They didn't want to be bothered with anything but emergencies." Abby giggled at this, but then frowned as she remembered her troubles with Summer. "So I sent her a reply from Hank," she said, "telling her to mind her own business. But that was a mistake." Once again she drained her wineglass and this time she poured the remains of the bottle into her glass. "I didn't realize they'd been having an actual affair. Summer didn't buy the fax. The tone wasn't right, she said. Goddamn it! She suspected Agnes had sent it herself—and she was sort of right. But she was arrogant. She made the mistake of confronting me with what she called 'inconsistencies'—ha!—she actually called me into her shop and laid out the evidence in front of me! What a twit."

"So you stabbed her," said Lorelei. "And you firebombed the place, nearly killing my sister."

"Where are my diamonds?" Abby asked. "Mike swore you had them, and I tend to believe him. He never could lie to me."

"Who's Mike?" asked Lorelei.

Abby sighed. "Listen," she said, in a reasonable tone, "there's no point arguing about all this." From her purse, she pulled a small can of lighter fluid. Her voice got suddenly hard. "Give them to me now or I set your little sister on fire."

Lorelei looked at Nixie's face, the long-lashed blue eyes filling with tears, the scatter of freckles standing out on her pale cheeks, the soft, coppery curls Lorelei had brushed so many times. The hands with their nimble little fingers.

"No," she said.

Nixie's eyes widened in terror, or was it disbelief? She made frantic noises, but the gag smothered her words. She struggled to point with her head toward the place where Rapunzel lay, but she was tied too tightly. Abby glanced once in that direction and, seeing nothing but a chewed-up old pet toy, ignored Nixie's desperate signals. She flicked the lighter and played with the switch, lengthening and shortening the flame.

"The cops are on their way," Lorelei said. "You'll be up on murder charges."

Abby smirked. "I don't think so. Little sis here will be just another casualty of the witch hunts. Do you know there is a souvenir of every single victim hidden away somewhere in the home of the Reverend Surefire? For little Nixie here, I thought I'd choose her distinctive red sneakers. Just one. Maybe plant it in his bedroom closet."

Lorelei tried to catch her sister's eye, but she couldn't convey what she knew, that if she gave the diamonds to Abby, Abby would light the fire anyway. But until she got the diamonds, Abby would keep them both alive. Abby had an addiction—and Lorelei knew all about it.

Suddenly, a loud burst of static made both Lorelei and Abby jump.

"Drop your weapon!" came a loud, amplified voice.

Abby leaped out of her chair, but she didn't let go of her gun. "Who is that?" she yelled at Lorelei. "Did you really call the fucking cops? You did! You idiot!" She crouched and waddled toward the window. She raised a hand to lift a corner of the curtain and the voice boomed again.

"Get away from the window!"

Abby jumped back. "Someone's out there with a fucking megaphone," she said. "And they can see right into the house! Shit." She looked around wildly, seeking the source of their knowledge.

"We are coming in the front door," another voice announced. It was so loud it sounded as if it was right in the room.

"Shit!" yelled Abby. She ran through the door out into the hall and Lorelei could hear her tearing wildly through the house in an attempt to escape out the back. But the cops weren't that stupid. If they were going to storm the place, they'd have surrounded the house first. Lorelei ran to the door and locked it, wedging a chair under the knob. She grabbed her gun and a pocket knife from the desk drawer. She cut the gag in two behind Nixie's head, careful not to nick her.

"Untie me, quick!" Nixie begged.

Lorelei tucked the gun in her dress pocket and worked at the knots binding Nixie's hands behind her back. Had Brian called the cops? How much did they know? Could Abby possibly escape? What would she say if they arrested her? The knots were too tight. She grabbed the pocket knife again and began to saw at the clothesline. As she freed

Nixie's hands, she was horrified to hear a creak behind her and, turning, to see the closet door begin to open. She reached for her gun but did not draw. If it was a cop—

Both sisters gasped as the door opened wider. A foot came forward. Imogene emerged, pale and shaken. She was holding the voice synthesizer in her hand. She dropped it and knelt beside Nixie. Without a word, she began to struggle with the knots that bound her feet.

"That was you?" Lorelei asked, incredulous. "Pretending to be the cops?"

Imogene nodded. "I just wanted her to leave," she said. Her lips quivered.

"You mean there's no cops out there?" Nixie whispered.

Imogene shook her head. She looked up into Nixie's eyes. "That was me saying all that," she said. "But we can call the real cops now."

"No," said Lorelei. She handed the pocket knife to Imogene. "Just get Nixie free." She picked up the rag doll and held it in her arms. "This is what Abby wants, Nix. And I'm going to give it to her."

"What are you saying? Rapunzel belongs to us!"

"Oh, no. She belongs to Joey Shaunigan," said Lorelei. "He deserves her. If we keep her, she'll only doom us."

"What *is* that?," Imogene asked, as she worked on the line that bound Nixie's ankles. "Some kind of voodoo doll?"

"Sort of," said Lorelei. She took her purse off her shoulder and placed its strap around Nixie's neck. "Don't let go of this," she said. "It has everything in it."

By everything, she meant a thousand in cash, the check from Waverley, which Nixie could cash through the PsyRen account, a lot of good jewelry, and an envelope full of false identification papers. Everything a girl might need to get a new start in life.

"I have to go now," Lorelei said. "You be careful. People will be looking for you."

"What do you mean *me*? What about you?"

"Listen carefully. I'm going out there and I'm going to give Rapunzel to Abby." She looked out the window. A beat-up lime-green Gremlin was parked in the driveway, blocking Lorelei's Mercedes. She would have seen it earlier if she'd come in the front. "I'm going to draw Abby away from here," she told Nixie. "I'll try and lead her over the Maryland Bridge and down to Portage Avenue. If we get that far, I'll turn west and keep going until the cops stop her. But you have to make sure the cops stop her. As soon as I leave, I want you to call Brian. Here's Abby's licence number." She scribbled it on a notepad. "But don't call the cops. They'll come after you. Call Brian. Describe Abby's car and tell him exactly where it's headed. Tell him the diamonds are in it. Can you do that?"

"Sure, but where are you—?"

"All we have to do is make sure the cops find Abby in possession of these very particular one-carat diamonds and Uncle Joey will be back in court before his parole hearing even comes up."

"But where are you going?" Nixie's small, pinched face was red, her eyes full of tears. Imogene cut through the line and freed Nixie's feet. Nixie threw her arms around Lorelei. "Don't go!" she said. She clung to Lorelei's neck with both hands, but her waist was still tied to the pole, and Lorelei was already pulling away, slipping from her grasp. She felt Nixie's fingers slide off her neck and then she turned and ran.

Lorelei was alone now. She crept out into the yard with her gun drawn, praying she wouldn't be sucked into a gunfight. She didn't know where Abby was hiding. She bent low, using the vehicles for cover, in case Abby was watching from the house. When she reached the Gremlin, she tossed Rapunzel in through its open window onto the floor in the back. Then she got into her own car and revved the engine, driving recklessly and noisily across the front lawn to get around Abby's car, smashing straight through Charlotte's tidy picket fence and into the street.

Abby, realizing there were no cops around, came tearing out the front door, gun in hand, and jumped in the Gremlin.

Lorelei waited until Abby's Gremlin turned into the street and came after her. Then she veered left onto Wellington Crescent and headed for the Maryland Bridge. Abby followed, closing in faster than Lorelei had thought possible. She wasn't used to car chases, but obviously Abby lived a different sort of lifestyle. As they passed the riverside park, Abby rammed the back of the Benz, sending Lorelei's front end into the left lane, bashing the fender of a family sedan full of kids. The driver swerved and leaned on his horn. Lorelei righted her vehicle just in time for Abby to ram her again. This time Lorelei maintained control and stepped harder on the gas. She must not fail, she told herself. She calculated what was going on in the larger world. Brian would have discovered her defection by now. Would he have gone to his brother with the photographs? She wasn't sure, but she didn't want to find out. She had to get a good lead on Abby before the cops closed in on her. She knew her life was in danger. But the consequences of failure could be worse than death. The last thing Lorelei wanted was to go to jail.

Lorelei could not afford to slow down as she neared the

entrance to the bridge. But as she passed the synagogue, approaching the intersection, cars were whizzing on and off the bridge, up and down Academy Road. Some evening event was letting out at the Catholic girls' school on the corner, and a steady stream of pedestrians was crossing less than half a block in front of her. Lorelei lost her nerve. She eased up on the gas. Abby accelerated. The Gremlin rammed the Benz from behind with such force it jumped the curb. Lorelei jerked the wheel to the right, and the car tore across the front lawn of the synagogue at terrifying speed, smashed into a grove of trees and came to rest, its hood hopelessly crumpled, against a stand of oaks. She felt her neck snap back against the headrest. The seat belt dug into her chest, cutting off her air supply. Then it was over. She was no longer in motion. Dazed, she fumbled for the latch of the seat belt and released herself. She opened the door and fell out onto the grass. Above her, the yellow moon spun in the dark sky. Fighting vertigo and nausea, she sat up and looked behind her. Abby's Gremlin had crashed on the meridian in the intersection, its driver's door crushed up against a light standard. Abby would be trapped inside, at least momentarily. A few minutes' grace.

"Hey! Are you all right?" Two men came running from the door of the synagogue, offering to help her. Behind them, she saw bright lights, people. Some kind of celebration was going on. A crowd of youngsters poured out the door to stare at the car wreck. Lorelei wrenched herself to her feet and raced across the lawn toward the bridge. Even as she ran for her life, she was already mourning the loss of her Mercedes-Benz. She knew she was never going to drive it again.

She ran down the south bank toward the water. The Assiniboine River flowed east toward its junction with the

Red a few miles away at the center of town. The Maryland was a double bridge, spanning the river twice. If Lorelei could get down to the overgrown bushes of the riverbank, she could elude Abby and in the darkness make her way west along the cement path to the spot on the riverbank where she'd tied up Waverley's canoe one very long hour ago. The party at the synagogue had spilled out onto the grounds and she'd have to dodge teenagers and their parents, not to mention the two men who were trying to help her. But she had no choice. She raced into the thick of the crowd, and then she heard Abby scream.

"Lorelei!"

She turned her head and collided with a teenage boy. He grasped her by the shoulders. "Lady, are you all right?" Behind him, Abby approached.

Abby's shirt was torn open and the right half of her face was covered in blood. She staggered forward, lurching like Frankenstein's monster. "Lorelei!" she yelled again. Her gun was drawn. She was ready to fire into the crowd of kids and parents.

"Abby, no!" Lorelei shouted. But it was useless. Abby was insane, her little mind focused on one tiny point, her nemesis. Lorelei doubled back and veered left, drawing Abby away from the crowd. Several people had seen the gun and were shouting now, their celebration forgotten as they tried to usher their children into the building.

Lorelei had nowhere to run but onto the east bridge. She had a good lead on Abby and was halfway across before Abby made it onto the bridge. A siren sounded in the distance. Possibly an ambulance on its way to the hospital across the river, but more likely a police car. This was a quiet neighborhood. A car chase, a wreck, and a crazed, bleeding woman with a gun would not go unreported. Lorelei had little chance of escape. She needed a hiding place. She leaned over the railing on the east side, to see if there was any way to climb down underneath. The railing jutted out around a narrow lookout platform bearing a streetlamp, but otherwise, there was not even a toehold. She hoisted herself up and over the railing and stood on the thin ledge, clinging with both hands to the rails, the long drop to the river behind her. It was too dark to see the surface of the river. She knew there were tall cement buttresses rising out of the water, supporting the bridge. A dim, pale shape below her seemed to be one of them, but she couldn't be sure. She tried to hold tight to the railing but her hands were shaking. She was weak with fever now, burning up and shivering at her core. In her delirium, she considered letting go. She might land in the cold, deep water below, with its infamous, dangerous undertow. Or she might miss and go hurtling into the side of the buttress, smashing her skull against the cement. As she hung there, dizzy and undecided, she saw Abby advancing along the bridge, her shiny black revolver held stiffly in front of her, ready to aim and fire.

"Drop your weapon," called a male voice, so loud it must have been coming through a megaphone. Abby turned around. The amplified voice called, "Freeze! Drop your weapon! Now!" This time it wasn't Imogene playing tricks. It was the real cops at last. Lots of them. Lorelei looked back through the railing at the site of the car crash. She saw flashing lights, a black and white, an ambulance, a news van. There was going to be a gunfight on the bridge, a shoot-out. If she survived, she would be arrested.

She let go of the railing with one hand and turned around, so she was facing away from the bridge. To the east, below the synagogue, lay the riverbank where Brian had first kissed her and she had first lied to him. She had seen him from up here that day. She had seen rosebushes and dappled sunlight. Poplar trees and a weeping birch. But now everything was dark. Faint thunder sounded in the distance. All around her she was surrounded by things she knew were there but could not see. For an instant, sheet lightning illuminated the sky and then everything was dark again. The tops of the trees on the opposite bank were dark. A dark wind blew the tears from her face.

Abby looked out over the railing, her eyes on her target, a woman she'd hated for twelve long years. She leaned over farther to get a better aim. The police weren't going to be able to stop her in time. She raised her arm and aimed.

The sound of the gunshot reverberated in the night.

Lorelei's body was airborne momentarily before it plunged toward the black, invisible water of the Assiniboine.

The moon was round and fat. What was it she'd told Waverley? In the days that followed the Moon of Takara, the veil between the living and the dead grew fragile. You could slip right through it.

Leaning up against her painted van in the parking lot of the animal clinic, Vivian crossed her arms in front of her chest, threw back her head, and stared at the sky. What was she doing here? Nixie was over two hours late to meet her. Vivian should have been long gone. She should have figured out by now that Nixie was a fake, a fraud, a nothing, a nobody.

Nixie watched her from the car. In the passenger seat, a subdued Imogene Trapp sat beside her, biting her nails and wondering what was going to happen next. Nixie had phoned Brian on his cell phone and delivered the message she was supposed to deliver. She had gathered a few small things from the house, laced up her sneakers, stepped out the door and become a fugitive. On impulse, she'd offered to take Imogene along. They'd hotwired a neighbor's car and come here, intending to pick up Bitsy and take her along into whatever lonesome future loomed ahead. Neither of them had anything to lose. Or that's what Nixie had thought in the moment. Suddenly she wasn't so sure.

A low rumble of thunder crossed the sky. Vivian lifted her eyes to the north, studying the clouds. She stepped away from the van, and for a second Nixie could see her own purple-spotted sleeping bag, rolled up and waiting for her in the passenger seat. Expecting her to keep her promise, to arrive. Lightning flashed and Nixie counted to four before the thunder sounded again. The storm was four miles away. Soon, the clouds would burst overhead. The heat wave that had plagued the city for four long weeks was about to break. She picked up the purse that Lorelei had given her and hooked it over her shoulder. Then she sat with her hands folded on top of the purse, the purse in her lap.

"Nixie?" said Imogene. "What are we doing here?"

Instead of answering, Nixie opened her door and stepped out of the stolen car. She entered the parking lot. Vivian's eyes were still on the sky. Nixie took one step forward. The rain began to fall.

"Nixie!" Imogene called. "Where are you going?"

Vivian looked up then and saw them. Vivian straightened and stepped forward, her pale face serious. She was obviously relieved to see Nixie. Yet not surprised. Not at all surprised. Nixie could see in her eyes that Vivian had never doubted she would come.

"Don't leave me here!" Imogene wailed.

"I'm not leaving you," Nixie said. She reached behind her and grasped Imogene's hand in her own. But she didn't turn around. She was looking at Vivian.

"Nixie!" Vivian called. "What happened? Are you all right?" She was walking quickly now. Coming toward Nixie. Moving toward her the way she had always been moving toward her, though Nixie had been slow to see it.

"Imogene?" Nixie asked. "How would you like to go out to the country for a while?"

Imogene didn't answer right away. But it didn't matter. Vivian closed her arms around Nixie's shoulders, and the patter of rain quickened and grew loud. Lightning flashed across Nixie's closed eyelids and she counted one two three before she heard the thunder again, this time a loud crack, as if the earth were splitting in two. The storm was closing in. Soon, the highway would be slick and dangerous, the prairie sky electric. But it would be warm in the painted van, and dry, and the windshield wipers would beat a rhythm like the beating of a heart all the long way north to Revelation Lake.

First Tommy arrived at the apartment with a chocolate cake and a gallon of butter chicken and then Rhonda showed up with a six-pack of beer and a box of crackers, so Brian didn't have to face the first terrible night alone.

Tommy tuned the television to a local channel and muted the sound until the news came on. "Sarisha and I thought it would be better if she stayed home with the boys," he said.

"Of course," said Brian. He pulled the tab off a can of beer and stared as the foam came bubbling up.

"Was she dead before she fell?" Rhonda asked. "Or did she drown?"

"I don't know," Brian said. "I got there too late. She was already gone."

"Look. There it is," said Rhonda. "Turn it up." She joined them on the couch.

Brian turned on the volume and pressed "record" on the video recorder. Over top of an image of the Maryland Bridge, taken from down on the riverbank, Kent Mason's voice recited the facts according to The News at Ten: "The Maryland Bridge was the scene earlier tonight of a shoot-out between police and warring criminals. Police say that two fraud artists, Lola Gold of Sacramento California, and Abigail Shaunigan of Winnipeg, were engaged in a dispute over the ownership of some rather rare and rather famous diamonds. That dispute ended in tragedy. The dramatic event was captured on camera by Channel Ten from the banks of the Assiniboine River."

The scene was chaotic. Police cars and their flashing lights, silhouettes of people running. The voices of police officers shouting commands through their megaphones. Then gunfire, and the camera zoomed in on the two women at the center of the action.

"As Lola Gold climbed the railing, apparently trying to hide behind the light standard, Shaunigan spotted her and advanced. Here is the moment of the shooting, caught on tape. A Channel Ten exclusive."

Brian, Tommy, and Rhonda all leaned forward, trying to see more clearly the shadowy figures on the videotape. Abby raised her arm and a shot rang out. Lorelei's body jerked and buckled. A second later, she was gone. The camera tried to follow the trajectory of her falling body.

"If you look under the bridge," Kent Mason's voice continued, "you can actually see the body of Lola Gold, falling from a height of thirty feet straight into the Assiniboine River."

A tiny shadow appeared to drop from under the bridge, and through the miracle of computer graphics, it stopped for an instant, and a little red circle appeared around it, so that you could tell what you were looking at, before the fall was completed. Then the picture disappeared, replaced by the face of Detective Lyle Larraby, who appeared to be answering questions at a press conference.

He said: "These are two individuals who are known to police. They have been known to police for some time. We first became apprised of the recent activity of Ms Gold thanks to a concerned citizen who came forward, and we took it from there. What's that? Yes, ma'am. These diamonds we recovered from the vehicle of Ms Shaunigan are items we have been wanting to find for some time. We believe they are material evidence in a cold case robbery homicide. That case is now reopened and we cannot comment on an ongoing investigation. Yes, ma'am, I can tell you that Ms Shaunigan is in custody tonight. She has been charged with murder and possession of stolen goods. Other charges are pending. No, sir. Ms Gold's body has not yet been recovered. It's dark out there and the current is strong. Police divers will begin a thorough search in the morning. We cannot estimate the likelihood of success at this time. All right. No more questions."

"That's it?" said Rhonda.

"I'll find out more tomorrow," Tommy said. He stood. "You're going to be all right?"

"Sure," said Brian.

"Sorry I have to go." Tommy looked at his feet. "Early day tomorrow."

"I'll walk you out."

"Do you mind if I stay a while?" Rhonda asked.

"Of course not," said Brian. "Make yourself at home."

At the door of the apartment, Tommy turned and gave his brother an awkward hug. "Look, don't romanticize this chick too much."

"Right."

"She betrayed you, Bri," Tommy said. "You gotta face the facts, man."

"Sure, Tommy. I know."

After Tommy went home and Rhonda finally drifted off to sleep on the couch, Brian rewound the tape and played again and again the scene of the shooting and Lorelei's tragic plunge from the bridge. He played it in slow motion, studying every frame. Just at the beginning, before she began to fall, he thought he could see her feet bounce upwards, as if she was taking a little, preliminary leap, like the high divers he'd seen on the Olympics. A split second later, she was hidden by one of the buttresses, and then she appeared again below the bridge, plummeting into the river. Brian pressed the pause button. In the middle of the television screen, the body of the woman he loved was a narrow smudge, the size of an exclamation mark.

He wasn't sure, but he thought she was falling headfirst, arms extended before her, legs taut, toes pointing toward the sky. Yes, he could see it, if he looked closely, and it was important. The streamlined posture of her body was a message. But he fell asleep before he could decipher it, the television remote dangling from his hand, so that all night the image of Lorelei remained on the screen, frozen in mid-dive.

In a cheap motel room outside of Devil's Lake, North Dakota, Lorelei woke from a dream of falling, her legs crashing against the bed, the wind knocked out of her. She lay on her back, wheezing for air, trying to remember the details of the dream, but they were gone. Nothing remained but the sensation of the fall itself. She looked at the bedside clock. The digital display was blinking midnight, its twelve and double zeros a sign of yet another power failure in a place where nothing worked. But she knew it was still the middle of the night. Two or three a.m., judging by the color of the thin wedge of sky she could see through a rip in the curtain. She rolled over, coughed, sat up. She wouldn't be getting back to sleep any time soon.

Wrapping the grubby sheet around her naked body, she walked to the chair by the window. She flipped on the television. Lit a cigarette. The newscaster said a few words about the long-range forecast, and then his voice was obscured by a burst of static. Lorelei muted the sound.

Since her dive from the bridge into the cold waters of the Assiniboine, she had been thrown deep into another world. She had crossed a line, and until it was safe to return, she would remain buried below the border. She was lucky she wasn't really dead. She'd been badly hurt and the river wasn't clean. Adrenalin had fueled her swim through the dark waters to the shore. Then she'd lain in the canoe and let the river current carry her east and away. Pain killers had kept her going for a day of driving. Then she'd been forced to stop to find a doctor. The wound where the bullet had grazed her hip was infected. Three of her ribs had been cracked in the car crash. The pneumonia, inevitably, had returned. For the first week of her afterlife in Devil's

Lake, she had sweated with a fever so severe she barely knew where she was.

Now she was convalescing, alone, in this room with its broken clock and its broken television, hoping her money would hold out until she recovered strength enough to work again. Maybe by the end of the year, once Waverley and Penny had married and settled in Victoria, it would be safe to return to Canada. For now, the veil between the living and the dead was too dangerous to breach. Yet sometimes Lorelei still believed she could see through that thick membrane. Transitory flashes. Brief, delirious glimpses of Brian. The muscles of his shoulders rising from the lake water as he swam toward her, his hand reaching out to grasp her ankle. How he had looked up at her then, a wild flicker, like green flame, in his dark eyes.

Sometimes she could see Nixie Nobody, even though Nixie wasn't there, even though Lorelei was wide awake, with her eyes wide open. She could see Nixie's breath in the cold air of northern Manitoba. Nixie was bareheaded, her orange curls darkening as the early dusk settled across the prairie. She kneeled on the grass, a broken bird in her small hands. Someone tall was walking toward her, to say it was time to come inside for the night. The image had the texture of a dream, but it wasn't a dream. Maybe it was simply a wish. Or maybe Lorelei had a gift, a kind of second sight that pulled the light toward her through the darkness of the long province that stretched between herself and her lost sister.

She remembered the weight of Nixie's fingers on the back of her neck, like ten sparrow feathers. She could feel those ten fingers lifting one by one from her skin, taking flight, and then Lorelei was hurtling again through that small piece of black, empty sky. That open space between bridge and water. She was falling. She would always be falling. She had a gift.

Catherine Hunter is a professor of English at the University of Winnipeg. She is the author of the thrillers *Where Shadows Burn* and *The Dead of Midnight* and the poetry collections *Lunar Wake, Latent Heat,* and *Necessary Crimes.* She lives in Winnipeg.